Shepherd Security – Operation Fallen Angel

Margaret Kay

This book is dedicated to the staff who work on 4 North.
You gave me amazing care while I was there in both January and May of 2019.
Please forgive any incorrect medical scenes. I am not a skilled professional as each of you are.
My thanks for the demanding job you do – and do so well!
Margaret

Alpha

Sister Elizabeth listened to the sounds of war in the distance. She could hear the muffled explosions, but she couldn't tell at first from which direction they came. Everything echoed through the valleys that lay between the many hills that rose from the desert floor.

This was a harsh and unforgiving landscape that suffered endless droughts. There were repeated religious uprisings and continuous political unrest, but the people who she'd come to know and care for here, were worth the fight. They had hope, faith, and love in their hearts. They were good people who survived against all odds and tried to eke out an existence in a desolate land that seemed hell-bent on denying them life.

Black smoke billowed from the hill a good five miles away. She kept her bright blue eyes trained on the hill while straining to identify that direction as the source when the next concussions echoed through the valley. Yes, that was where the fighting was taking place. It was a lot closer than she would have liked.

A sudden gust blew her black headscarf from her head. Her waist-long stick-straight, dishwater blond hair joined the scarf swirling in the scorching breeze. She clenched the scarf in one hand and gathered her hair as best she could, securing it in a tie at the base of her neck. Sweat trickled down her back, beneath the dark gray tunic she wore. Beneath, she wore a black tank top and a pair of athletic shorts. Not the customary wardrobe for a Sister, but she wasn't a typical Sister either.

In the twenty-four-years Sister Elizabeth had lived, the last three in this village had tested her faith in ways she would never have predicted. Even though she looked younger than her years, the people here, both fellow Sisters and locals, treated her with respect and trusted her as a medical professional with a deference she would never have received in the United States.

Sister Bernice John came up behind her. "Those poor people. My heart aches for those in that village."

"They are steadily moving closer, Sister," Elizabeth said.

"God will keep us safe. Surely you have faith?"

Elizabeth felt a pang of guilt in her heart. No, she didn't. She turned and faced Sister Bernice John, a woman she respected immensely. The Sister wore, as always, the traditional habit of their order. Sister Elizabeth on the other hand, dressed appropriately for the area.

"I've, um, stockpiled some supplies in the cave and fabricated a fake wall in the clinic up against the entrance to the cave in the hill. If they come to our village, we may not make it out, but I think we could hide and remain safe if we need to."

"Sister Elizabeth!" Bernice John reprimanded. "God will keep us safe. We will not flee. We will not hide. We will face what God sends us with courage and faith."

"And the children, and innocent women in our care? How can we demand the same of them? We've seen what Al-Shabaab does when they take a village. As Christians, we are targets. They're not like the militia, the warlords, and the pirates who have some degree of reverence for us, or in the very least fear reprisals in their own afterlives if they harm us. Can you really demand those children face these demons with the same courage we would?"

Another blast rolled through the valley and a boiling black cloud expanded over the faraway hill. Elizabeth knew that signified the death blow to that village. She turned away from Sister Bernice John, her Mother Superior over this small order, and returned to her medical clinic.

The Sisters of Mercy had been in this village, right at the border of Ethiopia and Somalia for years. There were sixteen Sisters serving the destitute in the area. They ran an orphanage, a school, and a clinic. Because of the strife in the area, their beds were full.

Elizabeth decided that, with or without permission, she would do what she could to stockpile the supplies they may need to survive. She knew the fighters would head their direction next. She knew she didn't have the faith she should, but a part of her had to believe that the idea to hide could be divine, a calling to survive.

"Sister Elizabeth!" Sister Bernice John exclaimed running into the clinic. It was several hours after nightfall. "The fighters attacked the next closest village. We have incoming casualties and a few dozen refugees fleeing that village. I fear they are leading Al-Shabaab to our doorstep, but we cannot turn them away."

Just then Sister Mary Michael burst into the room, leading a half-dozen women who carried children, several of them severely injured. "They tried to take the children," Sister Mary Michael said.

Sister Elizabeth motioned the women to the two exam tables she had. They sat and laid the four most seriously injured children on the tables. One of the women needed attention as well. She had several deep cuts on her face and arms that bled.

"Sister," Elizabeth said to Mary Michael. "Clean the wounds on the less serious injuries." She carefully examined the wounds on two young boys. They were both unconscious, but still alive. "These boys are both in critical condition. I need to take them to the treatment room and see what I can do."

Elizabeth trained at a community college in her hometown of Seattle and earned her Certified Nursing Assistant License. While working at a free clinic in one of the roughest neighborhoods in Seattle before her assignment with this mission, she learned far more from Sister Abigale, a doctor, than she had formally. Before she traveled to Africa, she already performed advanced medical procedures like starting IVs, dispensing medications, cleaning and bandaging wounds. She'd even assisted Sister Abigale when she dug bullets out of at least two-dozen shooting victims.

She had planned to become a registered nurse, but this assignment to Africa was one that she felt drawn to. Sister Abigale gave her the necessary recommendation to be chosen for the assignment. It was only supposed to be for two years and Elizabeth planned to return to school after it to continue her education. She wasn't sure what her plans were now, though. This experience had changed her, she knew that. She saw and thought about things differently than she had before coming to Africa. She supposed it was natural that the idealism she once felt was gone. After seeing what she'd seen here, how could it not?

She wasn't sure how the other Sisters who had been here for years still felt the way they did. Sister Karen, who served as this clinic's doctor, was steadfast in her belief that things in this region could change for the better. Sister Karen also gave her the confidence to attempt whatever was needed to save the innocent lives that came through the doors. Elizabeth had learned so much from Sister Karen that she carried on and practiced medicine every way she had to, to save lives. That was one of the things that kept her here, for now.

Sister Karen had suddenly been medevacked out six months earlier, after suffering a stroke. The request was in for a replacement doctor, but one had not been assigned yet. Her absence had delayed Elizabeth's departure, that, and Sister Bernice John's stubbornness in not wanting to let Elizabeth leave.

It took several hours for Elizabeth to stabilize the two young boys. She had to sedate them with ether, the only sedative she had. One, she dug out shrapnel from his chest. She stitched him up the best she could, hoping she'd found all the points he bled from. The other, suffered two broken legs. She set them and splinted them. He too had a number of deep cuts that she stitched, the most concerning at his clavicle.

"What on Earth happened to you two?" She asked the two unconscious boys.

"The barbarians tried to kill everyone," a young local woman said from the doorway. She had carried one of the boys into the clinic. Her clothes were saturated with blood.

"Are you injured?" Sister Elizabeth asked her.

"No, it is all that boy's blood."

"Is he your son?"

"No, I don't know who he is. This morning, many came seeking refuge in our village from their own, which had been attacked yesterday. No one seemed to claim these two children. But I believe they are brothers. They don't speak our tongue or English. I'm not sure where they are from."

"Your English is very good," Elizabeth complimented her.

"I worked at the U.S. Embassy in Addis Ababa as a translator. My father was a diplomat and made sure I learned English when I was young."

"What are you doing way out here? You are a long way from home."

The woman smiled fondly. "You are even farther, Sister. The man I married was from this area. We traveled here to visit family, and the fighting has kept us here far longer than planned. It just is not safe to travel the roads back to Addis Ababa at this time."

"They will sleep longer, but can I have you stay with them?" Sister Elizabeth asked. "I'd like to go check on the others."

"Certainly," the woman said.

Elizabeth returned to the main room. It was packed with the other Sisters, all the children and women who lived in the village, as well as the many who sought refuge. It was chaotic and crowded. There was a desperation in the collective. Outside, she heard shouting. She went to one of the windows and pushed the window covering aside. She stared into the dark night.

Her eyes landed on Sister Bernice John, as she came through the door. "What is it?"

"The fighters are nearly upon the village!"

"I just operated on the two boys, Sister," Elizabeth said. "If I try to move them, it will kill them."

"We're not going to evacuate. God will provide safety. We will shelter in place as you suggested. We're securing the buildings as much as we can. Everyone is gathering here. Show me this false wall you have fastened so we can herd everyone behind it."

Alexander 'Doc' Williams felt the vibration from his cell phone just as he heard the various alert tones of the phones belonging to his teammates in the room. Both Alpha and Delta Teams were there, and by the looks of it, every member got the alert. He viewed the screen. Just as expected, it was the Operations Center. The teams were being called in.

He downed the rest of his beer, Octoberfest, and shoved the last two forkfuls of jaeger schnitzel from his paper plate into his mouth. His eyes scanned the others. They were doing the same. A few had already dumped their plates in the trash and made their way over to Sienna and Garcia to say final congratulations on their new house. This was some housewarming party, with one of the hosts and nearly every guest getting called into work. Sienna knew what she was getting into though. She knew very well what the team did. Interrupted plans were just the new normal she'd have to get used to.

Behind Sienna, he saw Jackson give his six-month-old son a kiss goodbye. Then his lips went to Angel, his wife. So, Jackson had gotten scrambled too. That meant this was something big. Jackson had been pulling more shifts in the Ops Center recently than out on missions in an attempt to balance his time at home with being away. Doc didn't blame him. If he had a child, he couldn't imagine being away as often as the team was.

Doc stepped over to Sienna. "Congrats again." He gave her a hug. "I'll have Garcia's six, don't worry."

"You better."

Doc gave her a forced smile. Then he made his way to the door and followed several others out. He drove to HQ, the Shepherd Security Building. He followed the long line of vehicles down deep into subbasement two, and the secure parking area that was hidden behind a locked gate and two secure garage doors. He parked beside Danny 'Mother' Trio's pickup truck and pulled himself from behind the wheel of his SUV. He grabbed his bags from the back.

"This isn't going to be pretty," Danny said.

They entered the main facility door and joined the others in the Team Room, stowing their gear near their lockers. Cooper and Madison entered as he was about to go into the stairwell and head to five, to the main conference room where the mission briefing would take place.

"Do you have any idea what's up?" He asked Cooper. As number two in charge of the agency, Cooper often had information that no one else did.

Cooper shook his head no. "It's big if both teams were called in."

Doc nodded. Yes, he knew that. His adrenalin pumped through him as he charged up the stairs. The sounds of the heavy footfalls of the others echoed through the stairwell. He stepped off on five and followed his teammates into the main conference room. Shepherd waited there. He already had the monitor on, a map and mission particulars displayed. Africa, more specifically the border area of Somalia, Ethiopia, and Djibouti.

They all took their seats and waited. Jackson and Garcia entered five minutes later. Doc could tell Shepherd wanted to comment on their tardiness but knowing Garcia's housewarming party was interrupted by the alert, Shepherd was uncharacteristically quiet.

"Sorry to interrupt your party, but after you hear why, you'll agree this is important." His eyes settled on Jackson. "As you know, we have kept the area that Angel's mother is in on our radar. The base commander at Camp Lemonnier, Djibouti is aware of our interest. He notified me earlier today that a conflict has erupted on the border at their location. The village they are in has been overrun by hostiles, looks like Al-Shabaab.

Jackson's jaw clenched. "We're going in?"

Shepherd nodded. "You'll fly out within the hour." Then Shepherd went over the mission details. They'd fly into Andrews Air Force Base and board a C-17. They'd fly from there into Camp Lemonnier in Djibouti and use it as their base of operations in the area. "Evacuating the Sisters of Mercy and the civilians they protect is the mission. Do what you have to do to get in and out, engage the enemy as needed, but don't pursue them if they retreat."

Doc watched Jackson carefully. He could see the wheels turning in his friend's head. Jackson was already worrying about Angel. She'd be upset her mother was in danger. This would be a hell of a way for Jackson to meet his mother-in-law in person. They'd had a few video calls, but Angel's mother, Sister Bernice John, had been with the Sisters of Mercy on a humanitarian mission in Africa since long before Jackson met Angel.

"Can I call Angel and let her know?" Jackson asked.

"Negative," Shepherd replied. "I'll do it tomorrow when Lassiter can be there too."

Dr. Joe Lassiter was the team shrink. He knew Angel well and would be the best person to handle whatever Angel's emotions would be upon hearing the news. Doc was always impressed by how well Shepherd handled these things. Emotional issues were something that Shepherd inherently was tuned into, and that was before any of the men had women in their lives. Shepherd had always realized that they were human beings and the work they did strained even the most professional man amongst them. That was one of the many reasons that Doc was on this team.

"That's good," Jackson said. "Thanks."

Shepherd nodded. Then his eyes shifted to Madison. "Miller, upon arrival at Camp Lemonnier, you will act as the team liaison and remain at the base in their Ops Center directing operations while the team is in the field."

"What?" She demanded, bordering on insubordination. "You're sidelining me?"

"Stand down, Miller," Shepherd ordered. "We need someone there and you are the most logical person to fill that role."

"Because I'm the only woman?"

"No, because of your history manning combat Ops in the Middle East when you were in the Army." Shepherd's voice was sharp, the warning to let it go dripped from his words.

"Yes, sir," Madison replied.

Doc could tell she didn't like it one bit. And he was sure every man in the room knew that it was because she was a woman. The area they were going to, was continually plagued by civil unrest. Strict Sharia law was practiced in the parts of

Somalia that were under Al-Shabaab's control. Everywhere else, terrorist attacks, kidnappings, clan violence, and dangerous levels of violent crimes were the normal state of affairs. There was no effective police force present. And the waters near Somalia were full of pirates, who controlled villages on the coast. He agreed. This mission was no place for any woman.

His eyes shifted to Cooper, who stared straight ahead. Doc was sure Cooper was pleased Madison, his wife, would be nowhere near any of that shit. Or maybe Cooper had been the one to make the call on it. Safely on base, would be the only place Doc would want his wife, if he still had one. He mentally kicked his own ass. Mind back on the mission.

"That's it," Shepherd said. "Get your gear ready. Outfit with full combat gear and desert fatigues. I have Requisition Ryan packing up your ammo. He'll meet you in the garage. Be ready to roll within the hour. Be safe and go get them!"

Everyone stood and moved to the door. At the stairs, some went up, some went down. Doc took the stairs down one flight to four, to where his office was. Gary 'the Undertaker' Sloan, Delta Team's medic, was right behind him.

"Fucking Somalia," Sloan said. "I hate that place."

"Yeah, it's not my favorite place either," Doc agreed.

They each went into their offices. Doc grabbed his mission medical kit, which was always kept packed and ready. He picked through the supplies, double checking its contents. He had a little space left. Knowing they were going to an area where food was scarce, he added as many protein bars that would fit.

"Fighting is active along the border," Sloan yelled from his office. "What do you think, Doc, should we try to bring some whole blood?"

"We'll requisition a supply from the infirmary at Camp Lemonnier, but it probably wouldn't hurt to bring our own insulated bags for it." He grabbed his from the shelf.

Angel arrived for work at Shepherd Security with baby Sammy on Monday morning. Jackson and the team had been scrambled the day before. After the men's sudden departure, Angel stayed at Sienna's long after Michaela and Yvette left. They were the only other guests who hadn't been called into work. Sienna was doing very well with being with a man who did what their men did.

She found it odd that Jackson had not called her since he got called into work. She knew she would find out the details of the mission this morning. Shepherd would tell her. He always did. Angel took Sammy's jacket off and sat him in the activity chair which sat beside her desk. She logged into her computer and logged herself into the staff calendar. She saw that Shepherd was logged in, as well as Yvette and Michaela.

Before she could reach for her cell phone to text Shepherd, a message came in from him asking her to come to his office. She picked up baby Sammy and carried him through the inner hallway to Shepherd's office. His door was open, and he sat behind his desk. He rolled out from behind it as she entered the room. He extended his hands to take his little namesake.

He motioned to the guest chair which sat next to him. "How are you little man?" He held Sammy up in front of him and kissed his forehead. "How are you this morning?" He asked Angel.

"Good, a little concerned about the team, though. Jackson hasn't called since he deployed yesterday."

"I asked him not to," Shepherd said.

Angel stared at him in disbelief. He'd never done that before. She became even more confused when Lassiter came through the door.

"Hi, Angel," Lassiter said, greeting her with a hug. He took a seat beside her.

Angel glanced between the two men. "This can't be good. Is Jackson okay?"

Shepherd gave her a reassuring smile. "The entire team is fine."

"Then why?"

"Angel, the team deployed to Djibouti, Africa."

"I know. Yvette called into Ops after they got called in. They said the Army called in a favor from you."

"Yes and no," Shepherd replied. "Captain Marscin, the base commander knows of our interest in the village your mother and the Sisters of Mercy are in. They've been keeping an eye on the area. He called to let us know an armed conflict erupted in the area." He paused and his eyes flickered to Lassiter. "Angel, they lost contact with the Sisters and believe their position was overrun by unfriendly forces."

Angel took a deep breath. This was her worst nightmare coming true. She let the breath out slowly. "How soon will the team get there?"

"After we called them in, they left immediately for Andrews Air Force Base, where they caught a C-17. Flight time was approximately fourteen hours. I got confirmation that they landed in Djibouti an hour ago. They're gearing up and getting ready to deploy to the village. I would expect them to be onsite within the next few hours."

Angel nodded; her eyes locked onto Sammy. "What is their mission?"

"To find and evacuate the Sisters and any civilians in their care," Shepherd said. "Miller will remain in Ops at Camp Lemonnier coordinating the mission. She will also be in contact with our Ops Center throughout."

Angel nodded again. "You'll keep me informed?"

Lassiter squeezed her shoulder. "You know we will. When the mission is on, I will monitor the situation from the conference room and will keep you updated."

"Thanks, Joe," Angel said. It was never good for her to listen to mission operations live. "Okay, I better get to work." She stood and reached for Sammy.

"Angel, are you okay?" Shepherd asked, allowing her to take Sammy from his arms.

She beamed a fake smile at him as she hugged her son close to her. "I'm fine. The team will get my mom out."

"It's okay to be worried," Lassiter said softly.

"I know. And I am."

The eight men walked the flight line and boarded the helicopter. It would be a short flight to the drop zone. Doc sat on the bench with his back to the pilots. He had a clear view of every team member. He rummaged through his medical kit, one final check. His eyes went to Cooper, seated directly in front of him. Cooper's eyes were closed, and he was in his usual pre-mission meditation state.

Garcia, seated beside him, had his earbuds in, rocking out to the Stones or the Doors, no doubt. He was methodically checking over his weapons. His jaw was set, his lips drawn into a thin line. Jackson, further within the craft wore his earbuds as well. Country music was his go-to, to calm his pre-mission adrenaline. His eyes were focused on the picture of Angel and Sammy he kept in his helmet. Beside him, sat Lambchop. The Reverend had his phone in front of his face, reading Bible verses, no doubt. He'd broadcast a short prayer to the group as the helo was on final approach to the LZ.

Doc's eyes then went to the Birdman. He was the quirkiest of the group in his pre-mission ritual. He kissed his dog tags three times and then tucked them away. He checked each weapon, and then he kissed his dog tags one last time, followed by making the sign of the cross in classic Catholic fashion, spectacles, testicles, wallet, watch. Doc's lips curved into a grin watching the Birdman do his thing. The Cajun openly professed to being superstitious. If he got distracted and missed a step or did a step out of order, he started all over again. The team used to fuck with him, trying to make him goof up so he'd have to restart it.

The Undertaker sat beside the Birdman. Doc had watched him on countless missions. He didn't seem to have a pre-mission ritual, like the others. He talked and laughed with Mother, who attempted to play his word games on his phone. Doc knew Mother preferred to be left alone to play his games, but he would never ignore the Undertaker's joking banter. Maybe that was the pre-mission ritual the two of them followed?

Everyone knew that Mother was addicted to the games, a competitive streak in him drove him to build his vocabulary with several different word-a-day text messages coming to his phone. He often shared new words with the team, not to wow them with his impressive vocabulary, but to educate them. Mother had the spirit of a teacher in him.

"Three-minutes till the drop zone, standby," came the pilot's voice.

Immediately, Lambchop lowered his phone. Both Garcia and Jackson removed their earbuds. When Lambchop knew he had everyone's attention, he began. "Dear Lord, we, your humble servants ask that you protect us and all innocent civilians during the coming operation. Please let us find the Sisters and the women and children in their care, safe. Enable us to withdraw to the LZ without incident. We ask this in the name of your Son, Jesus Christ, Amen."

Amen resounded throughout the helicopter. Doc wasn't sure what would happen if Shepherd ever hired someone who objected to the pre-mission prayers. He actually wasn't sure if anyone on the team already did object. He was pretty sure Shepherd and Cooper both would tell any man who complained to keep it to himself if he had a problem with it. Doc wasn't overly religious, but he did believe in God. He found the pre-mission blessing comforting. Besides, he'd prefer to have the big man on their side and not against them.

Jackson and Sloan moved to the doors and took up sniper positions. The chopper set down in the small clearing as discussed in the pre-mission briefing. It would be a two click hike from the LZ to the village where the Sisters should be. The base in Djibouti last heard from them over twenty-four hours ago. Even though the Sisters planned to shelter in place, they could be anywhere by now, that's if they were still alive. But the village was a starting point.

Doc was the first to hop out of the chopper, his AR-15 held at the ready. He prostrated himself on the ground a few steps out, rifle trained in front of himself, his eyes scanning for threats. To his left, Cooper did the same, aiming his rifle in the other direction. It took only seconds for the eight men to disembark and for the helicopter to lift back into the sky, bank, and speed away. It cleared the area without incident.

The eight men made their way through the mixed landscape of rocky outcroppings with sparse vegetation, desert soil, and a few five-foot tall trees randomly growing in places that defied logic. The village was on the other side of the small rocky rise they would climb, which would keep them hidden from the view of any unfriendly forces that could still be in the area. They made good time traversing the rough terrain. It was late afternoon, and it was hot, a seasonal one-hundred five degrees. The rocks held the heat making the ground hot too.

"This is an awful place," Doc remarked aloud.

"A complete shit-hole," Sloan seconded. "I can't understand why anyone would fight over this place."

"Hey, maintain operational silence!" Cooper barked. He didn't like this place any more than anyone else but getting Angel's mom and the other Sisters out was the mission.

From the hillside, they viewed the village through binoculars. All looked quiet, but they knew that was seldom the case. At least it hadn't been burned as neighboring villages had.

"I don't see anyone moving, neither military nor civilian. It's quiet. Too quiet," Cooper said. He did see at least a dozen bodies on the ground.

"Thermal imaging from the satellite still shows no heat signatures," Madison broadcast. "I hope the Sisters are in the cave as they intended. If not, they aren't there." She didn't need to elaborate on the fact that they could be there and show no heat signatures if they were dead.

"Roger that, Xena," Cooper acknowledged. "Watch our six. We're heading in now."

"You better believe it," she replied through their comms. "Good hunting Alpha and Delta."

The men took up an assault formation, covering each other as they carefully moved in. They fanned out in teams of two, clearing each building as they came to it. Once in the center of the village, Cooper sent both Jackson and Sloan, the two snipers, onto different roofs to cover the team as they continued to clear the buildings.

The whole village appeared to be deserted. The buildings were looted, but were intact, not burned to the ground. There were a dozen bodies, their lives extinguished from gunshot wounds. They lay mostly in front of tiny homes.

Garcia approached a body that lay in front of the building that was designated as the orphanage during the briefing. "I have a Sister, multiple bullets in the back," Garcia broadcast.

"Is it Angel's mom, Razor?" Jackson asked, a lump in his throat. Through the scope he watched Garcia.

Garcia rolled the woman over. "Negative, this Sister is Hispanic and much younger."

Jackson breathed out a sigh of relief.

"At the entrance to the clinic. It literally is sitting right up against the rocky hill," Doc broadcast. He made eye contact with Cooper, who stood beside him.

"We're breaching it now," Cooper said. "Continue to search for unfriendlies or survivors. We won't have time to bury the dead."

Cooper went in first. His gun swept around the room while his eyes scanned every corner, every shadow. Doc was in right behind him, his AR-15 held tightly in his grasp ready to fire on any threat. The two men moved around the room slowly.

The room was hot, the air stuffy. Not a soul was in sight. They moved towards the back wall that would be up against the towering hill.

"Sister Bernice John," Cooper called. "We're here to get you out!"

There was the sound of movement in the corner. A portion of the wall moved. A petite woman wearing the traditional 'penguin' habit appeared in the opening. Her face was an older version of Angel's.

"Thank God," she said. "We are here, within the cave."

"Sister Bernice John?" Cooper asked.

"Yes," she confirmed with a warm smile. "Did Captain Marscin send you?"

"Yes. I'm sorry it took us so long to arrive."

"No apology needed. Until this morning there were enemy forces in the village. We have stayed hidden, but the children are getting restless."

Doc stepped forward. "Do you have any injured within, Sister?"

"We do. Many refugees from a nearby village came to us needing medical attention. Several of our own people didn't make it within before the enemy was upon us. Am I correct in fearing the worst?"

"I'm sorry, Sister. Yes, your village suffered several casualties."

Tears filled her eyes, and she nodded.

"Coop, the village is clear. We need to move those people out to the pickup rendezvous while we have some light left," the Undertaker broadcast. "I don't have any movement nearby, but I think we've gotten some attention a few hills to our west. I've got some movement that could indicate mobilization."

"Roger that. Xena, are you monitoring that situation?" He asked his wife.

"Roger Coop. Not sure if they are getting ready to head in your direction or if their sudden movement is coincidental, but I wouldn't take my time if I were you. If they become a threat, I will call in some air support, but let's not push our luck."

"Roger Xena." Cooper turned his attention back to Angel's mom. "We need to get your people together and move out quickly. This is our medic. He can take a look at your wounded."

She nodded, motioned to the two men to follow, and then went back through the secret doorway.

Doc followed her back through the hole in the wall and into the cave. Low voltage lamps illuminated the space. It was jam-packed with women and children, and supplies. The air was stifling, and it had the stench of body odor, urine, and feces.

"Oh, shit," he mumbled, pulling his scarf over his mouth. He could usually tolerate most smells, but it was overpowering.

"Yes, in those buckets," a waif of a girl said, pointing to the six buckets that lined the fake wall.

She was a white girl who appeared to be in her mid-teens. She had dirty dark blond hair that hung long in her face. She was short, not much over five foot. Her eyes drew his attention. Even in this low lighting the beautiful blue depths sparkled and held his gaze. They were focused on him in a way that bothered him.

"We need to move, fast," he said. "I'll evaluate the wounded as we move them."

"I have two patients that cannot be moved. It will kill them," she argued.

"We are all evacuating, now," he replied firmly.

"I'm not and neither are my patients."

"Sister Elizabeth," Sister Bernice John cut in. "Perhaps this medic can assist with your two most critically wounded."

"Yes, Sister," Elizabeth said. She returned her gaze to his. "They are back in the farthest chamber. I don't believe any of the wounded in this section to be too fragile to be moved."

Doc nodded to Cooper. Behind him, several other members of their team filed in to aid with the extraction of the many within the cave. Doc followed the young girl through a low and narrow cutout in the rocks that led into a second chamber. A curtain hung, which he pushed aside as he stood upright. There, on two metal tables laid her patients.

His gaze swept over their tiny bodies. Neither could have been older than five years old. She'd cleaned most of the blood from them, but they both had large stitched up wounds with scabbed blood. One of the boys looked as though he'd undergone open heart surgery. The other, besides a large wound at his collar bone, had both legs in crude splints. He couldn't believe the sight. The job done on them both had been done with a poor technique. The wounds weren't even bandaged. He was surprised the bleeding had stopped.

"You did this?" He demanded.

"Yes," she confirmed. "I used the remainder of the sutures I had and expended the antiseptic as well. Knowing I probably didn't kill all the germs with the sparse sanitizing I could do, I left the wounds unbandaged so I could watch for signs of infection."

"You're a doctor?" He asked.

"No, a nurse, but we have no doctor and these two would have died had I done nothing. They were both bleeding profusely when they arrived. I did my best," she insisted firmly and unapologetic.

A pang of remorse hit Doc, square in the chest. Of course, she had. She was obviously in way over her head. "And you did save them. I can strengthen your sutures and apply a proper level of antiseptic and then bandage the wounds. Will you assist?"

She nodded and moved in close as he opened his medical pack. He handed her a set of gloves and donned his. He found her to be a good assistant, knew the names of the instruments he asked for, handed them to him correctly, and jumped in when needed to help tie off or cut threads. She was a competent nurse but shouldn't have been the doctor in this village.

When finished, Doc took both boys vitals. They were both weak, very weak. He hated to admit it, but Sister Elizabeth was correct. Moving these two would kill them. Hell, just carrying them out of the cave would probably do it.

Cooper stuck his head into the room. "Doc, we're ready to move. Do you have these two stabilized?"

Doc gazed into Sister Elizabeth's ocean blue eyes. He saw a fire in them.

"They're too weak to move. You know that," she pled. "Go, I'll stay with them."

"Our mission is to get everyone out," Doc said.

"What does it matter if you kill them in the process?" Elizabeth demanded. "Come back for us in three days. If they make it, they'll be strong enough by then."

"We're not leaving anyone behind, Sister," Cooper said.

"She's right, Coop. We'll kill them if we move them now." Doc considered it for a long moment. "Come back to get us in three days. They'll be ready to be moved by then."

"We're not leaving anyone behind," Cooper insisted.

"And make sure someone empties those buckets of piss and shit. I can't stand the smell," Doc added.

"Doc, you're sure they can't be moved?"

"Coop, you need to move, you have incoming," Madison's voice came through their comms. "I'm calling in an airstrike, but I doubt we'll get them all."

"Roger, Xena." His eyes refocused on Doc. "You're sure?"

"Yeah, get everyone to safety. We'll hunker down and get these two strong enough to be moved."

Cooper nodded. "Stay on comms and we'll coordinate time off to save your batteries. Stay safe. We'll be back. I promise."

Doc nodded and then watched him leave, already regretting his decision to remain behind. His eyes met the young Sister's. She should have been scared shitless, but she looked defiant. "You just might have gotten us both killed."

"Thank you," she said in a small voice, "for staying to help. You are a skilled doctor. These boys have a better chance of survival with you here."

Bravo

The seven remaining members of Shepherd Security led the civilians out of the village and to the LZ. Madison called in the air strike. Missiles hit three of the four trucks, loaded with Al-Shabaab members. The explosion stunned the women and children that were evacuating. Many cried out and hit the ground when the Earth shook violently as the deafening concussion echoed through the canyon.

The fourth vehicle sped around the carnage and continued towards the village. After conducting a very brief search, and finding it vacant, the truck loaded with the fighters took the only other road out, the one the Shepherd Security personnel were on with the refugees, mostly women and children.

"You've got one truck with about a dozen heat signatures heading your way. Move your asses to the LZ!" Madison's voice came through the men's comms.

"Roger that, Xena," Cooper said. They were trying. Many of the civilians were injured or were young children that weren't capable of moving too quickly. "What's their ETA?"

"At your current speed, it's going to be close."

"Understood," Cooper said. "Keep me apprised of their twenty."

"Roger Coop," Madison replied.

Two Sikorsky UH-60 Black Hawk helicopters came into view, swiftly getting closer. The rotors kicked up the loose sandy dirt floor of the canyon and swirled it through the dry, hot air. Both birds landed. The men didn't waste a second. They hustled the civilians aboard, lifting those who needed assistance.

Sister Bernice John stopped in front of Jackson as she was about to climb in. Recognition washed over her features. "Jackson?" She shouted.

He smiled and nodded. "We'll catch up on board. We have to move, Sister!"

"Of course," she said and climbed in, assisted by her son-in-law.

"The hostiles are on the other side of that rise to your west," Madison announced. "I launched a second Hellfire. ETA two minutes. Keep your heads down."

Cooper and Lambchop took up cover positions, weapons aimed at the hill, in case the hostiles moved in faster than the drone. Over his shoulder, Cooper saw the last of the civilians climb onto the choppers.

The truck crested the rise. The incoming force fired at the first sight of them. Gunfire struck the helicopters, which were sitting ducks on the ground. Then the missile hit the truck. It exploded in a rolling fireball that sent debris a hundred feet in all directions as the earsplitting blast reverberated between the hills, shaking the ground.

Cooper and Lambchop climbed aboard taking up gunner positions with Mother and the Undertaker on their chopper. Cooper viewed the other bird. Jackson, the Birdman, and Garcia covered the doors on it. The birds flew out of Al-Shabaab territory, swiftly retreating further into the safety of Ethiopia before banking and heading towards Camp Lemonnier.

"The team is clear," Madison said. "Doc, are you safe at your twenty?"

"Safe enough," Doc replied. His eyes flickered to the young Sister. "We need to figure out a schedule to be off comms and save my battery power."

"Roger that, Doc. Go ahead and signoff now. We'll start out with a top of the hour rotation. Al-Shabaab is still trying to figure out what the hell hit them. I'm sure they believe the village is vacant. You're safe for a little while, but I'll be watching."

"Keep a good eye out, Xena. I'll be back online at the top of the hour."

Doc turned the comms off, knowing he was now cut off from his team. If Madison saw any threat, she would not be able to alert him. His gut twisted. Remaining here was one of the stupidest things he'd ever done. He took a seat on the narrow, hard cot beside the Sister. Then he opened his pack and removed two protein bars. He handed one to her.

She gave him a slight smile and took it. "Thank you," she said in a small voice. "Dear Lord, our provider, thank you for the salvation of rescue these men brought. And thank you for this sustenance for my body. I especially thank you, Father, for this doctor who brought it, who will help heal these children, in Your name, Amen."

Doc had opened his packaging and took a bite of his bar when she'd started speaking her blessing. He paused, watched, and listened, giving her the respect of her faith. He then watched as she tore the packaging on her protein bar open. She devoured it like she hadn't eaten in weeks, before he even took another bite.

"What's your name?" She asked after she had finished eating.

"Doc."

"No, your real name, what your mother named you."

"Alexander Williams, but I go by Doc."

"Alexander," she announced like she had just named him. She smiled pleasantly. "It's nice to meet you. I'm Elizabeth Shaw." She reached her right hand to him.

"It's nice to meet you too, Sister Elizabeth." He shook her hand.

"Just Elizabeth is fine." She glanced around nervously. "Way back here in this cavern we should be safe." Though she knew they were not. Not as long as they remained. She knew the violence in this region, the war, the lack of respect for human life.

Doc didn't like that it was as though she could sense his feelings and thoughts. That was exactly what he'd been telling himself. "I've got a couple motion detectors on me. I'm going to wire the fake wall and a second location within the main cave. You stay here and I'll be right back."

He came to his feet and wove his way through the narrow passageway and back to the main cave. He mounted his motion detectors and then extinguished six of the eight low wattage lamps. He carried the last two with him back to the chamber where Sister Elizabeth and their two patients waited. Then he sat up the rugged computer tablet that would monitor the motion detectors on the foot of one of the metal tables where the smallest of the two boys laid.

"What about power for it?" She asked, coming to her feet and coming in close to inspect the equipment.

"It's self-contained. The monitoring equipment draws very little power when idle. It only eats the juice when activated."

"And that can't power your other communication device?"

Doc smiled. She was a curious girl. Of course, he already knew that, a nurse performing surgery. This wisp of a girl was both curious and tenacious. He shook his head at that thought. "No, a different type of power is used. How old are you, anyway?"

She raised her chin into the air and stood a little taller. "I'm twenty-four years old. Why does that matter?"

Doc's lips ticked up into a grin. Jesus, she was a child. "It doesn't. It's just that you look like you're about fifteen. I was just wondering how old you were."

His words annoyed her. "I'm old enough," she said with an edge to her voice unbecoming a Sister. "I've been here three years."

"And what have you learned in the three years you've been here?" Doc asked as he continued configuring his equipment.

"The people of this region are strong and resilient. They want to survive and live free of conflict and tyranny."

"They're living in the wrong part of the world for that," Doc remarked cynically.

"Most of the militia, warlords, and pirates steer clear of us so the women and children who seek refuge with us are safe." She paused and chuckled. "They fear repercussions in their afterlives if they harm a Sister. They may not believe in the same God, but they respect that we are women of faith. But Al-Shabaab and Boko Haram, they're different. They are ruthless and radical."

"Yes, they are," Doc agreed, his tone dead serious. "If you Sisters hadn't hid, you'd all be dead or someone's concubine."

"Probably dead," she agreed.

With this admission, Doc saw her armor crumble. She knew she was in deep shit here; knew how close it had been, probably even knew how dangerous it was for them to remain for the next three days. "But you hid, and you survived." He'd throw her that bone.

"Yes," she confirmed with pride. "I just prayed they wouldn't burn our village to the ground as they did the others. We would have been overcome by the smoke and no doubt would have all perished in the cave."

Doc nodded. They'd been damned lucky. "Well, the others are all safe now. It's just the four of us we need to worry about for the next three days, or as soon as these two heal up enough for transport."

Elizabeth nodded wearily. The exhaustion of the past few days were overtaking her now that she was safe, well, sort of safe. She yawned deeply. "I haven't slept much. Do you mind if I?" She pointed to the cot.

"Sure," he said. "I've got them. Get some sleep."

She grabbed one of the lighter weight blankets and balled it up to use as a pillow as she reclined on the cot. This man's presence did bring her a feeling of safety and security. Knowing he would watch over her patients, she drifted off into a deep slumber almost immediately.

Elizabeth's calm state didn't last long. She soon found herself shivering, awake and in a near-frenzied state. She gasped for air while mentally telling herself to calm down and relax. She was safe.

"Shh, it's okay," Doc said, soothingly. He took hold of her wrist and took her pulse. It was racing. He knelt beside the cot. "Take slow, deep breaths."

She did as she was told. "I'm not sure how I can be cold as this cave is hotter than Hades, but I'm shivering."

"How long had you been awake?"

"I don't know, thirty or so hours."

Doc's lips twisted into a smirk. "You were running on adrenalin, hyping you up, until you went to sleep. You're just crashing now. It's a common response. Just keep breathing slowly and you'll be fine." He sat her hand back to the cot and moved away. Great, he had a third patient, just what he needed.

The two Black Hawk helicopters sat down in the darkness beside a hangar at Camp Lemonnier. All the Sisters and civilians, except for Sister Bernice John, were turned over to base personnel, who led them to temporary quarters where they would receive medical evaluations, meals, and bunks. Sister Bernice John would catch up with them later.

After introductions all around, including hugs of thanks from Angel's mom to each man, she and Jackson enabled a video chat with Angel, back at HQ. Angel held a sleeping baby Sammy up for his grandmother to see how big he had gotten.

"I wish I was there with you," Angel said. "Mom, when the team returns, can you come with them?"

"Oh, my Angel, I wish I could. The people we serve need us more than ever now. You are safe and healthy." She paused and smiled at Jackson. "Your husband and his coworkers see to that. My heart is at peace that you are in the very best place you can be in. Praise God that He delivered you to this man." She embraced Jackson.

"I worry about you, Mom," Angel said.

"God provides, Angel. Sister Elizabeth had a divine inspiration to prepare the cave we hid in. God saw to it that your husband and his group came to our rescue. I have faith, my child, and where there is faith, there is no fear."

That same old knot twisted in Angel's gut. She believed, but not as devoutly or as fully as her mother. She couldn't say if it was God or luck that enabled her mom and the others to survive, though she would prefer to believe it was God. Having been through her own moments of terror, Angel knew how much faith played a part in getting through a horrific ordeal. "You are an inspiration, Mother," Angel said. "I love you and I am so relieved that you are okay."

"I love you, my child," the Sister said with tears in her eyes. "I love that precious grandchild of mine." Her gaze then shifted to Jackson, who sat beside her. "And I love you, Ethan Jackson. You have proved yourself time and again to be the best man for my daughter." She embraced him and cried tears of relief, of joy, of love.

"I don't like it any more than you do, Big Bear," Cooper said, cell phone to his ear. He stood near the Lakota helicopter on the very busy flight line. He nodded at the Undertaker and Lambchop, who approached, gear in hand under the bright artificial lights.

"Then why did you leave a man behind? And a Sister?" Shepherd barked.

"There were two little boys in critical condition that couldn't be moved. We're monitoring that village and all the players in the area very closely. No one will even fart in that sector without us knowing. Razor, Mother, and Jax will take shifts in Ops with Xena. The Undertaker, Lambchop and I are getting ready to deploy closer to that village with a flight team at the ready whenever Doc notifies us those kids are okay to transport, or he's in trouble. Base personnel have friends over the border in Ethiopia. We'll wait there. We're not leaving Doc uncovered."

"I still don't like it," Shepherd remarked harshly. "But I trust Doc's medical assessment of those kids. Cover his six and keep me posted."

"Roger," Cooper replied, acknowledging Shepherd's order, and by the tone of Shepherd's voice there was no doubt it had been an order. He disconnected the call.

"Shepherd busting your balls?" Lambchop asked.

"He doesn't like that we left a man behind. If we hadn't needed every single one of us at the LZ with the civilians, I'd have stayed."

"I'm glad you didn't," Lambchop said, slapping Cooper on the shoulder. "I'd be the one making the report and getting my nuts crunched by Shepherd." The big man laughed and then climbed aboard the chopper.

When Elizabeth woke again, she felt rested and well, with none of the symptoms that had scared her. She rose from the cot and quietly approached the two exam tables and their sleeping patients. She closely examined each. They rested comfortably. She checked their wounds beneath the bandages. They looked clean and free of infection. She wondered when the last antibiotics had been administered. She checked her watch. How was it possible? She had slept ten hours!

Glancing around the cave, she found the stranger, the man named Alexander, seated on the floor with his back against his large pack. His eyes were closed. She approached him quietly. She stood less than a foot away, eyeing him to decide if he was asleep and if she should wake him. She needed to know what care had been given to her patients while she slept.

For the first time, she really looked at the face of this man who risked his own life to help with the two critically injured boys who slept on her exam tables. He was handsome in a rugged way. His face held sharp angles. He had a strong jaw that was covered in stubble. His cheekbones were chiseled and defined. His hair was shaved close, a very dark blonde with gray peppered in. He looked experienced and distinguished. She couldn't keep her lips from curving into a small smile as she viewed this warrior, this hero.

"It's rude to stare," his voice quietly said as his eyes popped open. "And dangerous to sneak up on a sleeping man."

"I'm sorry. I didn't mean to wake you," Elizabeth stammered. "I slept for over ten hours," she said, still surprised that had been the case. "The boys seem to be resting comfortably."

Doc stretched, elongating his sore back. He was getting too old for this shit. Each mission that had him in primitive conditions wore on him worse than the last. "I've kept the pain meds consistent in them, which has kept them asleep. I'm giving regular doses of the IV antibiotics as well. I will need to bring them to consciousness sometime in the next few hours. Do you speak their language?" He pulled himself from the ground and stood, towering over the petite Sister. He stretched in a few different directions.

Elizabeth gazed up at the man, at least a foot taller than herself. Of course, she was used to most every other adult and many children surpassing her height. But there was something different about his height and how it affected her. She watched him raise his hands over his head as he stretched. He had removed his overshirt and wore only a t-shirt, which clung to his carved frame. His arms were muscular and defined, even his forearms.

Elizabeth pulled her thoughts from his form, inappropriate. "I don't think so. The woman who brought them in said they had fled from another village that had been attacked. She didn't think they spoke her tongue or the regional clan dialect in the village she was in. She was from Addis Ababa, Ethiopia."

"She was pretty damn far from home. What the hell was she doing way out here?" Doc asked.

"If I may ask, please, do not use curses when it's unnecessary," Elizabeth said softly.

A gut check hit Doc. Yeah; he probably shouldn't swear in front of the Sister. "My bad, sorry. Habit. I'll watch it Sister."

"Really, just Elizabeth is fine," she insisted. "Anyway, the woman was visiting her husband's family's village when the violence broke out and was stuck there. I'm glad she was evacuated with the others. Your group was God-sent!"

Doc's lips pulled into a smirk, no, not God-sent, Captain Marscin from Camp Lemonnier-sent. He rummaged through his pack and pulled two more protein bars out. He handed one to the Sister. He knew there were local foods stockpiled in the other cave, mostly rice and other low nutrition foods. There were a few bananas, probably the only food that he deemed safe to eat. He would avoid the water that was in containers in the cave as well, even though Sister Elizabeth insisted it had gone through their water purifier and was safe. He had enough water on him to last him the few days he'd be there if he rationed it.

"God, thank you for this nutrition to maintain our bodies. Thank you for this man who brought this food and who continues to give professional care to these two young souls. I am grateful for so much. In Your name we pray, Amen." Elizabeth glanced up into the man's eyes after she completed the blessing. She saw warmth, but not an abiding faith. Prayers prior to a meal was not his way. No matter, she would continue to say a blessing aloud as long as he didn't protest.

Doc flashed the Sister a pleasant grin and then tore open the packaging of his protein bar. He still couldn't get past the fact that she looked like a teenager, so young, too young to be in this dangerous part of the world. He was intrigued though, that someone so young had dedicated herself to God in servitude as a Sister, to live in poverty and chastity.

"These bars taste good," Elizabeth said. "I read the nutritional label. There are more grams of protein in one bar than many in this region ingest in a whole month."

"They're a special military grade," Doc replied.

Elizabeth nodded. "I assumed so."

"I have enough in my bag for us both for the next few days."

"Once the boys are awake, I'd prefer my share go to them. I can make do with the bananas and rice in the cave."

"I have enough for the boys as well, once they are able to eat," Doc corrected his prior statement. He didn't like the idea of her sacrificing her portion.

"Very good," Elizabeth said. Conversation with this man was awkward. Of course, besides the topic of medicine, what did they have in common?

Charlie

Twenty-four more hours passed. Doc kept the boys stable, but the pain killers he administered whenever they cried, knocked them out too. Their wounds were healing but their vitals hadn't gotten any stronger. Doc napped in between checking in with his team at the top of every hour. He was tired and needed more than a fifty-minute nap.

Elizabeth could tell this quiet man was growing weary. "Teach me to use your communications equipment and I can check in with your team while you sleep," Elizabeth said. "We can take turns napping."

"I don't need to sleep. I'm fine," he insisted stubbornly.

"You look exhausted. If you were my patient, I'd recommend sleep."

Doc chuckled to himself. If he were her patient! Like he'd place himself in the care of a nurse who looked like she was a teenager. Never mind the fact too that she operated so far outside of her training, not that he didn't respect her for what she had done to save the two boys. He did. He also discovered she was obstinate and frustrating. Their interactions over the past thirty some hours proved that.

"Sister, you're far more tired than I am. I'm used to little sleep."

She scoffed at that. "Do not let the fact that I wear a habit mislead you into thinking I am weak. I am anything but."

Doc chuckled out loud. "Oh, Sister, trust me, I don't think you are weak. I pity the poor man that goes up against you."

She wasn't sure if he was mocking her or not. "And just because I don't seem as jaded or cynical as you, don't assume I don't know the circumstances of the world. I've seen hate and the disregard for human life. I've seen more than my years give me credit for. My education may not be formal, but it has been intensive, both in Seattle and here. I choose to see the good in the world and in people, but I also accept there is evil."

"I never meant to insinuate you are naïve, Sister. If you mistook anything I said, I apologize."

She evaluated his words, his tone of voice, and his facial expression. This man was hard to figure out. When, after a few quiet moments he flashed her a grin, she returned it. "If this goes on for several more days, at some point, you will need more than an hour of sleep at a time. I promise you, if anything happens while you sleep, I will wake you."

Doc knew she was right about that too, just as she had been right about the condition of these two boys. But he didn't want to admit that to her. He checked the boys again. The bigger of the two, with the most serious chest wounds had stronger vitals than the other one. He reexamined the wound at the little one's clavicle. The sutures held, and no infection was present. He checked his pulse in his femoral arteries since both legs were splinted. They too were there, weak, but there. He couldn't figure out why this one was faring more poorly, unless he had lost more blood volume in relation to his size.

At the top of the hour, Elizabeth watched closely as Doc turned his comms on and initiated communication with his team. She paid close attention to the words he used. After the brief two-minute exchange with someone named Xena, hearing only his side of the conversation, she watched him turn the comms back off. Then he resettled in the corner, on the floor, with his back planted firmly against his pack where he had slept every time.

Forty-five minutes later, she gently deactivated the alarm on his wristwatch, which woke him every fifty minutes. She took the comms, which he wore loose around his neck, and after checking the motion detection feed on the tablet, and seeing there was no movement in the cave, she retreated into the passageway that led to the main cavern. She was careful to stay far within that cavern, far from the motion detector so she wouldn't trip it.

At the top of the hour she turned the comms on and placed them in her ears. "Campground to Basecamp," she said, just as he had.

A female voice replied. "This is Basecamp, Campground, you sound as though your nuts have been cut off."

Elizabeth was surprised by this reply. "Just checking in. All is quiet at our twenty," she said, as he had earlier.

"Who is this and where is Doc?" The female voice demanded.

"This is the Sister," Elizabeth said. "And he's sleeping. He's done every check in. He was exhausted. But he's okay."

"Roger that. All is quiet, there is no activity near your Campground. Talk to you during the next check in. Basecamp out."

Elizabeth pulled the comms out of her ear and turned them off. That was anti-climactic. The woman on the other end wasn't as chatty with her as she normally was with Alexander. Elizabeth wasn't sure what she'd expected, but she felt let down for some reason.

Elizabeth repeated the check in seven more times. She watched the boys, administered antibiotics and painkillers to them, and she watched Alexander sleep, proud she had found a way to help him despite himself. She knew he really needed it.

On the eighth check in, the woman on the other end of the radio was a bit friendlier and chattier. "You'll need to wake Doc for the next check in," she said. "We're going to need to talk with him to plan your extraction."

"I will," Elizabeth said, guessing extraction meant getting them out. "I'm glad he was able to sleep this long. He hadn't for days. Are you the one he's called Xena?"

She heard a little laugh. "Yep, that's me, but if you're trying to envision me based on the iconic character, don't, I look nothing like her."

Elizabeth didn't know what the iconic character looked like. She had never been into pop culture when she was a teen as she'd already been with the Sisters then. She spent her time on biblical and scholarly pursuits. As an eighth grader, she was more well-read than most adults. "I'll keep that in mind," Elizabeth said. "Will I meet you when we extract?" She was careful to use the correct language.

"Roger," the woman replied. "We'll meet. Before we sign off, give me a status on the comms power."

Elizabeth removed the one side from her right ear and looked at the indicator. "It's below a quarter," she reported.

"Roger that. Tell Doc to make it one and a half rotations till next check in."

"Will do." Then Elizabeth signed off and powered the comms down. When she turned around to go back into the passageway that led into the cavern the others were in, she ran right into a solid form. She let out a surprised sound, not quite a scream.

"What the fuck?" Doc growled. He grabbed her by her upper arms. He pulled her through the narrow passageway and back into the little cavern they had been hunkered down in. Then he held her at arm's length with fire in his eyes.

Elizabeth gazed fearfully into Alexander's face. He looked mad but rested. She swallowed her fear. "You needed to sleep."

"I was out for over eight hours," his caustic voice enunciated. "Do you have any fucking clue how much danger you put us in?"

Elizabeth shook her head. "I checked in with your team at the top of every hour and I monitored the motion detection equipment."

Doc released her arms and grabbed the sides of his face while sighing out loud. "Elizabeth, you disabled my alarm on my watch."

"You needed to sleep, Alexander. You were exhausted."

"It wasn't your place to make that decision," he said, trying to calm himself.

"Everything remained quiet. I just got off the line with Xena, no one is in the vicinity. She's been watching." She gave him a moment. She could tell he was trying to calm his anger. "Battery power is under a quarter. She said to change the cycle to one and a half rotations, whatever that means. She told me to wake you for the next check in to plan our extraction."

Doc scrubbed his hand over his face and sighed out loud again. "Okay," he finally said. "But you don't do that again. Do you understand me?"

Elizabeth nodded her head yes. "But don't you feel better now that you've slept longer than an hour?"

Doc growled and stepped around her. He did, but he surely would not admit it to her. He grabbed his last bottle of water and two more protein bars from his pack. He handed one of the bars to her. He drank a quarter of the water, devoured the protein bar, and then checked the boys. Both had stronger vitals. Good, they could get out of there soon.

He checked his watch as he took a seat on the ground near his pack. It was just past zero-three hundred local time. A zero-four-thirty check in with Basecamp, and if it was all clear, they could be out of there by zero-six hundred. He set his alarm for zero-four-thirty. His anger softened. He gazed across the cavern at the young woman, perched on the edge of the cot, nibbling at her protein bar.

"Are you getting enough by just eating those?"

She smiled meekly, recognizing the olive branch he was extending. "I am. These are full of more nutrition than my body has had in one meal in years. I think I've adapted to the region and my body knows rice and bananas with very little meat is all it's going to get each day. I remember how hungry I felt when I first arrived, even after ingesting what is considered a meal around here."

Doc nodded. "It's appalling what over a quarter of the world is sustained on."

"It's even more appalling how ignorant many of the wealthy are. They do not understand what they have compared to the rest of the world."

"Amen to that, Sister," Doc agreed.

"When I first arrived and felt as though I was starving, I fed my soul with reading God's word when I wasn't ministering to those who sought refuge here."

Doc smirked and nodded. He didn't know many who could fend off a hungry belly by reading the Bible. He wondered how that worked for the little kids, like the ones on the exam tables. The continuous state of widespread hunger in this country was another reason he hated Somalia. Children starving to death depressed the hell out of him.

Elizabeth watched the thoughts play over Alexander's face. She couldn't make out what he was thinking. Nothing new. This man was an enigma to her. "So, what do you do to feed your soul?"

Doc gazed at her with a half-smirk, half-smile. No one talked that way, no one that he knew, anyway. His mother used to be a little on the poetic side, like that, when he was a little boy. His lips tipped into a full grin with thoughts about his mother. He hadn't seen his family or his home in Houston in years. He made the obligatory call home on major holidays and he usually kept those calls short. There were way too many unpleasant memories in Houston, memories he didn't want to invade his conscious thought.

"Every chance I get, I go fishing, which isn't often enough."

"Fishing," she repeated with a smile. "What is it about the act of fishing that you like?"

Doc sighed and stretched his legs out in front of him. "I don't know, me alone with the beauty of nature. No inane chatter, not another soul within miles. It's peaceful, quiet, and I can just be."

Elizabeth smiled and nodded. "I can understand the attraction it holds for you. I imagine you have seen a few too many of man's atrocities against each other." She spoke from experience. "I'm from Seattle. While I, and after I earned my CNA, I worked in the Sisters of Mercy's free clinic in South Park, which if you don't know Seattle, is one of the worse parts of the city. The crime rate there is very high. Most live in extreme poverty. And there is a lot of gang activity. The Sisters turn no one away. I learned to dig bullets out of people from the doctor there, one of the Sisters."

"And those patients went unreported to the authorities?" He tried to keep his judgement of that from showing.

Elizabeth nodded. "They had to have faith that they would remain anonymous or they wouldn't come for treatment. And if they didn't come for treatment, they'd most likely die."

Doc shook his head. "I was a Paramedic in Houston, before I joined the Army. I transported way too many young people who'd been shot. Such a waste. And of course, in the Army, over in the Sandbox, the wounded were always coming. Man's hatred for each other is a constant no matter where you're at."

Elizabeth nodded her head. "I hope you will be able to go fishing soon."

Doc gazed at her with an added level of respect. She got it, few others did. "What about you? What do Sister's do during their leisure time?"

Elizabeth chuckled. She locked eyes with him, appreciating the unique pale gray coloring of his irises. "I like to read and sing. I recently got hooked on crossword puzzles. The Sisters don't really have leisure time, they are always in ministry or studying the word of God. I'm no longer a Sister. I didn't take my final vows."

Doc stared at her with surprise. "What exactly does that mean?"

"When it was time for me to make it official, I didn't."

"I'm sorry," Doc said. "I'm not Catholic. I know there are steps and a timetable, but I don't know what those steps are."

"I declared my intention to serve at age sixteen, was sure I had the calling. At age eighteen, I officially joined the order. At age twenty, I made my first vows. I should have made my final vows last year, but I couldn't. Sister Bernice John counseled me this past year, and we prayed on it together. She put the paperwork to process me out on hold, believing I'd change my mind. I haven't. I don't have the faith I should have. I mistook the feeling of belonging with a calling."

Doc gazed at her with a mixture of feelings. "So, just like that, you decide after eight years of your life that you're not being called. Now what?"

"I need to leave. I'm more sure of it now than I have ever been. When we get picked up by your team, I will be firm with Sister Bernice John that it is time for me to go home, for my paperwork to be processed. I guess I'll need to figure out the rest of my life now. I'm not afraid of the future and my deep and abiding faith remains. I will always love God and my fellow man, just not as a Sister."

Doc didn't understand. She still sounded like a nun. Then his thoughts went to Lambchop, their resident reverend. Lambchop had that faith and still managed to be a hell of a SEAL, and a hell of a team member. Maybe her calling was more in the direction as Lambchop's. He knew there were limited roles for women in the Catholic church, and the whole celibacy thing for both men and women would be a deal breaker for him. Unable to figure out anything to say, Doc just nodded.

The older of the two boys mumbled words. He began to move his limbs. Doc rushed over to him. He was the one with the many wounds in his chest. "Hey, easy there, little guy," he said. He kept the boy from touching his bandaged wounds, which as the boy came more alert turned into a fight to control his hands. The boy shouted out words. "Do you speak his language?"

Elizabeth hovered at the head of his bed. "No, it sounds like one of the many clan dialects."

The boy was becoming more combative. Doc was worried he would tear his sutures. He grabbed both of the boy's hands and pinned them down, which frightened the boy and made him fight harder. He shouted out louder. Even though Doc didn't understand the words, he recognized the panic and fear in the boy's voice.

"It's okay, my child," Elizabeth said softly, leaning her now scarfed head into the boy's line of sight. The boy's eyes focused on hers.

Doc watched Elizabeth smile mildly. She ran the back of her fingers over the boy's cheek soothingly.

"You are fine, and we will not hurt you, precious one." She pressed a gentle kiss to his forehead, a motherly gesture no matter what language a person spoke.

Doc watched in fascination. She definitely had a way about her, a way that instantly disarmed the child. The boy stopped struggling. Doc relaxed his hold of the boy's hands.

"Tawfiiq," the boy exclaimed repeatedly.

Just then a flashing light and a low tone emitted from the rugged computer tablet Doc had set up on the foot of the other bed. "Fuck, the motion sensor," Doc said softly. "Help me get him quiet."

Doc moved to the other table and clicked on the keyboard, silencing the low tone.

"Shh!" Elizabeth said over him. "Al-Shabaab." She pointed towards the entry into the cavern, like the boy would know where she was pointing to.

The boy did know Al-Shabaab. He whimpered, his eyes went wide, and his pleading eyes never left Elizabeth.

"Shh," she repeated, her finger in front of her mouth making the universal gesture to be quiet.

"The fake wall shows movement," Doc whispered, standing beside her. He had his rifle clutched in his hand.

Elizabeth's wide eyes met his cold focused stare. Then her eyes darted around the cavern. There was nowhere else to hide. She watched Alexander take a step towards the passageway. "Come back to me, please," she whispered.

He glanced back at her and nodded.

She held the little boy's hand and tried to remain calm. A few minutes later, the second motion sensor showed movement on the tablet dashboard. *No, no, no,* she said in her head. She strained her ears to listen for any sound. Nothing. Certainly, if the enemy had breached the fake wall, she would have heard gunshots or at least a scuffle if they overtook Alexander.

The seconds dragged into minutes, and time played games with her senses, just like it had the entire time they hid before Alexander and his team rescued them. She stood motionless, listening intently, barely breathing for a long time. Finally, Alexander reentered the cavern.

"They've moved on, never entered the cave. From what I can tell, it was looters, taking anything that wasn't nailed down," Doc whispered as he came in close. Then he moved to the computer tablet and typed a few commands in, resetting the system. He checked his watch. "I'm due to check in with my team in five minutes. I'm going to go on early and check the status of our visitors."

Relief washed over Elizabeth, as did exhaustion. She watched him power his comms back up. He stood facing her as he talked.

"Doc to Xena."

"You're in early," Razor's voice came through Doc's comms, bringing a smile to his face.

"Just had some visitors, thought I'd let you know we didn't invite them in or entertain them."

Garcia laughed. "Glad to hear that. It sucked not having the ability to give you a heads up."

"I've got a couple motion sensors wired. They weren't too curious about the surroundings just the things they could take. Are they still in the area?"

"Affirmative, these guys are in no hurry. I'd stay as quiet as possible."

"My batteries are at under twenty percent. I'll be back on in twenty minutes to check the status of my visitors. We are ready to evac whenever you can get us out."

"Roger that," Garcia said.

They remained silent standing near the exam tables. The little boy stayed quiet as though he understood what was taking place. Twenty minutes later, Doc powered his comms back up. "Razor, you got a report on our visitors?"

"They are out of the area. You are clear, Campground."

Doc smiled and nodded at Elizabeth. "Roger that." He checked his watch again. It was just before zero-five hundred. "We are good for exfil as soon as a canoe can come by and pick us up."

"Good to hear, Doc. Coop and company are poised near your twenty, ready to swoop in and take you out. Primary LZ will be right in the middle of downtown," Razor said indicating the chopper would land right in the middle of the village. "Give me about twenty minutes to make the arrangements and I'll be back in touch."

"I'll go off comms till then. My power is damn-near depleted," Doc said, viewing the gage.

"Roger that Doc. Basecamp out."

"We're getting picked up, probably within the hour," Doc said to Elizabeth with a grin curving his face.

Elizabeth smiled too and relaxed. She thanked God.

"Tawfiiq," the boy said, sensing the easing of the tension in the adults.

Elizabeth's eyes met Doc's. "That's a name. Help me angle his head to see this other boy. The woman who brought them in thought they were brothers."

Because of his wounds, in order to turn his head, it meant rotating his entire body. Doc slid both his arms beneath the boy. Together, he and Elizabeth rolled the boy so he could view the other one.

"Tawfiiq," he said with obvious relief and then relaxed against Doc's arms.

Elizabeth leaned over him again. "Yes, Tawfiiq is fine." She pressed another kiss to his forehead. She caressed his cheek. Then she smiled at Doc. "This is what I'll miss no longer being a Sister."

"There are a lot of jobs you can do back home to comfort children that you don't have to be a Sister to do," Doc said.

"I haven't thought about it yet. My departure from here was always so far off, but now that it is about to happen, I guess I will have to give it some thought."

Doc took a few moments and packed things up. Twenty minutes later he logged back onto his comms and reestablished communications with Razor. "Are we clear to move closer to the cave opening? The last visitor destroyed part of the wall."

"Roger that, Doc. The bird is en route to your twenty, ETA, twenty minutes."

"Great to hear, Basecamp," Doc said. "Make sure the bird has a stretcher. I only need one."

"It does," Razor guaranteed.

Doc turned off the tablet monitoring the motion detectors and packed it away in his bag with everything else. He carried his bag to the main cavern. When he returned, he took hold of the older, alert boy. "I'll bring him out first, follow me so I can leave him with you while I get his little brother," he told Elizabeth.

She nodded and followed him from the cavern, glancing behind herself at it as if to say goodbye to it. It had hidden them and kept them safe. She felt an amazing relief wash over her. Doc sat the boy to one of the two exam tables Elizabeth had in the main cavern. Her eyes scanned the fake wall she'd fashioned. Yes, the looters had torn part of it down. They weren't completely exposed, but they weren't hidden well either. Good thing their ride out was on its way and there were no threats nearby.

Elizabeth got a cup of water and helped the boy sip. It had been several days that neither boy had been awake long enough to drink more than a few drops of water. Alexander had them both hooked up to IV fluids the entire time so they wouldn't be dehydrated. He'd just removed the tubing, but he'd left the needles taped into their tiny hands. She was sure the boys would receive good care at the U.S. Naval Base in Djibouti when they arrived there.

Doc reentered the main cave carrying the younger boy. He was still unconscious. He gently laid him onto the other exam table. He saw the anticipation and relief on Elizabeth's face. The anger he felt towards her for disabling his alarm and handling the check-ins by herself was gone. Stubborn girl!

The two of them made idle chatter to pass the time. The sound of engines approaching brought a smile to Elizabeth's face, but a worried frown to Doc's. "That's not a chopper. Campground to Basecamp," he spoke. There was no reply. "Basecamp, this is Campground." He took his comms off and viewed the battery level. "Fuck! They're dead."

Delta

"Campground, come in," Razor repeated with urgency. He shook his head at Jackson who sat beside him in the Operations Center at Camp Lemonnier. "Doc's comms were nearly dead when we last spoke. Sonofabitch! Coop, I can't raise Campground. He has no idea they have incoming."

"We've fallen back two clicks from his location. How soon can you get backup in here?"

"Not soon enough if it goes south. Sonofabitch!" Garcia repeated. "I only hope he recognizes the difference between truck engines and a chopper fast enough."

"How many heat signatures you got in those trucks? It would be nice to know how many Tangos we're dealing with," Cooper questioned.

"Well, we got four troop transport trucks with blurred heat signatures in the back of each. They could each be full, men sitting shoulder to shoulder or it could be a few men laying on the benches. It is early morning. They could be sleeping."

Now Cooper cursed. "Fuck, we're too close to lose them now."

"We're watching Coop," Garcia said.

"So are we from HQ," Yvette's voice came in. "Big Bear just came on and wants to know why an airstrike wasn't called in the second the threat was identified."

"Fuck," Garcia cursed off mic. Then he clicked back in to answer. "The convoy of trucks was observed entering the sector. Its original route had it heading south, but it veered off course and doubled back at the last minute and turned onto the road leading into the village."

"Can you neutralize the threat now?" Shepherd's voice came through.

"Negative, Big Bear. The trucks have regular Somali military markings. We don't have authorization to engage."

"Do we know if it is regular Somali military behind the wheel? From the briefings I've received, that cannot be taken as a given."

"Captain Marscin is attempting to get clarification with his Somali counterparts. We're at a standstill until then," Garcia reported.

"Fuck!" Shepherd exclaimed. He had a very bad feeling about this. Things were going south, fast.

The engine sounds cut almost directly in front of the clinic building the cave entrance was behind. Doc's eyes went to Elizabeth. He heard voices. Doc killed the two low wattage lights he had on, plunging them into darkness. It took a moment for his eyes to adjust so he could see the opening on the half torn-down fake wall in the shadowy morning light that was cast on it from within the clinic building. The voices grew louder. The men were now within the clinic building, moving closer. Then his eyes became glued to the part of the fake wall that was torn down. His rifle was held at the ready.

Elizabeth leaned into the boy's face and shushed him, finger in front of her pursed lips. She heard items being picked through in her clinic. More looters, she assumed. Would Alexander's team come in with the looters here and run them off? Or would they wait until these interlopers were gone before they came to get them? She felt lightheaded, barely breathing, afraid to make any noise.

The seconds dragged into minutes; the time passing once again warped. Elizabeth felt her heart beating wildly in her chest. The sounds from within the clinic were so loud. Surely, those within would find them. Her eyes went to Alexander. He held his rifle in both hands. What would happen if he did fire his weapon? How many were within, ready to gun them down? They didn't know who was there. They just knew it wasn't Alexander's people.

The fake wall moved. Doc's adrenalin, already high in his system, quadrupled. His finger hovered near the trigger. He wished he would have had time to get Elizabeth and the two boys on the floor. The voices near the wall chattered more loudly with each other. He made out four different voices. He could take them all out, but he didn't know how many friends they'd brought that were in different buildings in the village. He hoped Elizabeth would drop to the ground if any gunfire erupted.

"Ha sameyn toogasho!" The little boy called out. "Aabe!"

The fake wall was pushed in. Doc fired a burst of gunfire. Screams answered.

"Ha sameyn toogasho!" The little boy yelled louder. "Aabe!"

Elizabeth made out a few words, don't shoot and father. "Alexander! Don't shoot!"

"Don't shoot!" Was repeated from the inside of the clinic. It was said with a heavy Somali accent, but it was said in English.

"We won't shoot if you don't," Doc called out, still holding his rifle at the ready.

"Ha sameyn toogasho!" The little boy repeated. "Aabe!"

A bright light approached the opening. Elizabeth turned one of the low wattage lamps back on.

"Extinguish that," Doc commanded.

"Aabe is father," Elizabeth told him.

Her heart stopped when three men stepped through the opening into the cave. They wore military uniforms. Two of them had their guns trained on Doc. The third one wore officer insignia. They all stared at each other in silence for a few long beats.

"You speak English?" Elizabeth asked. "I am a Sister, and this is a doctor. We stayed behind because these two boys were too injured to be moved when Al-Shabaab attacked and the others fled."

The man ignored her. He approached the young boy. He spoke to him in rapid sentences in what Elizabeth recognized as one of the many clan dialects in Somali. The boy replied. The conversation went on for a few minutes. Then the man moved to examine the other boy.

"He lives?"

Doc nodded. "Yes. He's weak and unconscious, but he lives."

The officer's eyes swept between Elizabeth and Doc, who still held his rifle. The two men who had entered the cave with him had their guns trained on Doc. "Guns down," he told Doc.

Reluctantly, Doc complied. He sat his rifle to the ground, unholstered his two sidearms, and then raised his hands into the air. They hadn't shot him upon breaching the cave. He hoped that meant something. He wasn't sure how reliable or trustworthy the regular Somali military was, if that is who they were. He knew there were many factions that had broken from the regular military and acted as warlords over regions. And those factions were criminals.

"Bring them," the man in the officer's uniform said, motioning to the two boys.

Elizabeth's eyes were on Alexander's looking for direction. He moved in and scooped up the heavier of the two boys. He nodded to the other. "Can you get him okay?"

"Yes," she said.

She pulled her headscarf into place first and then lifted the little boy from the table. She followed Alexander from the cave, through the clinic, and out into the early morning light, squinting her eyes against its brightness. Three men were carried out of the clinic, bleeding. Doc had shot them.

Doc viewed the village. Four military troop transport trucks lined the road. About two dozen men milled around, weapons in hand. Some were in uniform, or in portions of uniforms, most were not. Even those in uniform looked rough, dirty, unkept. The men who'd entered the cave were the only ones who looked like regular military. A gnawing in the pit of Doc's stomach warned him that they were in a shitstorm of trouble.

The officer approached Doc. He grabbed his comms, which hung around his neck. "Djibouti?"

Doc nodded.

The officer broke the comms, tearing the wires and smashing what was left. He threw it to the ground. Then he pointed to the back of the lead truck in front of them. "In!"

"These boys might not make it in a truck," Elizabeth protested.

"Be quiet and do what they say," Doc corrected her.

"Alexander," she began to argue.

"Not another word, Sister!" Doc yelled, already moving towards the rear of the truck. These men did not need to know a helicopter was on its way for them.

She froze, an outraged expression on her face. When she saw the serious look on Alexander's, she suddenly became terrified. She knew of the many factions that broke away from the regular military, but even those factions had always given the Sisters deference. Something about this situation though made Alexander fearful. She accepted that his experience may make him realize things she didn't.

He nodded to the truck. She followed. He laid the boy to the bench and then he took the little one from her arms and climbed back in. The Somali officer pushed her in, none too gently.

"This is a Sisters of Mercy village," she told him, watching his face. His expression remained unchanged. He didn't care.

The three wounded men were loaded in next. "You will treat their injuries," the officer told them. He sat Doc's backpack onto the floor in front of them.

"Sister help me with these patients," Doc said, pulling her deeper within the truck.

She remained quiet; her eyes locked on his. They spent a good half hour treating the wounded men. Only one had a serious wound, a bullet in his abdomen. Doc applied a QuikClot bandage to it. He couldn't dig the bullet out. He was sure it would kill him. The other two just had flesh wounds. They'd be fine.

The truck filled with men. The officer was the last to get in. He sat near the rear of the truck. Then the truck rolled forward. Elizabeth held the littlest boy tightly in her arms. He was still unconscious. She tried her best to stabilize his broken and splinted limbs.

The truck bumped and lurched over the rocky terrain for well over two hours, picking up speed on the straightaways of the more established roads. Elizabeth was parched and exhausted before the truck pulled to a stop, the others behind it.

The men rose and jumped down. The officer motioned to them to get out. They were the only ones left in the truck.

"Let me get down first, then I'll help you," Doc said to her. His voice sounded scratchy.

He moved to the rear of the truck with the boy in his arms. The boy had lost consciousness again, but his sutures held, at least externally. A man stood ready. He took the boy from Doc.

"Be careful with him. He has extensive internal injuries."

The man nodded.

Doc wasn't sure if the man understood him or not. Then Doc looked around. They were in front of a large mansion style house. A dozen other buildings were scattered in the compound, that was surrounded by a twelve-foot high fence. He turned and helped Elizabeth down from the truck. She still cradled the smaller boy tightly in her arms. Another man came in and reached for the boy. The man who took the first child was gone.

"We've got him," Doc said, wrapping his arm around Elizabeth and the boy protectively.

One of the pseudo-soldiers pulled Doc away. A second hit him in the gut with the butt of his rifle. Doc groaned out and the rapid expulsion of air from his lungs amplified the sick sound. He doubled over.

"No!" Elizabeth yelled. Another soldier pointed his weapon at Elizabeth. The man took the boy from her arms. She ran to Alexander and wrapped her arms around him. He was still doubled over. "Are you okay?"

Doc tried to speak, but it came out as a grunt. When he stood, he had fire in his eyes. He took a second to catch his breath. "Where are the children? They need medical care!"

"They are no longer your concern," the officer said.

Doc let out a low growl and went for him, his hands around the man's throat.

Elizabeth watched in horror as one of the armed men struck Alexander in the head with the butt of his rifle and Alexander crumpled to the ground. She heard a scream, more of a screech, and she realized it had come from her. Her eyes went to the officer, standing smugly in front of her, Alexander's still form at his feet.

"Please don't hurt him any further. He's just trying to protect those children," she pled.

"Make your friend cooperate and no further harm will come to him," the officer said. Then he nodded to his men. Two of them lifted and dragged Alexander away. Another man took hold of Elizabeth's arm and pulled her to follow, towards the house.

The lobby of the home was lavish, wealth unimagined by all the people who sought refuge with the Sisters. She cooperated and walked up the grand staircase, following the men who dragged Alexander. At the top of the stairs the man holding her, released her and walked the length of the hall beside her.

They passed many doors, all closed. In a far corner, one of the men opened a door and motioned her in. She stepped into the room. It was a large bedroom. They dropped Alexander to the wood floor just within and then retreated, closing the door. She heard a lock engage.

Immediately she knelt beside Alexander. There was a laceration on his head where he'd been hit. The blood ran down saturating his t-shirt. She looked around the room. An open door on one of the walls revealed a bathroom. She went within and grabbed the two white washcloths from the stack of towels on the bench. There was a sink, running water. Then she noticed there was a toilet and a bathtub too. This was unheard of wealth for most in Somalia. She wet one of the cloths and rushed back to Alexander.

After cleaning Alexander's wound with the wet cloth, she grabbed one of the two pillows from the bed, used the dry washcloth as a bandage and positioned his head on the pillow. Then she sat beside him, said a prayer, and just held him, willing him to wake.

Doc felt pain everywhere as consciousness slowly came to him. He felt a soft caress on his cheek that traveled down his neck, across his shoulder, over his arm, before his hand was held. Then he felt a kiss press to his forehead.

"Alexander, please wake up."

Through the fog in his head, Doc heard the familiar voice. He struggled to remember where he was and whose voice it was. Slowly, realization dawned on him. He moaned as he fought to fully wake. Elizabeth and the two boys needed his protection.

Bright blue eyes, a sweet young face, and a relieved smile greeted him. He felt the soft caress return to his cheek.

"Thank God you're awake," Elizabeth said.

He tried to move, but she placed her hands on his chest, pressing down. "Stay still. You have a head wound. Do you remember what happened?"

Doc raised a hand and felt over his splitting head. Yeah, he remembered all right, he remembered everything. "Yeah. Are you okay?"

"I am. I didn't try to attack them like you did. But they took the boys. I don't know where they are."

Doc glanced around, confused by the surroundings. A well-furnished bedroom was not where he would think they would be. He brought his wrist to his face to view his watch. It was just past zero-nine-thirty. He hadn't been out that long.

"How bad is my head?"

"Just a superficial laceration, probably a mild concussion. It wasn't as bad as it could have been. What were you thinking, attacking that man?"

He knew she was right, again. "I guess I wasn't thinking."

"Please stop attacking them. I need you Alexander and I don't want to see you hurt anymore."

He took hold of her hand, which tenderly held his shoulder, and gave it a squeeze. "I'll cooperate unless there is a viable opening for escape for us. Do you have any idea who these guys are? What faction?"

"No, but I'm going to assume they split from the regular military, probably a clan militia. This region is full of them, warlords who control different areas. They usually give us Sisters reverence and don't interfere with our ministry too much. I'm going to assume that is why we are in a bedroom rather than a cell, or worse."

Doc nodded. The jamboree in his head was quieting. "Help me to sit up."

Elizabeth protested, but as he pulled himself up, she assisted. He scooted so his back rested against the bed. She readjusted the make-shift bandage on his head. The bleeding had stopped.

Then he looked around the room. He was surprised to see the bathroom against the far wall. He was sure this was the least lavish room in this mansion. Even so, this room was luxurious compared to how the vast majority of Somali's lived. Just the fact that there was indoor, modern plumbing, and glass windows boasted wealth.

He pulled at the bedcovers. The bed had both a top and a bottom sheet over a real mattress. Yes, the owner of this mansion had great wealth and had visited modern, wealthy cities. He looked up. A ceiling fan circulated the air. Power, a rare commodity in this country.

When he finally felt more stable, he had Elizabeth help him to his feet. He went to the door first.

"It's locked," Elizabeth said.

That was what he expected. But he examined it anyway. The doorknob was loose. There was no deadbolt. It must be secured with an exterior lock of some sort, most likely a sliding bolt action lock. He'd have to hear it open or close to be sure.

He looked out of each of the three open windows at the large compound, then the fourth within the bathroom. He saw over fifty armed men, many women, and even children. The women were fully covered wearing garments with long sleeves and headscarves. There were a dozen buildings, dozens of vehicles, even bulldozers and tractors, all within the twelve-foot high barbed wire fence. Interesting.

When he turned back to Elizabeth, she was sitting on the edge of the bed, watching him with pleading eyes. He forced a pleasant expression, trying to ease her worry. "I think we are somewhat safe, for now. If they meant us harm, we'd be in a cell or worse as you said. It's a thriving village out there, not that it isn't a militia camp too, the jury is still out on that."

Elizabeth nodded. "I just wish the boys were with us. I hope they haven't been harmed."

"That officer and the boy spoke in the cave. I have to think that boy is one of theirs. That gives me hope those boys are being tended."

"I hope by someone with some degree of medical knowledge," Elizabeth voiced.

Echo

Cooper pushed through the doors to the conference room just down the hall from the Operations Center at Camp Lemonnier. Lambchop and the Undertaker were but steps behind, keeping up with the rapid pace he set the second he jumped from the helicopter upon its return to the base.

He locked eyes with Madison. A meaningful nod was exchanged between the husband and wife. It would be noticed by only their team members as a sign of the love they shared. The remainder of the team plus a half-dozen men he didn't recognize were in the room.

Cooper's eyes went to the base intel officer who stood at the head of the conference table, the keyboard and mouse in front of him. Then Cooper's eyes went to the wall-mounted monitor displaying an aerial view of the compound his man, his friend, Doc was brought to.

"Tell me you have good intel on this compound so we can plan the mission to go in and get our man," Cooper said.

"Good enough," the intel officer said. He nodded to the four men who lined one side of the table. "Fire Team Green is at your disposal."

Cooper viewed the men, obvious Operators. Their designation was that of a Navy SEAL assault team. He nodded. "Thanks, we'll gladly take the assistance."

Madison took control of the keyboard. She tapped into the Shepherd Security tracker software and isolated Doc's. She overlaid the compound view with it. Doc's tracker was stationary in the northwest corner of the main house, an eighty-two-hundred square foot mansion.

"We won't know what floor of the building Doc is in, until we are on site with a handheld tracker locator, but we plan our mission for all variables," Cooper said. "Miller, you'll remain here in the Ops Center. Jackson and Sloan, you'll be strategically placed in sniper positions here and here," he said pointing to the two buildings to the north and the west of the target building. We'll breach the target building at these three points." He pointed them out. "Take out any and all who see you. We get our man and the Sister and then we retreat to the primary pick up point here." He pointed out the primary LZ. "Or the backup point." He pointed that out next. "We'll go in after dark. Get some sleep and be ready to move out at twenty-thirty."

The lock bolt slid open loudly on the door. The door swung open. Doc and Elizabeth both came to their feet but didn't move towards the man in the officer's uniform they were very familiar with. A man stood behind him, rifle in hand, aimed at them. Doc raised his hands into the air.

Another man entered. He carried a stack of neatly folded clothing. He sat them on the table near the door. A second man brought in a tray with some food and a bottle of water. He sat it on the table beside the clothing. Then they both backed out.

"Bathe and clean up and then dress in the fresh clothing. You have three hours until General Halima returns. I will be back for you then. He will make the decision on what is to be done with you, if you shall live to see tomorrow or not."

The door closed and Doc heard the lock slide closed. He went to the clothes and held each article up. A beautifully embellished dirac, a regional dress, in blues and purples and a matching dark blue headscarf was on top. Beneath, was a crisp, bright-white, cotton dress shirt, men's large. On the bottom of the pile were a pair of men's military dress pants in olive. He held them up. They appeared to be a few sizes too large for him. He found these formal articles of clothing confusing.

Elizabeth crumpled to the bed. She drew her legs up to her chest and hugged her knees. "General Abdi Ishmael Halima is known as one of the worse butchers in Somalia, even when he was a part of their regular military. He preaches death to non-Muslims but has never come into our region before. I don't know if he is with Al-Shabaab or Boka Hiram, but there are rumors he helps to fund them and helps to provide safe transport to them. This just went from bad to worse."

Doc sat beside her and drew her into an embrace. "At least we know who we're dealing with now. We plan our strategy accordingly."

"Our strategy?" She demanded. "We are his prisoners."

"We still approach this strategically. This man is used to complete power, right?" She nodded.

"And he commands complete respect through fear, right?"

"Yes. So, what do we do now?" She asked in a breathy voice accompanying the frown that was on her face.

"We give him that respect and do what they say. And most of all, I'd say, we don't go out of our way to piss them off."

"I'm not putting that dress on," Elizabeth spat.

"Now *that* would be going out of your way to piss them off." Doc shook his head. "You can bathe first, and I'll stand guard, and then you *are* going to put the dress on."

"You know what they're going to do to me, don't you? Do to us? They want me in that dress to look like a woman for a reason." She said no more. She didn't need to.

"If we can make it till nightfall, my team will mount a rescue operation," Doc said.

"How can you be sure?"

"I know my team. Trust me, they'll come in for us."

"How will they even know where to find us?" Elizabeth asked, not wanting to get her hopes up.

"They'll know exactly where we are, down to this very room. It'll be a surgical strike. They'll come in quiet and with precision and get us out. Don't worry, Elizabeth."

She shook her head, not believing him.

"There is a tracker planted under the skin in my shoulder," he said, tapping the spot in his upper back. "My team knows exactly where we are."

Elizabeth shook her head again, a frown drawing her lips down. "I am afraid nighttime will be too late. The General is due back in a few hours. I don't think they're going to wait that long to do to us what they're going to do to us."

Doc grabbed both of her hands. They trembled. "We need to cooperate with them and be strong. Live through whatever they do to us till rescue can come. We'll deal with healing from it after. I'm asking you to have faith in that, Elizabeth. Have faith in me and my team."

Tears filled her eyes. Faith was one thing that seemed to be in short supply inside her. She prayed to God to give her faith in Him on the truck ride here. So far, none had filled her. Her eyes wandered over this man's face. He was scruffy, had dark blonde and gray stubble over his cheeks and strong jaw. He had dirt on his face as well as some dried blood. But his light gray eyes bore into her with such conviction and strength, she couldn't help but believe in him and his team.

She nodded her head yes.

He pulled her to her feet. "I promise I'll keep you safe while you bathe. Close the door. I won't interrupt you."

Elizabeth removed her tunic and dropped it to the floor. Beneath, she wore a black tank top and those gray athletic shorts. Around her neck on a long lanyard was her passport in its protective pouch.

A grin formed on Doc's face. "This is how a Sister dresses beneath her habit?"

Elizabeth returned his small smile. "Well, this one, but I'm not a Sister any longer, remember?"

"Yeah, you probably don't want to tell our captors that." He fingered her passport. "I guess you wouldn't want to get caught anywhere in this country without it."

Elizabeth shook her head. "That was one piece of advice I heeded. Always have your U.S. Passport with you."

She hurried into the bathroom and closed the door. She drew the water in the tub as she disrobed. She did feel and smell terrible. She grabbed the bar soap from the sink and brought it into the bathtub. She used it on every inch of her body. She found small tubes of both shampoo and conditioner on the ledge against the wall. They were lightly scented, French. She used those as well.

Doc was surprised when the bathroom door reopened just twenty minutes after it had closed. Elizabeth emerged with a towel wrapped around her tiny frame and another around her head. A light, fresh scent wafted out with her as she stepped into the room.

"Your turn," she said softly.

Doc nodded, his eyes fixed on her pinkened cheeks, the exposed creamy white flesh of her neck and chest that was also flushed pink against the white towel she had wrapped tightly over her small bosom. She looked even younger; a child bundled in oversized towels.

"I'll be fast, so you are not alone and unprotected too long."

"I don't think it matters. We both know what they will do to me when the General returns. Now or then is irrelevant. You won't be able to protect me."

"You don't know for sure," he began to say.

She shook her head, silencing him. She'd been in this region long enough. She did know.

During the short ten minutes he was sealed behind the closed bathroom door, she put on the beautiful dirac. This one was finely crafted in a well-appointed fabric. It fell long to her ankles. Its sleeves were short, which she appreciated as the heat of the midday sun was warming the air. She finger-combed her hair and towel dried it.

When the bathroom door opened, she stopped and gazed at Alexander as though she'd never seen a man before. His chiseled torso glistened with water. A purple bruise in the middle of his stomach reminded her of the danger they were in. A towel was wrapped low around his waist, so low she saw the muscles of his abs point downward in a V into the towel. She'd never seen a man who was not injured dressed in as little as a towel before. He was not a patient standing before her. He was a man, a red-blooded, breathing, virile man. That was when a thought came to her that she knew was right.

"I just need the pants," he said, pointing to the pile of clothes. He took a few steps into the room, but was stopped by Elizabeth, who met him half-way.

"Alexander, will you do me a favor?"

Doc looked into her beautiful ocean-blue eyes, which were alive with something he couldn't identify. "If I can."

"We have a few hours before they will be back for us. We both know what they are going to do to me. I don't want to know abuse without ever knowing what a lover's touch feels like," she breathed out, her voice getting shakier as she spoke. "Will you make love to me?"

Doc's gut clenched tighter than it ever had. He fought the urge to shake his head no. "Elizabeth, you don't know that's what is going to happen."

She grabbed hold of his hands, which were firmly rooted on his hips. "I've been here three years. I know what the men here do, know how they treat women. Yes. I know what's going to happen." Her tear-filled eyes met his. "I've treated their injuries. I know fully well what is in store for my body. Please, Alexander. Show me passion before I know pain."

Doc raked his fingers through his wet locks. Holy hell. "Elizabeth, I'd be taking advantage of you, of this situation. You're a Sister for God's sake!"

"I'm not a Sister any longer. I decided over a year ago to leave the order. It is only an administrative filing recognizing me as one. Please, Alexander it would be for you too, before you die. You know what they'll do to you too. If this general is with Al-Shabaab, you'll be beheaded or burned alive, and that's after you are beaten and tortured. Please." She went silent when Alexander engulfed her in an embrace and held her to himself.

Doc held her tiny frame against his chest. Holy hell, what was he going to do? He couldn't have sex with this girl. He would not take advantage of her. Fuck, and she was a virgin on top of it. Nun or no nun, she was innocent and untouched. No, he would not be the man that would take that from her.

He felt her hands, reach around him and caress his back, felt her breath across his chest. Against his wishes, his dick reacted. He pushed her away and held her at arm's length. He gazed into her young face. Fuck, she looked young enough to be his daughter. "Elizabeth stop it. It's not going to happen. You're a nun. It would be wrong."

"I will be raped, brutalized, most likely killed. You would have that happen to me never knowing what it feels like to be held by a man, kissed, my body made to feel good? I've taken medical classes. I know the chemistry, have read about orgasms. Since deciding I wasn't being called to be a nun, I've thought about being with a man. I've never touched myself as masturbation is a sin," Elizabeth said, with a new-found bravery. "Please, in what could be your last act of protecting me, will you please show me what it feels like to be a woman?" She watched indecision play over his face. "Please, Alexander. I'm begging you."

Doc felt his resolve crumble, brick by brick, with each of her words. She had a right to go out on her own terms, if that was what was going to happen. And although he desperately tried to think of any other way this could play out, he couldn't. Elizabeth was right, again. They were both going to be tortured and killed. He also doubted they would live to see the rescue attempt by his team, which he was sure would happen after dark. Despite how wrong he felt this was, he found himself nodding yes.

A small smile curved Elizabeth's lips. He stepped into her and gently placed a soft kiss on them. He was surprised to feel it returned, hesitantly at first, but then with more vigor than he was anticipating. He held her, taking in the sensation of her body against his.

He pulled away, staring at her with half-hooded eyes. Her pupils were dilated, her jaw slack. "If you change your mind at any point, just say stop."

She shook her head. She would not change her mind. She knew this was what she wanted.

"I'll be gentle. I promise." His voice was soft.

"It will be a sin if we do not vow before God, our maker, to be faithful unto each other. We're both going to die here, Alexander, we both know that. Will you say vows with me before God?"

The knot in Doc's gut tightened so much it sucked the air from his chest and caused his heart to skip a beat. He nodded. He couldn't dispute they were going to die, something, in his line of work he always knew was a possibility. It was just that he never had to face it with such certainty, with such immediacy. Having sex without marriage was a sin in her mind. He would do whatever he could to protect her, and this would give her that protection in her afterlife. He nodded yes.

A gratified smile spread over her face. "Thank you," she whispered. She said the first thoughts that came to her mind. "I, Elizabeth, take you Alexander, to be my wedded husband, to have and to hold, forsaking all others, until death do us part before God, my creator."

Doc swallowed hard and his chest constricted. Memories of the last time, the first and only time he had said similar words flooded his head, as well as images of Victoria in her white gown contrasted by her dark hair, smiling. Then more images flashed through his mind. Victoria, against the white sheets of the hospital bed, the sonogram of his son, and the headstones. His breath caught in his chest. He hadn't thought about any of those things in more years than he could count. Tears filled his eyes as a crushing anxiety overtook him.

"Alexander, please," she pled.

He snapped from the memories and back into the room. He found that his hands held Elizabeth's arms tightly.

"It's the only way I can, otherwise, sex outside of marriage is a sin."

"We shouldn't do this," he said.

"We are both going to die horrible deaths in just a few hours. Please do this for me, Alexander." She felt a surreal courage, speaking the words, believing them, but hoping against hope that she was wrong.

Her words were pleading, as were her eyes. He was humbled how bravely she spoke. Yes, he too was sure that they would be killed. He wasn't sure if a Hail Mary was out there, but he wasn't going to bet on it either. This woman had more faith in her than anyone he knew. He could do this for her. He nodded yes. "I, Alexander take you Elizabeth to be my wife, before God as our witness. I will forsake all others until death do us part."

Then he kissed her again, his tongue parting her lips this time. He held her small frame against his and allowed his body to react. He pushed from his thoughts how young she looked as his hands felt over her. Her butt was firm and round, her breasts small, but perky and her nipples reacted to his touch. He trailed kisses down her neck and heard her sigh out loud, a womanly sound that was mixed with a pleasure-filled moan.

Elizabeth pushed the fear from her thoughts as she felt Alexander's kisses become more intense and as his hands touched her in intimate places. They were married before God. This was not a sin. This was a God-given pleasure married men and women enjoyed. And she knew the biology of it, about blood flow, erection and arousal.

That knowledge was nothing compared to the sensations his kisses elicited, especially on her neck. His fingers on her breasts brought about incredible arousal that was nearly overwhelming. Then his hand ran up her leg, flesh against flesh. It rose higher, over her knee and tingles shot into her very core as his hand lightly brushed her inner thigh. She couldn't help but moan out and shiver in response.

"Should I stop?" He whispered, his breath blowing over her ear.

She could barely think, let alone answer.

"Elizabeth, should I stop?" He repeated, hoping her answer would not be yes. This was wrong. There was no doubt about it. But his dick was rock-hard. His whole body hummed in anticipation of having her.

"Dear Lord in Heaven, what you are making my body feel is indescribable. I never knew," she paused mid-sentence and moaned as his hand made contact with her between her legs, his warm hand on her in a way that no one ever had. She felt his finger penetrate her and she whimpered, her whole-body trembling.

Doc found her wet and hot to his touch. Her body quivered and her breath panted. He slid his index finger inside her. Fuck, if she wasn't the tightest thing he'd ever felt. He moaned out unconsciously, his already hard member becoming steel at the thought of going where his finger was, going where no man had been.

He brought his lips back to hers and kissed her again like he'd never kissed anyone in his life. He knew he was overwhelming her senses. Her hands gripped his shoulders so tightly he was sure he'd have marks. But he couldn't stop himself. She felt too good to stop. He pulled her dress up and pulled his towel free. He pressed his anxious dick to her, skin to skin between her legs. He wouldn't penetrate her yet, she wasn't ready, but he wanted her to feel him at her entrance. If anything would freak her out and panic her, it was that. She gasped but didn't tell him to stop.

Elizabeth knew what was poking her as soon as he made contact with her, skin to skin, and the full weight of his body on hers. She pulled her lips away from his to drag in a deep breath. She felt as though she were suffocating. An excitement laced with terror gripped her. Their intimate parts were aligned. He pressed to her with a hardness that she knew meant he was ready to make love to her.

When he pulled away, she was confused. He pulled her to her feet and took the dress from her, leaving her standing naked before him. Her eyes went to his hard member, jutting out proudly before him. Then they went back to his eyes, the embarrassment she felt that his eyes raked over her bareness, flushed her cheeks pink.

"Your body is beautiful," he said in a raspy voice.

She cringed when he angled his head, his mouth taking her breast and nipple. Then, he moved to the other. He directed her to sit on the edge of the bed and then lie all the way back, her butt just dangling over the edge. She felt his hands cup each butt cheek as he dropped to his knees before her, spreading her legs with his body between them. Now she wanted to die of embarrassment. He pressed a kiss to the inside of each thigh right near her private parts.

"You know about orgasms?" His voice whispered, his breath blowing over her lips.

She trembled from the intensity of it. "Yes," she forced out.

"I'm going to give you one before I make love to you, so you are nice and wet," he said in a seductive voice that instantly increased the moisture between her legs.

Then he licked, lapped, sucked, and nibbled while his finger entered her with gentle strokes, stretching her, so when his dick penetrated her it wouldn't be as painful. Her scent and her taste were addictive. He soon forgot she was untouched, the purposeful reserved lovemaking he'd planned was replaced with his ravenous hunger to have her. Her whole body trembled. She quaked with a release that gripped her so strongly that she cried out as a deluge coated his fingers.

Before her mind registered what had happened, she felt him enter her very slowly. He groaned out a sound unlike she'd ever heard. It was a sound that she knew meant he was in the grips of a sensation so intense, an experience so overwhelming that he was having a near out of body experience. There was a brief stabbing pain followed by only the awareness of being stretched and pulled apart as he pushed deeper within her. It wasn't comfortable.

Doc was lost to the sensations, the perfect wet, hot, vice grip around him. He moved slowly, burying himself all the way inside her before he remembered where he was and with whom. He pulled out and then pushed back in, gasping every inch of the way. He felt her tense.

"Breathe and relax your muscles," he whispered. "It'll feel better in a second."

At first, it didn't become more comfortable for her. As he went in and out, she felt raw, stretched, pulled apart. It wasn't until he increased speed, went deeper with grunts vocalizing, nearing his own orgasm, that the friction on her caused that incredible sensation to return. She could feel him throbbing inside her. She knew the moment he orgasmed.

The stillness in his body when he was through shouted complete relaxation. Although he breathed heavily, every other aspect was serene. After a few minutes, he rolled further onto the bed, drawing her onto his chest as he rolled.

Doc stroked his fingers over Elizabeth's cheek. Her eyes were closed, and she gripped him with trust and affection. Her long, dark blond hair was spread over his chest in a thin sheet that clung to him. Her tiny frame was pressed to his, their legs still entwined.

His thoughts, against his wishes, flashed images of Victoria's thick, dark hair over his chest from so long ago, her body, full and womanly, a stark contrast to Elizabeth's. Everything about Victoria was drastically different than every trait that made Elizabeth the person she was. Polar opposites assaulted his consciousness.

"I do," her full red lips spoke, a smile beaming at him with sassy confidence. Her white wedding gown hugging all her feminine curves, the tall, brass organ pipes of the church rising behind her. Victoria, on their wedding day.

Doc shook the images from his mind. He checked his wristwatch. Their captors would return in less than an hour. They needed to get up and get dressed as instructed. They needed to talk. He needed to coach Elizabeth so they had a snowball's chance in hell of surviving until his team could mount a rescue that evening.

"Elizabeth," he spoke as he gently shook her. "We need to get dressed."

She opened her eyes and gazed into his. "One more kiss, please?"

She didn't want this moment to end. It had been all she had hoped it would be, the act, intense with emotions. The connection with him was strong, just as she had always imagined it would be after making love with a man. And the appreciation she felt that he had agreed to do this, consumed her.

Doc took her cheeks between his hands. He gifted her with a kiss that under any other circumstances would have kept them both in bed for a very long time. "We need to get up," he said when their lips parted.

Reluctantly, Elizabeth rose. After quickly washing herself off in the bathroom, she reentered the room with the towel wrapped around herself. Like it mattered! Alexander had seen and felt over every inch of her body. It was a heady feeling, knowing she had shared that type of intimacy with him.

Doc went into the bathroom behind her. He cleaned himself up quickly. His shorts were disgusting, he would not put them back on. He had not been provided with underclothing. He slid the pants over his naked butt. They were of a fine fabric. They were at least two sizes too large. He'd use his own belt.

He reentered the room to find Elizabeth dressed, the dirac flowing down to the floor, the headscarf in place. The dress was short-sleeved. He found that odd. The women he viewed out the window were fully covered, and Elizabeth had said the General was Muslim.

Doc pulled the dress shirt on and then his dirty socks, followed by his combat boots, chuckling at the contrast. What the fuck was this about? Why the formal clothing?

Doc pointed at Elizabeth's boots. "Put them on." If the opportunity for escape presented itself, she'd have to be able to run.

She sat on the edge of the bed and pulled her dirty socks back on and then her boots. "This all feels so surreal."

Doc nodded. His thoughts exactly. All of it was surreal, contradictions that were almost comical. He was most likely going to die going commando in some strange man's military dress pants. And even the size of them, so large, what Somali wore pants that large? Most Somali's were rail-thin, starving to death.

Foxtrot

The officer and three of his men returned at the appointed hour. "You will cooperate?"

"We will," Doc said.

Doc took hold of Elizabeth's upper arm and led her from the room, following the officer and one of his men. The two others fell in behind them, rifles aimed at their backs. They walked the length of the hallway and back down the main staircase.

At least forty people fussed about the entry and the formal dining room to the left of the staircase. Plates were set formally, crystal goblets sat on the table over fine linens. Trays of food were then brought out and sat on the table. The officer halted them in the foyer, in what became a growing line of bodies.

Elizabeth soon realized she was the only woman in the gathering. The other women who had been scurrying about were nowhere to be seen. Her eyes met Alexander's questioningly. He seemed as confused as she was. All at once all the women appeared in a line and fell in behind the one Elizabeth and the men were in. They bowed their heads.

The front doors swung open, held by a man on each side. Striding through was a large man in decorated military dress. Doc judged his size to match the pants he wore. He found that even more confusing. It was obvious that he was the master of the house. By the activity and the reverence, the others showed, you'd think God himself was walking into the foyer.

"Welcome home General," the officer proclaimed.

"Is all prepared as requested," the General asked.

"Yes, your excellency," the officer replied.

Doc wanted to laugh out loud. Jesus! Your excellency. Seriously? This General had a mighty high opinion of himself. He'd have to feed that. Then he realized they had spoken in English. This was for his and Elizabeth's benefit.

The General greeted many of the others in line and spoke briefly with them in Somali. Then he stepped in front of Doc and Elizabeth. He eyed them both up and down with an unreadable, but unfriendly expression on his face.

"I am General Abdi Ishmael Halima," he said with authority. "Do you know who I am?"

Doc nodded. Elizabeth froze and stared at him with fear.

The corner of the General's lip ticked up. "You've given my men some problems."

"I'm sorry for that, General. We do not mean to cause you any problems," Doc said as meekly as he could force his voice to sound.

The General angled his view to Elizabeth. She avoided eye contact. "You are one of the Sisters from the village?"

"Yes, General," she replied respectfully. "I am also a nurse and this man is a doctor."

"You stayed to treat two injured boys?"

"Yes, General," she repeated with a slight bow to her head.

The General used his index finger to raise her chin until she looked him in the eyes. "Do you know who those boys are?" The large man demanded.

"It doesn't matter," Elizabeth said humbly trying to keep her voice even. His finger on her chin sent fear into every cell in her body. "They are children of God who needed healing and protection. We would not leave them and moving them to evacuate with the others would have killed them."

"You both sacrificed yourselves for these two boys?" He scoffed.

Doc stood taller. "We stayed to ensure their welfare. They were alive when your men took them. If you would allow it, I'd like to see my patients to be assured they are well."

The General laughed. "Those boys are with my personal doctor. Those boys are my sons."

Doc and Elizabeth exchanged surprised stares. Holy hell. Doc's eyes went back to the General's. "Have you seen them since you've been back? Are they okay? We've been very worried about them."

An amused smile formed on the General's lips. "I have and they are. I thank you for the care you gave them and the concern you still show. My enemies would wish death to them."

Doc shook his head. "We are not your enemies." He pointed to Elizabeth. "The Sisters of Mercy took them in and would have even if they'd known who they were."

"Enough," the General announced. "We eat." He motioned towards the dining room, which became filled with activity at his pronouncement.

Again, Doc and Elizabeth exchanged surprised stares.

"Move," the officer said, pressing his hand into Doc's back. "Stand where the General tells you. Do not sit until after his excellency does."

"Here," the General said, his eyes on Doc. He motioned to the chair to his left. "And the Sister shall sit beside you, doctor."

General Halima took his seat. Doc and Elizabeth watched the others and only sat when they did. Doc slid Elizabeth's chair beneath her before he took his seat. The General said the Dua, which was repeated by the other men at the table. All platters were offered to the General first by the women, who came to the table and took the platters up. They circulated around the table beginning with Doc after the General.

Doc was hungry, but suspicious of the food. The water it was washed with alone could give him a nasty intestinal bug. But he knew better than to offend so he took a serving of each offered dish. Wine was poured in the large goblet in front of each person. Doc knew the fermented beverage had a better chance of not causing illness.

"General Halima, thank you for this hospitality. The Sister and I thank you for your kindness," Doc said, still trying to figure out what was happening.

Elizabeth was starving, but too nervous to eat. Would the fact that they cared for his sons really mean the General wouldn't hurt them? And if he was going to kill them, why the niceties? Why feed them dinner? She forced herself to take bite after bite. The wine in the glass was strong. Combined with the afternoon heat, she quickly found herself getting lightheaded.

"You are a military man," the General said to Doc. "Your contributions to my army's supplies are appreciated."

Doc was confused. "My contributions?"

The officer who had taken them laughed. "Your pack, weapons, and equipment. The General's personal doctor has found your donated medical supplies helpful in treating the General's sons."

"Yes," Doc said. "I am glad the doctor has been able to use those supplies to help your sons, General."

"As a military man, you appreciate rules of engagement, treatment of prisoners, and the need for discipline." He leaned closer to Doc as he spoke, an act definitely meant to intimidate.

Doc didn't like where this conversation was going. "Yes, sir, I do. I also realize there are extenuating circumstances that necessitate compassion and the relaxing of those rules on occasion. It's what makes us human when others are animals." He hoped he hadn't overplayed his role with that statement.

"So, as a military man, do you make accommodations for personal reasons?"

Doc knew he had to go all in on this one. "Yes, sir, I do. When it comes to family or my team, I definitely make accommodations. Strength is important. But I believe we must take care of those who take care of our own and by the same thought, I believe those who hurt our own must be dealt with harshly. Al-Shabaab attacked the village your sons were in and caused their injuries. The Sisters took them in. Sister Elizabeth and I cared for them."

"So, you believe I should show the two of you mercy?"

Doc knew it was the moment of truth. This man admired strength and respect. Doc knew he had to respond appropriately. "Not mercy, sir, a fair response to the situation at hand."

General Halima eyed him curiously. "You have courage. Or do you wrongly believe that I will not have you executed because you are a doctor?"

"General Halima, I know our disposition is completely in your hands. I defer to you with respect and humility." Doc bowed his head.

Elizabeth couldn't breathe. She prayed harder than she ever had, made a few bargains with God, and hoped Alexander knew what he was doing. Had he ever been in a similar situation? Or was he winging it?

"You have been silent, Sister," Halima said, startling her out of her prayers.

"I am a guest in your country, General. I follow the customs as best as I am able."

"And we do not want to hear from females in Somalia?" He asked with antagonism.

"General, that is not what I meant. I defer the handling of these matters to you and the doctor, a fellow military man. I have no experience in these things and I too realize that our disposition is in your hands. You are a strong leader and are known throughout the region as fair."

"A western woman who knows her place!" He paused and laughed. "It's nice to know you exist. My son told me of your kisses to his brow, the tender touch you gave him that despite the fact he could not understand your words assured him he was safe. He saw his mother murdered. I'll deal with those fighters soon. They will die miserable deaths!" He slapped Doc on the back. "I too believe that we should deal with those who hurt my family. harshly."

Doc nodded, still not sure where he stood with the General, waiting for the boom to lower.

"Eat, both of you," the General said, motioning to their picked at plates.

Doc wondered if this was his last meal. He forced himself to take a few healthy bites. The food was good. The wine was not. He glanced sideways at Elizabeth. She too ate several large forkfuls of food at his prompting. General Halima then engaged in conversation in Somali with others at the table. Doc and Elizabeth exchanged a few nervous glances with each other.

At the end of the meal the women cleared the plates. Halima motioned to one of the men who brought a cell phone to him. He handed it to Doc. "You will not dial this until you are in the designated location." He motioned to the man who had brought it to him. "This man will show you a map. You will be provided a vehicle. You are to drive there. You may contact your people to pick you up once you arrive there, but not before. If you contact them prior to reaching that location, you will both be killed. For the care you gave my sons, I am granting you both amnesty. Go and do not return to my country. Be sure none of your men ever return here. I will treat them as the enemies they are, if they do."

A stunned Doc took the cell phone and bowed his head. "Thank you, General Halima. You have my word of compliance of your terms."

Halima came to his feet. He pointed to the man who brought the phone. "Go with him now."

Doc and Elizabeth instantly stood. They followed the man to the foyer. He produced a map from beneath his draped shirt. He pointed out the route, speaking in Somali. Doc knew the terrain well enough to figure out where he was being ordered to go.

Halima stood by the doorway into the lavish dining room. The other men stood behind him. "Go and do not return."

"Yes, sir," Doc said.

The man who had pointed out the route opened the front door and spoke words Doc didn't understand. He pointed to a Jeep, which sat directly in front of the residence.

"We're to take the Jeep?" He asked Halima.

The big man nodded his head yes.

As they walked out the front door, Doc positioned himself behind Elizabeth. If shots were going to be fired, he wanted them to impact his back and give her a chance. He placed his hand on the small of her back and nudged her forward. She was walking very slowly. He could feel the fear radiating from her. Outside, he took hold of her upper arm to guide her towards the awaiting Jeep, still doing all he could to use his body to shield hers.

"Remember," Abdi Ishmael Halima called from the doorway, "do not alert your friends of your location until you are in the clearing. I guarantee safe passage. My debt to you for saving my sons is now repaid. Do not return. Amnesty will not be granted to you in the future."

Elizabeth slowed and turned her head.

"Keep walking and don't look back," Doc said to her. Then he turned his head to view the General when he reached the jeep. "Thank you, General Halima. I promise no one will return."

He pushed Elizabeth into the Jeep and slid into the driver's seat beside her. "Let's hope this thing doesn't blow up when I turn the engine over," he mumbled. "If you haven't been saying prayers all along, now would be a good time to, Sister."

Elizabeth didn't correct him on the fact that she was no longer a Sister. "I won't stop until we are safely at the U.S. base in Djibouti."

Doc sucked in a breath and turned the engine over. He shifted into drive and pulled away. He kept his eyes peeled on the countryside as he drove the designated route. The air swirling around them was at least one-hundred-ten degrees. The sunshine beating down on them in the open Jeep was intense and blinding. Doc knew his eyes would be shot from the brightness before they reached the clearing.

Thirty minutes later, they arrived. He parked near a clump of rocks. He turned the engine off and turned to her. "Move when I move and quickly get out and crouch down behind those rocks."

She nodded her understanding of his directions.

He opened the door, looking around and listening intently. Elizabeth opened her door too. Though he knew if they were to be killed out here, a sniper could be far away on one of the hills. He'd be dead before he heard the gunshot. Then he got out of the vehicle and moved to the front of it, assuming if there was a sniper, he'd be in front of them. He may buy Elizabeth some time to get behind the rocks.

No shot came. After she was safely hidden, he moved there as well. Only then did he open the phone Halima had given him and he dialed his home Ops, the number designated for Operators on non-agency devices in trouble.

"Go," was Yvette's one-word answer.

"Situation zero-one, Control. Doc, requesting immediate extract for two." He kept his voice even as he spoke even though his heart was racing. He'd never had to declare an emergency before.

"Roger that, Doc, got your location, twenty klicks northwest of Harirad. Bringing the team online now."

There was a click, then a twenty second pause, then another click. "Doc, situation zero-one, please reconfirm," Madison's voice came over the line.

"Roger, Xena, zero-one, requesting immediate extract for two. I don't know how long the window will be open, you better make it fast."

"Roger Doc," Madison said. "A chopper has been at the ready. ETA to your location forty minutes."

His eyes met Elizabeth's. "The chopper is on its way."

"Any other instructions, Doc?" Madison asked.

"Yeah, tell the pilot to lift off as soon as we're in. Don't wait for us to buckle in."

"Roger that," Madison replied.

"Can you scan the immediate area for hostiles?"

"That's a negative. The landscape itself is so hot, I'm not getting any heat signature difference off you versus the surrounding landscape. The area is measuring in excess of ninety degrees. I barely have you."

"Roger that, Xena," Doc replied. "We'll sit tight. Forty minutes, huh?"

Even though they crouched behind the clump of rocks that were heated to at least ninety degrees, a shiver ran through Elizabeth. They'd have to wait forty minutes. What if this was a trap to shoot down the helicopter? What if they were luring a few others to their deaths as well? She still couldn't believe they had just walked out of there and drove away in one of the General's vehicles. He was known for being ruthless. Did the fact that they had saved his sons really mean he would let them live? She had a hard time believing that. The irony of her lack of faith was all too apparent to her.

"When the chopper lands, we are going to run to it as fast as we can," Doc said, giving her hand a squeeze. "I'll help you in and you'd better move quick and make room for me."

Elizabeth nodded again.

Doc felt the sweat running down every inch of his body. It felt as though he sat crouched in a blast furnace. The sun beat down, the rocks emitted heat. He had to believe this is what hell felt like.

The forty-minute wait was excruciating. Finally, the sound of a chopper was heard faintly. It got louder and then came into sight, the sun gleaming from its hull as it approached. With a scorching whirlwind it sat down, kicking up the desert sand. Doc held Elizabeth's hand firmly and ran full-out towards the bird. Cooper, Lambchop, and the Undertaker leaned out the door, rifles at the ready.

When they reached the door, Doc pushed Elizabeth in. Cooper assisted to haul her aboard. Then Doc climbed in, rolling across the flooring as the chopper lifted, ascending quickly, banking to its right. Through the open doorway, Doc saw the desert landscape disappear, replaced completely with a beautiful, cloudless blue sky.

Then the Undertaker closed the door. Doc rolled further in, onto his feet and then pulled himself to the seat beside Elizabeth. She was holding on tightly. He fastened her seat belt, then his own, and then grabbed a set of the headphones for himself. He pulled them on before he did the same for her.

"Welcome back," Cooper said, a hand to Doc's shoulder.

Doc leaned his head against the headrest, gazing into Cooper's eyes. "I've never been happier to see you, Cooper."

He heard his three teammates chuckle.

"Do either of you have any medical needs?" Sloan asked.

"No, we're fine," Doc replied.

Elizabeth leaned her head back and closed her eyes. She said a prayer for continued safe transport back to the U.S. base. She hadn't even realized she was clutching Doc's hand until he squeezed it back.

"I think you can relax now," Doc said.

She opened her eyes at the sound of his voice and viewed the three men who stood before them in camouflage and full combat gear. They were all armed. She forced a brave smile as her eyes met Doc's. "Sorry." She loosened her grip.

"Sister Elizabeth, this is Cooper, Sloan, and our team reverend, Landon Johnson," Doc introduced, pointing them each out.

"It's nice to officially meet you, Sister," Cooper said, smiling with recognition.

She nodded and forced a small smile. She remembered him from the cave and the evacuation of the others, though he too looked scruffier than he had with a face that hadn't been shaved in days. She noticed that he too looked very tired. She didn't remember the two other men.

"You two had us worried," the Undertaker said. "By the way, Doc, all the injured we evacuated are doing fine. How are the two boys?"

"They made it," Doc reported without elaborating.

"How in the fuck did you negotiate a release?" the Undertaker asked.

"We watched your tracker get moved to General Abdi Ishmael Halima's fortified estate. We were planning a rescue mission when you phoned in," Cooper said. "Shit, Doc, we were calculating casualties of a rescue mission."

"Hell, if the two boys didn't turn out to be the General's sons. What were the fucking odds?" Doc replied with a head shake. "We were granted safe passage for the medical care we gave that saved their lives," Doc added falling into old habits of swearing, forgetting Elizabeth heard the conversation. "Halima made it clear it was a onetime granting of safe passage." Doc shook his head again, still in disbelief they had walked out of there. "I kept waiting for the gunfire that would fucking end us."

"God was with you," Lambchop said. "Let's not test that too many times in the future, my friend." He clasped Doc on the shoulder.

Elizabeth listened to the exchange between the men finding comfort in it, even though the language was vulgar. The reverend knelt in front of her. He was a big man. His biceps swelled from beneath the camouflage shirt that was rolled up as far on his arms that his muscles would allow. He took her hand gently in his.

"Sister, God delivered you both safely." He laid a hand onto Doc's shoulder and then bowed his head. "Heavenly Father, we thank you for Your protection of your son, Doc and your faithful servant, Sister Elizabeth. We thank you they were delivered safely to us and that we were able to retrieve them without further bloodshed. Please bless the people in this region that want to live in peace in Your name. Amen."

"Amen," Elizabeth repeated. Then she dropped her head down into her hands, cupped her face and cried. The realization that they'd made it, against all odds, hit her. They'd made it out alive. She felt Alexander embrace her.

"It's okay, Elizabeth. We made it," Doc said as he wrapped an arm around her.

He drew her in close and just held her all the way back to the base. Several times she gazed at him with questioning eyes. He knew what was on her mind. It was on his too, except, his thoughts were also painfully bombarded with memories from his past. Horrible memories he hadn't thought about in well over a decade and a half swirled through his thoughts mixing with the commitment he'd sworn to Elizabeth in those dark moments when they thought they'd be killed.

Golf

The chopper sat down beside a hangar. Doc led Elizabeth the short distance, following Cooper into the building. Within, the remainder of the team were gathered. They all rushed to greet Doc, welcoming him back. Elizabeth stood back, an outsider, alone, and out of place. Madison came over to her after giving Doc a hug.

"Sister Elizabeth, I'm Madison, also known as Xena. Are you okay?" She took hold of both of Elizabeth's hands. Gazing into the young woman's eyes, Madison saw exhaustion and something else she couldn't identify in the blue depths.

"It is nice to meet you. You are kind, thank you. I am unharmed."

Madison forced a smile and nodded. "You may be unharmed, but are you okay? This had to be frightening."

Elizabeth's lips quivered. "Yes, very. Where are the Sisters? I'd like to say goodbye to them and arrange my transportation home, back to the United States."

"Goodbye? You're leaving them?"

"Yes, my time here has come to an end. I wish to go home."

"Let me see what I can do," Madison said. "And I'll arrange for you to see the Sisters."

Elizabeth watched the taller woman walk away with confidence and purpose. The loose blond bun at the back of her neck bounced with each step. She watched her stop in front of the man named Cooper, who Alexander had told her was in charge of the unit. They were too far away for her to hear what was said though.

Alexander still talked with several of the men. His back was to her. She wished he would turn and look in her direction. She needed to see the expression on his face. They needed to talk. He had to know she planned to return to the United States.

She watched as Cooper and Madison then stepped over to the group of men Alexander talked with. After a few moments, Alexander finally turned and looked at her. His eyes focused on her for a long moment, before he again turned his back to her. She wasn't sure what that meant. She wanted, no, she needed to talk with him alone. They were married in God's eyes and that wasn't something she took lightly.

Cooper approached her, walking with purpose. "Sister, I understand you need transport back to the United States."

"Yes. Madison said she'd get me reunited with the Sisters so I can say goodbye. Sister Bernice John will know how I can get home."

"We can help you with that," Cooper said with a smile. "The team will be heading out in about an hour. They're refueling our plane now. There are extra seats if you want to catch a ride with us."

"That would be very much appreciated," Elizabeth said with a genuine smile. Perhaps, Alexander did want her to remain with him.

Across the room, Madison was on the phone. She couldn't help but watch the young Sister. She looked like a fish out of water. Her eyes though still had that look, haunted almost. She was on the verge of tears and Madison could tell she was doing everything she could to hold it together. After she hung up the phone, she returned to the corner Sister Elizabeth had remained in.

"The Sisters are on their way here now," Madison said. She pointed to a door on the far wall. "This room is off limits to them, but you can see them in that room."

"Thank you. And thank you also for talking with Mr. Cooper to allow me to travel home with your group."

"Of course, we're going that direction anyway, so why not? There is no reason we can't take you as far as we're going. Where is home?"

"Seattle," Elizabeth said. "What about you?"

"Our headquarters is near Chicago. We'll take the C-17 into Andrews Air Force Base and transfer there to our own plane."

Elizabeth nodded. Chicago. Alexander's home was near Chicago. She'd never been there. She'd never been anywhere but Seattle and Africa. She almost laughed aloud at this ridiculous revelation. She followed Madison across the hangar to the door. The other men followed them through it, hearing the other Sisters would be coming to say goodbye.

The small room became crowded and loud with the fourteen other Sisters and every member of the Shepherd Security team. One Sister hadn't made it into the cave and had been killed by Al-Shabaab when the village was attacked. Sister Maria was a faithful servant of God and she was a friend of Elizabeth's. Elizabeth cried upon hearing the news of Sister Maria's death. At least it had been from a gunshot. It could have been a lot worse; Elizabeth knew. That gave her some solace.

Jackson and Sister Bernice John embraced. "Goodbye, Sister," he said. "Please be safe. Angel would really like you to come visit and hold your grandson, you know. Are you sure you don't want to hitch a ride with us now? You could always come back later."

"Thank you for the offer. I do long to hold Sammy, but there are so many other of God's children here who need me more. Sammy has all of you to hold him. The children here have no one but us and I cannot turn my back on them."

"I understand, Sister," Jackson said. More importantly, Angel understood.

"Take good care of my daughter and grandson," Bernice John said.

"You better believe I do," Jackson said. He gave her another hug.

"You are a good man and I am so very pleased I got to meet you in person. Safe travels home to you and your team and thank you again for coming to our aid."

"You're welcome, Sister."

Elizabeth said goodbye to each of the Sisters and embraced each one. They said their goodbyes to the team as well and then filed out of the door. Sister Bernice John was the only one left. A lump formed in Elizabeth's throat. "I will miss you, Sister." She and Bernice John joined hands.

"Elizabeth, are you sure about this?" Bernice John asked.

Elizabeth nodded. Tears filled her eyes. "I was sure when I gave you notice I could not take my final vows last year and I am even more sure now." She hugged Sister Bernice John, who had been a strong source of faith in her life. She felt as though she had let Sister Bernice down, but she knew she didn't have the unwavering belief she should have, to remain in the order. "I didn't have faith, Sister. In the moments of darkness, my heart didn't believe in the Lord," she confessed.

"You will always be in my thoughts and prayers. Please stay in touch with me and let me know how you are doing."

"I promise I will," Elizabeth swore. That was a vow she knew she could keep.

"Where will you go? Back to Seattle?"

Elizabeth's eyes went to Doc. "I don't know yet."

The women embraced again, and Bernice John left her after saying a prayer with Elizabeth for safe travel. Elizabeth watched the Sister leave, closing the door behind her. She felt Alexander behind her before turning her head to look. When she did, she wished she hadn't. His eyes were focused on her with no warmth in them. His face was fixed in an unfriendly cast.

"We need to talk," Doc said.

She noticed that they were alone in the room. "It appears we are alone. Please say what you have arranged this private moment to tell me."

Doc ran his hand over his stubbled chin. Damn her, did she have to make this harder on him? He'd given this a lot of thought. It was the right thing to do, for her. "Elizabeth, we survived. Against all odds, we survived. We said things and did things, thinking we surely would be killed that we wouldn't have under any other circumstances, things we shouldn't have, things we cannot hold to."

Elizabeth felt her heart shatter in her chest. "I release you from the vows you made to me, Alexander." Tears filled her eyes. She would not beg him to stay with her. She would not beg him for anything. Pride was a sin, she knew, but her pride would not allow her to beg him to fulfill the vows they made before God. If he didn't want to make a life with her, she didn't want him there. She would make a life on her own.

Doc nodded. This is what he wanted, was what he was going to talk with her about. They weren't married, didn't have a relationship that would continue. But how could her statement make him feel even worse than he already did? "Elizabeth, you will find someone who you will love with everything you are, and I hope you will remember me with fond feelings when that happens."

Elizabeth spoke with soft, breathy words. "I will always have fond feelings when I think of you, Alexander. Can we stay in touch?" She knew the answer before Alexander spoke. His face took on a dark cast, his body stiffened.

"That is not a viable option. This is what I do, Elizabeth. This is my job. I'm not easily reachable, never know where I'm going to be."

She nodded. "I understand," she said. But she didn't. In this modern age of cell phones and computers, he could stay in contact with her, but his answer showed he didn't want to. She wouldn't beg.

She turned away, her shattered heart aching. She bit back the disappointment and forced the tears to stay in her eyes. They had sworn their vows before God. She could release him, but she'd never release herself. They were married in God's eyes and they made love, consummating the union. He might be able to walk away from it, but she couldn't.

"Elizabeth, it's for the best," he said to her back.

Elizabeth shook her head without turning back to look at him. She opened the door and stepped through, rejoining the others in the hangar. Her eyes met Cooper's, who smiled at her pleasantly.

"Madison will lend you fatigues, Sister. The lift is from regular Air Force, so everyone has to appear to be active duty. Civilians are prohibited under most circumstances," Cooper said.

Elisabeth nodded. She didn't like the idea of lying about her identity, but this was the fastest and easiest way to get her back to the United States. She didn't correct him addressing her as Sister. It really didn't matter. She followed Madison to where her bag was across the room. She glanced back and saw that Alexander was watching her. He was going through a bag and pulling clothing out too.

"Are you okay?" Madison asked her quietly.

Her eyes came back to Madison. "Just very tired, thank you."

Madison handed her a large stack of clothes. "It gets cold with altitude. These base layers will help to keep you warm." She smiled. "You'll sweat like you're in hell as we walk to the plane, but you'll be thankful for them when we reach twenty-eight thousand feet."

"Thank you." Elizabeth said with a small smile as she took the clothing.

"There are bunks for the pilots behind the cockpit. After we take off, you should be able to lay down. The seats we'll be sitting in are not very comfortable."

"That would be appreciated, if no one else needs one. Whenever someone does, I will gladly move," Elizabeth volunteered.

Madison motioned her into the bathroom. Elizabeth put the borrowed clothes on. Madison was six inches taller and her body was more muscular. The clothes were baggy. She cuffed the extra length at the bottom of the pants and at the wrists. Then she rejoined the others. They were all picking up their gear. Madison handed a bag with food and water bottles in it to her, to carry. The eight men and two women walked the short distance across the tarmac to the awaiting C-17.

"After you, Sister," Doc said, pausing at the stairs leading up to the plane. He motioned her forward.

"I'm not a Sister any longer. You know that better than anyone, Alexander."

A pain shot into Doc's heart. Yeah, he did know, and he was partially to blame for that. He merely nodded.

They took the first ten sidewall seats along the fuselage. The cargo area was fully loaded with crates, boxes, and a Humvee. They would be the only passengers on this flight. As far as the crew knew, they were all regular military. Elizabeth's boots would be the only thing to give them away, if anyone noticed. So far, no one had.

Doc was forced by boarding order to take a seat beside Elizabeth. She looked nervous and he assumed she felt out of place as well as hurt by his rejection. The sidewall seats were physically uncomfortable to sit in, but he knew she wouldn't complain. He wished the accommodations were more comfortable for her. She'd been through enough.

Madison sat on the other side of her, Cooper beside Madison. Doc envied Cooper. He had his career, his woman, his life, just as he wanted it. Jackson did too for that matter, as did Garcia. Doc had that once, fucked it up, and would never have it again.

The engines revved, and the plane began to roll forward. Once airborne it would get cold. He would give his insulated blanket to Elizabeth. The rattling of the plane and its cargo got louder as the C-17 thundered down the runway. It lifted, nose in the air and then banked sharply to the left.

Elizabeth gripped the seat beneath her, the very uncomfortable seat. After the plane leveled off, she let it go, and clasped her hands in her lap. She stared straight ahead and concentrated on quieting her thoughts. Sixteen hours and one quick stop to refuel in Germany and she'd be home. She still wasn't sure how she'd get home to Seattle from either Maryland or Chicago, but she'd be back in the United States at least. She could always get a job waiting tables or something wherever she was until she had enough money for a bus or a train ticket.

Doc closed his eyes and pretended to sleep to avoid eye contact with Cooper, who watched him with an alarming focus. He knew Cooper would have Lassiter on alert, who would meet them at the office the moment they arrived. He understood the protocol of having the team shrink clear the team after an Op, but he could honestly say this time, he wasn't up for it. He needed time alone to process everything that had happened and all the memories that had flooded his mind.

He felt movement beside him. Elizabeth was getting up. He cracked his eyes open and watched Madison lead her up the ladder to the flight crew bunks. She was exhausted, and she'd be more comfortable there. He was glad Madison thought of it as he sure as hell had not.

Elizabeth followed Madison. They climbed the steep and narrow staircase. She appreciated Madison thinking of this for her. The air was getting cool. She'd been warned it would be a cold flight. She hoped there would be a blanket she could use. When they reached the bunk area, disappointment washed over her. The crew bunks were two small metal shelves, each with a thin mattress. A curtain for privacy hung open. The inside wall, the head and foot panels were the same metal. The worse part of it was that the height of each bunk was so low it resembled a coffin. Tears filled her eyes.

"What's the matter?" Madison asked.

"I'm sorry. I'm not sure I can lay here." She offered no more of an explanation.

Madison wasn't sure what the issue was, and Elizabeth said no more. She waited a moment, while Elizabeth eyed the bunks. "Wait here." Madison left her and returned to the others. She approached Doc, who appeared to be sleeping. She laid a hand to his shoulder and shook him. "Doc!"

Doc felt Madison's hand on his shoulder and heard her voice muffled by the earplugs and the noise within the aircraft. He contemplated ignoring her, hoping she'd go away, but he knew he couldn't do that. He opened his eyes and gazed into hers.

"Something is up with Elizabeth. I think you need to come."

His eyes flickered to the stairs, debating it.

"Doc, now," Madison repeated forcefully after a few seconds.

He unbuckled his restraint and came to his feet. He mounted the ladder, without looking behind himself to see if Madison followed or not. She didn't. When he reached the two-bunk area, Elizabeth stood in front of him, her back to him.

"Elizabeth, what's wrong?" He asked.

She didn't turn to face him, she just shook her head no. When he spun her around, he saw tears in her eyes.

"Elizabeth, what is it?"

"It's so small. It's like a metal coffin and it looks like it would be cold. I don't mean to be ungrateful."

"Wait here," he said and then returned to the main cargo floor of the aircraft.

He pulled his thermal blanket from his bag and brought it back to the bunk area. He spread the blanket over the bunk. Then he rolled in and under the blanket. He laid on his side, his back to the metal wall. He tucked the blanket behind him because yes, the metal was cold.

He patted the mattress beside him. "Lay down with me."

Elizabeth felt foolish, and she worried Alexander would think she was being manipulative or deceptive. He had pulled away from her since they were back with his team. She wasn't sure why he acted so differently now, except that she knew he regretted the sexual act they shared. She didn't. It had been incredible, and she was glad that it had been with him. She would always remember him and her first time, and it wouldn't be tainted with the circumstances, just the emotions she still felt when she thought about it.

"Elizabeth, lay down," he repeated.

She rolled into the space, her back pressed against his chest. He pulled the blanket over her and wrapped an arm around her waist. How he held her, was comforting. Very quickly, she warmed and relaxed. Exhaustion overtook her, and she fell asleep.

Doc lay awake long after he was sure Elizabeth was asleep. Her small form was nestled against him. He fought the urge to enjoy how it felt. Even though she obviously needed comforting, it was wrong of him to get something out of it. And he surely didn't want to encourage her that there was any hope of a relationship between them. That would not be in her best interest. Period.

At some point, Doc fell asleep. It was a shallow and restless sleep. Even with the ear plugs, and the noise of the plane, he heard when the curtain was pulled open. He opened his eyes and was staring into Cooper's.

"We'll be descending into Ramstein to refuel in a few minutes."

Doc nodded. Cooper's eyes flickered to Elizabeth's face and then back to his. He saw the condemnation across Cooper's features. Yeah, he shouldn't be here with her this way. Tell him something he didn't know. Without another word, Cooper turned around and left.

Cooper descended the ladder and walked up to Garcia, who sat with his eyes closed, earbuds in. He kicked Garcia's foot, instantly causing his eyes to snap open. "I want to know everything about Sister Elizabeth Shaw that you can find."

Garcia got a WTF look on his face.

"Just do it and get a report to me before we land at Andrews."

Elizabeth rolled over, so she faced Alexander. "What time is it?"

Doc brought his wrist up to his eyes to view his watch. "Nearly twenty-two hundred. We need to retake our seats for our landing into Ramstein."

"I slept great. Thank you for staying with me." She pulled herself from the bunk and waited for him.

He motioned her to the steep stepladder. "Can you make it down, or do you want me to go first and spot you?"

She glanced down it. It was so steep. "Can you go first?"

He nodded and climbed down. He waited and watched her. She did fine by herself.

She pointed to the door to the lavatory. "Do I have time to use it?"

"Yeah, it should be fine."

When she reopened the door and stepped back into the body of the plane, Doc was already fastened into his seat. She took her seat beside him. She wondered if there was anything she could say to him to make this less awkward. The truth was, she enjoyed waking beside him and she would miss him when they parted. The marriage vows she had taken meant something to her. She could grow to love him, she was sure. But she did what Alexander wanted her to do. She released him from the ones he had made.

She retook her very uncomfortable seat and fastened herself in, just as the nose dipped and the steep descent began. Doc produced another blanket and draped it over her. She noticed the others were all covered in blankets as well. Most appeared to be sleeping. The craft shuddered and shook violently as it landed. The strapped in cargo, clanked and banged, threatening to break free from their lashings.

The refueling didn't take long, less than an hour. Before Elizabeth knew it, the aircraft was thundering back down the runway. She swallowed hard to clear her ears as it climbed straight up, noticing that most of the others still appeared to be sleeping. How could that be? Even Madison's eyes had remained closed the entire time. The one exception was the man named Garcia. He was on his laptop, clicking the keys and reading whatever was on his screen with a sharp focus.

After the aircraft leveled off, Garcia unfastened his restraint. He approached Cooper and kicked his foot, returning the favor. He'd been in a deep sleep when Cooper woke him earlier. Cooper's eyes snapped open. Garcia nodded towards the galley closet. Cooper followed him to it.

"Elizabeth Shaw declined to take her final vows and become a Sister of Mercy and has been a novitiate for several years longer than normal. The paperwork to process her out of the order was on hold. Angel's mom is the nun in charge of the group in that village and Sister Bernice John thought it possible Elizabeth would change her mind."

"What's in Seattle?" Cooper asked.

"That's where Elizabeth is from, but from what I found, there isn't much there waiting for her. Her mother died when she was twelve. She has a brother, Robert Shaw, four years older than she is. He's in the state pen, serving a ten-year sentence for B and E. He had a long juvie record, and multiple arrests as an adult. There is no father listed on her birth certificate, her brother's either. When her mom died, she was taken into the Sisters of Mercy Orphanage."

"Does she have any kind of bank account?"

"I found a savings account opened when she was a child. She has two-hundred-fifty dollars in it."

"Education?" Cooper asked.

"She's a smart cookie, graduated top five percent of her class from the Seattle Public School System, then went to a community college's CNA vocational program on a scholarship and earned top grades, graduated and passed the state's licensing. She was already pledged to the Sisters at that point and worked at their free clinic in one of the worst areas of the city. Then they sent her to Africa. She was only twenty-one years old when she went over."

Cooper shook his head disapprovingly, sending a twenty-one-year-old to a war-torn hell-hole. "Anything else?"

Garcia shrugged. "There's nothing else, no social media presence."

"No other assets?"

Garcia shook his head no. "Nothing. She barely exists in any records."

"Okay, thanks," Cooper said. He pulled his phone from his pocket and tapped out a text message to Shepherd as Garcia retook his seat.

The flight landed at Edwards Airforce Base, pulled into a hangar, and they all deplaned. Elizabeth watched the others numbly. She was exhausted. She had slept for a few hours in the uncomfortable seat, but it hadn't been a restful sleep.

"Sister Elizabeth," Cooper said. "This airman will escort you from here. My team is transferring to our ride home."

Elizabeth's eyes flickered to Doc for a moment. His face was impassive. Would he even say goodbye to her? "Thank you for everything, Mr. Cooper." She presented her right hand.

Cooper pulled the money he had collected from all the others from his pocket and placed it into her hand, instead of shaking it. "For you, for expenses while you travel home to Seattle and to get settled."

She looked at the bills. "It's not necessary and far too generous of you." Embarrassed feelings she recognized from her childhood surged through her as she realized there had to be more than five hundred dollars in her hand.

"The entire team pitched in." His eyes went to Madison. "We know you don't have any money on you."

"I can find my way to a shelter and get a job to earn what I need to get to Seattle," Elizabeth insisted.

"Or you can take the money, say thank you, and let this Airman escort you to the airport where a plane ticket to Seattle in your name waits for you," Madison said.

"This is too much," she murmured, shaking her head. She couldn't even make eye contact with anyone, least of all Alexander. The shame of needing their money was too much.

"Elizabeth," she heard Alexander's voice. She still didn't look at him. "We don't operate that way, letting someone off in a strange city with no money. Your ride home with us is all the way to your home in Seattle."

"Thank you, all." She gazed back into Cooper's eyes. "I will earn this amount and repay you at some point in the future. I promise." She shoved the bills into a pocket of the borrowed pants she wore.

"That isn't necessary," she heard Doc's voice say.

She nodded just to end this.

"Airman, swing by the base's Exchange on the way please. Her bag got misplaced during our mission and she has no civvies," Madison said.

"Yes, ma'am."

"You have enough there to buy whatever you need," Madison said. Then she stepped forward and hugged Elizabeth. "Take care of yourself."

"Thank you, Madison. You have been most kind."

When they parted, Cooper stepped into her and gave her a brief squeeze. "Safe travels home, Sister."

"Thank you for everything," she murmured.

The Reverend folded his large arms around her next. "God be with you, Sister."

"And also, with you," she said robotically.

One by one each of the men said their goodbyes and then walked across the hangar to another plane. Her eyes met Alexander's. He was the only one left. "Goodbye, Alexander," she murmured.

"You'll be fine, Elizabeth. You're a strong woman." He wrapped his arms around her and held her for a brief moment. Then he stepped away, followed the others, and didn't look back.

Hotel

Doc dropped his gear in the Team Room and then took the stairs to the fourth floor, to his office. He stowed his secondary pack of medical gear and personal articles that had been left at the base in Djibouti when they went into Somalia. He was not looking forward to the paperwork he would have to fill out on all the equipment that he 'donated' to the General's group. He heard Sloan doing the same in his office across the hall. He took his time, not in a hurry to see Lassiter. He was dreading it. Way too many memories had forced their way into his consciousness, memories he thought he had banished, memories he didn't want to discuss with Lassiter.

"Hey," Sloan said, poking his head into his office. "I'll check over all the medical supplies in the office tomorrow and place an order with Ryan. If there is anything you need that won't be obvious to me, let me know and I'll get it ordered. What do you think? Will Lassiter have you off a few days to a week?"

Doc frowned. He didn't want to discuss this. "At least," he muttered.

"Okay, well, I'm taking off. Have a good few days."

"Yeah, you too," Doc acknowledged.

He sat in his chair and stared at absolutely nothing for a long time until his phone chirped, a text message. Lassiter. He closed his eyes for a second and breathed deeply. Yeah, he knew he was due to see him. He glanced at his watch. Correction, he was past due, expected a half hour ago.

He pulled himself out of his thoughts and pulled his butt from the chair. He made his way through the inner office area to the entrance to Lassiter's office suite. He found Lassiter sipping coffee in his kitchenette. He deposited himself in a chair across the table from Lassiter.

"You don't want any coffee?"

Doc shook his head no.

Joe sipped his coffee again, his eyes focused on Doc's. "So, what happened?"

Doc's lips pulled into a frown. "I need two weeks off to go fishing."

Joe Lassiter nodded his head. "Two weeks is doable."

Doc came to his feet.

"Whoa! Not until we talk."

Doc ran his fingers through his hair. It was getting longer than he liked it. "Joe, can we let it lay for a few weeks?"

"You know that isn't the way this works."

Doc wandered over in front of the window and gazed out. "When we arrived at the village to evacuate everyone, Sister Elizabeth wouldn't leave. She'd just performed spaghetti surgery on two young boys. Moving them would have killed them. I stayed with her, tidied up and strengthened her sutures, and gave the boys painkillers and antibiotics. Then it was a waiting game until they'd be strong enough to be moved."

Joe eyed him suspiciously as he waited for more that wasn't coming. "That's it?"

"Until the General's people came by for the third time and we got taken."

"You waited three days, were just about to evac with the boys when you were taken."

"Yeah. We would have been home free if one of the kids didn't call out."

"How'd it go for those three days?"

"It was routine."

Doc heard Joe snort out a disbelieving snicker. His eyes remained fixed on the mall parking lot. The silence in the room remained for several long minutes. Doc knew that Lassiter would wait him out for more. He didn't have it in him. Not right now, anyway.

He closed his eyes and saw Elizabeth's face standing in that hangar. He hadn't even said a proper goodbye to her. That had been shitty. After everything they'd been through, everything they'd shared, he didn't give her the words she needed as they parted. He told her what he needed to say to make himself feel better. A strong woman? He'd told her she was a strong woman. What the fuck would that mean to her?

"Joe, I need two weeks, a lake, my fishing gear, quiet that only being out in the middle of nowhere can bring me, then I'll be ready for this. You've known me a long time. I need you to trust me that I know what I need."

Joe Lassiter considered Doc's words for a quiet moment. "Answer one question, then I'll let it lay for two weeks."

Doc nodded his head, his back still to Joe.

"Did you think and accept that you were going to die?"

A sick feeling washed over Doc. His heart clenched in his chest and he had to force himself to draw in a breath. "Yeah."

The sound of the chair scooting back from the table resounded loudly through the otherwise quiet room. Doc heard every one of Joe's footfalls on the tile floor as he closed the distance. Joe's hand on the back of his shoulder was heavy.

"You've got your two weeks. Clear your head and get it back on straight. And you know how to reach me if you need to in the interim."

"Yeah," Doc again muttered.

The floatplane landed on the mirror-smooth lake. The sun was high in the noonday sky reflecting off the water and intensifying the brilliant orange and auburn colors that surrounded the large, four-thousand-acre lake. Lac Vieux Desert Lake, up where Wisconsin met Michigan's Upper Peninsula, was his little slice of heaven. There were more fish than people in this area, just how he liked it.

The boat taxied up to the dock, a rickety wood structure Doc hadn't set foot on in way too many years but was as familiar to him as an old friend. They were on the side of the lake away from the resorts, an isolated area with only a dozen cabins scattered through the trees and out of each other's line of sight. The pilot helped him to quickly transfer his half-dozen bags and cases onto the wood dock.

"Your cabin is number four, about a twenty-minute hike up the north trail," the pilot said, pointing at the footpath that was obvious in the tree line. The sign that was staked there, 'North Trail, Cabins One through Eight', was new since the last time he'd been here. It wasn't necessary. He knew the way.

"Yeah, I know where it is."

Dave, the pilot, eyed him curiously. "I've been the only pilot bringing in fishermen for the last five years. I've never brought you in."

"It's been a while since I've been here, too long."

"Well, not much has changed. You've got my phone number for an emergency. Secure your food, there are bears up here. And be ready for pickup by eleven a.m. two weeks from today."

"Yeah, got it, thanks," Doc said.

"You may want to check your cell signal before I go, to be sure."

"I have a satellite phone. It's good," Doc assured him. "I'll see you in two weeks. I'll be packed and ready at eleven hundred."

"Okay," the pilot said, nodding. He turned and got back into his cockpit.

Doc watched the floatplane gain speed as it pulled away from the dock. It pulled into the air, the sun gleaming off the fuselage before it banked south and grew smaller and smaller against the brilliant cobalt sky, finally disappearing from Doc's view.

Doc gazed up at the beautiful night sky and breathed in the cool air. It was going down to a crisp thirty degrees tonight. It had taken nearly the entire two weeks, but he finally felt at peace. Tomorrow would be his last day to fish and enjoy the solitude, his pickup scheduled for the day after. He added a log to the fire and then sat back in front of the dancing flames. The longer he sat and thought about it, the more decided he became that he would extend his trip by a week. He needed it. He deserved it. And he certainly had plenty of vacation time banked.

As soon as he decided, he called the floatplane pilot to pushout the pickup by a week and authorize a charge of an additional week cabin rental to be billed to his credit card. Then he placed the call to Shepherd, not caring what time it was.

"Shepherd," he answered on the second ring.

"Hi Shep." He didn't need to tell Shepherd he was still at the lake, out in the middle of nowhere. The evening tracker report would already have been given to Shepherd so he would know.

"What can I do for you, Doc?"

"I'm taking an additional week off, put me down for vacation."

Silence hung on the open line. "Is that a fact?" Shepherd asked after an appropriate wait.

Doc could hear the tone in his voice. Shepherd didn't like being told. Asking for the time would have been a more proper way of handling it. "It took me this long to get my head on straight. Now I want to enjoy fishing."

"Did you already reschedule your transportation?"

"Yeah," he replied.

"I guess that's decided then. Follow up with Lassiter when you're supposed to, and I'll see you when he releases you to return to full duty."

"Thanks," Doc said, feeling anything but thankful.

He knew how he handled it had been shitty. Just as he had handled the goodbye with Elizabeth. He wondered how she was. He knew she had made it to Seattle. The thought of her staying at the Sisters of Mercy shelter bothered him. Her whole life had been a hard-luck story. He wished he could have done more for her.

One thing he had come to in the past two weeks was that he was not responsible for her. Just because he had slept with her and they had nearly died together, that didn't make him responsible for her nor did it mean they had a relationship. The vows they had said to each other before he made love to her were based on the fact that they were going to die, and she had released him from those vows. It meant nothing.

The other thing he had come to grips with was the fact that he could have died, should have died, was damn lucky he hadn't died. It wasn't just this mission, of course. The potential for his death was there on each and every mission he went out on. He knew that but had never had to accept the fact that he was going to be killed, probably tortured in the worse ways possible. That realization and acceptance changed something inside him that he was only now coming to grips with.

The regrets he had about the past, regrets regarding Victoria, so many years ago, bubbled to the surface. He could still picture her in his mind, even though he wished he could banish all traces of her from his soul. That was a long time ago. He thought time healed all wounds. Well, it hadn't healed this one. He was trying to accept that just maybe, this one would never heal, and that was the reason he would never be in a relationship with any woman ever again, especially not someone as young, naïve, and sweet as Elizabeth. No, someone like him was the last thing she needed in her life.

He sat out enjoying the fire, gazing at the cloudless, dark sky for hours. His demons quieted, and he was able to think about pleasant things, the upcoming week of additional fishing in the fresh air surrounded by nature. He was glad he would take the extra week. The season was winding down. Soon, fall would give way to winter.

Winter. His thoughts jumped to the first stanza of the poem that was burned into his brain...We must live through the weary winter if we would value spring, and the woods must be cold and silent, before the robins sing, by Agnes L. Pratt, the poem that represents the Infants Remembered in Silence Organization. Damn, Victoria for sharing that poem and that organization with him. His thoughts turned dark again with too many memories flooding his consciousness.

Doc heard the floatplane approach but thought nothing of it. Dave was probably just picking up the two men in the cabin nearest his. He had spoken with them the day before and they were packing up and going home today. He hoped another group wasn't being brought in to occupy that cabin. He liked his quiet evenings alone by the fire. The two men who had been there were quiet themselves.

His line tugged and his thoughts were brought back to his task at hand. He didn't think any more of it. He enjoyed the remainder of his day on the lake.

Satisfied with the day's catch, Doc packed his gear up and headed towards his cabin. He had three large Walleye in his cooler, his legal limit for the day, enough for dinner, breakfast, and lunch tomorrow. To him, the whole point of the fishing trip was to catch enough for all his meals. The day had been a beautiful and unseasonably warm fifty-eight degrees, sunny, with a light breeze. He had enjoyed being on the lake, alone with his thoughts and at peace. These extra few days were exactly what he needed.

After he docked his boat, he trekked through the woods, on the path back to his cabin. His thoughts were light. He felt happy and content. Until his cabin came into sight, more specifically, Joe Lassiter sitting in front of the lit fire in front of his cabin. Holy. Hell.

"Hi Doc. You're back earlier than I thought you'd be. Did you have a successful catch?" Joe greeted with a shit-eating grin on his scarred face.

"Joe, what are you doing here?" He demanded, like he didn't know.

"We had an appointment, that you missed. So, I came to you."

Doc muttered a few obscenities under his breath. He passed by Lassiter and the fire and brought his gear to the cabin porch. He went inside and put his gear away. Then he slipped on warmer clothes as the temperature would quickly fall once the sun went down. He grabbed his equipment to clean and cook the fish. He noticed a large pack with a sleeping bag attached to it and a heavy winter coat on the old plaid couch. Lassiter's. He was planning to stay here with him. He let fly a new string of curses.

He went back out and brought the cooler over near the fire. "Looks like you've made yourself at home. Since you'll be eating, you can help clean the fish." He sat on the stump across from Lassiter.

"I brought eggs and bacon for the morning. Figured since you extended your trip you would have burned through all of your supplies by now."

"I will gladly enjoy your breakfast. But you're cooking it," Doc said.

Lassiter's lips ticked into a grin. He grabbed two beers from the cooler at his feet. He handed one to Doc. "And just so you know, the sooner you talk, the sooner I'll leave."

"I would like the end of my fishing trip to be in solitude," Doc said. He focused on cleaning the fish and filleting it. Lassiter let him be quiet with his thoughts. When he finished, he held up two of the fillets. "Looks good, doesn't it?"

Lassiter smiled and nodded towards the pan on Doc's lap that was filled with fillets. "Looks like enough there for your whole team."

Doc smirked. Smooth. "I hope to have a haul when I go back, will host a dinner for the team."

"What about their women?"

"Sure, whatever," Doc agreed.

"Tell me about Sister Elizabeth, who it turns out wasn't a Sister."

Doc clenched his eyes shut. He reopened them and fixed them on the fillets, which he then salted and peppered and wrapped in foil. "She was a child. Looked to be about fifteen."

"She's a twenty-four-year-old woman."

"What else do you know about her?" Doc asked. He laid the foil containing the fish onto the coals in the firepit.

"She's back in Seattle, doesn't have much there but an older brother in prison."

"She's had a hard-luck life," Doc paused and shook his head. "But the thing is, she doesn't seem to know it."

"Ah, the grateful type."

"Yeah, and sweet, and hardheaded. She was right those boys couldn't be moved. It would have killed them. If it wasn't for her, I would have moved them to get everyone out. That was the mission."

"So, those boys turned out to be the warlord's sons," Lassiter said.

"Yeah, didn't see that one coming."

"What happened after you and the boys were taken?" Lassiter asked.

"Do you want the long or short version?"

"I want the version that includes what you're beating yourself up about."

"We were sure we were going to be killed, tortured, brutalized, do not pass go, do not collect two-hundred dollars, just two-hundred broken bones or stab wounds."

Doctor Lassiter waited while Doc turned the tin foil packets. Doc took a drink of the beer and then returned the bottle to the ground by his feet. Lassiter took a drink of his as well, his eyes focused on Doc.

Doc stood and pulled on his flannel jacket. The sun was setting, and the temperature was dropping quickly. "Elizabeth was sure she'd be raped. She was a virgin. She didn't want to know abuse without ever knowing what it was like to be loved by a man. She begged me to," his voice trailed off. He lifted his beer and drank the remainder of the bottle in one pull.

"So, you had sex with her?"

"I made love to her," Doc corrected him. "There was nothing sleezy about it."

"I apologize," Lassiter said. "I didn't mean to imply it was anything less than what it was."

Doc shook his head. "She's young enough to be my daughter. Her first time should have been with someone she loved, was in a relationship with."

"She didn't want it to be a brutal rape by a warlord. I'm sure she appreciated you for it."

Doc let loose a whole new rant of vulgar adjectives, mostly focused at himself. "She's a child, for fuck's sake. You know what that makes me, don't you?"

Lassiter let out a burst of sarcastic laughter. "Jesus, Doc. She's twenty-four years old."

"You don't understand," Doc argued.

"Make me," Lassiter challenged.

Doc was silent, messing with the tinfoil containing the fish fillets again. He nodded towards the cabin. "Make yourself useful and go get us a couple of plates and forks."

Lassiter brought himself to his feet and went to the cabin. He had his heavier coat with him too when he returned. The night chill was creeping in. He held the plates while Doc retrieved the fish. He opened the packets and checked several fillets before leaving them on the plates.

"You got another beer in there for me?" Doc asked Lassiter.

Lassiter handed it over. "You got more to go with your story?"

A frown curved over Doc's face. He took several bites of fish before he answered. "Yeah. Because she is Catholic, and since we were convinced we were going to die, we said vows, promising to be faithful, marrying each other with no witness, just before God."

Lassiter took a bite of the fish, digesting that piece of info from Doc. "It's good," he said. Then he took another before speaking again. "So, your wife is in Seattle."

"No, my wife is dead. Victoria was my wife, and I killed her. I'm not going to do the same to that innocent young thing in Seattle."

Lassiter narrowed his eyes on Doc. "I thought we dealt with this. You did not kill Victoria."

"I didn't pull the trigger, but I didn't stop her from doing it to herself either."

"Everyone deals with grief in their own way. You weren't there for her because you shut down, poured yourself into your work. That was your way. But you didn't kill her."

Doc squeezed his eyes shut. He could still see that sonogram image of his baby in his head. A day later, a drunk driver, Victoria in the ICU, and no more baby. "I shouldn't have transferred to active duty and stayed deployed after. I should have gone home to her. She needed me and I let her down."

Lassiter nodded. "You were twenty-five years old. A kid yourself. At some point, you're going to have to forgive yourself."

"I don't deserve forgiveness," Doc said.

"What about Elizabeth? What does she deserve?"

"A life without someone like me in it," Doc shot back without missing a beat. "She doesn't need an old man who has seen what I've seen, lost everything as I have. She deserves someone young and hopeful with a future, someone capable of loving her."

"Doc, what happened to Victoria and your unborn child was tragic. No, you weren't there for Victoria, but did you think for even a second that she would take her own life?"

"Beforehand, no. I didn't think twice about it. But looking back after, the signs of the depression were there clear as day. I was too wrapped up in my own grief to see it though."

"You weren't looking. You were focusing on saving the lives you could, the men getting shot and blown up on the battlefield. It was your defense mechanism for dealing with the one you couldn't save, your child," Lassiter said.

Doc never thought about it in those terms. After the car accident he flew home to Houston. He had a two-week emergency leave to sit next to Victoria's bedside. They planned their unborn child's funeral. They cried together. They mourned the loss of any future possibility of having a child together. The damage to her uterus required it be removed or she would have died too.

"Her mother brought her home from the hospital after I was back in the Sandbox and stayed with her. She was supposed to see a counselor. I thought she was." Doc put another log on the fire. He gazed up at the sky, now pitch-black behind the many constellations that graced the heavens. It was a stunning display.

"It's natural you'd think of Victoria after taking vows with Elizabeth."

Doc snorted out sad laughter, tears filling his eyes. "Life is cruel. I hadn't thought about any of this for a long time, was doing just fine. I sure as hell didn't need any of this shit coming back, especially now."

"But now that it's back, you need to deal with it."

Doc nodded. "I am in my own way. It took the first two weeks up here to get my head back on straight."

"And now that it is, what have you figured out?"

"Well, for starters, I don't owe Elizabeth anything. She's a sweet kid, but we don't have a relationship. We don't have a future. I'm not in love with her. Hell, I'm not sure I'm capable of loving any woman."

"That's a whole other discussion we'll get to later. Regarding this last Op, what else have you figured out?"

"Everyone, including me, is going to die. I can take precautions, but the timing is not in my control. When my number's up, it's up."

"You've always known that. You've seen more death than most," Lassiter reminded him.

"This was different. It was the first time I truly thought it was going to be lights out, my number up. I accepted that and made my peace with it."

"So, if you made peace with it, what's the issue?"

Doc sighed. "I don't know."

Lassiter waited a beat for Doc to continue. He didn't. "I'm calling bullshit on that. You've had two weeks to think about it and work it out."

"Joe, can we let this lay for now?"

Lassiter laughed. "You're not getting off that easy." He watched Doc add another log to the fire. "Give me something substantial. Something that justifies two plus weeks up here without talking to me. You know why this protocol is in place. I gave you time to get your shit together, trusting you wouldn't blow your brains out up here."

Doc shook his head. He knew what it was, what he didn't want to fess up to. He stared into the dancing flames of the fire and avoided eye contact as he spoke. "I was a total douchebag, with Elizabeth. I shouldn't have slept with her, shouldn't have married her, and I sure as fuck treated her shitty when we left her at Andrews. I told myself it was for her own good, that I left her the way I did, but I could have done it differently. You should have seen the look on her face. I hurt her and that was wrong. What the fuck is wrong with me?"

Lassiter was satisfied they were finally getting to the core of what was eating at Doc. "Let's break this down one at a time. Why shouldn't you have slept with her? And don't give me that she's a kid. She's not. She's a twenty-four-year-old woman."

"She was a nun, innocent, a virgin. Under any other circumstances she never would have slept with me or anyone else."

"But the circumstances were important to the context. What if you had said no, and she was indeed raped, brutalized, and killed as you both expected would happen?"

Doc ran his fingers through his hair and grabbed his temples with both hands. "I know, that's what makes this maddening."

"Doc was she really that innocent? She was serving in a hellhole. Certainly, she was more experienced than you are giving her credit for."

Doc gazed at him with a laser-focused stare. "Yes, and no. She had seen enough to be jaded but chose not to be. She knew all about sex, the mechanics and chemistry of it, but had never had it."

"Did you enjoy it?" Lassiter asked.

"What the hell is wrong with you, asking that?"

Lassiter chuckled. "You did and you're beating yourself up for it." He watched Doc for a few seconds. He had a fire in his eyes, a self-loathing fire, and a gut-eating agony. "No, you're not beating yourself up. You're crucifying yourself for it."

"I'm not discussing this with you anymore."

"For now. We'll move on to why you shouldn't have married her."

"That's fucking obvious, isn't it?"

"Enlighten me," Lassiter prompted.

"I only did it to sleep with her. She's Catholic. If we weren't married, in God's eyes it would have been a sin."

"And again, if you'd both been killed, it wouldn't be an issue. That was the context you said those vows to her."

"She released me from the vows after we were set free," Doc murmured.

"Did she release herself?" Lassiter asked.

Doc shook his head. "I doubt it." The truth was he didn't know. He hadn't bothered to ask her.

"Hardly seems fair," Lassiter remarked. "I can see why this is eating at you."

"I don't love her, Joe, am not right for her. Hell, I didn't even ask her what she wanted when we left Africa. I just told her what it wasn't going to be for me and sent her on her way."

"Is that how you could have handled it better to not hurt her?"

"Yeah, that and more. I handed her cash because she didn't have a dime on her to make it home. Cooper messaged Shepherd, who arranged an airline ticket for her. He took up a collection from the team. I gave her every cent I had on me. She had the clothes on her back that Madison gave her. That was it."

"What else could you have done?"

"I could have brought her back with me and let her stay at my place, bought her some clothes and stuff she needed, let her get on her feet before she went back to Seattle. I could have been kind and not so eager to get rid of her."

"Why didn't you?" Joe pressed.

"I didn't want her to think we had a future and I damn sure didn't want to sleep with her again."

"Which would have happened if you had her at your place."

Doc shook his head not wanting to admit it. But he knew Lassiter would know if he spoke anything but the truth. "Probably."

Lassiter smirked. "You are allowed to move on from Victoria, you know."

"That's not what this is about," Doc insisted.

"You have not had one real relationship since her, have you?"

"And I still haven't."

"Yeah, you sent Elizabeth away to be sure of it." Lassiter paused watching Doc again. This wouldn't be an easy fix. Doc had well over a decade of self-loathing regarding Victoria's death he hadn't really dealt with. He'd buried it, pushed his self-guilt down so far that even Lassiter hadn't known it was there. Well, now he did, and Doc would deal with it. He'd make sure of it.

"It was for her own good."

"So, you've said." He grabbed the last two beers from the bag. He handed Doc one and then twisted the top off his. He sucked down a drink. "But what I haven't heard yet, is what is it you really want."

"To be left alone."

Lassiter grinned. "We both know that's not going to happen." He took a drink. "Jackson, Cooper, Garcia, all the members of your team have a woman in their lives. Doesn't that make you feel at least," he began.

"No," Doc interrupted. "It doesn't make me want what they have."

"It can be done, a woman, a child, while doing this job."

"I think I've hurt Elizabeth enough. She sure as shit doesn't need any more from me."

"Hum, you seem fixated on that woman being Elizabeth. That wasn't what I was saying," Lassiter remarked.

"What do you want from me, Joe? Tell me what you want to hear, and I'll say it."

Lassiter laughed. "You know that isn't how this works. You, my friend, have some work to do to forgive yourself before you can even think about being in a relationship. You were right about that when you said she doesn't need any more from you, not in your current state, anyway. There is no room for her or anyone while you are carrying around what you are. And I'm not going to let you bury it again. It's out now and damn it, Doc, you're going to deal with it this time."

Fine, just fucking fine, Doc thought.

Indigo

"Do you feel ready to be back?"

"Return me to duty, let me go fishing for another few weeks, I don't particularly give a shit," Doc said. He stood in front of the window in Lassiter's kitchen, gazing out at the mall parking lot again. It had been three weeks since they got back from Africa. It felt more like a year.

Lassiter eyed him suspiciously. That wasn't the reply he was expecting. "Are you ready to be back? That's the question. Have you worked out what you needed to work out that initially made you request two weeks from me?"

Doc gazed at the ceiling as though the correct answer would display in bold black letters over the white tiles. "I'd like to say I have. I have mostly, but," he paused for a long couple of beats. "Look Joe, I won't try to BS you. Way too many thoughts about the car accident and Victoria's suicide came back, thoughts I thought were dealt with long ago."

"Dealt with or buried?" Joe asked.

Doc shook his head. "When we talked up at the cabin, you gave me some things to think about. I never thought that I was compensating, helping those to survive that I could. But yeah, that's exactly what I was doing. Out there, there was so much death, it was like it helped me to accept that our baby had died, that death was normal, expected. I don't know."

Lassiter nodded. Now they were making progress. "And the vows you made to Elizabeth, did they bring back your married life or your vows to Victoria?"

Doc shook his head. "You know, not at first. But memories crept in. Her youth and innocence were not what Victoria was at all." He let loose a string of curses. He paused, frowned, and shook his head. "Victoria was no angel before we got together. We had sex in my truck in the bar parking lot the night I met her. I was captivated by her. She was beautiful, sassy, and so confident. When I popped the question, I was so worried she'd say no, but she didn't. But then life got complicated, and I joined the National Guard for the extra money. I knew deployment to the Sandbox was a possibility and sure as hell, eight months later our unit got called up. We didn't know she was pregnant when I left." He paused and chuckled. "I think she got pregnant the night before I shipped out."

Lassiter smiled and nodded to encourage him to continue.

"When I got the call from her, I was thrilled. But what we were going through over there was pure hell. The attacks and roadside IEDs caused casualties that never stopped coming. I found myself caring less about home and what was going on with Victoria, than I did about what was going on over in the Sandbox. I changed. And after her car accident, all I cared about was learning all I could to save more lives. I checked out on her. And the worst part is, I can't say it had anything to do with my unborn child's death. I can't say it wouldn't have happened had he lived and been born."

"Well, you'll never know because that is what happened. And don't discount how life changing it is to serve overseas in a combat zone, especially as a medic."

"I know," Doc agreed.

"Do you feel you're still that person you changed into, or do you think you could be a checked-in caring partner?"

Doc shook his head. "I don't want to find out and I sure as hell don't want to subject anyone else to a life with me if I can't."

"So, if you know for sure or are at least sure you don't want to find out then why did this thing with Elizabeth dredge all this up? Or was it something specific to Elizabeth?"

"I don't fucking know. Figuring that out is your job, isn't it?"

Lassiter chuckled again. "It's a joint project."

"Why do I get the feeling we're not done with this?"

"Probably because we're not." Lassiter grinned. "When we talked last, you said that you know you hurt Elizabeth, but it was for her own good. The question I have for you is how it made you feel? What were you thinking about?"

Doc's steely gray eyes focused on Joe Lassiter. "I felt nothing. I thought nothing. I did what was best for her."

Lassiter doubted that. Doc was a master at burying what he didn't want to think about. He didn't want Doc to bury these feelings about Elizabeth too, but he knew when to push and when not to. And this was not a time to push Doc. He knew the man well enough to know that.

"Do you remember when we talked after the Inverness Academy job?" Lassiter asked. Doc nodded. "When we talked about the dead girl and the one you had to sedate, did you think about your child at all during any of that?"

Doc shook his head. "I've never thought about Daniel during any mission. He was never a living breathing child and I've never envisioned him as one. He's in my memories as that sonogram image, nothing more."

Lassiter doubted that too. "Doc, I think it's best you come back to work as long as we touch bases regularly. You need to get back into your routine, get back to work. When we talk next, I want you to be able to tell me how you felt when you said goodbye to Elizabeth. I want to hear real feelings, real thoughts that went through your head. This bullshit that it was for her own good won't fly."

Doc just stared at him. He didn't speak, didn't argue it. When he left Lassiter's office he went to his own. It was a place that was as comfortable to him as his home. Both places felt foreign to him now. He'd gotten back from his fishing trip the previous evening and after stowing his fishing gear, he just wandered around his small condo. All he wanted to do was to go back to that cabin.

Joe Lassiter reported to Shepherd. He carefully considered what words he would use beforehand. "I recommend Doc be returned to full duty, provided he continues to have very regular sessions with me, and he is observed when in the field." He paused and shook his head. "No benefit of the doubt shall be given to him. If any actions are suspect, he is to be immediately pulled."

Shepherd rubbed his fingers over his pounding forehead and temples. "If you're worried, why return him to full duty?"

"Because in this situation, I feel it would be more harmful to him to be off."

"I usually don't press, but you've got to give me more, Joe. His self-mandated three-week leave is unprecedented."

"Sam, you need to trust me. This one is going to take some time."

Shepherd's eyebrows raised. His stare was unwavering.

"You know I won't divulge the details," Lassiter said.

They had a staring contest for another thirty seconds.

"I didn't do my job, Sam. I thought some issues were resolved. They weren't. He buried things that have now resurfaced and I'm not going to allow him to not resolve them this time."

Shepherd nodded. "I trust you, Joe, you know that. I'll need to bring Cooper in on this for that observation. Keep me informed of the progress."

"You got it," Joe promised. "I'll meet with Cooper regarding this too, so he'll know what to look for. The dynamics of Alpha Team have changed dramatically over the past few years. The members are at different points in their lives now. You may need to reassess team assignments at some point."

Shepherd leaned over his desk. "Is that solely based on the Doc situation or are you picking this moment to bring up other team issues?"

Lassiter nodded. "Both. I'm just planting the idea for you to be aware that it may be needed at some point. Do I think you need to do anything now? No."

Shepherd eyed him suspiciously. How could the relationship statuses of Doc's teammates have a bearing on his team assignment? Shepherd knew Doc had been disappointed with Cooper and Madison for the relationship that developed between them, against protocol, and he initially had been pissed that Jackson hadn't been fired for getting involved with Angel during that mission, another huge breach of protocol. He thought though, that Doc had been okay with both after the fact. He hadn't even reacted to Garcia getting involved with Sienna.

Then his thoughts clicked in a different direction. "Joe, are Cooper and Miller still okay working together on the team?"

Lassiter nodded. "That isn't an issue, for anyone on the team."

"I know Jackson wants more time at home, is that part of the issue? I thought with the shifts in Ops we were accommodating him well enough."

Lassiter's lips tugged up into a grin. "Sam, stop fishing. You don't have an issue yet. I'll let you know when you do, just know I feel it's on the horizon."

Joe Lassiter came to his feet, indicating he was done with this conversation.

Doc's first few days of the first week back, were quiet. He flew under the radar and avoided his teammates as much as he could. By Thursday though, he found himself sitting in a pre-Op mission briefing. He felt mentally distracted and detached.

A wealthy man was kidnapped, his bodyguards shot, ransom demands received. The man's attorney's contracted Shepherd Security to handle the ransom drop and recovery of the man. They'd located where he was being held and were going in to get him. Doc forced himself to pay attention to the building layout and the mission particulars, who would go in which door, how many Tangos to expect, the usual.

"The last proof of life was twelve hours ago," Shepherd's voice broke through Doc's thoughts. "Let's hope this is a rescue mission and not a recovery mission. Doc, you know what types of injuries you may be in for."

Doc nodded.

"Okay, that's it. Go get him," Shepherd said.

Doc followed his teammates from the room. Cooper and Madison were both going on this one, as were Garcia and Jackson. They took the stairs to subbasement two, to the Team Room to grab their gear, assault rifles, body armor, black fatigues. He watched the others exchange joking banter as they packed up. It should have felt familiar and comforting. It didn't. It irritated the hell out of him.

Then he followed them as they headed out to the garage and the two awaiting SUVs that Requisition Ryan would have already stocked with ammo for their mission.

Cooper stopped and turned to face Doc, blocking his path. "Are you okay?"

"Yeah, why do you ask?"

"You've been quiet. Didn't you have a good fishing trip?"

Doc felt his lip tick into a smirk. "No, the fishing was good, just too short."

Cooper raised an eyebrow in response to that statement. "Are you mentally checked in and ready for this mission?"

That was when Doc knew Lassiter had talked with Cooper about him. He knew Lassiter would never share any details with anyone, not even Shepherd, but Cooper had been told to watch him. That pissed him off and he knew one misstep and he'd be put on leave by Lassiter, and not to go fishing either. He stared Cooper down. "Yeah, I'm checked in and ready."

Cooper nodded. He turned around and exited into the parking garage. Doc followed. They transferred to the company LearJet and changed into their fatigues en route. There would be two vehicles waiting at the airfield for them to drive to the mission site, an abandoned warehouse in a mostly vacant industrial area of Detroit.

It was dusk as the plane descended. Doc did a final check of his medical supplies. He knew exactly where everything was and that he had everything he would need. It was just a habit to do one more check before they began a mission, just like his teammates had their own habits. Cooper meditated, Garcia zoned out to classic rock, Madison did what she called chair yoga, contorting her body in a variety of uncomfortable looking stretches, and Jackson stared at a picture of Angel and Sammy while blasting country music through his headphones.

After a bumpy touchdown at Coleman A. Young International Airport in Detroit, the team deplaned in a private hangar out of view from any curious onlookers. They transferred their gear quickly into the two black-tinted windowed SUVs. Cooper drove one of the vehicles, Jackson the other. Doc rode with Jackson and Garcia on purpose. He didn't want to be under Cooper's scrutiny.

The two SUVs drove near the abandoned automobile plant, where they identified that their victim, Dax Winchester, was being held. From a block north of the building, the team viewed the large metal structure that loomed like a haunted skeleton in the darkness across what had been the parking lot area. It now had more tall grass growing than the field to the south of the building. Graffiti decorated the building. Most of the windows were broken. This entire area was eerily quiet, abandoned, urban blight at its worst.

Cooper lowered his binoculars. "It's quiet. Intel says four Tangos. Not sure where they are, but they're not walking the perimeter. Control, do you have thermal imaging for us?"

"Negative, the metal building is blocking all heat signatures within," BT's voice came.

Cooper's eyes swept over the others. "Okay, we do this the old-fashioned way. We'll all go in together through the north entrance." His breath left puffs of steam in the frigid air. He nodded to Jackson. "As soon as we're inside, find a high point and give us some cover."

Jackson nodded, sniper rifle in hand.

"Garcia and Madison, you'll break and go west. Doc and I will veer east. Clear each room, cover each other and don't take any unnecessary risks. If the Tangos are armed, drop them. They've already shown they won't hesitate to fire, and we don't want to give them any opportunities."

The five of them made their way to the building moving stealthily through the night, night vision goggles in place. They slipped into the building silently and broke off into their assigned teams. The interior was dark. It was a cloudy evening so not even the moon or stars shone through the few windows.

Cooper and Doc wove themselves deeper within the metal labyrinth. The factory floor had been gutted long ago, but the interior offices had cubicles, desks, and file cabinets. One room led to another in the icy darkness. There were coat closets, conference rooms, and break rooms to search. It was slow going.

On the other side of the factory, Madison and Garcia zigzagged their way through what had been stockrooms, with empty shelving in rows that rose up to the ceiling. They found nothing after over an hour of searching.

"Coop, we've cleared this level. We're making our way back to the middle of the plant, to the west stairwell," Garcia reported.

"Roger that, Razor. Go up, we'll go down. Our area is clear as well," Cooper replied. "Jax, you got anything?"

From high on a catwalk over the middle of the factory floor, Jackson replied. "Negative, Coop. There isn't anything moving but you and a couple of field mice trying to stay warm. Jesus, is it cold in here!"

Cooper's lips tipped into a grin. He removed his NVGs and his eyes focused on Doc. "Don't tell me fishing is better than this and you didn't miss this shit?" His voice whispered.

Doc gave him a sarcastic smirk. "Yeah, clearing an abandoned factory in subzero temps is better than a lake and my fishing gear."

Coop chuckled softly. He repositioned his NVGs and nodded towards the stairwell on the other side of the wide hallway. They crept down the metal staircase. They cleared the rooms they came to before turning the corner and getting a halo of light from up ahead. They removed their NVGs and let their eyes adapt.

"We have a lighting source ahead," Cooper transmitted. "We're moving in slowly."

"Roger that," BT at HQ acknowledged.

Doc followed Cooper, his new FERFRANS SOAR gripped tightly in both his hands. He was still pissed his tried-and-true weapons had been 'donated' to General Halima's forces. All in all, the FERFRANS was a good assault rifle, accurate, reliable, and comfortable in his hands. The paperwork to replace his gear hadn't been too much of a hassle and Shepherd had pretty much given him carte blanche to order whatever he wanted. It wasn't every day one of them lost all their gear the way he had.

The light grew brighter as they approached. From around the next corner, they heard a radio playing obnoxious rap music, male voices, and laughter, amateurs. They inched closer to the corner. Cooper looked Doc in the eyes, shifted his eyes right towards the corner, down, then back to Doc. His lips mouthed the words, three, two, one, go.

Then he thrust himself around the corner into the open. Doc followed, dropping to a knee beside Cooper. Two men were seated at a table. They reached for their weapons. They didn't reach them in time. Four silenced rounds, two each from Doc and Cooper's weapons stopped the men dead.

A door behind the dead men opened. A man exited the bathroom, carelessly wielding his Remington R-15 Predator rifle. It took a costly second for him to realize what was in front of him. Four rounds hit him, center mass, again two from each man's weapon. The rifle clanked to the cement floor as he hit it, face down.

Cooper and Doc moved in close. They moved the weapons from near the dead men at the table and they kicked the rifle from near the dead man on the floor. Then the stench hit them.

"Jesus, not sure what that boy ate as his last meal, but that's rank," Doc remarked.

"What the fuck are you guys doing out there?" A voice demanded from behind the door to their left. It opened. A man, as wide as he was tall filled the opening. He reached for the handgun shoved in the front of his low-slung blue jeans.

"Leave it," Cooper ordered.

The man didn't listen. He didn't get the gun from its tight restraint before Cooper dropped him as well. He fell beside the space heater that glowed orange warming the area to a balmy sixty degrees.

Cooper moved near him, kicked him onto his back and disarmed him. It didn't matter. He wouldn't be a threat. No life remained. "Four Tangos neutralized," he broadcast.

"Did you find the target yet?" BT asked.

"Negative," Doc replied. "We're still searching." He was sure the man would be close by. He stepped over the dead man and into the room, into the noticeably warmer room that had a sofa, lights, and a television. Two doors were on the far wall.

He opened the first one, throwing it open with his left hand, his right aiming his CZ-97 .45 ACP into the empty closet. He moved to the second door. It was locked. By this time, Cooper was beside him. He went back to fat-boy on the floor and unclipped the keyring from his belt. He tried four keys before the one that unlocked the door slid into the keyhole. He unlocked it and threw the door wide.

Within, on a futon in the dark room was their target, Dax Winchester, self-made billionaire. He wasn't bound or gagged. He started at the sudden appearance of his rescuers, but quickly recovered and came to his feet.

"Mr. Winchester, are you okay?" Cooper asked.

He nodded. "Took you long enough. Three fucking days I've been in this shit-hole with these lowlife thugs!"

"Do you have any medical needs," Doc asked.

"Just malnutrition. The bastards only gave me junk food."

"Target acquired," Cooper broadcast. "He's unharmed."

"You're welcome," Doc said to their victim sarcastically.

"We'll escort you out," Cooper said. "The four men guarding you are dead, and we have to go past them. Did you see anyone else?"

"I don't give a shit the four homeboys are dead. Those fucking gang-bangers were wasting the air we breathe. None of them were smart enough to orchestrate my kidnapping. Please tell me you know who was behind it?"

Cooper and Doc exchanged glances. "We'll work that one out after we've got you to safety," Cooper said. "Razor, Xena, be advised we are bringing our victim out. Meet us at the east stairwell. Jax, hold position."

"Roger, Coop," Garcia replied. "Third level west is clear. We are headed in that direction now."

"Roger, Coop," Jackson echoed.

No other threats were on site. After Garcia and Madison met up with Doc and Cooper, escorting their victim, and it was assured all was quiet, Jackson came down from his perch. The five of them surrounded Winchester and walked him across the grassy parking lot, back towards their SUVs.

"HQ notify LEOs we have four fatalities in the southeast corner of basement level one."

"Don't you have a coat for me? It's fucking freezing out here."

"There will be blankets in the car," Doc said.

"Better have a hell of a heater," Winchester said in disgust. "What kind of rescue is this?"

"Look, asshole!" Doc sneered, his face leaning into their victim's personal space. "These men left their families to come rescue you, risking their own personal safety. The least you could do is be grateful."

"I'm sure you're being paid very well, if I know my attorneys. Besides, this is your job, isn't it?"

Doc raised a fist, ready to deck this piece of shit.

"Whoa!" Jackson said, grabbing Doc's arm. He pulled him away, turning Doc so his back was to their victim. "I want to teach him a lesson on appreciation too, but this isn't you, Doc."

Cooper came in close. "What the fuck? Stifle that!" He exclaimed in a hushed tone.

Doc looked back. Garcia and Madison were leading their smart-mouthed, ungrateful, arrogant victim to their SUVs. His eyes locked with Cooper's. "I wasn't going to punch him. I wanted to. But I wouldn't have."

Cooper smirked and shook his head. "Whatever is going on with you, you need to resolve it. Get your head on straight. You'll be up with Lassiter as soon as we get back."

Then Cooper walked away. It was a punch to Doc's gut. He'd been accused of being grumpy in the past. Okay, he'd been accused of a lot worse personality traits than grumpiness, but he'd never been called out by Cooper for it. Not like this.

When they arrived at HQ just after three-hundred hours. Doc went straight to Lassiter's office. He'd never been one to dodge his responsibilities. This was no different. He'd fucked up and now it was time to face the music. Lassiter. And explain his actions.

He found Lassiter in his office seated at his desk. "I want to grab a cup of coffee," Doc said.

Lassiter rose and followed Doc into his kitchen. He grabbed himself a water bottle. He had hopes of grabbing a few hours' sleep on his couch after talking with Doc. Cooper had sent a detailed report via email after texting Lassiter to request his presence upon their return.

Before Doc's cup even finished brewing, Lassiter began. "So, what happened? Why am I here?"

"Our victim was an ass. I said some things Cooper took exception to."

"He was the victim, the one you went into rescue."

"That arrogant fucking douchebag deserved my harsh words. It could have been worse; he could have been removing my size eleven from up his ass."

"Cooper reports you raised a fist. He said Jackson restrained you."

"I wasn't going to hit the rich pretty-boy. I wanted him to know he was out of line though, put a little fear into him."

"He'd been kidnapped. You don't think that put fear into him?"

"Not the way he was acting," Doc replied.

"And how was that?"

"That we were obviously beneath him, so it was okay the team risked their lives to save his sorry ass. Never mind we killed four men to rescue him. It was just our jobs, according to Mr. Silver-Spoon."

Lassiter decided it was time he changed the subject. "So, he wasn't grateful, like Elizabeth had been. You still have to answer for that, you know. What did you feel when you sent her away? And don't tell me nothing."

"Joe, I felt bad. I hurt her. I admit that. I just felt I had to make it clear we had no relationship."

Lassiter stared intently at Doc, waiting for more. When Doc didn't continue, he broke the silence. "So, those vows you exchanged with her meant nothing to you?"

Doc let out a loud, measured breath. "At the risk of sounding like a complete prick, no, didn't mean a damn thing."

Lassiter stared in silence at Doc longer, trying to evaluate if he was telling the truth. He could usually tell. Maybe it was that Doc was being honest, and he just didn't want to believe it. Or maybe, Doc was already burying his feelings regarding it.

"She's a nice kid, but she's just a kid, and don't give me any shit about her age. That's not what I mean when I say she's a kid. It's her experience level."

"You don't think serving in a place like Somalia has given her more experience in life than most others her age?"

"In some ways, but not in others. Look Joe, she only earned her CNA, and she was doing surgery over there, attempting things vastly outside of her training." He paused, shook his head, and muttered a few more curses. "When I first saw the condition of the one boy's chest, I thought my head would explode. But she did whatever she could do to save lives. I respect that. Then she opens her mouth and she's like, oh golly shucks mister, I've never done more than hold a boy's hand and get a kiss on the cheek, now please make love to me so I know a lover's touch before I know abuse. What the hell was I supposed to do with that?"

Joe's lips pulled into a grin. He knew there weren't many people outside of the team that Doc would say he respected. He wouldn't point that out though. "Seems to me you decided to make love to her. That's what went down, wasn't it?"

"You know I wrestled with that one. I didn't just say, yeah, great, let's fuck."

"So, it wasn't the act that messed with your head as much as the vows you exchanged?"

Doc grabbed his head and growled. "It was all of it, the whole fucked up situation. I know those vows meant everything to her, were the only way she could have sex so it wouldn't be a sin in God's eyes. You can take the girl out of the convent, but you can't take the convent out of the girl. We were both one hundred percent sure we were going to be tortured and killed. How could I say no to her?"

"Saying no under those circumstances would have been what a complete prick would have done. You met her needs on her terms to help her come to grips with what was sure to be a very unpleasant end of her life. There is nothing in that to be beating yourself up over. So, the real question then, is why are you?"

Doc shook his head. "When we were flying out of there, after our release, I held her in my arms, and she stared at me with puppy-dog eyes. I know I was in shock that we were walking away alive. I can't even imagine what she was feeling. But in that moment, I knew I had to make sure she realized we didn't have any future. There was no relationship."

"You thought about pushing her away in that moment, when you were evacuated? Your first thought while holding this woman whose virginity you had taken, who you had made love to just a few hours earlier, was to make it damn clear to her that you had no relationship?"

"Pretty damn cold, don't you think?" Doc asked.

"I'm wondering which one of you it was, that you were so hell-bent on convincing, her or yourself?"

"I was clear in my thinking. She had to know those vows were only because we were going to die."

"I remember that moment when I accepted that I was going to die," Lassiter said. "I almost welcomed it at that point. Accepting that changes a man. That's why I let you have your two weeks without talking with me."

Doc knew of Joe Lassiter's past, his capture, torture, rape, and near death at the hands of enemy insurgents in Afghanistan. He lost his leg to an infection that could have been treated if he'd been rescued sooner. He knew how many years it took Lassiter to recover physically and how many more years it took him to get over the psychological scars that the ordeal left on him. Joe spoke from a place of experience, of understanding. Doc respected that.

"And I appreciated it, if I said so or not. I know I don't feel the same about some things as I did before, like rescuing ungrateful, arrogant bastards."

"And if he'd been another Elizabeth, innocent and thankful, would that have been different?"

"Yeah, those are the people I do this job for, otherwise it sure as hell wouldn't be worth it."

"You've been doing this for a long time, on both active duty and for Shepherd Security. Maybe it's time for a break?" Lassiter suggested, watching Doc very carefully for his reaction. It wasn't what he expected.

"Is that what you think? That I need a break?" Doc demanded. "Are you going to fucking bench me, Lassiter?"

"No, I definitely think you need to work. Another leave of absence would do you no good. At some point you need to decide for yourself though if this job is worth it to you, regardless of the people you think you're doing it for. If you're not doing it for yourself, that's when it's time to hang it up."

Doc froze and stared at Joe Lassiter like he had two heads. He hadn't thought about who he did the job for in a very long time. The truth was, he didn't know anymore. He hadn't questioned it before Africa. It was his job, his life, what defined him, regardless who the target was or who they were rescuing.

The brotherhood he shared with his teammates sustained him. Shepherd's approach to the job, what he focused on, how he supported the team were a huge part of why he was here. But since he had accepted, truly accepted he was going to die in one of the most unpleasant ways, none of it crept into his consciousness or if it did, it didn't matter.

Doc rubbed his forehead. "My teammates have always been my family. We share a common purpose, a common experience. We did until Africa. I feel different now, have experienced something I don't think many of them have. I've never asked Garcia if while under as Razor, either time, he was sure he would die. Or Miller, while she was out and unprotected after her covert base of operations was hit, I don't know if she felt like I do."

"But I did," Lassiter said. "I know what you're feeling. I was there. I'm pretty sure Shepherd and Angel felt sure they would be killed, accepted it. Isn't that enough?"

Doc shook his head. He hadn't even thought of Shepherd and Angel or what they had gone through. "I guess it should be. It sets me apart from my team though, the members of Alpha."

"Until one of them go through it at the same level you did. Then they won't feel set apart. They will have commonality with you."

"Do you really think another member may be in a spot that they truly accept it's going to be their end?"

"I think if a man does the job long enough, then yes, he will face and accept his death is imminent like we have. He may not make it out alive like we did though. I'd say we were both damn lucky," Lassiter said.

Doc knew he was right. They were alive, they were more than lucky. "Why does everything feel so different now?" Doc asked after a long silence. "Why don't I feel alive?"

"You feel disconnected, separate," Lassiter stated.

Doc nodded.

Lassiter knew Doc had finally turned a corner. The path back would show itself to Doc, but he would need to be patient with himself. It wouldn't be an overnight fix. "It takes time, Doc. You accepted you were going to die, now you need to remember how to live."

Doc laughed a sick sound. "It shouldn't be this way."

"Give it time."

Juliette

The weeks passed. Another mission came and went. Doc found himself sitting in Lassiter's kitchen again. He'd really thought he'd watched his P's and Q's this time. Cooper didn't agree. Doc couldn't help but chuckle a sarcastic laugh when Lassiter asked him, "what happened this time?"

"I really don't know why I'm here this time, Joe," Doc said. "I didn't threaten anyone. I did my job. I even had a beer with the team after, on the flight home."

Joe Lassiter ran his hand through his hair. Then he rubbed his chin. "Do you think you engaged with your team? And don't give me this bullshit you had a beer with them. Did you say two words to anyone outside of discussing the mission or through your comms coordinating movements? During that beer, tell me one thing anyone said."

Doc rubbed his eyes and gripped the bridge of his nose, as if either movement would make him recall words he hadn't listened to. "Jackson told us the new sounds Sammy is babbling." It was a guess. Jackson always told them every new sound or action baby Sammy did.

"What sound was it?"

"How the fuck am I supposed to remember? It's a new babble every day."

"And Cooper? What did he share with the team on that flight?"

Doc breathed out a heavy sigh. "I have no fucking clue, to any of it. So, don't ask me about Garcia or Madison. If either said anything, I sure as shit don't know what they said."

"You need to actively engage, Doc. It's like a muscle. If you don't use it, it won't strengthen."

"I know you said it would take time, but I'm done with this shit. Maybe this is the new me. Maybe I don't need to strengthen anything. People change all the time. Maybe I'll change back, maybe I won't. I can't be anyone other than who I am, and this is who I feel like now." Doc shot to his feet. He stormed out of the room. He was pretty sure Lassiter would give him a day or two reprieve, but that was it.

Four days later Doc found himself in a meeting with Shepherd, Cooper, and Lassiter. He was sure he was going to be fired. Shepherd glared at him from across his desk. Cooper stood beside Shepherd; his arms folded over his chest. Lassiter sat beside him, but he didn't look any friendlier than Shepherd or Cooper.

"Our mental health protocols are in place for good reason, Doc," Shepherd said. "It's been over two months since the Op in Africa."

"I don't see much difference in you," Cooper said. "You've been a royal pain in the ass since we plucked you and Sister Elizabeth out of that valley. Did the heat out there do irreparable damage to your head?"

Doc felt his lips twist into the granddaddy of all smirks. He wanted to tell them all to go fuck themselves. "I do my job. What's the damned problem?"

"They call it a team for a reason. You haven't come to one out of the office thing, no football games, no poker nights, not even Thanksgiving dinner at Angel and Jackson's. Christmas is a few days away. Will you be around for our office Christmas Party?" Cooper blasted him.

"I've never missed Christmas with the team when we aren't working. I'll be there. I already told Angel to count me in."

"I'm more concerned with your conduct when you are with the team. Cooper tell Doc what you told me you wanted him to know," Lassiter prompted.

"When you're with the team, like on this last mission, you're like a damned robot," Cooper said.

"When's the last time you worked out in the gym?" Shepherd asked without missing a beat. He already knew the answer. Before Africa. "And remember, I see all the logs. If it were any other team member, you'd be all over his ass for not engaging in PT for over two months."

Doc huffed out a sigh. "I know. I'm still working on being back." He glanced sideways at Lassiter. He knew Lassiter would never disclose what was weighing on him, why he was still having issues. He both appreciated that and hated Lassiter for it. If Lassiter had told Shepherd and Cooper, he was sure he would be granted more leeway.

"And you didn't complete your last post-mission eval with Lassiter," Shepherd said, pointing to Joe. "You walked out on him, what, four days ago?"

"He never called me back for another meeting."

Joe Lassiter laughed. "You know the protocol. Coming back was on you. You're the one who walked out on me."

Doc nodded. "I know." He faced Lassiter. "I'm sorry, Joe. This afternoon. I'll be into see you this afternoon."

"You'd better. Alpha Team has another mission just after the New Year and you're not going if Lassiter doesn't clear you. We'll bring the Undertaker or Powder in to have a medic. You need to decide if you want this job, Doc, because from where I'm sitting, I can't tell."

Shepherd's words cut deep. He'd always considered Shepherd a friend as well as a boss. They had a different relationship than Shepherd had with most of the other men, except maybe Cooper and Lassiter. Even now, Doc felt like an outsider. When would this get easier? When would he feel like himself again? "I want this job, Shep. I just need a little more time to get my head on straight."

Shepherd's eyes flickered to Lassiter. Damn the good doctor for not sharing details. Shepherd had no idea what the issue was, so he had no idea if more time should be granted or not. Then his eyes went to Doc. "Your team leaves on its next mission January fourth. Get your head on straight by then or notify me that we need to fill your spot with another medic. Something's got to give, Doc."

Doc nodded. He knew Shepherd was right.

"Do you want to take leave and go home to your family over the Christmas holiday?" Shepherd asked.

Doc winced. Fuck, if that wouldn't make it worse. Houston was the last place he needed to be. His eyes went to Lassiter. "No, I need to be here with the team. I'll pull it together, Shepherd. I want this job."

Shepherd nodded, his eyes going back and forth between Doc and Lassiter. "Resolve this, gentlemen."

Doc and Lassiter rose. They'd just been dismissed.

"I have time now," Lassiter offered.

"Yeah," Doc agreed. He followed Lassiter down the flight of stairs to four.

After Doc and Lassiter left, Cooper wandered around the room. "I have to say, if it were anyone other than Doc, I'd say fire him. I just don't know what could have gone down that caused this. Doc is so damn, un-Doc-like."

Shepherd stared hard at Cooper. "So, you have no idea either?"

"No," Cooper said, shaking his head. "All that Lassiter gave me was that issues from Doc's past that he thought had been dealt with have resurfaced. I don't know what the fuck that's about."

"And no one on the team has asked him?" Shepherd said as more of a suggestion.

"Madison tried. He shut her down fast."

"I'd normally say whatever transpires between Lassiter and one of the men is off limits, but in this situation," Shepherd paused and shook his head.

"I say we give Lassiter and Doc the two weeks to work it out. I'll want Sloan on standby for the next mission. Maybe benching Doc will be enough to force him to resolve it, whatever it is."

"Yeah," Shepherd agreed.

Elizabeth checked her mail slot, thrilled to see an envelope in it. She recognized the perfect handwriting that addressed it to her. Her smile spread on her face. She'd been waiting anxiously for this letter for a month. She charged up the narrow staircase and hurried down the dark hallway. "Merry Christmas," she greeted the many she passed. "You are coming to the sanctuary for the service later this evening, aren't you?" She asked each.

The Sisters of Mercy shelter was full. In the basement cots were set up for the single men, leaving these dormitory-style rooms for women, children, and families only. She had one of the smallest of the rooms, tucked in the farthest corner. She didn't mind. It was quiet there, and she didn't need much space.

Upon reaching her door, she unlocked it and hurried into the eight by eight space. She sat cross-legged on the twin-sized bed that was covered with a dark blue blanket. She tore open the letter.

My Dearest Elizabeth,

I have prayed for you daily since your departure. I have missed you, your enthusiasm, and your smile. But I understand your decision to leave. I've prayed on your request and have supplied the information you requested below.

Elizabeth skipped the remainder of the written letter and scanned to the bottom of the page. It was there. Her heart seized up for a moment. She knew she had to act on it. That was why she had written Sister Bernice John to begin with. She banished from her mind all thoughts of not doing it.

She went to the tiny dresser of drawers and pulled the small jar from under her clothes. She opened it and dumped the cash on the bed. She recounted it. She knew she could make the missing amount in tips at the diner over the few days following Christmas if she picked up double shifts. Now that she had the information, she knew she had to act fast on it.

Then she grabbed the notebook from the top of the dresser and shuffled through the Continuing Education requirements from the state again. She'd only completed two units since she'd been back from Africa. There were so many credits needed to reinstate her nursing license, not that Sister Abigale, the doctor in the Sisters of Mercy Free Clinic, cared if she was licensed or not. She appreciated the advanced skills that Elizabeth had.

Elizabeth tucked the letter in the notebook. She'd finish reading it later. She dropped to her knees in front of her bed and clasped her hands in prayer. "Dear Heavenly Father, please let my plans be the correct path, your path. I am trying to do the right thing in your eyes, but I know I fall short. I pray to you, God, please bring my heart peace. I pray in the name of your son, Jesus Christ, my savior. Amen."

She spent the next two hours working the dinner line, serving those who came to the shelter for the free Christmas dinner. There were many regulars she recognized. She greeted all with a warm smile if she knew them or not. She worked beside Sisters, residents, and volunteers.

"Sister Elizabeth, can you help me get another pan of the ham?" Sister Mary Theresa asked. "Oh, I'm sorry. I keep doing that."

Elizabeth embraced her. "Sister, it is fine. There is no apology needed." The two women went through the swinging doors into the kitchen. Lined up on the counter were several large tinfoil trays of food. After all the others were fed, Elizabeth would get a plate for herself.

"I do not mean to pry Elizabeth, but why did you leave the order? You seem the same, you do the same things the rest of us do."

"I know you may not be able to understand, Sister, but it is not my calling. I thought it was, but I was mistaken. Clarity came to me while I served in Africa."

"You still wear your wedding band," Sister Mary Theresa pointed out.

"This no longer signifies I'm married to God. I married a man while I was in Africa. Perhaps I shouldn't wear this particular ring though." She slipped it from her finger and pushed it into her jeans pocket.

"I don't understand. You married someone but you are not with him?"

"It's complicated," Elizabeth confessed. "We are from different worlds. That's all I can say to explain it." She took hold of the tray and carried it back through to the dining area.

Later that night, the Christmas Mass was wonderful. The sanctuary was packed. Even though Elizabeth enjoyed it, she couldn't keep her mind from straying to thoughts about Alexander. She thought of him daily, prayed for his safety, and longed to hear from him. He knew where she was. If he wanted to get in touch with her, he could. Even though he had been clear when they parted that he wanted nothing to do with her, she still hoped he would change his mind.

Tonight, on this holy night, she prayed that he was safe and with people he cared about, people who cared about him. She knew the work he did was dangerous. She prayed he was still alive. Even that she couldn't be sure of.

She stood with the choir and sang the Christmas songs she knew and loved. The song, Silent Night, always made her cry. Tonight, was no different, except this year, thoughts of Alexander, and her wish that he had a calm and peaceful night made her cry harder than ever. She prayed he would sleep well tonight, wherever he was.

The Christmas holiday gave a much-needed break to most of the Shepherd Security team members. The office was decorated, presents were wrapped and placed under the Christmas Tree in the rec room. The majority of the gifts were for baby Sammy in anticipation of the little boy's first Christmas.

A buffet-style meal was catered in. Charlie Team even took a break from the Power Grid Project and came into the office for Christmas Eve and Christmas Day. Lambchop held a special midnight service, attended by all. It was followed by the gift exchange.

Doc knew he was under scrutiny. He did everything he could to participate. He bought gifts, opened his and smiled, gave thanks, and threw out sarcastic barbs where appropriate. His thoughts drifted to Elizabeth more than a few times, wondering if she had anyone to spend this holiday with.

For the first time, Doc thought about the Christmases missed with his own son, who'd never had a chance at life. Holding Sammy in his arms, he paced away from the others and stared out into the darkness as tears gathered in his eyes. His gaze wandered over the little boy's features, wondering if his own son would have had dark hair like Victoria or if he would have been blonde as he had been as a child.

Angel came over a few minutes later. She saw the moisture in Doc's eyes. "I know something has bothered you for a few months. If I can help in any way, I'd like to."

Doc swallowed hard. If only. He blinked the unshed tears away. "Thanks, Angel. I appreciate that." He placed a kiss on Sammy's forehead and held him up over his shoulder. "I think this is just what I need. For being up so late, he's doing great. You and Jackson are lucky. Don't ever allow yourselves to lose sight of what you have."

Angel rested her hand on Doc's shoulder. She wished she could help him. It was obvious to her that something was really bothering him. He'd never held Sammy so tightly to himself. "We won't. I promise. Jackson and Sammy are my world."

Doc smiled. Angel was something special, the way she fit into the team, the relationship she had with Shepherd, the love she shared with Jackson. He felt bad for being down on Jackson for having the relationship with her in the beginning. He supported Jackson being fired back then. What a fool he had been. Jackson proved himself a hundred times over from the very beginning, taking a shot at the man who held a gun to Angel's head, knowing he could have killed her had she even flinched. Jackson had more guts than he did.

"It shows. You are a great wife to Jackson and an even better mother to this little boy. Jackson is one lucky man."

Angel rose on tiptoes and placed a chaste kiss on Doc's cheek. "I know you talk with Lassiter, but if you ever want a woman's perspective let me know." She smiled wide.

Doc smirked. "I'll keep that in mind."

"Jackson has been worried about you since Africa. The whole team has. Something changed you, Doc. You know what I went through and how long it took me to be okay. Don't let anyone here tell you there is a timetable. There isn't. Just because Shepherd carried on with what others saw as little fuss, doesn't mean he wasn't dealing with the same issues I was. He just hid it better than I did. If holding Sammy helps you, then do it as often as you need. And if you aren't ready to adhere to anyone's timetable tell them to go fuck themselves. Whatever it is, it's yours, not anyone else's. Take the time you need."

Doc choked up. Angel did understand, probably better than the rest of his team. "Thanks, Angel. Yeah, let me hold on to Sammy a while longer. He's almost asleep."

Angel nodded and returned to the noisy, active area of the room. Doc remained in the dark corner feeling more at peace than he had in months.

Kilo

Elizabeth readjusted her backpack on her shoulders. The right strap needed to be tightened. It had loosened up, and it kept slipping down her arm. She read the gold lettering on the black door in front of her. Shepherd Security. Her destination. Would Alexander be there? Would he talk with her? Now that she was standing here, she was afraid he would not.

Sister Bernice John had been so kind to her, both during her time with the Sisters in Africa and in the letter, she received just over a week earlier, giving her this location. It had taken a month to receive the letter back. She wished she could talk with Sister Bernice John in person and tell her everything. The friendships she had formed with the Sisters while in Africa was something she dearly missed now, being part of that family. Working at the clinic now was different even though it was also run by the Sisters. Or maybe it was because she was no longer a Sister. She was no longer one of them.

She took a deep breath and pulled the door open. She stepped inside the waiting room. The reception desk was empty. She checked her watch. It was four p.m. on a Wednesday afternoon. Certainly, the office wasn't closed. She approached the glass window and peered through it. Just then a pretty, black-haired woman appeared, who she recognized as Angel from Sister Bernice John's photos of her daughter.

"Hi, may I help you?" Angel asked, her voice coming through a speaker. She hadn't slid the glass open.

Elizabeth smiled at her. "You're Angel. I would recognize you anywhere. I'm a friend of your mother, Sister Bernice John. My name is Elizabeth. I was with your mom in Africa."

Angel's eyes went wide in surprise. Yes, she knew who Elizabeth was, and she knew there was a history with Doc. She and everyone else on the team suspected Doc, and this woman had shared something that rocked Doc to his core when they were hiding out and captured. Doc had not been the same since he returned from that mission. Everyone at Shepherd Security knew that.

"Sister Elizabeth," Angel said with a surprised smile. "Is everything okay with my mom?"

Elizabeth noted that Angel still had not slid the glass open. Nor had she moved to the door to let her in. "It's just Elizabeth. I'm no longer a Sister. I left the order. And

I assume that your mother is just fine. I received a letter from her last week and all seemed well."

"Okay," Angel said, seeming more confused. "I'm sorry, one moment please." Angel lifted her cell phone from the desk, hit dial, and brought it to her ear.

"Shepherd."

"I have a woman claiming to be Sister Elizabeth from Africa standing in the outer office."

"Hold while I bring Ops in." There was a pause. "Why am I contacting you and not the other way around?" Shepherd barked when Yvette came on the line. He switched his monitor over to the camera view to display the young woman who stood before the glass partition.

"We are running a threat assessment now," Yvette replied. "I just accessed footage with Sister Elizabeth on it. Facial recognition is running." There was a chime. "Got a positive result, but we may want to deploy someone who was on that mission to the lobby to validate."

Shepherd clicked into the team calendar. Miller, Cooper, Jackson, and Doc were all in the office. He knew that Delta team had just returned from an Op. They had entered the building from the private underground parking garage. They were still in the Team Room stowing their gear. He added Cooper to the call. "Coop, there is a visitor that needs validating in the lobby."

"I'm on my way," Cooper replied. He ended the call and glanced at Madison, who sat beside him on the couch in his office. "Shepherd needs me to validate a visitor."

"That's cryptic," Madison replied. She rose as well and followed him from the room.

"It'll be just a moment," Angel said through the speaker to Elizabeth.

Elizabeth was even more confused. She hadn't asked to see Alexander. She had merely greeted Angel. She felt more anxious about this now. Just then, Cooper and Madison appeared beside Angel. She smiled warmly in recognition.

They both returned her smile before moving out of view. The inner door was then opened.

"Elizabeth," Madison greeted. "How are you?"

Elizabeth was relieved by Madison's warm greeting and hug. Cooper gave her a quick embrace when Madison released her. Her raw nerves calmed until she saw the pistols holstered on both of their belts. Why would they be carrying guns in the office?

Several thoughts shot through her mind. Madison had been kind to her, which she would never forget. Remembering that helped to calm her nerves. They had all been armed in Africa, even the pastor, she reminded herself. She had the loaner clothes in her backpack to return. She didn't have the money they had lent her. She only had enough in her wallet to make it back to Seattle.

"What are you doing here? And how did you find us?" Cooper asked as he ushered her within the inner office.

Angel came up to her and gave her a hug as well. "It is nice to meet you, Elizabeth. My mom has spoken of you. She really misses you."

Elizabeth let out a nervous sigh accompanying a big smile. "I love your mother and I miss her and the other Sisters very much." She turned her attention back to Cooper. "It was Sister Bernice John who told me where to find you. I must speak with Alexander. It's important."

Madison and Cooper exchanged looks. This was a huge breach in their security. They couldn't believe Angel's mom would have given their location out. This would have to be addressed.

"Sister Bernice John knows what this is about. I promise you it is important, important enough for her to risk her daughter by telling me where to find you. Please, is Alexander here and may I speak with him?" Elizabeth pressed, her voice tense.

Cooper's phone chirped. "One moment," he said before answering his phone. As expected, it was Shepherd. "Yes, identity is confirmed."

"What is she doing here and how did she find us?" Shepherd demanded.

"I'll report in person shortly," Cooper said. He knew something had happened that had completely changed Doc. The man was not himself, hadn't been since Africa. He dialed Doc. "Report to the kitchen on five. It's not a medical."

"On my way," Doc replied.

"Please, come with me," Cooper said, motioning to Elizabeth to follow him.

Madison came up beside him. "Are you sure this is a good idea?"

"Nope, but I don't think he should be told she's here either."

Elizabeth heard them whisper but couldn't make out what they said as she followed the short distance into the kitchen. Angel followed behind her.

"Can I get you a cup of coffee or tea?" Angel offered.

"No thank you. I am fine," Elizabeth replied politely. Her eyes met Cooper's. "Is he on his way now?"

"Yes," Cooper said, watching her closely. She was nervous. That was obvious.

"Thank you," she said robotically, saying what was appropriate. She shrugged off her heavy backpack and sat it on one of the chairs, but she left her thin winter coat on. She nervously glanced around the room as they waited.

Cooper stood near the door. He was all Doc saw as he came down the hall. "Hey, what's up?"

Cooper motioned him into the kitchen.

He stopped dead when his eyes landed on Elizabeth.

"You have a visitor," Cooper said.

"Elizabeth, are you all right?"

"Hello Alexander," she greeted softly, her apprehension tripling by being in the same room with him.

"I asked you if you are okay," he repeated.

Elizabeth's eyes swept over the others. "May I have a moment alone with Alexander, please?"

"Of course," Madison answered. She followed Angel and Cooper from the room and closed the door to give them privacy.

"What do you think that's about?" Angel asked.

Both Cooper and Madison shook their heads. They didn't have a clue either. It couldn't be good, that was clear. Elizabeth looked frightened and nervous. Doc looked like a deer in the headlights, and not happy about it.

Doc and Elizabeth stood awkwardly staring at each other for several long seconds before he spoke. "Elizabeth, what are you doing here?"

Elizabeth swallowed hard and sucked in a deep breath for courage. She blew it out loudly. "I do not expect anything from you. But I felt you had the right to know that I am pregnant, with your child."

His eyes went wide, and all the oxygen got sucked from his lungs. A feather could have knocked him over.

There, she said it, just as she had rehearsed in her head since finding out. He stood still; his wide eyes focused on her. His face held no other emotions, and he didn't say a word. The silence stretched into more than a minute before he finally spoke.

"Are you sure?" He asked.

Her lips pulled into a small grin. "Yes, I'm sure. It's quite a simple test, not that my symptoms weren't conclusive on their own."

"I'm sorry. That was a stupid question. Of course, you would be sure."

"So, that's all I came to tell you." She stared at him, keeping her hope tamped down.

He ran his fingers through his hair as he stared at her. She looked petrified. "We were in Africa nearly three months ago. How long have you known?"

"For just over a month, six weeks maybe," she replied.

He shook his head. "Elizabeth, why didn't you get in touch with me as soon as you knew? You could have called the office."

"I didn't know where you were. I wrote Sister Bernice John, and it took a month to get a letter back from her with this location. Besides, I had to save up the money to afford the train ticket. It was nearly two-hundred dollars."

This made no sense to Doc. "Save up? Where were you working?"

"Well, to be given room and board at the shelter, I worked in the free clinic I used to work at, that is run by the Sisters. To have spending money, I waited tables at a neighborhood diner."

A pang of guilt hit Doc like a Mac truck barreling through his chest. She worked two jobs to afford a lousy train ticket to come see him to personally deliver this news. "Elizabeth, you didn't need to work waiting tables to afford to be able to travel here. I would have come to where you were if you told me you were pregnant, or I would have bought you a plane ticket."

"I made it here didn't I?" She said defiantly. "Besides, I wasn't sure you would talk to me. When we parted, you made it clear that you didn't want anything to do with me."

"Aww, honey, I did what I thought was best for you."

"How could that have been best for me? I thought what we did meant something. I thought you at least liked me as a person." Her calm demeanor quickly crumbled. And she had told herself a thousand times that no matter what, she wouldn't beg him, wouldn't cry, wouldn't show him she was upset, or that she wanted him in her life.

That Mac truck exploded in his chest, shredding his heart. He wrapped his arms around Elizabeth's tiny frame. "It meant a lot, honey, more that you know. And I do like you. I haven't been able to forget about you or the time we spent together." It felt good to confess this to her.

"Then why?" She whispered.

"It's a very long story and has nothing to do with you. It's all on me." He rubbed her back gently. What the fuck was he going to do now? "Please don't cry, honey."

"I'm sorry," she said, pulling away. "As I said, I don't expect anything from you. I just believed you had the right to know and to hear it from me in person."

"What do you mean you expect nothing from me? It's my child. I'm going to take care of you, of both of you."

"That's kind of you, but unnecessary. I'm not afraid of hard work. I can take care of," she started to argue, but he interrupted her.

"I'm not being kind and it is necessary. Damn-it Elizabeth, let me take care of this. This is my responsibility."

"I don't see this as a mistake or a bad thing. We created a life. A life that is inside me." She paused as tears filled her eyes, but she jutted her chin out and raised it. "I love this child and don't want you or anyone else in its life that is there out of responsibility or guilt." She knew that sinful pride was flaring again. But she would not beg him, for anything.

Doc jammed his hands into his hips. He was fucking this up, royally. He breathed out the heavy weight from his chest. "Let's put this on pause for just a second." He went to the cabinet and grabbed two cups. He brewed an herbal tea for her, and then a coffee for himself. He pointed to a chair. "Please sit."

She nodded and complied. He sat the cup in front of her and then took the seat beside her. She took a sip. When her eyes met his, she noticed he was watching her with a sharp focus. "What?"

"I have thought about you often. And I am sorry about how I was when we parted. I promise you an explanation in time, when I'm ready. I have a past that has haunted me, Elizabeth. As I said, how it was when we parted was on me, not you."

Elizabeth nodded. "Fair enough."

"What are your plans?" He knew she was hardheaded and independent. He couldn't dictate anything to her. And after how he had treated her, he knew he would have to ask her to stay. He hoped she would. He absolutely didn't want her going back to Seattle.

She shrugged. "I have two-hundred thirty dollars to get me back to Seattle."

He shook his head no. "Please stay."

She nodded. This was what she had hoped for. Well, part of it.

"You can stay at my place. We'll work this out."

"I'm not sure how we'll do that."

She looked like she was going to cry again. "Stay right here," Doc said. "Will you do that for me?"

She nodded her head yes.

Doc opened the door and saw Angel in the hallway holding baby Sammy in her arms. "Angel, can you keep Elizabeth company for a minute?"

"Sure," Angel agreed stepping towards the kitchen.

"And don't let her leave," Doc whispered as he passed her. He went out through the public entrance and took the stairs down to the lobby.

Elizabeth glanced up at Angel and the baby as they entered the kitchen. He had grown so much from the last picture she had seen of him that Angel sent her mom in Africa. Elizabeth smiled wide; her hand unconsciously gripped her own abdomen. "He's precious," she said coming to her feet.

Angel grinned. "This little man is my world." Doc's words to not let her leave hit her. She didn't know what was going on, but she knew how to keep her from leaving. She leaned Sammy towards Elizabeth. "Can you hold him for a second while I make myself a cup of tea?"

"Certainly," Elizabeth said with a smile, taking him from her arms. "You are a handsome guy, aren't you? Your mommy and daddy are blessed to have such a good boy."

"Yes, he is, and I am truly blessed," Angel said. After her cup of tea brewed, she brought it to the table. "May I join you until Doc returns?"

"Yes, thank you," Elizabeth said, handing the little boy back to his mother. She wondered if her child would be a boy or a girl. She hadn't allowed herself to think too much about it before now.

When Doc returned, Angel was seated at the table with Elizabeth. They were both sipping tea and talking about Angel's mom. "Thanks, Angel." He nodded towards the door. "If you don't mind."

Angel came to her feet. "Not at all." She smiled at Elizabeth. "It was nice chatting. Hopefully, we'll have many more opportunities to get to know each other better."

Elizabeth nodded and came to her feet. "I'd like that." She watched Angel leave and close the door behind herself.

Doc took Elizabeth's hands in his and slid the decorative gold band he'd just bought at the jewelry shop in the lobby onto the ring finger of her left hand. "We're doing this out of order. But the ring belongs there."

"Alexander, what are you doing?"

"We said our vows in Africa before we made love and consummated our union. We'll get the marriage license at the county building tomorrow, and have Lambchop sign it on Friday, when it's valid. We are husband and wife, Elizabeth. I want you to stay here with me as my wife. I want to be with you during this pregnancy and after."

She was stunned. This was more than she hoped for. "You don't have to do this." Her voice was soft.

"Yes, I do. I want to make this right, want you to understand we're in this together."

New tears filled her eyes. Happy tears this time. She nodded her head yes. Then he drew her in close and held her. "Come on," he said when he released her. "Let's go home."

She smiled and nodded.

He lifted her backpack from the chair. It had to weigh twenty pounds. When he reopened the door, the hallway was empty. He had the backpack in one hand, her hand in his other. He led her to Angel's desk, where she sat. Sammy was in his activity chair at her feet.

"Where's Cooper?"

"In with Shepherd," Angel replied.

Doc nodded and then led her back through the suite towards the back corner where Shepherd's office was. The door was closed. He gently backed her against the hallway wall. "Wait here for me." He pressed a soft kiss to her forehead and sat her backpack at her feet. "I'm going to check out with my boss and then take you home."

Her lips trembled. "Okay," she said softly.

Doc gave Shepherd's door one loud rap and then opened it without being invited in. He closed it behind himself. Cooper stood in front of Shepherd's desk. He turned to look at Doc with a 'what the fuck' expression on his face.

"Doc, what the hell is going on?" Shepherd demanded.

"I'm leaving for the night, taking Elizabeth home with me. And I need to take tomorrow off. She and I need to go to the county building and get a marriage license."

Cooper and Shepherd exchanged surprised glances. Shepherd shook his head. "What the hell?"

"You're marrying her?" Cooper asked a beat later.

"She's Catholic and pregnant with my child."

Cooper's trademark smirk formed on his face. "You slept with her in Africa during the mission."

"Look, I'm not proud of it, but I'm trying to make it right now. She's alone in this world, got nobody else."

"So, this explains why you've been a pain in the ass since Africa," Cooper said.

Doc ran his hand through his hair and then slid it down his tense neck. He massaged it for a second. "It's complicated, and yes, this is one of the reasons I've been a pain in the ass."

Shepherd's gaze shifted to Cooper. "We can push the next mission off a few days. Contact the client."

Cooper nodded and then turned his attention back to Doc. "Will you be ready to go by Monday?"

Doc nodded. "Yeah, I'll have my affairs handled by then."

Shepherd nodded. "Take tomorrow off and Friday too, if you need it."

Doc nodded again. "I'll need her added to our medical insurance and get a secure phone issued to her before I go on this next mission."

"Anything else?" Shepherd asked. The annoyance in his voice was obvious.

"I'll want to install a tracker in her, and have it monitored in Ops, just like the other women."

Shepherd's lips drew into a thin line. "You do realize we don't really have a protocol for this."

"I guess we better write one then. And I'll want her to meet Sienna too. She's going to need support from the other wives with me gone."

Cooper and Shepherd exchanged glances again. Shepherd was not pleased. "You'll need to talk with Garcia about that one. As far as the other items, Cooper and I will discuss them and get back to you."

Doc nodded. "Fair enough."

Doc left Shepherd's office, closing the door behind himself and he rejoined Elizabeth. She stood where he left her. "Come on," he said, nodding to the stairs. "I'm checked out for the day." He led her down to four. He needed to get his gear from his office before he left.

She watched as he pressed his palm to the scan pad and entered his code into the door lock. She was intrigued by the security. She followed him to his office. There were four offices in the area marked with a plaque that said 'Medical'.

Beside the door was a name plaque that read 'Williams'. That's right, Alexander Williams was his full name. *Elizabeth Williams*, she ran through her thoughts, giving the name a mental test run. Her eyes flickered to the wedding band he had put on her finger. It wasn't that different from the band she wore as a Sister, indicating she was married to God. This one was wider and had a delicate floral design etched on it. It was pretty.

Her eyes swept over his office. It looked just like any medical office room she'd ever been in. She watched as he opened a few cabinets and packed various supplies into a large backpack. It was only then that the flannel shirt he wore untucked, shifted to the side, and she noticed the gun on his right hip. She would have to ask about it, but she wouldn't ask now.

"Okay, I'm ready," Doc said. He grabbed a very warm looking coat from the hook behind the door and put it on.

She put her coat on, as well. It wasn't that warm. She froze on her way to this office. January in Chicago was colder than she thought it would be. She bought the warmest coat the Goodwill Store had that fit her. She'd just have to add more layers beneath.

Doc carried both their backpacks and led her down the stairs to subbasement two. She followed him, still surprised and curious about all the security. She followed him across the large underground parking lot, that had at least twenty cars and SUVs parked in it, to a newer dark blue SUV. He sat the backpacks on the backseat. She climbed into the passenger side. The garage wasn't cold, and neither was the car, she noticed. It wasn't over fifty degrees, but it wasn't below zero like it was outside.

Elizabeth pressed her back against the comfortable leather heated seat in Alexander's big SUV, but she wasn't relaxed. The double garage doors and security gate to exit the parking garage was something like she'd never seen. She wasn't sure who this group was. Sister Bernice John had referred to them as some sort of paramilitary, whatever that meant. Again, she tamped down her curiosity and tucked away the many questions that ran through her mind.

They drove in silence. The radio wasn't even on. She tried to take note of the street names and the route he took. He pulled into the lot of a big, fancy grocery store and parked.

"We were supposed to leave on a mission Friday. I spoke with my boss on the way out and we'll push it off till Monday so I can get you settled in my place, but I don't have enough fresh food in the house for us both. They have good premade meals and sides. If it's okay, I thought we'd just pick up something to bring home for dinner and probably something for breakfast too. Then we can do a proper shopping trip to stock the house for you tomorrow."

The parking lot light shone through the window illuminating Alexander's face. Elizabeth studied his face as he spoke, trying to judge his mood regarding his words. "I'm sorry your team's plans changed because of me. It's not necessary. I can fend for myself."

Doc felt his lips tug into a grin. "It's no trouble. Besides, there is a lot to do to get you settled beside the marriage license. We need to add you to the team's medical insurance to cover your pregnancy, get you a secure cell phone so we can be in contact while I'm away, and I need to be sure you have everything you need at my place. I also want you to meet Garcia's girlfriend. She and Angel will be a good support system for you while I'm away."

"How long will you be gone?"

"Maybe two weeks."

A pang of disappointment hit Elizabeth. She'd only have a few days with him and then he'd be gone for two weeks, half a month. She hid how she felt and forced a smile. "Okay, whatever you think is best."

"Come on," Doc said nodding to the grocery store.

He got out of the SUV. She followed and walked beside him, pulling her coat more tightly around her. The frigid wind went right through her, chilling her instantly. No, this coat was not meant for the cold winter temperatures in Chicago. And she needed a winter hat and gloves too. If she was staying, she could use the money she earmarked for the return train ticket to buy adequate clothing.

Once inside the huge store, he led her to the prepared deli case. The amount of food and the variety surprised her. She didn't shop in places like this. They had large perch fillets encrusted with pecans. For no additional cost, they would cook them.

"Do you like perch?" He asked pointing to the fillets in the case.

Elizabeth saw the price. "They are very expensive," she replied softly.

"Maybe," Doc replied. "But they will cook them while we do the remainder of our shopping. Do you like pecans and perch? That's the only question."

"I'm sure they will be very good."

Doc placed the order. They would be ready and packaged in fifteen minutes. "Okay, now a couple of sides, then we'll go over by the breakfast stuff."

At the sides bar he picked a couple of twice-baked potatoes and a hot fresh vegetable medley in a light butter sauce. He loaded the containers into the hand basket he carried.

She paused, checking the price for each container. Her eyes met his. "I'll pay for half of everything we buy. My wallet is in my backpack in the car though, so I'll have to pay you later."

Doc breathed out a frustrated sigh. "Elizabeth, you are not paying half of anything. I've got this." He knew they'd have to talk about living arrangements and finances. He knew her financial situation. She had to understand that he wouldn't expect her to pay for anything. He had more than enough money to take care of them both and the baby after it came.

Elizabeth didn't understand Alexander's tone of voice. Why wasn't he pleased that she would pitch in her half of the expenses? She didn't want him to be upset with her after he had so kindly asked her to stay and file a real marriage license. "Okay, thank you."

Doc also loaded an expensive container of cleaned fresh fruit into the basket as well as a dozen eggs, a loaf of nine grain bread, a gallon of overpriced organic milk, and a package of turkey sausage. Then they went back to the deli counter and picked up their prepared fish. Elizabeth had to admit it smelled very good.

They checked out. The total bill for these few items was larger than what she normally spent on an entire week's groceries. Elizabeth watched Alexander pay with a debit card. She never had one. She didn't have a bank account either, paid cash for whatever she needed. It was easier that way.

Then they climbed back into his car and drove the five minutes to his condo complex. He parked in the attached one-car garage and they entered through the interior door that led into the kitchen. She watched him enter a code into the security system.

"I'll get you set up with your own code tomorrow."

"Thank you," she muttered, confused by this too.

Her eyes then swept the interior of his home. The kitchen was small but had nice stainless-steel appliances, granite countertops, and dark gray cabinets. A small table and chairs sat at the far end. He sat the backpacks onto the floor near the table and then took the grocery bags from her and sat them onto the counter. He unpacked the contents. She watched him put the fish and sides onto the table. Everything else went into the refrigerator. He grabbed two water bottles from the fridge and sat them on the table too. Then he opened a cabinet and drawers, getting plates and silverware.

He motioned to the table.

She smiled and followed him over. From the table, she saw into his living room. It was a manly room, with black leather couches and black glass tables. The walls were painted white with several black frames with pictures of lakes and streams with fishermen. On a large five shelf bookshelf near the front door sat a bunch of fishing gear. A small smile came to her lips as her eyes scanned the room. "This is nice. It's what I would picture your house to look like, knowing you."

Doc chuckled. "I'll have to find a different place for my fishing gear."

"You don't need to change anything for me, Alexander. I don't take up much space."

Yeah, they needed to have a talk about living arrangements, finances, a lot of things. He served up the dinner onto the plates and slid one over to her. He picked up his fork, but noticed she bowed her head. She remained quiet, but he knew she was silently saying a blessing. "Did you want to say that blessing aloud?"

She smiled. "Some habits remain, I guess. God, thank you for this food and for Alexander's kindness. Thank you for allowing me to safely make it to him to share the joyous news of the new life. We thank you in the name of Your son, Jesus Christ, Amen."

When she finished, she gazed into Alexander's eyes.

He reached across the table and took hold of her hand. "It's going to take time for us to be comfortable, you know. But I want you to be who you are. If you want us to say grace before a meal, we'll say grace."

"Thank you. And I'm sorry this is so awkward." Her eyes shifted to their joined hands. She liked the feeling of him holding her hand, liked the connection to him. She had missed him since Africa.

"It'll get easier." He released her hand and took a bite of his food. After several quiet moments of them both just eating, he took a drink of water and then continued. "I'll clear a few drawers for you in my dresser and make some room in the closet for you too until we can get to the store and buy you your own dresser. Will we have to make a trip to Seattle to get your things or will someone send them to you?"

She pointed to her backpack. "There are no things. Everything I own is in my bag."

"Everything?"

"Yes," she said with a small smile. "I don't need much, have never had much in the way of material things. I will need to use some laundry facilities though, maybe tomorrow."

Doc pointed to the bi-fold closet doors on the wall farthest from the door to the garage. "Washer and dryer are in there."

"How very nice that you have your own facilities in your home." She smiled awkwardly.

"Our home, Elizabeth. Please try to think of this as ours."

She forced a smile. He knew it was forced.

"I've never had much. It has never bothered me, except when people have offered me charity. That was one of the things that drew me to the Sisters of Mercy. I thought I was being called to be a Sister, but I know it was just being accepted and being with others who didn't have anything material to speak of. It was a wonderful family where I felt accepted and cared for. The facilities were owned by no one and by all of us at the same time. I was given a room, but I never felt like it was mine. It was part of the collective, identical in most ways to everyone else's rooms."

"I'm not offering you charity. You do understand that, don't you?"

"I don't want to be a burden to you. I don't expect you to pay for everything for me. I plan to get a job and contribute fully."

Doc ran his hand over his tense neck. "We have great hospitals, medical centers, and private practices in the area. Will you get your nursing license here in Illinois?"

"I was working on getting my Continuing Education Credits up to date in Seattle, before I realized I was pregnant. I was in Africa for just under four years. I'm way behind."

"You know, Elizabeth, you are a hell of a lot better than a CNA. During this pregnancy would be the perfect time to go back to school full time and get your RN or go even further if you want. We have some of the best nursing and medical schools in the country in the Chicago area. There are three extension campuses located right near the office."

Elizabeth bit her lower lip. "That takes money, which I don't have, and I don't want to take out any student loans."

"Elizabeth, I have enough money for us both. I'd see it as an investment in your future earning potential and an investment in your happiness. Happy momma, happy baby."

Elizabeth laughed out loud, feeling more at ease than she had since she arrived in Chicago. "I can work, and I plan to while I'm reestablishing my nursing license here."

"Where are you thinking?" Doc asked as he helped himself to another serving of vegetables. He held the spoon out, offering her more as well.

She smiled and nodded. "There are a lot of restaurants in this area, certainly I can get a job waiting tables at one of them."

"Absolutely not," Doc replied without thinking about it. Her surprised expression shocked him. "I mean, oh, honey," he said. "I'm sorry. I don't mean to sound like a snob, but no wife of mine is going to work that hard on her feet while pregnant with my child. Damn-it, Elizabeth, I can afford for you to have an easier life than that."

"Thank you. I appreciate the thought, but I didn't come here to take advantage of you financially."

"I would never think you capable of taking advantage of me in any way. Let me make your life easier. That's all I want to do."

"You are a good man, Alexander Williams. Of course, I knew that about you when I first met you and you wouldn't risk those boys' lives." She paused and smiled a warm grin at him. "We have a few days before you leave for work. Can we talk about this later, when maybe it's a bit more comfortable between us?"

"Absolutely," Doc agreed. He hoped in a few days she would understand he could afford to support her, and she'd relax about money.

"So, Angel and Jackson had a good obstetrician. I'd like you to see the same doctor."

She nodded. "Sure, whatever you want."

Her agreeableness was starting to annoy Doc. Where was the little spitfire who argued with him in Africa? "Have you seen an obstetrician yet?"

She nodded. "Sister Abigale is a doctor at the free clinic. I saw her once to confirm the pregnancy."

"Once?" He asked. Only once? And she was nearly three months pregnant! His head was about to explode.

"There isn't much that needs to be done the first few months."

"You are taking prenatal vitamins, aren't you?" Doc was careful to keep his tone even.

"Of course, I am. She's a good doctor."

"I'm sure she's very competent. I just want the best for you."

She was quiet for a moment. "I know this is very awkward, for us both. But I have faith that as we get to know each other better, it will get more comfortable. We went through something together that few others have ever had to face, and I can't help but believe that experience will pave the way for us to work out okay."

Doc nodded. That and a hell of a lot of therapy. Lassiter was about to give up on him, he knew that. The last few months had been hell on Earth for him, the memories and regrets overwhelming him. And now this. An instant wife and a baby on the way. But he knew this was the right thing to do, for Elizabeth. And honestly, the thought of not being with her through this pregnancy and maybe missing out on the birth of his child, was unbearable. If he didn't have her here with him, he knew he would regret it for the rest of his life and no amount of therapy would ever help him resolve that.

Doc rose and did the only thing that felt right. He went to her and pressed a kiss to the top of her head. Then he pulled her to her feet and embraced her. "I believe that too. I ask that you have patience with me."

"Of course," she agreed. She didn't understand why he'd ask but then remembered him saying he had a past that haunted him. He'd also said that how he treated her was on him, not her. She hoped in time, he'd open up and trust her enough to tell her.

Lima

After they cleaned up the dishes, Doc gave her a tour of his condo. It was a small place. It was a short tour. It had one full bathroom, with a tub and shower and one bedroom. He brought her backpack in and sat it on the bench at the foot of the king-sized bed. The walls were a pale light gray, the floor the same dark gray hard wood as the rest of the condo. A comforter was spread over the large bed. It was black. There were no pictures on the walls of his bedroom.

"I'll let you have the bed and I'll sleep on the couch," Doc said unsure of how to handle this.

"I'm not going to take your bed," she insisted. "Besides, it looks big enough for us both, unless you don't want to lay with me, and if that's the case, I'll take the couch."

"It's not that I don't want to sleep with you. I didn't want to assume anything."

She laughed sarcastically. "Alexander, I'm pregnant with your child. Why would you think I wouldn't want to share a bed with you? Besides, am I or am I not your wife? Or is that going to be in name only? Because you felt you needed to do the right thing?"

Doc embraced her and held her while he tried to come up with the right words. This had gone poorly so far. "Elizabeth, I'm not going to take advantage of you. Marrying you is the right thing to do. We're having a child together and you are Catholic. I want to be here for you. I want us to experience this together. I won't abandon you. As far as our relationship, let's see how it plays out, how it develops. What I will promise you is that I will give it my all. I will be honest with you and I will do my best to be the partner you want and need."

Well, that was a lot more than she would have asked for. "Thank you, Alexander. That means a lot to me. I honestly had no expectations when I came here. I just thought you had the right to know."

"You had to hope I'd at least take responsibility."

"I did. I hoped you would, but I wouldn't have forced it on you. I'm not afraid of the thought of raising this child alone."

"You're not going to be raising this child alone. I promise I'll be here."

She felt new tears forming in her eyes. He was a good man, and she felt so much gratitude that he would be there for her. "I'm curious. You haven't asked for proof that I'm pregnant or that it's yours."

Doc smiled at that. "I trust you. You would never lie about anything. If you say you're pregnant and its mine, I fully believe it. Besides, I know we made love without any protection."

"I'm not sorry about that. There is a life inside me, a life we created. Maybe this was God's plan for me all along, and maybe yours too."

Doc nodded. "Yeah, maybe."

"If it's all right with you, I'm going to lay down now. I didn't sleep so great on the train and I'm tired."

"Of course," Doc said.

"Will you lay down with me?"

"Are you sure?" He asked uncertain if it was really the best thing to do or not.

She nodded yes. "I'm cold. I remember on the flight back. I was so cold, and you held me, which warmed me up." *And made me feel safe and cared for*, she thought but wouldn't vocalize. Besides, they were married. Why wouldn't they share a bed? She didn't understand his reluctance.

Doc stepped into her and wrapped his arms around her. He kicked himself for not realizing she might be tired and cold. She'd spent nearly two days on a train and her coat was thin, too thin for Chicago winters. He'd have to buy her a new one before he left too. He added that to the growing to-do list in his head.

Doc turned the heated mattress pad on while she was using the bathroom. When she reentered the room, she wore a pair of flannel pants and a long-sleeved t-shirt. His lips tugged into a frown. Wearing that, she looked even younger. Holy hell. "I turned the mattress pad on to heat the bed up for you."

"A heated mattress pad, wow, that's pretty cool," she said with a smile. She didn't know they made such things. She pointed to the side of the bed with the nightstand. "I assume this is your side?"

He nodded and watched her walk to the foot of the bed, intending to go to the other side. He pulled the comforter and sheet back. "Why don't you slide in this side and just leave me enough room to join you."

She smiled wide, a genuine smile. "Thank you, Alexander." She crawled in and stopped near the middle of the bed.

He viewed her, her beautiful blue eyes sparkling with delight, a happy smile on her face. He still could not reconcile that she looked like a child. *Twenty-four years old*, he repeated in his head. And just because he was going to lay with her, didn't mean he was going to have sex with her.

He stripped his heavy flannel shirt off, leaving the t-shirt he wore beneath, and then he set his gun and his cell phone onto his nightstand and plugged the phone in to charge. His flannel sleeping pants were at the foot of the bed where he'd left them that morning. He turned his back to her, dropped his jeans and shorts, and pulled his sleeping pants on. Then he reclined. He rolled to his side and gazed into her face. He allowed himself to think about how beautiful a baby would be with her eyes, her freckles.

"I can already feel the bed heating," she said. "I guess I didn't realize how cold it is here in Chicago, compared to Seattle."

"Yes. Now through March is the coldest part of the winter. I noticed your coat is thin. We'll go shopping and get you some warmer clothes this weekend." He saw in her eyes that she was about to protest that he would spend money on her. "And don't even argue with me about this. You need a warm coat and heavy clothes to make it through a Chicago winter. Let me buy what you need. Tomorrow we'll swing by the bank and add you to my bank accounts too. Maybe when you see how much I have in my account you will relax."

She shook her head, not liking it. "A thrift store or a Goodwill Store shouldn't be too expensive."

Doc wasn't sure what he would have to do for her to realize that how she was used to living, was below the poverty level. It wasn't how he lived nor was it how he would have the woman carrying his child live. "When we go shopping just promise me you won't look at any price tags. You'll buy what you like."

"Alexander, please understand. I don't want to be a burden."

"Aww, honey, you aren't a burden. Let me buy you things and spoil you. I want you to have everything you've never had, things you deserve. I make a good living and can afford to. Besides, when this baby comes, I'll be buying him or her more than you can imagine."

"This child will be very lucky just to have you in its life. Just as I am. You are my hero, Alexander."

"Stop right there, honey, I'm not a hero."

"You're my hero. You stayed with me to help those two boys. The others would have forced me to leave and would have endangered or killed those boys by moving them when it wasn't medically safe to do so. And after we were captured, you definitely were my hero. I lost my faith, was sure we would both die horrible deaths. That confirmed for me that leaving the Sisterhood was the right thing for me to do. It could have been a moment that my faith returned, and I trusted in God, but I didn't."

"It looked dark. I was sure we were going to be killed too. I've been in a lot of tight situations over the years, but this was the first time I accepted I was going to die."

"That was the only reason you slept with me, wasn't it? I know you're not attracted to me; know you didn't want to." There, she said it. She knew that was the reason he had not wanted to lie down with her, why he hadn't wanted her with him after they were rescued.

Doc closed his eyes. He wasn't ready to have this conversation with her. He considered his words carefully. "Your first time should have been with someone you loved. I felt as though I took advantage of you."

"You didn't take advantage of me. You did as I asked, as I begged. And as far as the part about someone I love, I know I can grow to love you. You are a good man, Alexander, and you have been kind to me. Maybe I'm naïve, but if we both love this child, how can we not have feelings for each other?"

Doc's heart felt full at that moment; in a way it hadn't felt in years. "You are not naïve. You are right on about that one. And let's get one thing straight. I *am* attracted to you. You are as beautiful on the inside as you are on the outside."

And with that statement he did the only thing that made sense. He kissed her, really kissed her. Even as his tongue penetrated her lips, he told himself he'd stop, he wouldn't make love to her. Soon, his thoughts went blank and all he focused on was how good it felt to kiss her, how good it felt for his hands to caress over her, to feel her frame pulled in tightly against his. Her age no longer mattered, nor did he think about the fact that she'd only had sex one time before, with him. His self-loathing for taking advantage of her vanished, and he did what felt right. He stripped her clothes away, and he made love to her, slowly, deliberately, passionately.

Elizabeth's nerves calmed as they kissed. She loved the feeling of Alexander holding her. And when he began to disrobe her, she was excited that she would again know what it felt like to have him touch her intimately. She wanted their marriage to be real. She wanted to know that he could love her and when he kissed her and touched her this way, she felt he could. Over the past few months, she had dreamed about another romantic interlude as she reveled in the memories of the love they made in Africa.

Very quickly, she found herself panting, the sensations from his touch incredible. His lips left hers and he kissed her everywhere, down her neck, over her breasts. His fingers were between her legs, bringing her pleasure that before they had made love in Africa, she didn't know could exist. His lips trailed kisses down her abdomen. He kissed the inside of each thigh that he pressed apart. She gasped out; the sensation overwhelming.

Doc held her long after he had made love to her. This time, thoughts of Victoria didn't assault him. He stroked over Elizabeth's long, soft hair, held her body against his, feeling the difference the pregnancy had brought. Her breasts were fuller, her hips and rear womanlier, and then there was the tummy, already protruding a little with the life inside her.

He wasn't sure how comfortable the blue jeans were that she wore. They looked tight. She'd need maternity clothes soon. He'd take her to the mall the next day and go shopping. She would not be getting any of her clothes at Goodwill or the Salvation Army stores. He smiled to himself at the thought of spoiling her with all the new clothes she needed.

Holding her and making love to her had been the least awkward moments since being reunited. For the first time since Africa, Doc drifted off to sleep easily. He slept well all night, another state that had escaped him the past few months.

The next morning, they woke to the sound of the snowplow. The yellow flashing lights invaded the room through the edges of the shades over the bedroom windows. After Doc explained to her what it was, he watched her jump out of bed, hastily pull her clothes on, and rush to the window. She pulled the curtains and opened the blinds. Then she stared out with hypnotic fascination. Big flakes were driven sideways by the wind. Elizabeth had only seen snow a few times before in her life, but nothing like the snowstorm that was raging outside the window.

"Wow, there's already a lot on the ground," she said excitedly.

Doc had forgotten it was in the forecast. He sat up and gazed at her. Her face was lit with enthusiasm and with the first light of the day, which was diffused through the snowstorm. She was beautiful, bright blue eyes, clear, creamy white skin, and hair that he knew was soft to the touch. Yeah, and she was way too young.

He held a hand out to her. "Close the blinds and come back to bed."

She smiled and did so right away. Doc helped her to resettle in bed, propped up in a sitting position. He tucked the covers around her. Then he pulled on a warm base layer shirt and his sleeping pants. He grabbed his phone and weapon from the bedside table, shoving them into the deep pants pockets. Her eyes followed his movements. He saw the unasked questions play over her face. He knew they had to discuss his job.

"I'm going to use the bathroom and then get us a cup of herbal tea. I'll only be a few minutes."

When he returned, she sat with her legs pretzeled beneath her where he'd left her, even though he heard her use the bathroom while he brewed the tea. He handed her cup to her. He sat his cup on the nightstand and then sat his gun, phone, and his wallet containing his FBI ID and badge beside it. Then he sat in front of her, facing her, his bent leg pressing against hers.

Her eyes were still on his gun and phone.

"We need to talk about that," he said.

Her eyes came to his, and she nodded.

"I am required to be armed at all times, for my job. Even in establishments that say no gun, I carry concealed. And I am always required to be available via phone, as well. I take them into the bathroom with me, sit them on a shelf beside the shower, sleep with them next to my bed as you noticed."

"So, you're basically on call twenty-four hours a day, every day?"

"Yes and no. If we're not away on a mission, we have dedicated times we know our team is on call and can request days or times that we are truly off, like for all your doctor visits, when we book childbirth classes, and when we have this baby. Those times will be blocked so I won't be on call. But some things that go down are so big we get scrambled regardless if our team is up or not. That's why I keep a basic medical kit with me always as well. Often, we meet at one of our airfields and someone from the office brings the weapons and ammo, our body armor, anything we may need."

She was almost afraid to ask the questions that ran through her mind.

"What we do is top secret. Nobody, and I mean nobody, can know. You can never tell a friend or a family member. You can only talk about it with those associated with the team like Angel or Garcia's girlfriend, Sienna. I want you to meet her before we go on this next mission. She and Angel will be good support for you while I'm away."

"Who exactly are you? Sister Bernice John referred to you as paramilitary. I don't understand what that means though."

"We all came from regular military, special forces mostly. Officially we are no longer active duty, but we did take the same oath and we do interface directly with our regular military, as you saw at the bases in Djibouti and at Andrews. We get sanctioned through regular military channels, but we act independently and take on jobs that often our regular military aren't allowed to."

"Like mercenaries?"

"No, more like a private security team." He grabbed his wallet. "We also all carry official US Federal credentials." He opened it and showed her his badge and FBI ID.

"Is that real?"

Doc nodded. "It was issued by the FBI and stands up to any scrutiny. It's what allows us to carry concealed even in bars and schools where guns are banned."

"So, you're an FBI Agent?"

"On paper only to give us some official standing while operating domestically."

If Elizabeth thought she understood, that feeling quickly slipped away. "Can you arrest people?"

Doc nodded. "Yes, and if I'm in a jam, the Deputy Director of the FBI will vouch for me, officially citing that I am assigned to a special task force."

"Does everyone who works at Shepherd Security have an FBI badge?"

"Just the Operators." He saw her confusion at that word. "Just those of us who operate in the field, but we all carry different federal credentials. Cooper carries CIA creds, Jackson and Garcia both have DEA badges."

"Madison is one of these Operators?" She asked.

"Yeah, she carries FBI creds too." He watched her process that. "I holster my gun either on my hip, in the small of my back, or in a boot. Try to remember that so you don't feel it and react when we are in public. And if I ever have to draw my weapon and you're with me, I need you to know that it is a dire situation and you have to do exactly what I tell you, be that drop to the ground, get behind me, or run."

She nodded nervously. She wondered how often that would happen.

"And I want to teach you to shoot and handle a weapon so you're comfortable with it. Then we'll work on getting you your concealed carry license. I'll want you to be armed at all times to protect yourself and our child when I'm not with you."

"Protect me from what?"

Doc blew out a heavy breath. "Elizabeth, the dangers that are out there, that most people don't know about could find you. I just want you safe at all times."

She didn't understand what that meant. "Does Angel carry a gun?"

"Yes, and she knows how to use it very well."

This sent chills down Elizabeth's spine. "Will your job put me in danger?" Her voice was a mere whisper.

"It could. But it also gives us a lot of tools to keep you safe. My car is monitored in our Operations Center and the key fobs have panic buttons that will alert Ops too. We have a state-of-the-art security system installed here in the condo, and at every team member's residence. If you're in danger when you enter, all you have to do is enter the code one-two-three-four, and Ops is alerted. There will be a half dozen armed agents coming through the door in minutes. That would be one of those situations if I'm off I would get scrambled for, to help a team member in danger."

He could tell she had nearly hit overload. He took his cup and sipped his tea.

Then he continued, to wrap up the last of what he thought she needed to know. "The special, secure phone the office will issue to you will allow us to talk when I am away. Our Operations Center will always know where it is because it is monitored. Often, when Jackson is away, Angel stays at the office. There is an apartment on the ninth floor as well as a guest room in Shepherd's penthouse. If you ever didn't want to be here, or if we fear there is a credible threat against you, you would stay there. But on average, no, my job won't put you in danger."

She stared fearfully at him.

"I promise, it will be a rarity that my job will put you in danger. I just want you to be aware of these things."

She took another drink of her tea.

"Talk to me Elizabeth. What are you thinking?" He asked after a minute had passed.

"I don't know how I feel about being tracked by your office through my phone."

"It's not to invade your privacy. It's to keep you safe and give me peace of mind when I'm on a mission. We're like a big family, Elizabeth. It's just a way for the family to watch out for you."

If she disliked the idea of her phone being tracked, she was going to hate the tracker he wanted to install in her shoulder. He'd save that discussion for later when they were at the office. He watched her take a long sip from her cup. Then she sat it onto the nightstand. The cup was empty.

"I didn't even ask you, are you having any morning sickness?"

"I did for about a month. It wasn't too bad as long as I had some tea or nibbled on some crackers as soon as I woke up."

"I'm sorry I wasn't there to make you your tea. I just want to take care of you Elizabeth."

She gazed deeply into his beautiful, pale gray eyes. Then her eyes wandered over his chiseled, manly face. "If we have a boy, I hope he is as attractive as you are and is as kind." She leaned forward and pressed a gentle kiss to his lips. Her fingers traced over his cheeks. "I can be okay with all of this. Just give me a little time to get used to it."

His lips tugged into a grin. "I know you can. The other women will help you too."

"Are there any other wives or girlfriends?"

"No, just Angel and Sienna, and of course Madison."

"Madison? She's one of you."

"Yes, and she'll be a good friend and give support to you too. She is married to Cooper, so that makes her one of the wives."

"They're married?" Elizabeth asked. Wow, that was a surprise. "I would never have guessed that."

"Yeah, they met when we hired her to be our first female Operator about a year and a half ago."

"So, your teammates are your friends, outside of work?"

Doc smiled. "Yeah, best friends, more than that, they're like brothers. We spend a lot of time together when we're off duty. That's why I want you to meet Sienna right away too." He was thoughtful for a few quiet seconds. "We might want to consider moving over near them. Jackson and Garcia live in townhouses in the same complex, across the street from each other."

"You want to move? But this is your home."

Doc smiled wider. "We'll be okay here until the baby is maybe six months old, but we'll need a bigger place so this baby can have its own room."

"This home is very nice, Alexander. It has enough space. Kids just need love and caring parents. They don't need their own room."

He took hold of her hands. "This place is fine for one or two of us. Kids do need their own room, a yard to play in, a playground in the area. The townhouse complex they live in is a great kid-friendly neighborhood. There is a pool and playground, sidewalks, and an elementary school in walking distance. This complex doesn't have any of those things. We can watch for a good unit to come on the market and take our time. I'm not saying I want to buy a new place tomorrow."

Elizabeth and her brother Bobby never had their own rooms, never had any of those things that Alexander thought were needed. They grew up in a one-bedroom apartment in a bad neighborhood. She slept sometimes in the tiny bedroom with either her mom or Bobby. Sometimes she slept on the couch or the floor.

She pushed through the memories and thought about being able to provide to her child those things Alexander said were important. She wanted him or her to have a better life, an easier life than she had had. She never wanted her child to feel ashamed when strangers gave them charity. She especially wanted to be able to buy her child Christmas gifts and not be listed on a giving tree at some church.

"Elizabeth, talk to me. Why do you look sad?"

"Not sad, hopeful," she said. "But at the same time, I don't want you to think you have to buy a bigger place because of me and this baby. This baby will be lucky, no matter where we live because he or she will have you as a father."

Doc kissed her. This time it was a deep, passionate kiss. He knew he was going to make love to her again, but he also wanted to finish this conversation. Just as he was about to lay her down, he pulled away just a few inches.

"This baby will be very lucky to have you as a mom. And I want only the best for the two of you. Living near Jackson and Garcia will be a good environment for all of us. But we have some time. We don't need to rush it."

She reached her lips to his and kissed him with everything she had in her. He was a good man, a kind man. He wanted to take care of her and the baby. That was enough to make her love him, if she didn't already. Honestly, she wasn't sure if she loved him or not. She'd thought about him every day while she was in Seattle, even before she realized she was pregnant. And after she knew she was pregnant with his child, she replayed in her head every second they had spent together trying to figure out if he could possibly have feelings for her. She knew even then that she had feelings for him.

Given how he was now, she was still very confused why he had acted the way he did after they were rescued. Why had he regretted having sexual relations with her? She knew he did. How could he not have felt bound by the vows they exchanged before God? She released him from his because she knew that was what he wanted. It wasn't what she wanted though, and she hadn't been brave enough to fight for him and a future together. As she kissed him, she knew she'd eventually ask him. But not now.

She paid attention to what he liked, what made him moan. Kissing his neck made him breathe hard. She knew from basic human biology that her hand on his penis would feel as good to him as his hands caressing her between her legs did. She ran her hand down his tight abdomen, skin on skin. First, she rubbed the front of his flannel pants. He moaned loudly and his mouth took hers more aggressively. Then she got brave and plunged her hand beneath them. She felt the silky soft skin of his member, his hard, erect member.

He gasped out and arched his head back when she made contact with him. "Oh fuck, Elizabeth," he groaned. He pulled his pants down to his thighs to give her more space to work over his cock.

A smile curved her lips. She liked that she was able to bring him pleasure. She wanted to make him feel as good as he did her. She wasn't brave enough to attempt oral sex on him. She'd have to do some research online to find out how best to do it to bring about the greatest sensation. She massaged him, stroked his shaft, and kissed his neck and ears.

Doc was assaulted with so many erotic sensations from Elizabeth's hand and her lips. The only thing that would have made this better would be if he could watch her hand work over him. He was just about to come, lost in how stimulating if felt. He stopped her hand, grabbing it with his.

"Clothes off," he growled. His hands then pulled at her top and her bottoms. Then he tore his all the way off too. He flipped her to her back. He hung his face over hers as he settled between her legs. "I want to look into those beautiful blue eyes as I make love to you. Don't close them or look away."

Elizabeth kept her eyes on his as requested. The honesty of the moment as he penetrated her was overpowering, a connection unlike any she'd ever felt. He moaned, his eyes half-closing in a sensual bliss. In the depth of his eyes, she saw his soul, open and raw. She saw affection that could be love. She watched his facial expressions. It was erotic, watching his pleasure morph into what almost looked like pain as he plunged harder, deeper, and faster into her. She knew he was about to orgasm. Sweat beaded on his forehead.

The moment he came, his head snapped back, and his eyes rolled to the back of his head. She watched him in fascination. The sensation of him throbbing deep inside of her was exciting, bringing her closer to her own climax. He collapsed onto her; his entire body coated with a sheen of sweat. She heard his heavy breathing beside her ear, felt his racing heartbeat over hers.

After a few minutes he rolled off her and his hand reached down between her knees. His eyes reaffixed on hers. "Your turn and keep your eyes open and on mine as long as you can. I want to watch your eyes as I make you come."

As his hand worked over her and she felt the incredible sensations. His eyes invading hers made her feel stripped down, her soul open to him in the most intimate and vulnerable way. He quickly brought her to an orgasm so intense she screamed out, but he didn't stop his ministrations. He kept the rhythm up, making her cry out, overwhelmed by the assault on the little bundle of nerves. Her whole body quaked as her mind exploded, fireworks exploding behind her closed eyes, a lightning bolt jolting her everywhere.

The next awareness coming to her was being held tightly to him. She still breathed hard; her senses felt numb. *Oh dear Lord, thank you,* was all she could think. She wasn't capable of speaking yet, nor did she know what she'd say. The connection they'd just shared was overpowering. She now understood why a sexual relationship was special. To share this with another human being was something only to be shared with someone you could be naked down to your very soul with, open, and honest in all ways.

She felt a kiss press to her cheek. Then Alexander's lips took hers again. He kissed her deeply, passionately. When he pulled his lips away, she forced her eyes open to gaze into his. A soft smile curved her lips. "I fantasized about us making love again while I was in Seattle, but it was never that intense."

Doc chuckled. "We'll see if we can top that tonight, but right now, I think we need to get up and get going. We have a lot to do today."

"We do?"

"After we both clean up and have breakfast, we need to get the marriage license from the county building. Then we're going shopping to get you a warm coat and some other clothes you need. We need to go to the bank and then stop in at the office."

Mike

While they each showered, cooked breakfast and ate, Doc sent and received several text messages on his phone. He messaged Lambchop to be sure he'd be at the office. There was no need to tell him the situation, Lambchop's first text back said congratulations! Are you bringing the marriage license to me? Doc's lips curved into a grin.

He text-messaged Angel, telling her the situation, though he was sure that was unnecessary. He was sure everyone at the office knew about Elizabeth and the baby. He asked her to provide support to Elizabeth. The reply was immediate and affirmative, gushing with congratulations on both the marriage and pregnancy. He chuckled as he read it.

A message displayed from Shepherd, requesting a meeting that afternoon. Doc accepted it, hoping all his requests would be granted. At least Shepherd had come to a decision. Then a message came from Lassiter, with a meeting invitation an hour after the meeting with Shepherd. He shouldn't have been surprised.

Elizabeth saw Alexander texting but didn't ask any questions. She'd never had a cell phone, not that it mattered. All her friends were Sisters, who didn't have one either. She'd have no one to talk or text with, not that she could have afforded the cost of one. She realized Alexander had this whole life she didn't understand and wasn't a part of. She wondered if she would eventually feel more comfortable with it all.

For Doc, the contentment he'd felt in bed with Elizabeth was quickly replaced with that awkwardness. Even in preparing breakfast, did she like scrambled eggs? How about turkey sausage? He really didn't know much about her, nor did she know him. In a lot of ways, they were complete strangers, complete strangers who had lived through something neither of them thought they would, complete strangers who created a baby. And now he was going to legally marry her, and she would live with him.

As they drove to the county building, the silence in the car was uncomfortable. Doc turned the radio on. "What kind of music do you like?"

"I've never listened to too much music besides what is played in church. What do you normally listen to?"

"Mostly, this station, Tom Petty Radio. I've always liked him, solo, with the Heartbreakers, the Travelling Wilburys, even with Mudcrutch."

Elizabeth didn't know who he was or any of the others he mentioned. "Then let's listen to this so I can see if I like it." She wanted to like what he did so they would have some commonality. She didn't like being so different and she wanted to be a part of his world. She did realize it would take time, and she was very grateful he had asked her to stay and wanted to make their marriage legal.

When they reached the county building, Elizabeth was surprised when Alexander took her hand as they walked in. The snow had stopped, but the wind blew cold. His gloved hand kept her hand warmer than the other one that she had stuffed into the shallow coat pocket. She smiled at him as he opened the door for her.

The process of getting the license was fast. They were in and out of the building in fifteen minutes. Doc took hold of her hand on the way out as well. The pavement was slick, and he didn't want her to fall. He knew he was going to be insane when it came to her safety. He'd feel better after they went to see an obstetrician. He noticed she didn't have on good winter boots. She was wearing those same nun-boots from Africa. He added winter boots, and every day wear boots and shoes to his mental shopping list.

He drove to the big mall next. For the next two hours they shopped for clothes, shoes, boots, a heavy winter coat, underclothing, even pajamas for her. Elizabeth had major sticker-shock and had to be talked into every purchase by Doc. "Elizabeth, this is what things cost and what normal people pay for them. I have the money and I want to spend it on you."

She could not vocalize all the thoughts that ran through her head. Not only was each item very expensive, they were from trendy stores, the newest fashion, and he bought her way too many items. She'd never needed more than two pairs of pants before, but he insisted on buying her ten. He bought her at least a dozen sweaters, another eight long-sleeved shirts, and three sweatshirts. The winter coat alone was over two-hundred dollars! And there was no reason at all that she needed four pairs of shoes and two pairs of boots.

When they walked out of the last store, both their hands loaded with bags, Doc couldn't figure out why she was so quiet and frowning. "Don't you like the clothes?" He asked. "I'm sorry if I talked you into styles that you don't like."

"Alexander, I can't believe the amount of money you just spent. I feel terrible about it. I get it, you don't like my clothes, want me in nicer things. What? Do I embarrass you?"

Doc felt a blow like someone had punched him in the gut. "No, you don't embarrass me. Why would you think that?"

"Those clothes were from stores I would never have even dreamed about shopping in. And the shoes and boots, I feel embarrassed you bought me six pairs. I only have one set of feet!"

"Elizabeth, even I have more than six pairs of shoes."

"And the bras," she said with embarrassment. "The department store had bras that were less expensive, Victoria Secret, for God's sake! I did not need fifty-dollar bras."

"No, but you needed to be expertly measured with accommodations for how your breasts will grow during your pregnancy and Victoria Secret does that. They are the bra experts. The one you are wearing is too tight. Even I can see that."

"How do you know what Victoria Secret does?"

"I was texting with Angel this morning. She told me we needed to go there."

"You talked with Angel about my bras?" She was mortified.

Doc halted her at the bench near the exit door. He sat the bags he was carrying to it and took those from her hands, setting them to fill the bench. He leaned in close, his lips to her ear. "Angel and I are very good friends, as is Madison. I'm a stupid guy that doesn't know anything about women's clothing, except that yours are getting too tight. I knew you didn't want me to spend much on these things for you, so I asked Angel what stores to go to. I knew you would never suggest we go into Victoria Secret, and forgive me for wanting to see you in sexy, lacy, pretty bras and panties."

She blushed and looked around to see if anyone was close enough to have heard. She was relieved that no one was. "They are pretty, and I do like them," she admitted. "But Alexander, those maternity clothes are over five-hundred dollars. I'll only wear them for six months! That is such a waste of money."

Doc gave her a sly smile. "Well, six months with *this* baby."

Elizabeth was surprised by his statement. Would he really want more children with her? The thought that they would have more kids and be a real family, filled her with hope that Alexander would grow to love her. She smiled wide. "Okay, the maternity clothes are comfortable."

"Okay, so no more frowning. Just be happy with your new clothes."

"Okay," she agreed.

Doc pulled his knife from his pocket and cut the tags from her coat, boots, hat, scarf, and glove set. "Wear the new winter stuff and put your coat and boots into this bag. It's cold out and more snow is due this afternoon."

She did as he said and was surprised how warm she was when they stepped back out into the chilly air. He drove across the parking lot to a restaurant and asked her if it would be okay for lunch. It was a chain restaurant. She'd never eaten in one though. When she saw the prices in the menu she again paused. A hamburger was fifteen dollars! Everything on the healthy menu was over twenty dollars. That was where Alexander was ordering from.

"You can have anything you want, but this is the section with the healthiest items. It shouldn't surprise you that I will want you to eat as healthy as possible, so our baby is healthy. I'm going to apologize in advance that I'm going to be crazy about your health and safety." He chuckled out loud.

She pulled her hair to the side of her head and twisted it into a braid unconsciously. She reviewed the healthy menu again and decided to order what he had. Then she looked up at him. "I'll want to be as healthy as I can be too. I like that you care so much about our baby."

"I care about both of you," he corrected her.

The bank was the next stop. They took seats within the personal banker's office. Doc presented his ID and prompted Elizabeth to do the same. "I need to add my wife to my accounts and get a debit and credit card issued to her."

"I don't need a credit card, Alexander," Elizabeth protested.

The young personal banker took their IDs.

Doc ignored her. "And if you could do me a favor and bring my checking account up and turn the monitor so we can see it, I'd appreciate it."

"Certainly," the man said. After a few keystrokes, he turned the monitor. "I just need to add you to the signature card," He said to Elizabeth.

"Can you give us a moment alone to go over my account?" Doc asked, surprising the young banker.

"Um, of course. I can use this time to get the supplies I need. I can issue her debit card, but the credit card comes from offsite, and has to be mailed to you, Mr. Williams."

"No problem," Doc said.

The man left, closing his glass office door behind him. His keyboard was on the far side of the desk. He'd watch through the door to be sure neither of them touched the keyboard. Alexander Williams was a long-term customer with high-balance accounts. Not the type of customer he wanted to piss off.

Doc pointed to each deposit on the screen. "These deposits are my paychecks."

Elizabeth was shocked by the numbers she saw displayed on the computer screen. Her mind reviewed the dates, every two weeks.

"This withdraw is the bank automatically transferring out ten-thousand to my money market account, when the balance rises over fifteen thousand. It's what I have it programmed to do, no sense leaving that much in a checking account. I also have a regular savings account and other investments."

Alexander had more money than anyone she knew. "Okay, you make enough to pay for what you bought me, but that doesn't mean you should have spent that much."

"I work damn hard for the money I make. I put my life on the line doing my job, and damn-it, I'll spend whatever I want on whatever I want to spend it on, be it two-hundred dollars on a coat for you or five-hundred dollars on maternity clothes." His voice was strong.

She didn't know what to say to that. She merely nodded. A part of her felt flattered that he wanted to spend his money on her, even though she saw it as excessive. A small smile pulled at her lips.

He took her hand and when he spoke again, his voice softened. "So, now will you relax about money and know we have enough to support us both and this baby?"

Her smile grew and she nodded.

"The only thing I will ask is that if you are going to spend more than three-hundred dollars at one time is that we discuss it first."

"Oh, good heavens, I would never spend three-hundred dollars at one time."

Doc chuckled. Sure, she would! "Okay. We're good then?"

"We are, and I'm sorry," she began.

"No sorry needed," he cut her off. He motioned to the personal banker who skulked just steps outside the door.

When they finished adding her and her debit card was issued, he brought her to the ATM and told her how to use it. He made her withdraw two-hundred dollars. He made her put it in her purse. She'd need cash for when he was gone.

"And if you spend it and need more, you go to any one of these bank branches and use the ATM. Try to only take money from this bank though, so we avoid fees."

"Okay, I promise, but I can't see needing more than this for the two weeks you will be away."

"And if you go out with Angel or Sienna while I'm gone, use the debit card if you can, rather than your cash. Just about everywhere takes debit, all stores, restaurants, even the movies."

"Oh, okay," she agreed, wondering if she'd ever feel comfortable with all of this.

From there, they drove to the Shepherd Security Building. She again watched in fascination the security steps he went through as they passed through the gate and two garage doors into the private parking area in the second sub-basement. He again put his hand to the scan pad and entered his code to call the elevator.

"I'll need to meet with a few people while we're here, so I'll probably leave you with Angel a couple times," Doc said as he pressed four on the elevator panel.

"If you are off work the next two days, why are we here?" Elizabeth asked.

Doc chuckled to himself. He wouldn't tell her it was because he basically lived at the office when he wasn't away on a mission. He knew that would have to change. "We need to get your cell phone from Garcia, and give the marriage license to Lambchop, so he can sign it and file it for us tomorrow when it's legal. I need to speak with my boss, Shepherd, and I have a second short meeting I have to be in. Besides, I did want to show you around and introduce you to a few people."

Even though he answered in detail, for some reason, she thought he was being evasive. "Okay, I was just curious." She flashed him a reassuring smile.

They stopped on four and left their coats and her purse in his office. Then they took the stairs up to five, exiting across from the elevator. Elizabeth remembered this hallway from the day before. She followed Alexander through the hall. They passed by the kitchen where she and Alexander had talked. A few feet farther, they came to Angel's desk.

Doc knew she would feel out of place. He hoped hanging out with Angel while he was meeting with Shepherd and then with Lassiter, that she would be okay. That was another reason he needed to talk with Garcia, he needed to arrange an introduction to Sienna. This would all be so different for Elizabeth. She would need as much support as he could find for her. He wished he wasn't leaving for two weeks in just a few days.

"Hi," Angel greeted them with a smile.

They both returned her greeting.

"Doc, I thought you were taking a few days off."

"I am. I'm just in for a quick meeting with Shepherd," Doc said. He wouldn't mention that Lassiter had contacted him that morning, setting an appointment with him as well. Angel would know that from the calendars, and he didn't want to explain Lassiter to Elizabeth.

"I hear congratulations are in order. I am so thrilled Sammy will have another little one to play with." Angel stood and first hugged Elizabeth, much to her surprise, and then Doc.

"Thanks, Angel," Doc said.

"Yes, thank you," Elizabeth repeated. She wanted to tell Angel that they had said vows, that this wasn't a child conceived out of wedlock.

"Jackson and I thought that we'd have everyone from the team over for pizza tomorrow night. That way you can get to know everyone better, Elizabeth. Are you two free?"

Elizabeth's eyes went to Alexander's.

"Yes, we are and that would be great," Doc replied. "I was going to suggest we all got together this weekend. Have you mentioned it to anyone else?"

"No, we wanted to be sure you were free first," Angel replied. "But I'll get right on it." She pointed to the conference room. "Doc, why don't you drag a chair out for Elizabeth. She can hang out with me while you're in your meeting. I know you are due in with Shepherd soon."

Doc glanced at his watch. He was due in Shepherd's office in three minutes. His eyes met Angel's. She gave him a smirk of recognition. She of course knew of his appointment with Shepherd. She knew everyone's calendars.

"Thanks." He gave Elizabeth's arm a squeeze and then stepped away. He brought her a chair and then headed down the hallway. He approached Shepherd's door considering the words he'd use to convince Shepherd if any of his requests were declined. This time, he knocked and waited.

"Come," Shepherd's muffled voice said.

Doc opened the door and stepped inside. Shepherd was alone in his office. He'd expected to see Cooper there as well.

Shepherd motioned to the guest chair in front of his desk. He sat behind his big desk in the corner of the floor to ceiling windows as usual. Shepherd had a very comfortable seating area with leather couches that he never used anymore. Doc supposed it was all the same to Shepherd. He sat in his wheelchair all the time anyway, and it was probably too much of a pain in the ass to transfer to a couch or a different chair, though Doc knew that Shepherd did have quite a bit of feeling in his lower back, his butt, and legs. The bullet fragment had only caused partial paralysis.

Doc sat in the chair and waited for Shepherd to glance up from his laptop.

A good thirty seconds later Shepherd looked up at Doc. "Thanks for coming in today to meet."

"Of course," Doc said. "Did you and Cooper come to any decisions on my requests regarding Elizabeth?"

Shepherd shuffled through a pile of papers. He handed one over. "This is to add her to the company insurance policies as a dependent. You can do so immediately. We have a clause allowing domestic partners as well as spouses. It will be in effect twenty-four hours after we submit it. Two hundred a pay period will be deducted from your paycheck to cover her. After the baby is born, it jumps to three twenty for the family rate, which will cover as many kids as you have."

Doc chuckled. "She isn't even past the first trimester yet. Let's not get ahead of ourselves, by talking about multiple kids, okay?"

The corner of Shepherd's lips tipped up. "Did you know before yesterday?"

Doc shook his head. "Hadn't a clue. I didn't expect to ever see her again."

"Is she what your problem has been since the mission in Africa?" Shepherd asked.

"Part of it," Doc replied.

"Jesus, Doc, so you broke protocol, given the fact your other teammates on Alpha all broke this one too, it's not that big of a deal."

"It is to me, Shep. You know how I feel about this protocol. I know why it's there. All I can say to justify it is that there were extenuating circumstances. Elizabeth and I truly thought we were going to be killed. She was sure she would be brutally raped.

She wanted to." Doc stopped himself mid-sentence. "Oh, Christ, Shepherd. I'm sorry." Talking about any of this with Shepherd was the last thing he planned to do, and he knew it would be the last thing Shepherd would want to hear. That was what Lassiter was on the payroll for.

"It's okay and I understand. When Angel and I were held, even though I knew the team would be on its way, I made peace with the fact that I'd be shot and killed, chained in that hangar like a dog."

"I finally got past the fact that I was going to die, just recently."

"It changes a man," Shepherd remarked while dragging his hand through his jet-black hair.

"Yeah," Doc agreed.

"So, sleeping with her and accepting you were going to die were making you a pain in the ass the last few months. Anything else?"

"Did Lassiter tell you?" Doc asked.

Shepherd's lips tugged into a grin. "You know Lassiter better than that. He didn't tell me a damned thing."

"Her age is also a huge issue for me, Shep. Jesus, look at her. Even though she's twenty-four she looks like a damned teenager. We were at the mall today and I know more than a few of the salesclerk's thought she was my daughter and not my wife."

A big smile curved over Shepherd's face. "And that's a problem?

"Yes, it is," Doc insisted. He shook his head. "It's something I'll just have to get past. But I'll talk with Lassiter about that."

"You're seeing him this afternoon," Shepherd said it as a statement.

Doc was sure Shepherd was the one who arranged it. "Yes."

"I also authorized the agency phone for Elizabeth. It made sense as you will need a secure line to talk with her when you are away on missions. You need to explain to her who we are and what we do, and especially impress upon her the covert nature of our work."

"She and I already had that conversation this morning. She knows we carry official federal creds, are armed at all times, and that she cannot ever talk with anyone outside of the agency about any aspect of the job. She understands. I don't think it will be a problem."

"See Garcia before you leave. He's loading her phone. She will have a direct line to Ops too. After sleeping on it, I decided it made sense for dependents to have the same security as agency personnel. Explain to her the panic code and that she should contact Ops if she's ever in trouble."

"Thank you, Shepherd. Knowing she's covered, I won't worry about her while I'm in the field."

"We needed a protocol for dependents. This just forced it to the top of the to-do pile. I authorize the tracker too. Sienna already has one since she was part of a mission. Did you know Garcia issued her a phone?"

A smirk curved over Doc's lips. Yeah, everyone on the team knew that, but Shepherd, evidently. "I guess I did. I knew Garcia wouldn't be talking to her on a nonsecure line."

"I hadn't given it any thought. That's on me, not planning for dependents. Besides Lassiter, no one had any. But things are changing. I suspect Garcia won't be too far behind you and Jackson. He's already told me he and Sienna will get married and have kids within the next year."

This didn't surprise Doc. With the way Garcia doted on Sammy, it was obvious the man loved the kid and wanted one of his own. And everyone knew Sienna wanted a few. It was only a matter of time. They'd just met six months prior during Garcia's undercover Op that Sienna crashed. He knew Sienna wanted to wait what she judged as an appropriate amount of time since her first husband was murdered, before she took a second, like anyone associated with Shepherd Security cared.

Doc went back to Angel's desk when he left Shepherd. He text-messaged Garcia. He was in the workroom next to Ops, just finishing with Elizabeth's phone. "I'll bring her back in a bit, if that's okay. I have one more meeting in about a half-hour."

Angel nodded. "We'll leave the chair here. I'm showing her some basic stuff. If Shepherd agrees I was thinking she could be a back-up for me." She smiled at Elizabeth. "Just until she decides what she wants to do or figures out her schedule."

"I told Angel you think I should go back to school and get a higher degree. She thinks it's a great idea," Elizabeth said. "She even showed me where those nearby extension campuses are that you told me about. We were just looking up admissions requirements." She pointed at Angel's monitor.

"A person absolutely needs a bachelor's degree," Angel said. "And while going to school, she would probably have the availability to provide some coverage as a receptionist. I know the guys hate it when I'm out and they have to cover this desk."

Doc chuckled. Wow, Angel was a powerful ally. He'd have to remember that. "I like that idea, but only if it's something you're interested in, Elizabeth."

She nodded. "Yes, I'll have to think about it, but I like the idea of helping out here."

Doc smiled. "Garcia is waiting for us to give you your phone and then we will drop our marriage license with Lambchop."

Elizabeth came to her feet. He led her back through the hallway and to the Elevator. They took it up to the eighth floor and stepped out into the empty hallway. Elizabeth wondered why it seemed so vacant. All the doors they passed were closed. The first open one they came to, was the workroom. Garcia was within.

"Hey, I'm just finishing up with it," he greeted. Then he smiled and shook his head. "I can't believe you beat me to it." He rose and shook Doc's hand, pulling him in for a shoulder bump. "Congrats man!"

Elizabeth stood back, watching them. Alexander had nice and supportive friends from what she saw so far. She found herself grinning when Garcia turned to her. She was surprised when he engulfed her in a hug.

"And congratulations to you, Elizabeth. Welcome to the family. That's what we are, you know."

"Thank you. Yes, that is what Alexander has said. He thinks of all of you as his family." As the embrace ended, she noticed his pistol, holstered in plain sight on his hip. Alexander's was in the small of his back today. She knew it would just take time to get used to it.

"I can't wait for you to meet Sienna," Garcia said. "She's an elementary school teacher." His eyes met Doc's. "We're still talking about when we will get married. I think she's crazy that we need to wait any longer, like anyone cares how long we've known each other. I know she wants a baby, hell, maybe I'll substitute placebos for her birth control pills. Certainly, if she's pregnant, she'll marry me sooner." Garcia laughed. "Can you hook me up with some sugar pills Doc?"

Elizabeth was surprised by his words. He seemed very accepting of the situation she and Alexander were in, as was Angel. She wondered if it would be a nonissue for all his friends. Was pregnancy out of wedlock really so accepted with people?

"Oh, no, I wouldn't want to be blasted with Sienna's wrath if she ever found out." Doc laughed.

Garcia showed Elizabeth how to use the phone. "You have unlimited voice, text, and data as part of the plan so don't worry about any of that."

Elizabeth had never had a cell phone before. She'd have to go online and Google exactly what all that meant. "Thank you. I appreciate it."

He pointed out the address book. He had it programmed with Alexander's phone number as well as Angel's and Madison's, his own and Sienna's. There were a lot of names of people she didn't know. He pointed out the Ops Center phone number. "If you're ever in trouble, even a flat tire, call Ops. Madison, Jackson, and I man it when we're not in the field. Ops is available twenty-four-by-seven. Someone is always available to help you with anything you need. We'll take you next door to Ops and introduce you to Yvette and BT. They're on today."

Doc smiled and nodded. He really appreciated Garcia going out of his way to make this easy for Elizabeth and welcome her. He watched Elizabeth slip the phone into the back pocket of her pants. They followed Garcia from the room.

Elizabeth watched in fascination as Garcia did the palmprint scan and entering of the code thing that Alexander had done to have access to the stairwell the previous day and to gain entrance this morning to the elevator in the basement where they'd parked. She wondered why, within this secure building, this room had the added security, until she entered the room behind him and saw what the room was.

Monitors lined the walls. A large one in the center showed an aerial view of what looked like a warehouse next to an expressway. Multiple computers sat on the desk with more buttons and dials than she'd ever seen in person. Two people were within, wearing headsets and staring at different monitors. The man, who had his back to her, had black hair and wide shoulders.

"Roger that, Charlie. I've got you on satellite. The perimeter is clear," he said.

The woman turned and looked their way. She had bright red hair, worn short and spiked up. She was older, in her forties. She smiled and held her index finger up. "Affirmative. I'll have that for you by fifteen-hundred." Then she clicked a short burst on the keyboard. She sat her headphones to the desk and turned back to them. "You must be Elizabeth," she said, closing the distance with her right hand outstretched. "I'm Yvette. It's nice to meet you."

Elizabeth returned her smile and shook her hand. "It's nice to meet you too," she replied.

"I'd like to say I've heard a lot about you over the past few months, but I haven't." She smacked Doc in the stomach, hard. "Grumpy shorts here, hasn't really said much to anyone about anything since he got back from Africa. But now that we know he had unfinished business with you, it makes sense why he was such a pain in the ass!"

Doc groaned. "Thanks, Yvette." That was the last thing he needed Elizabeth to hear.

The other man in the room turned their direction. "Don't let Yvette scare you off, Elizabeth," he said. "It's nice to meet you. I'm BT." He smiled warmly, his lips surrounded by a full mustache and beard.

Elizabeth returned his smile. "Hi. It's nice to meet you too."

"I just finished programming her agency issued phone. She's tied into Ops just as Sienna is."

Yvette nodded. Her eyes went to Doc's. "Will she have a tracker for us to monitor as well?"

Doc wished she hadn't asked. He hadn't had that conversation with Elizabeth yet. "Yeah, I'll get you the ID for it later today." He planned to install it while they were there at the office. He noticed Elizabeth was looking at him with unasked questions.

Elizabeth was confused. Alexander had said the phone would be tracked by Ops. Certainly, the ID number was available. Why hadn't Garcia taken care of that? She removed her phone from her back pocket.

Doc leaned in close to her. "We'll talk about it later," he whispered, directing her hand to replace the phone in her pocket.

"Yeah, we got the phone," Yvette said. "I was surprised that Shepherd had to think about it." Her eyes went to Garcia. "You never told him you provided an agency phone to Sienna, did you?" She laughed a full belly laugh when Garcia shrugged innocently.

Doc ended the Ops visit then, ushering her back into the hallway. He stopped and poked his head into Madison's office a few steps farther down the hall. "Hey."

Madison rose from her chair and crossed the room. She gave Doc a hug. "Congrats. Cooper and I are happy for you." Then she turned to Elizabeth and wrapped her arms around her. "Congratulations and welcome. I should have known there was something between you two. Do you know yet if you're having a boy or a girl?"

"No," Elizabeth said. Her eyes went to Alexander. They hadn't talked about if they wanted to find out the gender of the baby. They hadn't talked about a lot of things.

"It's probably too soon," Madison said dismissively. "Anyway, we're happy for you." She pointed back to her computer. "I've got to get back on. If I don't pass this test, we won't be official for the next mission. We'll see you guys Friday night at Angel and Jackson's house."

Doc chuckled to himself. So, Angel had already notified the team about the get together Friday night. Angel hadn't wasted any time. Doc appreciated these people, who were his family, more than ever. They all embraced his news, welcomed Elizabeth and made this easier than it could have been.

November

Elizabeth watched Alexander close the door to Madison's office. He led her around the corner. Several doors were open. They went to one and stepped into an office. Seated at the desk was the muscled black man who was the team pastor. He smiled warmly at them.

"Ah, Mr. and Mrs. Williams." He stood and closed the distance.

Elizabeth noticed that he too openly wore a pistol holstered on his hip. Yes, this was definitely going to take some getting used to.

He took them both in a hug at the same time. "Praise be to God for the new life created. You will let me baptize your baby, won't you?" His gaze met Elizabeth's. "I'm not Catholic, but God knows I am a devout Christian."

That was something else she and Alexander hadn't discussed. She wasn't sure how she felt about her baby not being baptized Catholic. Of course, she was married outside of the Catholic Church to a non-Catholic. "Given the situation, I'm not sure that matters."

"Elizabeth," Lambchop said, taking both her hands. "God loves you and your child. You said vows to God, not to the Catholic God, just to God."

Elizabeth nodded. He made a lot of sense. "I believe the union Alexander and I pledged before God is legitimate. It doesn't have to be within the Catholic Church to be legitimate, so the baptism of our child doesn't need to be either." She gave him a natural smile. "I would be honored if you baptized our baby."

Doc wrapped his arms around her and gave her a squeeze. He knew this was major for her. They hadn't discussed her faith and how it applied to their union and this baby. "Agreed," he said. "But first things first, the marriage license." He released Elizabeth and pulled the document from his pocket. He handed it to Lambchop.

Lambchop reviewed it. "We can sign it and date it for tomorrow and I'll file it tomorrow afternoon. Have you thought about who you'd like to sign as your witnesses?"

Doc hadn't thought at all about it, forgot it would even be needed. He made eye contact with Elizabeth. "How about Angel and Jackson?"

Elizabeth nodded. Angel was a good choice as she was Sister Bernice John's daughter, but she was okay with whoever Alexander would choose.

Doc removed his phone from his pocket and sent a text message to them both. Their affirmative replies popped in immediately. "They'll be here in a few minutes."

"We could do a short ceremony in the lounge and have anyone in the office who is available come," Lambchop suggested.

"No," Doc said right away. He glanced at Elizabeth. "Unless you want it." His gaze shifted back to Lambchop. "We said our vows in Africa. As far as I'm concerned, that was when we were married."

Lambchop focused his gaze on Elizabeth questioningly. "Are those your thoughts too?"

"I don't know any of the others, except Madison and Cooper. If Alexander doesn't want anyone else to witness us signing the license to make it legal, I'm good with that."

"Hold on," Doc said. "How about we have the rest of Alpha Team witness it too?" He owed that to his team.

"Delta was also in Africa," Lambchop reminded him.

"Okay, but just the two teams," Doc agreed.

"Not Shepherd?" Lambchop asked.

"Damn, this is getting bigger by the moment. Lambchop, we're just going to sign the damn piece of paper."

Lambchop smiled. "You know me better than that. There will be some words, a prayer, and a reaffirmation by the both of you before I sign that license."

Doc groaned.

Ten minutes later, Alpha and Delta Teams were assembled in the lounge outside of Cooper's office. At Lambchop's prompting, Angel did send a message to everyone in the office announcing the ceremony. Soon, a larger crowd than Doc anticipated and wanted was present.

Shepherd rolled into the room and up to Doc and Elizabeth.

"Elizabeth, this is the man responsible for this agency and everything we do, Colonel Sam Shepherd," Doc introduced.

She was surprised by the wheelchair. No one had mentioned that before. "Hello, Colonel, it's nice to meet you."

"It's nice to meet you too, Elizabeth," Shepherd said, shaking her hand. "And just Shepherd is fine." He nodded at Lambchop, signaling him to get this moving.

Lambchop had his stole around his neck, his Bible in his hand. He glanced at those assembled, who stood in a semicircle around him, Doc, and Elizabeth. "Today we gather to recognize a solemn vow these two children of God made to our Lord. While in Africa, Alexander and Elizabeth swore their faithfulness in God's holy ordinance, to live as husband and wife until death parted them. Today, we recognize this bond and celebrate it. Marriage is a union blessed by God. Elizabeth, Alexander, please join hands."

Doc didn't even realize that he stood there beside Elizabeth without even holding her hand. Damn, could he be any more thoughtless? He beamed a smile at her after he had taken both her hands in his.

"Elizabeth, Alexander, you said your vows before only God as your witness months ago. I am asking you to reaffirm your vows now, before these witnesses and God. Elizabeth, please go first."

Elizabeth felt a pang of something grip her chest. "I, Elizabeth Shaw took you as my husband, promising to forsake all others until we are parted by death, and today, I reaffirm those vows. I promise to work every day to make this marriage successful, to be the best wife and mother I can be, and to support you in all ways."

Doc was glad Elizabeth had gone first, to help him formulate what his vows should be. He glanced at Lambchop, who nodded it was his turn. "I, Doc, Alexander Williams vowed to you before God as our only witness to be your husband. I promised then, and I promise now, to be faithful to you until we are parted by death. I too promise you that I will work every day to make this marriage successful. I promise you my honesty and my loyalty. I will always be here for you Elizabeth. I will be the best husband and father I can be." His heart felt full, speaking these words to her. The fact that he said these vows in front of his friends, his family, affected him in a way he wouldn't have predicted. He knew he would do everything he could to be what she needed him to be. He wouldn't let her down again.

Lambchop opened his Bible to the bookmarked page. "There are many passages in the Bible that talk about the blessed union of marriage. This is one of my favorites and I think appropriate to this union. From **Ephesians 4:2-3**: With all humility and gentleness, with patience, bearing with one another in love, eager to maintain the unity of the Spirit in the bond of peace." He closed the book. "Elizabeth, Alexander, be gentle with one another. Have patience and humility. Maintain this unity you have sworn before God, our Father, and let your hearts be open to all the bounties the Lord has in store for you. Amen."

Elizabeth had hung on Reverend Johnson's every word, forgetting there was anyone else in the room. She felt at peace and full of the Lord's spirit unlike she had in the past few years. "Amen."

Claps, whistles, and cheers resounded through the room, snapping Elizabeth out of her own mind. She was surprised when Alexander leaned in and kissed her. They were congratulated by each person in the room. Alexander introduced her to those she didn't know. She knew she'd never remember all their names.

Soon the room was cleared out with only Lambchop, Doc and Elizabeth, and Jackson and Angel present. They all signed the license.

"That was a beautiful ceremony," Angel told Lambchop, taking him in a brief embrace. Then her eyes turned to Elizabeth. "Jackson and I were married by him in this room too."

"You were?" Elizabeth asked.

"Yes. Jackson surprised me and had my aunt and cousin here, telling them for the first time that I was alive. My aunt was a second mother to me so it was the most special wedding gift Jackson could have given me." Angel grinned the biggest smile at the memory.

"Your mom mourned the loss of your life when she thought you were dead, but her abiding faith also had her celebrating that you were with God and that she'd see you when she went to heaven. Her faith is amazing. Of all the Sisters I've known, your mother has this way about her that inspires a person to believe deeper, to serve with more selflessness, and to love all of God's creatures to depths that few can. I love your mother as my second mother, just as you do your aunt."

Angel embraced Elizabeth. "I know you are very special to her too. Thank you for asking Jackson and me to sign your license as your witnesses. It means a lot to me."

"Us too," Doc said. "Angel, I'm going to leave Elizabeth with you again. I have another meeting."

Angel nodded. She knew he was due to see Lassiter.

Doc dropped himself into the chair opposite Lassiter after he'd grabbed a water bottle from the refrigerator in the kitchen. They were in Lassiter's office. "I'm off on a vacation day, you know."

Lassiter chuckled. "But you were coming in to get Elizabeth's phone and for you to meet with Shepherd."

"Did you also know that Elizabeth and I went to the courthouse this morning and got a marriage license? Lambchop will file it tomorrow when it's legal."

Lassiter's lips tipped into a grin. "I suspected it."

"Jesus, does everyone know everything around here?"

"Are you asking me if I was summoned to Shepherd's office as soon as you left yesterday afternoon?"

Doc nodded.

"You know I was."

"I really pissed him off, didn't I?"

"I'd say he was more worried than anything, but you do know he prefers to be asked rather than being told."

Doc let fly a string of curses. After he shook his head he continued. "I know. And I know you're all about to give up on me. This whole fucked up situation has turned me inside out the last few months."

"You're marrying her and taking responsibility. You have a baby on the way. Does that help to straighten you out or is that going to push you farther over the edge?"

Doc shook his head. "I honestly don't know. But I'm doing the right thing for her."

"As opposed to how you left it with her when you left Africa."

Doc nodded.

"How are things between you and Elizabeth?"

"Awkward as hell. Except when we're in bed."

Lassiter's raised eyebrow gave Doc pause.

Doc rubbed his temples. He hadn't planned to talk with Lassiter about that. It just slipped out. "I told myself I wasn't going to sleep with her last night, but it just kind of happened."

"How did it happen?" Lassiter pressed.

Damned Lassiter. Doc knew he wasn't going to let him get away with anything. Well, technically he had for over two months. "She was cold, showed up here in a lightweight coat. I bought her a good heavy one this morning, and a hat and gloves too. She didn't even have those either. So, last night she asked me to lay with her and hold her, because she was cold."

"And one thing led to another?" Lassiter asked.

"Yeah."

"She's already pregnant with your child, it's not like you could get her anymore pregnant."

Doc shook his head.

"And you're making the marriage legal. She's your wife. Why wouldn't you sleep with her?"

"We were at the mall this morning. She had nothing, showed up with a backpack containing everything she owns. She didn't have many clothes heavy enough for a Chicago winter. I know everyone who saw us was sure I was her father. She's too damned young for me, Joe."

"You are not the only older man who's ever been with a younger woman. I don't understand why this is such an issue for you."

"It just doesn't feel right. I had to convince her to buy nice things. We were in Victoria Secret. I don't think she's ever had bras or panties that weren't white and cheap. I felt like a dirty old man, dressing this young thing up in sexy undergarments for me to take advantage of. It felt disgusting, and I didn't like it."

"Could this be more about you feeling old, than about her youth? You turn forty soon. You're the oldest man on the team, other than Shepherd, and you have had gray in your hair since you were thirty-two. Forty is a number that bothers a lot of men," Lassiter suggested.

"Fuck you," Doc groaned. "And you don't need to remind me about my upcoming birthday."

Lassiter chuckled. Doc just answered his question. "Just think about it. I don't think you have gotten to the root at what's bothering you about the age difference, and since she'll be a part of your life, I think you need to get over it."

"I know I do," Doc agreed. "The thing is, I want to love her. She deserves that. But I don't. I would never have picked someone so young and inexperienced."

"Do you believe love can develop over time?"

"I'm not sure what I believe beyond that I want to do the right thing for her, be there for her and this baby. She said she didn't come expecting anything from me, just thought I had the right to know." He paused and shook his head again. "She would have gone on her way and raised our baby in poverty all by herself."

"So, that's the only reason you stepped up, because it was the right thing to do?"

"I wasn't with Victoria at all during her pregnancy. I was in the Sandbox the entire six months. I'm not going to miss it this time or miss the birth of my child. I guess my reasons are a bit more selfish, not that I didn't know I had to do the right thing for her. It was also that I didn't want to miss this."

"Nothing wrong with that. Nothing wrong with any of this. And for the record, neither Shepherd nor I am ready to give up on you. You've been working through a lot. I told Shepherd immediately after we spoke when you returned from Africa that this was going to take some time."

"I appreciate you didn't tell him what my issues were. I always appreciate that you hold confidences so well. I have to believe that Shepherd would have pushed."

Lassiter laughed. "You know the man well. But don't worry. I can handle him. You have the weekend off. Take the time to get to know Elizabeth and make this new marriage and kid thing a positive for you. And if you find it's pushing you farther over the edge, get your ass back in here and talk with me about it."

Doc laughed. "It's weird. She's a complete stranger in some ways, a close lover in others."

"Have you told Elizabeth about Victoria?" Lassiter asked.

"No," Doc replied softly. "I did tell her the way I acted when we parted was on me, had nothing to do with her and that I am haunted from my past. I'm not ready to tell her about all that yet."

"I'd suggest you don't let it go too long before you have that conversation."

"I know, something else I owe her. I honestly don't even know how to begin all the conversations I need to have with her."

Lassiter nodded. He reached into his desk and pulled out a stack of what looked like playing cards. He handed them to Doc. "It's a game, but I think it could help you, seeing your time with her is limited before this next mission."

Doc turned the cards over, so the underside was visible. He fingered through several, reading the text on each card. They were 'get-to-know-you' questions, favorite food, favorite color, most beloved childhood memories. "I don't get it, scripted conversation?"

Lassiter chuckled. "Prompts to learn things about each other. You can play several ways. Ask each other or guess what each other's right answers could be. You could try to top each other with the most outlandish answers. That's always worth a good laugh. You could even make it more interesting and play the game naked and in bed."

"Jesus, Joe," Doc spat. He handed the cards back.

"Keep them." Lassiter reached into his desk and pulled out a second deck. "These are off-limits questions, for the most honest conversations." He flipped the top card over and read the text. "What did you really think of me the first time you saw me? And if that changed, what made it?"

"Oh, hell no," Doc spat. "I see no reason to tell her I thought she looked like a damned teenager that needed to be grounded or turned over my knee, and not in a sexual way. Nor does she need to know that I still think she looks way too young for me."

"Broaden your thoughts beyond appearances. You saw her as a capable nurse at one point. That would be the focus on what changed and why. It won't hurt to remind yourself what you liked about her by telling her," Lassiter said. "And it might be just what she needs to hear. Challenge yourself to come up with truths that don't focus on the physical or on age."

Doc nodded. Yes, he saw how this could be helpful. He took the second set of cards from Lassiter and slid them into the pocket of his flannel shirt with the first. "I'll give it a shot. You're right that we do need to get to know each other so things aren't so fucking awkward."

"Conversation, lots of conversation," Lassiter said.

"Yeah," Doc agreed.

The moment Doc had been dreading followed shortly thereafter. He went to Angel's desk to get Elizabeth. They returned to his office. Elizabeth picked up her coat and purse from the chair, assuming they were preparing to leave.

Doc halted her. "Elizabeth, there is one more thing." He knew she wouldn't like the idea of it. "Remember when I told you that I have a tracker implanted in my shoulder so that my team would be able to find me at all times?"

Elizabeth nodded.

"It's monitored in Ops. Everyone has one, Shepherd, Yvette, all the team members, even Angel and Sienna. I'd like to implant one in you too, so I know you will always be safe."

Elizabeth shook her head no, immediately. She didn't even have to think about it. "Isn't it enough they track my phone?" Now it made sense what Yvette had been talking about. It wasn't the ID for the phone tracker she had been asking for.

"No, if anything ever happens to you, a perp could separate you from your phone very easily. If you are ever in trouble, I don't ever want to not know where you are. I can't help you if I can't find you."

"No, Alexander. I won't agree to it."

Doc sat, took both her hands, and pulled her into his lap. "Elizabeth, please. I can't do my job unless I know you are being watched out for. This is the only way I will know that you are safe."

"And Angel and Sienna are okay with this?"

"They weren't at first," he admitted. "Sister Bernice John told you that Angel went through a lot, didn't she?"

Elizabeth nodded.

"She could identify the man who was in charge during the bombing at the events center where she worked. We were getting ready to go after him and his group and Angel was put into the Witness Protection Program with the U.S. Marshals. Shepherd went along, to help protect her, because she and Jackson were already together at that point. It was a last-minute decision on Shepherd's part. One of the Marshals sold her out and delivered her right to that man. It was only because of the trackers in them both that we knew something was wrong, the only way we found them, the only reason they are both still alive. We got there just in time to save Shepherd. He'd been shot."

Chills gripped Elizabeth. She didn't know any of that had happened to Angel. She wasn't sure Angel's mother knew the extent of what had happened to her either. "Is that why Shepherd is in the wheelchair?"

"Yes, the bullet fragmented and caused partial paralysis. But had it not been for the trackers, we never would have known they had been moved or to where. Neither of their phones were brought with them."

Elizabeth nodded. "Will you want to put one of these trackers in our baby too?"

"Yeah, I wish I could, but it's not safe to do so in developing muscles. Not till he or she is an adult. We do have other tech, an ankle bracelet that Jackson and Angel's baby wears at all times. We'll have the same thing for our baby."

Elizabeth sat rigid on his lap. She shook her head no again. "I don't like any of this."

"I'm sorry, Elizabeth. I know this is a lot to take in. Most people are lucky enough to not know what dangers are out there. Unfortunately, my group knows all too well, and we have to do what we do to mitigate those dangers for ourselves and those we care about."

Elizabeth's face took on an incredulous expression. "Are there any other surprises? Any other little bits of information that you're going to drop on me? If so, let's get them all out right now."

Doc shook his head. "I'm sorry, Elizabeth. I know this has been a lot. Why do you think I separated myself from you after we were rescued? I know this isn't your world."

"Fine, inject me with it," she said bravely. "This *is* my world now and I need to deal with it. As I told you this morning, I can be okay with all of this, I just need time to get used to it."

He pressed a kiss to her lips. "I know you can. I'll numb the spot with a topical numbing gel and then we'll ice it when we get home."

She nodded.

He took a picture of the serial number on the tracker with his phone to send to Ops after it was successfully installed. Elizabeth gasped out when he injected it into her shoulder. He saw tears in her eyes from the sudden, intense pain, but she bit them back. She handled it like a trooper, and he was proud of her. He'd seen Operators cry from it.

"Roger, Doc," Yvette said. "Receiving the signal."

"Great, thanks Yvette." He discontinued the call. He picked up Elizabeth's coat and held it up for her to slip her arms in. "Come on, let's go home and ice that."

Oscar

Elizabeth appeared in the bedroom doorway and smiled nervously at Doc. "What do you think? Is this outfit appropriate for pizza at your friend's house?"

Doc returned her smile. He hated that he had made her feel insecure about her wardrobe. He noticed that she wore the maternity leggings and the long blue sweater he'd bought her. "You look perfect. Are you warm and comfortable? That's all that matters."

"Yes, I'm glad the salesperson talked me into the leggings. They are very comfortable, and this sweater is so soft and warm. Thank you for buying these for me, Alexander."

He patted the couch beside him. He took hold of her hands when she sat. "You look beautiful and no thanks are needed." He kissed her lips briefly, but passionately. "I'm glad you're here with me. I like you living with me. And I'm happy we're going to go over to be with the team tonight. I know you will like Sienna. She's been good for Garcia."

"Thank you," she said with a genuine smile. "These last few days have been unexpectedly wonderful. I'm going to miss you while you're gone."

"I'll call as often as I can, and we can play some more of those cards." He smiled. They had played for a few hours that afternoon, all the ways Lassiter had suggested. The naked in bed, off-limits questions after they made love led to honest and meaningful conversations. "It'll only be for a couple of weeks." He knew it would be a long few weeks for her and he would be worried about her the whole time he was gone. "Besides, you have your homework to keep you busy while I'm away."

She giggled. She had decided that morning on a college with an extension campus nearby to get her Bachelor of Science in Nursing Degree. While Alexander was away, she would fill out the application and have the transcripts sent from the community college she attended in Seattle. It was too late to start in the few short weeks before the Spring Semester began, but she could enroll at the local community college for the classes she still needed. They even had online courses in many subjects so she wouldn't necessarily have to go to the campus.

Elizabeth felt nervous on the drive to Angel and Jackson's home. She knew it was foolish. They all knew she was pregnant, and Alexander promised her none of them would judge her. And so far, none of them had. Angel surely had not. She seemed genuinely happy for her and Alexander. She'd met everyone who'd be there, except Sienna. So, what was she anxious about? She wished she knew.

She held Alexander's hand as he led her up the sidewalk. It was cold out, but the new coat, hat, scarf, and gloves kept her warm. The front door was cracked open behind the storm door. She watched Alexander open it and push the door in without knocking. He stepped into the entry, pulling her in behind him.

"Hi," he greeted as he stepped into the house. Jackson and Garcia sat on the couch facing the lit, brick fireplace. Angel and Sienna were in the kitchen behind them. He held up the six pack of beer he'd brought. "As requested."

"Very good," Jackson said, coming to his feet. He took the beer from him. "Thanks for stopping to get it. I thought I had enough, or I would have picked up more on my way home." He pointed to the railing on the staircase that led to the second floor. "Just throw your coats there."

Doc took Elizabeth's coat and dropped it and his over the railing. He took his boots off and stepped into the living room. Elizabeth did the same and followed. Angel and Sienna met them halfway. Sienna greeted her with a hug as did Angel.

"We're having wine," Angel told Elizabeth, "but I have soda."

"Just a glass of water is fine," Elizabeth said.

Angel got a glass from the cabinet. "Ice?"

"Yes, please," Elizabeth replied. "That was something I really missed while I was in Africa, really cold water." Baby Sammy was seated in his highchair. Elizabeth approached him. "Hello there little one."

"You can take him out of his highchair. He just finished eating. He should be ready to go down for the night after Madison and Cooper get here. They would be mad if I put him down before they arrived."

Elizabeth took the baby into her arms. She felt over Sammy's ankles. Beneath one of his little blue socks she felt the bulge from the metal. She pulled the sock off and examined the beautiful, stainless steel ankle bracelet. The chain was a rugged serpentine pattern and there was a rounded plate with the inscription, 'Mommy's Angel'.

"I wish the tracker could be below his skin, like ours are," Angel said, much to Elizabeth's surprise. "I have nightmares he gets taken, and the perps cut the anklet from him and we can't find him."

"I'm sorry," Elizabeth said, replacing the sock. "Alexander just told me about the trackers yesterday. I wanted to see what it looked like. I should have asked first."

Angel took Sammy from Elizabeth and pulled the sock back from his little foot, holding his leg out towards Elizabeth. "It's unobtrusive, a cute design, and it keeps him safe. Michaela at the office adds links as it gets snug. There is no clasp so someone would have to cut it off. If anything ever happens to him, that would buy us some time to find him."

"Alexander told me our child will have the same tracker."

Angel nodded. "How does your shoulder feel? Yours got injected yesterday, didn't it?"

"It's just a little sore." Elizabeth's eyes went between Angel and Sienna. "I still don't like the idea of it, but Alexander insisted he'd do nothing but worry about me if I didn't have it."

"Just like Angel, I thanked God they put it in me. I'm not sure I'd be here now, if I didn't have it," Sienna said.

Garcia came up behind Sienna on his way to the refrigerator to get another beer. He wrapped his arms around her and nuzzled his head against hers. "You'd be here with me no matter what, sweetheart." He pressed a kiss to her cheek.

"Trust us," Angel said. "The tracker is a good thing. I hope the day never comes when you need them to find you, but if it does, you're covered."

The front door opened, and Madison and Cooper came through. After they both hugged baby Sammy, Angel carried him upstairs to put him to bed. The others all settled on the couch and the chairs in the living room, beverages in hand.

"What do you like on your pizza, Elizabeth?" Jackson asked, his cell phone in hand. "I know what everyone else likes. We're ordering an extra-large veggie for the girls, a second all meat extra-large for the rest of us except Garcia who eats his with ham and pineapple." He shook his head and pretended to stick his finger down his throat while making a barfy-face.

"Hey, hey, don't knock it till you've tried it. You've never even had a bite of the very yummy Hawaiian Pizza," Garcia said, pointing at Jackson.

The others laughed.

"There will be more than enough if anyone wants to try a piece," Garcia offered. He was getting a large so he would have leftovers for lunch all weekend.

"There is more than enough of all the pies we are ordering, but if you want anything special, let me know, Elizabeth," Jackson said.

"I think, if it is alright, that I'd like to try a little of each. I've only had cheese pizza before, but I like most foods."

Doc was sure that she'd only had cheese pizza because the cost of toppings was extra. "Perfect," he said nodding at Jackson to speed this along. He didn't want her to feel self-conscious that she'd never had pizza with toppings.

Jackson ordered the pizzas. Delivery would be in forty minutes. Angel rejoined them as all the men opened their wallets and handed bills over to Jackson to cover the cost of the pizzas. She had the baby monitor in her hand. She sat it on the fireplace mantel.

"Shepherd approved Elizabeth training to help cover the public reception desk," Cooper said.

"Fantastic!" Angel said.

"Shepherd authorized up to thirty hours each week for the next three weeks," Cooper added.

"We'll come up with a training schedule," Angel said, her eyes on Elizabeth.

"I'll have to check the bus schedule to see what times work."

"The bus schedule?" Angel asked. "Doc, you'll leave your car for her, won't you?"

"I don't drive," Elizabeth said.

"You don't have a driver's license?" Sienna asked, surprised.

"No, but I know there is a city bus. There is a stop only a block away from the condo. I can figure out transfers. I know there is a stop near the office. I'll be fine."

Garcia, Cooper and Jackson's heads snapped to view Doc. They all knew him well enough to know that she would not be taking the city bus. When he said nothing, the three men exchanged surprised glances. Each of them wanted to say something, but knew it was not their place. Cooper though, planned to talk with Doc about it privately. She absolutely should not be taking the city bus. She had to get her driver's license.

"Why don't you stay with me in our guest room while they are away on the mission?" Sienna asked. "Angel and I spend a lot of time together in the evening when they're gone. You can hang out with us."

"Thank you, but that's not necessary," Elizabeth said.

"No, that's a great idea," Angel jumped in. "It'll be easier. Since you'll be working at the office, you can just ride in with me."

"And in the evenings, you can help me grade papers. I've always taught kindergarten, prior to this year. There is a lot of prep work in kindergarten, but not much evening grading. This year I'm teaching fourth grade, and let me tell you, the amount of homework I have every night is astounding. I could really use your help."

"Unless you'd rather be at the condo to get settled in," Angel offered.

Elizabeth's eyes flickered to Alexander. She felt she should have approval before she answered.

"Actually, I was thinking Elizabeth and I should move into the neighborhood, for this very reason," Doc said. It bothered him that Elizabeth looked to him, rather than answering. They would have to talk about that. He wanted her to know that he supported whatever she wanted to do. She didn't need to ask his permission for anything. "Well for Elizabeth to be near the two of you when we go on a mission and because this is a good neighborhood for kids."

"And your place is only a one bedroom," Angel said. "You absolutely are going to have to move. I'll keep my ears open for anyone who is going to sell, Maybe I can find you a unit before it's listed with a realtor and save you a commission."

"I will too," Sienna said. "Several of the teachers at school live in the area. I'll put the word out with them too."

"That would be great," Doc said. "And Sienna, that is a very kind offer for Elizabeth to stay with you." He took hold of Elizabeth's hand. "I think it's a great idea, honey, but it's your choice. You could get to know both Sienna and Angel better and help Sienna with the papers she has to grade at night."

"You can stay here too," Angel said. "But you'd probably sleep better at Sienna's. Sammy is cutting some teeth and has been up crying half the night the last week."

Elizabeth smiled politely. "You are both very kind. I'd like that and it would make a lot of things much easier."

"Yes, it will," Doc agreed. He gave Sienna a wink. "I can drop her by on the way to the office Monday morning. We have to be in by zero-six-hundred, way before Angel gets in."

"Plan on picking me up," Garcia said. "We can ride in together."

"Hey, while they're gone, let's do a spa day next weekend. I can see if my aunt will babysit Sammy," Angel suggested excitedly. "Doc, you better leave her an extra five-hundred for it."

"No freaking way!" Madison exclaimed. "You are not going without me. Wait till we're back."

Angel laughed. "Will you be back by the following weekend?"

"The mission may run into it. Make the reservations for three weeks out, please! We'll do a full day with the lunch special. I love those little finger sandwiches they serve," Madison said.

Elizabeth didn't say a word. A whole day at a spa that would cost five hundred dollars? No, she would not be attending.

"My highlights could use refreshing," Sienna said, running her fingers through her shoulder-length brown hair. Her eyes landed on Elizabeth. She looked like she needed some convincing. "Your ends could use a trim, too. We normally get manicures and pedicures, facials, massages, and get our hair done. And they always do our makeup too."

"Oh, yes, please," Cooper said. "The last time you ladies went; Madison came home with every inch of her body incredibly soft from whatever lotion or oil they massage you with."

Madison laughed. "I'll want to go out for dinner that night. I'll have them give my hair a blowout. We won't be spending the afternoon and night in bed again."

"Blondie, you come home looking and feeling as sexy as you did last time and I'm not going to be capable of letting you out of bed." He laughed and hugged her affectionately.

Elizabeth sat silent as the others laughed. Wow, she would never have guessed from how these two interacted in Africa that they had this type of relationship.

"I'll tell you what, you add in a Brazilian wax and we'll go out for dinner," Cooper suggested, with a sly grin on his lips.

"*I'll tell you what*, you get one first without crying like a baby, and then I'll get one," Madison countered.

Now everyone roared with laughter, everyone but Elizabeth.

Angel's laughing eyes settled on Elizabeth. "Sorry, you probably don't know what that is, do you?" She brought her phone up to her face, Googled it, and handed it over to Elizabeth. "I forgot you have spent the last three years in a remote village in Africa. Plus, my mom wouldn't know what it is, either."

Elizabeth read the description. "Oh, good heavens. People pay to have this done to themselves?" Her eyes popped up and scanned the group. "And people provide this service, doing this to complete strangers?"

Everyone laughed. Doc embraced her. "Shocking isn't it? No one is coming anywhere near my ass with hot wax!"

They laughed even harder. This time Elizabeth joined in. From that point on, Elizabeth felt more relaxed. The pizza arrived, and she tried a piece of each kind, deciding she liked the Hawaiian the best.

"Finally," Garcia said, reaching his fist towards Elizabeth.

She laughed and tapped his fist with hers. She had seen the men do fist bumps, so she knew what to do. "Yes, none of you know what you're missing. Ham and pineapple are great on the pizza."

The others scoffed at that.

"I know what we should do. We make dinner reservations for the eight of us after our spa appointments and we will meet you guys there," Madison said. "Angel do get in touch with your aunt and arrange to have Jackson drop Sammy there on his way to the restaurant. That way we all get a night out."

"Really, you get a spa day and I have to get all dressed up too?" Cooper moaned.

Everyone but Elizabeth knew he was just giving Madison a hard time.

"Yes, and we both know you compete with me for who looks prettier when we get all dressed up." She turned to Elizabeth. "Don't let him fool you. This man right here primps more than any woman!"

"Primps? I beg your pardon," Cooper disagreed.

He was answered by the other men agreeing with Madison.

When the evening was over and they left, it was with hugs all around. Elizabeth was looking forward to her stay with Sienna and her training with Angel at the office. "I had a good time tonight," Elizabeth told Alexander after they backed out of the driveway.

"The Cooper and Madison show is all in fun. I should have warned you," Doc said.

"I don't understand," Elizabeth confessed.

"When away from work, Cooper and Madison trade barbs like that all the time. They entertain the rest of us, that's for sure. As far as dinner out, all Madison has to do is suggest it and Cooper is all over it. He does anything she wants. As far as I know, he's never told her no to anything. His moaning and groaning about getting dressed up was all for show."

"They were completely different in Africa."

Doc laughed. "Yeah, when on duty or at the office no one would even guess they are together. I surely didn't and when it came out that they were in a relationship, you could have knocked me over with a feather. That was a huge breach in protocol, and I was really pissed at them both. But once I saw they could keep it separate, and I saw how deeply they cared for each other; I respected their relationship."

"So, their relationship broke the rules?"

"Yep. So did Jackson and Angel's, Garcia and Sienna's, and ours. There has always been a no fraternization policy. No involvement with anyone associated with a mission, and no relationships between agency personnel."

"But no one has gotten into trouble?"

Doc shrugged. "That depends on your definition of in trouble. It's frowned upon. Shepherd has considered each breach on its own merits. Any of us could have been fired for our actions. Thankfully, Shepherd hasn't fired anyone yet."

Elizabeth considered that for a moment. That spoke volumes to her how much each of the other couples truly loved each other. To risk their jobs to be with the person they loved was inspirational. Alexander risked his job for her too. It gave her hope that she and Alexander would feel that way about each other someday.

"Are you excited about the spa day you girls have planned?" Alexander asked, breaking in on her thoughts.

She glanced at him. The oncoming cars headlights illuminated his handsome face. "I will not be going and spending that much money."

His head jerked to view her. "Elizabeth, of course you are." He brought his eyes back to the road. "We're not having the same money conversation again." He felt himself losing patience with her.

"Five hundred dollars for one day! That is a sin, Alexander."

"I'm pretty sure it's not a sin, not any more than masturbation is."

"It's widely accepted that self-pleasure is sinful."

"Elizabeth, you're not a Sister any longer." He regretted the words as soon as they left his mouth. "What I mean to say is, women go to the spa. They spend money, a lot of money on themselves. It's not something you do every day, it's something special. I spend a hell of a lot more than that on my fishing gear and trips. Spending money to enjoy life is what normal people do. It's why we work hard."

"You want me to spend that much money on getting my hair done and other frivolous things?"

Doc laughed. "I want you to go out with the ladies and have a wonderful day. Try it. If you don't enjoy it, you don't ever have to go again, but I don't want your decision to be based on cost." He reached over and took hold of her hand. "Look, Elizabeth, I want you to make your own decisions on things. You don't need to ask me permission for anything, but I don't want you deciding not to do anything based on cost."

"I've never done any of those things, a massage, a manicure, or pedicure," she admitted after a few quiet seconds. "My mom trimmed my hair. After she was gone, I learned how to do it for myself."

"Then it's high time you experience them. I love a good massage. I think you might too."

Elizabeth gazed out the window feeling even more different. Every time she thought she would fit in; she was reminded she was not like Alexander and his friends. She felt Alexander squeeze her hand.

"Elizabeth, it's okay that you've never done any of those things, just don't let that fact stop you from trying them."

Without turning to look at him she nodded her head yes.

They were stopped at a red light. Doc saw her head nod and was concerned because she had her head turned away. "Honey," he said, pulling on her hand. Her head snapped back, her gaze on him. She looked sad. He forced a smile. "I want you to try everything. I want you to enjoy your life and not let anything stop you from becoming the person you were always meant to be. I happen to think you are pretty special. You're my wife and will be the mother of my child. I don't want to see you sad for any reason."

Tears flooded Elizabeth's eyes even though she tried desperately not to cry. "You don't understand what it's like to not have any money, Alexander. My mom did the best she could. We didn't have material things, but we never lacked love and attention from her. My mom would never understand all the money you spent on this coat or the clothes for me and she certainly wouldn't understand five hundred dollars for spa appointments all in one day. I'm embarrassed by how much of your money has been spent on me."

"Then I am very sorry she is gone because I would have done the same for her just because she was your mother. And you're right. I don't know what it's like. There was only one time in my life finances were tight and that was over fifteen years ago. Please do not be embarrassed. That is not my intention. I honestly haven't thought twice about it."

His words made Elizabeth cry harder. He was so generous. She believed him, believed he would have spent his money on her mother too. "I'm sorry. I am trying to not think about the cost of things. This isn't my world."

"It is now, honey," he said squeezing her hand again. "Please don't cry. I had a good time with you tonight. I don't want our night out to end this way."

"I had a good time too. I really like everyone."

"It was very nice of Sienna to invite you to stay with her while we are away. I'm glad you will be with both her and Angel. I won't worry about you as much with you there." Elizabeth didn't say anything when he paused. "I hope I didn't twist your arm too much to agree to it. I noticed you didn't give her an answer until I said something."

"I wanted to be sure it was all right with you before I agreed."

"Elizabeth, listen to me. You don't ever need my permission for anything."

Papa

"I'll miss you," Elizabeth whispered when their lips parted.

"I'll call and text when I can. I don't expect we'll go dark during the first week, but you never know," Doc replied. It was zero-five-thirty. He glanced out the windshield at Garcia and Sienna's front door. He placed one more kiss on her lips and then nodded towards the house.

He grabbed her over-stuffed backpack, the laptop case for the new laptop he'd bought her the day before, and the bag of perishable groceries they'd packed up. He held her hand, walking her to the front door. A fine dusting of fresh snow coated everything. Garcia opened the door as they neared.

"Morning," Garcia greeted sleepily. He took the backpack from Doc. "I'll run this up to the guest room." He pointed to the kitchen. "Sienna's still in the shower, but coffee is on if you want a cup, Elizabeth." He had a travel mug in his hand.

"No, thank you. I generally have herbal tea. I brought my own."

"Make yourself at home and open the cabinets to find a mug if you want to make yourself a cup." Then he disappeared up the stairs.

Elizabeth glanced around. This unit was very similar to Angel and Jackson's home in its layout. They were both end units.

When Garcia came back down the stairs, a large chocolate lab trotted down the stairs beside him. "Hope you're not allergic to dogs. I don't think we mentioned Bailey."

Elizabeth put her hand down for the dog to sniff and then she patted the dog's head. "No, I'm not. He or she is beautiful."

"She, and yes, she is a sweetie," Garcia agreed. "Come on girl, let's go out." He brought her to the sliding glass door in the kitchen, opened it and sent her out alone into the small, fenced-in backyard. "You don't have to go out with her, and she will go to the door and bark when she has to go out."

"Got it," Elizabeth said from within the kitchen. She found the mugs and selected one. She dropped the tea bag in and filled it with tap water.

"Go ahead and put the food away in the fridge anyplace you find space." Doc had texted Garcia and told him they would bring the perishable food items from the condo with them. After a few minutes he went to the kitchen door and let the dog in, using the towel that hung from a hook beside it to wipe her feet. "Anyway, make yourself at home. Sienna will be down in about a half-hour." He put on his coat and picked up his multiple bags from the couch.

Doc gave Elizabeth one more kiss as Garcia gathered his gear. And then the two of them left, closing the door behind them. Elizabeth watched the headlights of Alexander's car retreat down the driveway through the open blinds on the front window. She stood at the window watching its taillights as the car pulled away until it was out of sight.

When her tea was done, she sat on the couch and turned the television on. She liked to watch the news in the morning. Bailey jumped on the couch and settled in beside her. "I sure hope you're allowed up here."

A half-hour later, Sienna came down the stairs wearing a robe and with a towel wrapped around her wet head. Her makeup was on, Elizabeth noticed, and she held a coffee mug in her hand. "Good morning," Sienna greeted. "Good, I see you've made yourself at home."

"Good morning, yes, thank you."

Sienna patted Bailey's head as she walked by. "I just need a refill on coffee while I finish getting ready for school. I leave around seven-fifteen. I'll show you your room before I leave and make sure you are logged into the internet. You're not going into the office with Angel until tomorrow, right?"

"No, not till tomorrow. Are you sure you don't mind me just hanging out all day here?"

Sienna laughed. "Not at all. You can let Bailey in and out and make sure she has plenty of water. She'll love the company."

Elizabeth's hand stroked over her soft fur. "She's a sweetie."

Sienna turned back, filled cup in hand. "She is. I'll be home for lunch. I always come home to let her out."

"Let me know what time and I'll make us lunch," Elizabeth offered.

"That would be great, thank you, but don't go to too much trouble. I usually just have a sandwich, soup, or a salad. Make yourself at home and feel free to rummage through any cabinets for whatever you need." She disappeared back up the stairs.

Doc sipped his coffee, his eyes on the large monitor mounted on the wall. Montana in the dead of winter! Whose fucked-up idea was it to accept this case in January? Of course, the client had approached them in December, and they'd put him off this long, not that December would have been any better.

"As you all know, Rick Walters and his wife Janey, the owners, will be the only people who will know who we are, besides our liaison at the Department of Defense," Cooper said. "Rick is the president and Janey is the head of HR. It's a privately-owned company, structured as a partnership with the two of them, so there is no board of directors or anyone else to have to deal with."

"On the flight out, make sure you familiarize yourself with the newest information we just received from the client and from what Ops has dug up on the original audit team and on the organization's competitors. It's been pushed through to your tablets. You've all had enough time to read the packet on the facility, the inhouse suspects, and your covers, so we won't go over that," Shepherd added. Then his eyes fixed on Doc. "Your role will be key, Doc. None of their employee screening records are online. They are all in paper files only, so Ops couldn't look at any of them. You need to audit one hundred percent of the files and meet as many employees as you can to verify."

Doc nodded. "I'll work closely with Jackson and cross-reference them against the HR records as well."

Shepherd nodded. It was good to have Doc back focused.

"Shepherd, what has the original DoD Audit Team been told?" Jackson asked.

"Just that they were pulled off this audit for several higher priority DoD Audits and this one was outsourced as it was classified as low priority due to their clean audit history. Their schedules have been booked out for the next six months."

"The Department of Defense takes audit interference very seriously. Blackmailing a DoD supplier with threats of making them fail a crucial audit could put inferior equipment in the hands of our soldiers. And if the Tango actually has the ability to tamper with the audit results, not only is that serious, but it will disqualify Walters Tactical Equipment from retaining its current DoD contracts, which will put them out of business," Cooper added.

"Our clients, the Walters', took an enormous risk by contacting us and refusing to pay the blackmail per our instructions. Let's figure this one out folks. Miller passed her DoD audit paperwork, so this audit will be official. Good work, Miller. In addition to that, she and Garcia did a lot over the last month to get this one ready. Smith and Trio will stay on it from here while you're on site," Shepherd said.

Garcia nodded. Good. Caleb Smith had good digital recon skills. He was most valuable in that capacity. He'd been pulled into the role of an Ops analyst, but behind the scenes was more his forte. He'd helped with a good deal of the info on competitors that they had dug up as well as helped test the Walters Tactical Equipment firewall for a way in. They hadn't found one. Their security appeared adequate, but Garcia and his team would continue to test that.

"So, Delta will remain at HQ the entire time we are out?" Madison asked.

Shepherd nodded. "With three of you who man Ops out, I need Mother and Lambchop to pull shifts. Plus, Delta's been in the field nearly nonstop since last July, except over the holidays. They're due to receive training updates and they need to hit the range and requalify with weapons."

"Their next mission is pending, so the quicker we can wrap this up, the better," Cooper added. "We booked two weeks for this, because that is the on-site timeframe of a normal audit."

"When you finish it, provided they pass and you haven't identified a suspect, it will get submitted up through the normal channels and we'll see if it changes before it reaches audit oversight."

Doc saw the frown on Shepherd's lips as he spoke. The man would be very disappointed if the blackmailer was part of the DoD audit chain. But at least they'd know.

"Okay, that's it. Go get them," Shepherd said. "Requisition Ryan has packed you the ammo for sidearms and ARs only."

Alpha Team stood and filed out of the room. After gathering their gear from the Team Room, they went out to the garage and the awaiting SUVs. They loaded the back ends with their gear and fifteen minutes later the two vehicles were driving towards the rising sun and their hangar at the Chicago Executive Airport.

Cooper glanced sideways at Doc. "You aren't really going to let Elizabeth take a city bus, are you?"

Doc smirked. His eyes flickered over his shoulder to Madison, who sat in the backseat behind Cooper. "Madison, I know you don't know her well, but what do you think Elizabeth's reaction would be if I tell her what she can and cannot do?"

Madison laughed out loud. "Yeah, Coop, that would not go over well."

"Our relationship is complicated," Doc said after a few quiet seconds. "Not only is she using these two weeks we are gone to train at the office, she's applying to a nursing school for the fall semester, registering at the local community college for a couple of classes she needs before she can start her bachelor's program, and she's studying the rules of the road. When I get back, I hope she can pass the test for her temporary driver's license. I'll then teach her to drive."

"That's ambitious, but it doesn't explain the city bus thing," Cooper remarked.

"She's been resistant to some of my suggestions. I've gone through Angel and Sienna to nudge her. She's got this enormous chip on her shoulder about spending my money and fending for herself. She's always taken public transportation, doesn't see anything wrong with it. I can't very well diss it or issue orders that she can't use it, so I've figured out a way to operate around her very stubborn personality."

Now, the corner of Cooper's lips twisted into a smirk. "So, Sienna's invitation to stay with her?"

"Yes, it was something I spoke with Garcia about prior to pizza night. What, do you think I'm crazy? That I'd leave her at my place for two weeks alone? And have her take public transportation everywhere she needed to go." Doc shook his head. "No way in hell was that going to happen."

Cooper laughed. It was good to have the old Doc back. More than that, with Doc in a relationship, the same as the rest of them, it brought a greater level of connection back to the team. He'd noticed that Friday night. He knew Doc had felt like the third wheel whenever they were all together, the only one without a woman. He hoped this would solve all the issues that had Doc out of sorts since the mission to Africa.

The team arrived on site at the large structure that housed the Walters Tactical Equipment Company later that afternoon, identifying themselves as the DoD Audit Team that was expected. The receptionist brought them to the main conference room, where they waited for Rick and Janey Walters.

They came through the door together, an unlikely couple. Rick, a tough ex-Marine, still rough around the edges. He was clothed in worn blue jeans and a waffle-weave Henley beneath a flannel shirt, both rolled up to reveal thick forearms covered in tattoos. Janey, an aging former beauty queen was decked out to the nines in a deep purple suit with a black silk blouse beneath. Her blond hair was worn long and loose, her makeup applied professionally.

After introductions all around, they got down to business. "You have access to anything you want," Rick said. "Just get this bastard who's threatened to put us out of business."

Janey laid her perfectly manicured hand to her husband's forearm. "Rick, we don't know it is any of our employees. I still believe a competitor is a more likely suspect." Her voice was laced with a southern accent.

"Well, whoever it is, we'll do our best to find them. Those in the DoD audit stream are even suspect at this point," Cooper said.

"This conference room has been blocked out for your team's use for the next two weeks, which is what we would normally do for the regular auditors. We've had the same team here the last four years, have even had them out to the house for dinner. I have a really hard time believing it could be any of them," Janey said. "One of them, even reached out to us when they were reassigned and offered his help if we needed it with the new audit team."

Cooper and Madison exchanged glances. He took the information on which member had contacted them. He'd have HQ run that person to ground. "We'll see what we turn up and will keep you informed."

The team got to work. Each person was strategically deployed to different areas of the company to gather records to audit. Doc was sent to audit the medical division and its ongoing drug screening program. Madison, in her short, tight, skirt was sent to the QC area of the manufacturing floor on purpose to interface with the completely male team. Garcia of course would conduct the IT Audit. Cooper went to the accounts payable/accounts receivable area to conduct a thorough financial audit. And Jackson went with Janey to HR to pull all HR and hiring records.

Later that evening, after the team returned to the hotel where they were staying, Doc called Elizabeth. It was late in Chicago and he hoped he wouldn't wake her.

"Hi, I was hoping you'd call," her cheerful voice answered.

"Hi, yourself. I'm glad I didn't wake you."

"No, I just came up to my room. Sienna wasn't kidding when she said how much homework she has every night. After we had dinner with Angel and visited with her for a while, we graded papers for over two hours!"

Doc chuckled. And he had been worried about Elizabeth? She sounded happy and was kept busy. "So, you had a good day then?"

Elizabeth went on to tell Doc about her day in detail. He laid on the bed listening to her with a smile on his face the entire time. He was impressed how much of her to-do list she had gotten done while Sienna was at school all day. She recounted how she had conversations with both Angel and Sienna through text-messages all day. She loved Sienna's dog and felt very comfortable at Sienna and Garcia's house.

Doc recounted his day without giving any details or using any names. "I hope this can be wrapped up sooner than two weeks, but it doesn't look promising."

"It's okay. I understand. This is your job, Alexander. I know you will be away a lot. I can be okay with this."

Doc chuckled. "I know you can. And this one isn't dangerous. I don't want you to worry about me." He knew the potential for danger was always there and the team would be on guard, but he wasn't in a war zone, there were no enemy hostiles identified, and no one was shooting at them.

"That's what Angel said. She promised me that you guys all look out for each other and that you all have had the best training. She really has faith in the team."

"She's not wrong," Doc said. "Before I go, I wanted to wish you luck tomorrow. You'll be working at the office tomorrow, won't you?"

"Yes. I'm very excited. And then after work, Angel is going to bring me to the community college. I have to be there in person to sign some things and buy my books. I did decide to take both classes online. I don't like the idea of committing to be there during set times. Angel helped convince me that when you are home, I'll want to be with you rather than sitting in class."

Doc's lips pulled into a smile. "I like that. I'll be gone for work a lot Elizabeth but when I'm home, I will want to spend the time with you."

"I was really disappointed when you told me you would be going out of town for work right away when I first got here, but I'm okay with this. The fact that you can call me while you're gone, makes it okay."

"I will try to every day. Hey, before I go, let's play a card," Doc said. "One from my deck." He had the off-limits questions. She had the get-to-know-you deck.

"Okay," she agreed excitedly. She sat up and crossed her legs beneath herself on the bed.

Doc had read through them all and strategically selected this one. He didn't need to read it from the card. He had it memorized. "Fast forward one year from today. We're having this conversation under these same circumstances. Tell me what you envision our lives to look like different from today."

Elizabeth giggled. "Well, our baby would be six months old. You're away on a mission, and he or she is sleeping in their crib in their own room. We live on the same block as Angel and Sienna. I'm home at our place, but we had dinner over at Angel's because the team is away."

Doc waited. When she said no more, he took his turn. "I've been looking at pictures on my phone of you and our baby all day, missing you. You are the perfect wife for my job, and you are an amazing mother to our child. I never worry about you when I'm gone because I know you can handle anything that comes your way."

Elizabeth smiled wide into her phone. "I like the confidence you have in me. I like what our future looks like, Alexander." She felt her emotions trying to take over. She'd never been an emotional mess like she had become since getting pregnant, stupid hormones!

"Me too," he said.

She swallowed her emotions. The phone line had been quiet for long enough that it felt awkward. "I should go. I have to get up early for work tomorrow."

"Sleep well," he said. "And have a good day."

"Good night," she replied.

She stared at her phone long after she'd disconnected. It was senseless, but she already missed him. She'd only slept beside him the last five nights, but the thought of laying in this bed alone felt wrong. A small smile came to her lips as she remembered it wasn't just lying in bed with him. It was making love, as they had every night and every morning since she'd been there. It was snuggling with him and the incredible sensation of safety that surrounded her as surely as his arms did.

Alpha Team's first four days on site were routine. They were settling in, pulling records, meeting the employees. Late in the afternoon that fourth day, they settled around the conference room table. Cooper sighed in disgust and threw the file he was reviewing over to Madison. "I need you to double check my calculations. Unless my math is way off, I have no idea how Rick and Janey are making payroll. Their bids on these contracts were so low, I don't see how they are turning a profit."

The others all gazed at him in surprise.

"They pay their people above average wages. Janey says it's to retain good help and reduce turnover, and it must be working, they haven't lost a single employee to anything but retirement in two years," Jackson said.

"They've increased staff, doubling it every two years since getting the government contracts," Doc added. "First, they added a second manufacturing and QA shift, and last year they added a third shift."

"Janey's talking about a swing shift to be added next year in the shipping and receiving department," Jackson informed them.

"The numbers aren't adding up," Cooper said with a headshake. "Something is very wrong, and I would think it would have been obvious last year when the auditors were here too."

Madison dug into the financial records Cooper had reviewed for the next hour and had Garcia do some digging into their bank records too. "Coop's right. The numbers don't shake out. Garcia went back before they bid on the first government contract, and there was a huge infusion of cash into the business accounts six months before the first contract was awarded to them. They've been drawing that balance down, but the way they have tried to cover it with the internal transfers is suspicious."

"Very suspicious," Garcia agreed.

"Would that be enough to cause them to fail the audit?" Jackson asked.

"It's a question and a conversation in the very least," Cooper replied. "But if there is anything sketchy about the financing, yeah, that would be enough."

"So, the auditors on site prior years should have noticed it?" Jackson asked.

"Given that a CPA was on site as part of the audit team, I would think so. I'm okay with numbers, but the guy with the DoD has a master's in forensic accounting. I would think he would have figured it out a lot faster than I did," Cooper said. He ran his hand through his short-clipped hair re-spiking the front. "Doc, Jackson, are you sure the staffing has been as consistent as it looks?"

Doc and Jackson exchanged glances. "Well, we haven't met the crews on second or third shift yet, but on paper, it all looks right," Doc said. "The one thing that doesn't seem plausible is the one-hundred percent clean piss tests. No company attains that. There's always one or two fuck ups who don't think they're going to get popped."

"Is their screening completely at random?"

"It appears to be. I found no discernable pattern," Doc answered.

"And not to judge books by their covers, but more than a few of their employees look like stoners," Jackson said. "One guy even has cannabis leaves tattooed on his neck." He selected the proper HR file and tossed it to Cooper. "Third shift guy."

Cooper opened the file and laughed out loud. He held the picture up for the others to see.

"No arrest record on him," Jackson added.

Cooper chuckled. "That's hard to believe." His eyes settled on Garcia. "Have you verified fingerprints to names and database records?"

"That was the first thing I did. These employees shake out to who they're supposed to be, verified through outside sources. I ran everyone through the Nationwide Criminal with SSN Trace with Alias Database, the Sex Offender Registry, the Global Criminal Watch List, the Federal Criminal Database. I also ran everyone for Nationwide Wants and Warrants, and through CODIS and AFIS."

Cooper shook his head again. Doc could tell he was getting frustrated. "Anything else suspicious?"

"Just that no one has hit on me," Madison said. "My short-skirted ass has walked all over that manufacturing floor and not a single man has even flirted with me." She shrugged. "Maybe I'm losing my sex appeal."

"Never!" Cooper said with an exaggerated expression of disbelief on his face.

"I'd like Jackson and me to confront Janey Walters on the clean piss tests," Doc said.

Cooper nodded. "I say we divide the Walters' up and confront them both with the same questions to see what answers we get."

They spent the next twenty minutes scripting out the questions each team would ask the separated couple. Cooper, Madison, and Garcia would grill Rick while Doc and Jackson would have a not so routine HR meeting with Janey. Their questions would be identical and then the team would meet after to compare notes.

It was after hours when the team found the Walters' getting ready to leave for the day. The team insisted on meeting with them each, right then and there. After their meetings with each, they reconvened.

"Rick claims to know nothing about anything HR related," Cooper said.

"And Janey has the same ignorance regarding R&D and the manufacturing process," Jackson replied.

"I don't believe either of them," Garcia said. "I don't teach fourth grade, but I can tell you everything about Sienna's job."

"Unless they don't talk about work after they are home," Doc suggested.

"Come on, Madison and I never stop discussing work."

"I don't think it's possible to work together and not talk about it when your home," Madison agreed.

They went over the answers to the questions, one by one.

"Rick can describe how the random piss tests are determined but said the company doctor is in charge of collecting them and sending them to the offsite laboratory," Cooper said.

"Hum, that's odd. Janey said she's in charge of pulling the names every week for the tests, but she is not present for them. That's left to the company doctor. And the company doctor, Dr. Rod Stanley, is the one who runs the tests. They don't get sent offsite," Jackson said.

"I'd like to interview the good doctor first thing tomorrow morning and see what he says," Doc said. "There's something about the guy I don't like."

Cooper nodded. "Do it."

"What don't you like about him?" Madison asked. This was the first they were hearing about Doc's feeling.

"I can't put my finger on it. He has been cooperative, opened all the records to me, answered all my questions. But he's downplayed his role, minimized how much he does, referred to himself as a dispenser of Tylenol as his main function. Most doctors don't do that."

"Come to think of it," Jackson said, "that's another thing that is odd. Their safety record is too good. Not a single Work-Comp claim in three years. I wish I would have thought about that before we interviewed the owners."

"We can go back at them with that one in the next round. I have a feeling we will be talking with them again," Cooper said. His gaze went back to Jackson and Doc. "Rick explained the cash infusion just over four years ago as inheritance money invested in the business so they could go after government contracts, knew it was the only way to be solvent enough to qualify. He anticipated a few years of loss based on their bids."

"Janey stated nearly the same thing, but she didn't call it an inheritance. She called it her mamma's money," Doc said, feigning Janey's southern accent on the last two words. He chuckled.

Garcia clicked the keys on his laptop. A few seconds later he looked up. "Janey Walters' mamma is alive and well in a retirement villa in Naples, Florida."

"Inheritance, my ass!" Madison exclaimed. "These clients of ours are either stupid or under the influence of something if they think they can slip all of this past us."

"Oh, and Miss Janey claims they have an aggressive anti-drug education policy. That is why no one has gotten popped," Doc said. "Their employees just don't use, plain and simple." His voice easily shifted to the southern accent again.

Garcia let out a sarcastic sound. "Every company has employees that use. Cannabis leaves tat-guy smokes. I guarantee you."

"You need to be with Doc and Jackson when they meet the remainder of the employees. I want you to take a few smoke breaks with every shift too. You better stop and get a pack on the way back to the hotel tonight," Cooper ordered. "And while you're at it, be a pig regarding Madison too. See if any of the guys jump on your bandwagon. My wife is hot. No one flirting with her or hitting on her is beyond suspicious."

Everyone laughed.

"And wear a short-sleeved shirt tomorrow so your tats show, and no tie," Cooper added. "The more you can look like one of them, the better the chance you have that someone will get comfortable and slip up."

Garcia nodded.

"Let's get out of here," Cooper ordered, coming to his feet. "We'll be back at zero-five-hundred. I want us to come in, unannounced, during the last few hours of third shift."

Quebec

Doc rode with Garcia on the way back to the hotel. It was past nineteen-hundred hours. The convenience store he would stop in was beside a salad and sandwich shop. That was what Doc wanted for dinner, a salad with grilled chicken atop it. They had been eating unhealthy fare the last few days. Lunch had been pizza ordered in.

"When next you talk to Sienna, thank her for me. Elizabeth has enjoyed staying with her and helping her grade her papers. I really appreciate her having Elizabeth. I would have worried too much about her had she stayed alone at my condo."

"No worries," Garcia said. "Sienna has enjoyed it and having Elizabeth there is keeping her company too. I think Elizabeth is spoiling her though, she has had lunch made for Sienna when she comes home during her lunch break." He chuckled. "And I'm hoping it's softening Sienna so that she'll finally agree to marry me and get pregnant. I'm going to really push her when we get back. I think this wanting to wait shit is fucking ridiculous."

Doc wasn't sure why he was pushing so hard. "Why the hurry?"

"I just want to get on with my life," Garcia said. "I spent more years under as Razor when I was with the DEA than I ever wanted. And going back under last year," he paused and shook his head. "Fuck man, that was six months of my life I will never get back. Besides, from the second I was with Sienna; I knew she was it. And it wasn't just because the sex was so good."

Doc wished he felt the same. He wanted to feel that way about Elizabeth. He just didn't. Hell, the sex wasn't even great as he was focused on trying to be gentle with her because she was so inexperienced and pregnant. He rubbed his forehead and then his hand slid to his tense neck.

"Explain," Garcia prompted.

"Explain what?"

Garcia laughed sarcastically. "You, my brother, are not on the same page. Everything about this, from the second you got back to the hangar in Djibouti through now has been off. I know none of us pushed you when you were obviously going through some bad shit after we got back, but maybe we should have. I have eyes. I know you're not in love with that girl you married."

Doc sighed out loud. "I'm doing the right thing by marrying her. She's pregnant with my kid."

"Yeah, explain that one."

Now Doc laughed sarcastically. "I really need to explain to you, of all people, how she got pregnant?"

"Fuck you," Garcia threw back. "You follow regs. It's who you are. And I'll never believe you took advantage of that young thing, unlike what I did as Razor with Sienna. I was a fucking predator, not that she was innocent."

"Elizabeth was, innocent."

"I assumed," Garcia said. "Is that what your problem has been?"

"Partly."

Garcia waited. "Out with it. What else gave you such a serious mind-fuck? Because that's what it's been from where I'm sitting."

Doc stared out his side window. "When under as Razor, did you ever think you were done, that there was no way you were getting out of a spot alive?"

Garcia pulled into a parking spot in front of the store. He put the car in park. He faced Doc. "More times than I'd like to admit. It's a dark place, accepting you're going to die. I was really fucked up from it for a while, well, that and all the drugs that were in my system. You've been talking with Lassiter, haven't you?"

"Yeah," Doc admitted. "I actually feel better about a lot of things now that Elizabeth is with me and I know about the baby."

Garcia's lips curved into a grin. "No longer a Sister, no longer innocent. Please tell me you're at least enjoying the more primal side of married life with that sweet little thing in your bed."

Doc let fly a string of curses. "You don't get it. She was a virgin. She was as innocent as they come, with the Sisters' since she was twelve years old."

"She's no longer a Sister, she's no longer a virgin, and she sure as hell isn't twelve years old any longer. What's the problem?"

Doc felt an irrational anger build. "We're done here." He removed his seatbelt and took hold of the car door, leaning up.

Garcia grabbed him and slammed him back into his seat. "We're not done here. What is your fucking problem?" Garcia stared him down. "Are you telling me you haven't slept with her since she got here?"

"No, I've slept with her," Doc defended.

A wry grin spread over Garcia's lips. "Missionary sex, nice and easy like you did with the virgin. That's all you've done. Isn't it? You've held yourself back."

Doc let a whole new string of curses loose using the word fuck as a noun, a verb, an adjective, and an adverb in the same rant.

Garcia laughed. "That's it." He nodded knowingly. "You've got to turn yourself loose. She can take it. When we get back, fuck her without thinking about it. Just do what feels right. You'll feel a lot better from it. You're married to her; your baby is inside her. That's your territory man, claim it."

"She's pregnant."

"Talk with Jackson about that. It doesn't matter. Certainly, you know sex won't hurt the baby."

"Do you understand innocent and untouched?"

"Maybe the first time you touched her, not now," Garcia said.

"I don't want to scare her."

Garcia laughed. "Sounds like you still have an issue with that."

"With what?" Doc demanded.

"That you were her first. What, did she freak out?"

"No, she handled it well. She's been fine every time," Doc admitted.

"Then what's the problem?" Garcia insisted.

Doc just shook his head.

"You have the problem, not her. I guarantee you she may not have had sex before you, but she knew about it. Where she's worked, she knows a lot more than you give her credit for. She's not as innocent as you've built her up to be."

"She was a nun," Doc said.

"You're hung up on that. Do you have any idea what she saw in that free clinic in Seattle? How about in that African village? It's not like she was cloistered in some monastery. She's seen more than most, I guarantee it."

"So, what am I supposed to do with that?" Doc asked.

"You do understand you have an opportunity, don't you?"

Doc scoffed at that. "What possible opportunity do I have?"

"To teach her how to be the woman you want her to be. If you only have missionary sex, that's all she's going to think sex is. Don't flatter yourself that you'll hurt her if you do it in any other positions."

"Fuck you," Doc spat.

Garcia laughed. "Just think about it. At some point your wild side is going to come out. You can't keep that beast caged forever." He nodded to add emphasis. Then he got out of the car. "Hey, get me a beef sandwich and some chips," he yelled to Doc's back as he approached the door to the sandwich shop.

"I'll get you grilled chicken, it's healthier," Doc yelled back.

The next morning at zero-five hundred, the five of them parked in front of the Walters Tactical Equipment Company. They all had their assignments. Cooper headed to the conference room, which was near both Rick and Janey's offices. He'd watch for them to arrive. He wasn't sure what time they usually got in, but they had both already arrived at the office the previous four days before the team did. The four other members of the team headed to the production floor to surprise the third shift.

Rick Walters was already on the manufacturing floor conferring with his third shift supervisor when the team arrived. He momentarily seemed disturbed by their unexpected presence but covered it up quickly. The team saw right through him and insisted on introductions and access to the employees.

"Of course," Rick agreed. "I wish I'd known though. We are struggling with a manufacturing deadline. There were some equipment problems overnight. I got the call from Chuck," he said motioning to his third shift supervisor, "two hours ago."

Chuck Geist, the third shift supervisor, was a crusty old Marine buddy of Rick Walters. He had a head full of thick gray hair. He was a medium skinned black man, who Jackson knew from his employee file to be sixty-seven years old.

"We'll try not to interrupt operations too much," Jackson assured them. "I just need to verify onsite identities to the personnel files."

Rick and Chuck exchanged glances.

"Unless that's a problem?" Doc asked.

"Not at all," Rick assured them.

"And I'm going to go validate the QA team and their processes on this shift," Madison said with a smile. Today she wore tight blue jeans and a clingy red sweater.

Jackson, Garcia, and Doc watched the employees as she strutted away, across the manufacturing floor. They noticed more than a few sets of eyes follow her from the room, including Rick Walters' appreciative gaze.

Hum. That was interesting, Doc thought. His gaze met Rick Walters' eyes after Madison had disappeared from view. Walters knew he was busted. He flashed Doc a brief and defiant shit-eating grin. Doc found that even more interesting.

They met the employees, validating workers to their employee files. Cannabis tattoo guy, Jason Piedmont, was at work. He talked with Garcia during the last smoke break of the shift. Garcia's DEA instincts were on high alert while they chatted.

Garcia chuckled as the twenty-nine-year-old, long-haired, heavily tattooed, heavy metal guitarist crushed out his smoke and then headed back to his machine. Piedmont openly professed to missing his drug of choice. "But hey, you gotta follow the rules to earn some bank," he'd said. "I damn near lost my woman and kid. She wasn't into the starving artist thing and told me it was time I grew the fuck up and supported her. So, I did."

Garcia judged that he was clean. There was one third shift employee though that Garcia suspected was using something, probably not weed though. Cecily Mays was twitchy. She didn't make eye contact with him and she sure as hell didn't say two words to him during the smoke break. He'd been around addicts enough to know that she was using something highly addictive. He would talk with Doc. She would definitely be included in the next drug screening.

The company doctor, Dr. Rod Stanley, arrived at zero-eight hundred. Doc had been waiting in his office for him for an hour. Doc grilled him about the drug screening protocols. He learned that Janey Walters ran a third-party, off-site, secure software program on Friday afternoon each week before she left for the night. Not only did the program pull employee numbers at random for testing the following week, it also randomized which day the testing would take place. Ten employees were selected each week.

Dr. Rod would get an email the day before the testing was to take place, so he would know which day to come in at six a.m. to administer the tests to any third shift employees selected. He was not given the employee ID numbers to match up to employee names until the day of the testing. That was delivered to him via email at five a.m. on the testing day.

Testing was done on site using integrated test cups that have a flat panel results window to easily identify failing test results. The cups tested for thirteen commonly abused drugs. Selected employees would be searched to ensure they had no liquids on them. They would take the cup into a designated screening room with no water source.

From what Doc was hearing, they were adhering to DoD protocols. He still wouldn't buy a one-hundred percent pass rate, though. "You'll have to let me know next week, what day is testing day. I need to be present to validate the process as part of the audit."

"That's not necessary you know," Dr. Rod scoffed. "Our past audit team never needed to be present to validate we adhered to DoD protocols."

"Is that a problem if I am?" Doc asked.

"Yeah, it is. The only reason you'd want to be here, is if you don't trust that I am following the guidelines at time of collection. What the hell?" He demanded.

"Whoa, easy there, Doctor," Doc said. "I don't mean to insult you. There is a new requirement in the audit review for this. Any auditors going forward must be present at the time of collection for the audit to be verified."

"Oh, sorry, I wasn't aware of that change."

"No hard feelings," Doc said. He left the good doctor's office amused by his reaction. Yeah, the company doctor did not want to have his shoulder looked over. That could only mean one thing as far as Doc was concerned.

Janey Walters didn't arrive until zero-nine hundred hours. She already knew the team was on-site early. Her husband had text messaged her. She and her husband called the team together in the conference room immediately.

"What the hell?" Rick Walters demanded after he'd closed the door. "Between the inquisitions last night when your team pulled the divide-and-conquer tactic on us and the early morning surprise visit, we're starting to think you suspect us of something. We called you, remember?"

Doc watched Cooper's jaw clench. Doc knew he was pissed.

"Inconsistencies," Cooper said.

"What inconsistencies?" Walters questioned with outrage.

Cooper nodded to Madison.

"Your internal transfers to cover expenses are suspicious at best. You undercut the bids for the government contracts so low, you are barely turning a profit and just to make payroll, you are drawing down funds that were infused into your company four years ago."

"We already explained that," Janey drawled. "My mamma gave us our inheritance when she sold her home in Atlanta and moved to the little villa, in Naples. We knew it would be tight for a few years with the growth we were planning if we got the DoD contracts. We knew we needed that money."

"Then why the shell game of moving it around?" Cooper asked.

Rick and Janey exchanged glances. "Mamma stipulated the funds could not be used for the business' operations. She wanted it to be our little nest egg for retirement. She's never had faith in Rick's business sense."

"Do you deny you're barely turning a profit?" Cooper asked.

Rick Walters leaned across the table. "We are solvent. That is the only stipulation in the DoD contracts. We predict we'll pull out in front during Q-three this year. Too much took place in taxation that we didn't anticipate this year to get there sooner. Our original estimates had us in the black during the Q-one, but thanks to both the Federal Government and the State of Montana raping small businesses, it isn't going to happen."

"Certainly, these things are not enough to fail an audit?" Janey asked.

"It depends how it's presented," Cooper said. "But I agree, there has to be more of a smoking gun the blackmailer was referring to."

"And how is it neither of you seem to know about the other person's side of the house? Rick, I don't buy for one second you know nothing about the HR functions. And Janey, you are way too involved to know nothing about R&D and the daily manufacturing process," Madison said.

"Look, we nearly got divorced two years ago because we both kept putting our fingers in each other's pies. Our therapist made us draw strict boundaries. I do not get involved in Rick's side of the house, ever. And he steers clear of everything HR. It's the only way we can stay married."

Doc watched Garcia take notes. He'd be online verifying both statements Janey Walters made as soon as possible. He wasn't surprised when Garcia started typing on his keyboard. He was probably already searching bank records to confirm payments to a marriage counselor. Doc's lips ticked into a grin as he listened to the tap, tap, tap on the laptop's keys.

Cooper nodded to Doc. "The piss tests."

"What about them?" Janey asked.

"No company achieves a one-hundred percent pass rate, ever."

"Oh, this again. I explained it to you last night. We have an aggressive anti-drug education program."

"Excuse me, ma'am," Garcia interrupted. "No company has that good of an education program. No company has that good of a screening process with new hires. No company is immune from the national epidemic of drug abuse. I met your third shift team. I can guarantee you at least two of them are using something."

Janey's face showed shock. "You tell me who and we will test them when they walk in the door tonight."

"We'll add my suspects to the screening, next week," Garcia said.

"I will be with Dr. Rod next week when your program spits out the lucky employees and we'll add a few of our own in," Doc said.

"If you are referring to Jason P., I know he looks like a pothead. Hell, he was a pothead prior to coming to work here. His stepdad is on first shift, an old Marine buddy of mine. If I didn't know his dad, I'd never have hired him. But he's clean now and a good worker."

"He's got a wife and the cutest little baby girl keeping him from using drugs," Janey added. "We have a company picnic every year and the families all come. We know our employees. They are like family to us. I don't like the inference that we have drug users we don't know about. Part of our education plan tells an employee if they are struggling with addiction to come to me. We will put them off on FMLA until they are clean and can come back to work drug-free."

"Have you had any employees take advantage of that offer?" Doc asked.

"Yeah, I didn't see anything in anyone's employee files about that," Jackson added.

Janey sat up straighter and raised her chin into the air. "We would never have recorded that in an employee file." She looked like she was considering it. She huffed out. "Four employees have. They were drug tested upon their return and passed. They have passed every screening since."

"You know I'm going to need those names," Doc said. "It goes no further than me."

The program spit out the ten employee numbers on Thursday morning the next week. It was zero-five-thirty. Doc sat beside Dr. Rod as he filled in the names next to the numbers. Doc validated the names against the employee numbers from a second source sheet. So far, so good.

Garcia had identified a total of six employees he thought from observation could be using. Only one of them had come up in the random selection. "I have five more employees we are adding," he told Dr. Rod. The four employees who had voluntarily come forward to Janey and were placed on FMLA while they were in rehab were not on the list.

Dr. Rod shot Doc a sharp sideways glance. Either the man was not happy with Doc's interference or he needed his morning coffee. "Fine." He took the slip of paper from Doc and eyed the names. "Jason P. is clean. I can guarantee that."

Doc shrugged.

Dr. Rod gathered four collection cups for the third shift employees on the list. He labeled them and then sat them on his desk. Then he placed a call to the third shift supervisor, requesting the four employees report to his office immediately for screening.

Cecily Mays, the employee Garcia categorized as acting twitchy came through the door first. Her behavior was no different as Doc observed her. She refused to make eye contact with Doc. Instead, her almost pleading eyes stayed locked with Dr. Rod's.

Doc wasn't surprised when she tested positive for heroin.

"Cecily, did you take one of your husband's Vicodin pills for that tooth ache? Vicodin will test positive as an opioid."

"Yes, yesterday morning when I got home from work, so I could sleep. You know this tooth is killing me." Her eyes flashed to Doc. "I'm in the middle of a root canal and got an infection."

Doc's eyes narrowed on Dr. Rod. That was blatant coaching.

"Cecily, we've talked about this before. You can't share his back medicine. Go on back to work now and have Chuck send the next victim back." He winked at her. He scanned the results into the system and made the physician's override notations.

"Thank you, Dr. Rod," she said and then slipped from the office.

"Are you shitting me?" Doc demanded.

"Come on. She's a good kid. Don't tell me you would bust her for an honest mistake? A lot of people out here don't go to the doctor for minor issues. They use what's in the house. This is a little town, not the big city like I gather you are used to."

Doc made notations on his tablet, which was all the authority an auditor had. He would speak with Janey about this and he would want that same employee retested on Friday morning. The next three workers came in one at a time. They all passed their tests, including Jason P.

First shift had six workers on the list. One of them failed for marijuana. Dr. Rod tried to explain that one away as the employee spending too much time with her elderly father, who has a medical marijuana card for cancer, while he smoked.

"Secondhand smoke, my ass!" Doc said, borrowing Madison's catch phrase.

Doc stuck around for the start of the second shift. Five of their team were on the list. Garcia kept the keys to the second rental car and stuck around as well. He was still conducting some of his own tests against the company's firewall and servers. The others left, heading back to the hotel.

Two of the five second shift employees failed. Dr. Rod tried to explain those two fails away as well, writing overrides. This was definitely enough for Walters Tactical Equipment to fail this audit. Doc had to wonder if Dr. Rod was the blackmailer, exacting his revenge that the funds had not been paid.

"Fifteen piss tests, and four people failed," Doc said. "I can't believe there has been a clean record. There were no overrides previously in the records, so I have to ask you what the hell is going on?"

"I think you're jumping to conclusions," Dr. Rod said. He checked his watch. "Can we meet with Janey tomorrow and talk this through? I know she's already left for the day. I know you'll understand and agree with my decision when you see the information in its entirety."

"In its entirety?" Doc demanded. "It's black and white, pass or fail." Doc's head was about to explode.

"I'm going home," Dr. Rod said, picking his keys up from his desk. "I will see you in Janey's office at nine a.m."

Doc watched him walk out the door. He wanted to put him against the fucking wall. From where Doc stood, Dr. Rod falsified the records today, so he had to wonder how else the records had been falsified in the past. Now *that* was enough to make Walters Tactical Equipment fail their audit.

Doc pulled his phone out and dialed Garcia. "Hey, look deeper into Dr. Rod's financial records. Look to see if he needs cash, if he has gambling debts, owes back taxes, anything that could make him the blackmailer."

"I did a cursory financial review on all employees, and nothing flagged on him, but I'll do a deeper dive tonight from the hotel. Are you ready to go?"

"Yeah, I'll meet you out by the car."

Doc grabbed his coat and his backpack and headed towards the exit. He pushed the door out and was hit by a cold north wind. Garcia was nowhere in sight.

"Fuck this," he cursed aloud.

No, he would not wait by the car till Garcia got his ass out there with the keys. He quickly ducked back within the building, closing the door as he retreated. At that same moment, the unmistakable sound of a shotgun firing, blasted the serenity of the frigid night. Its birdshot peppered a five-foot section of the metal door and walls. Doc heard the sharp impact of the many rounds hitting where he had just been standing. He drew his .45 from the small of his back.

"Son of a bitch!" He cursed aloud. Then he grabbed his cell phone and hit redial with the thumb of his left hand. He held it to his ear as he rushed down the hallway that led to the manufacturing floor. He'd go through it and exit the building at the front entrance.

"Patience, I'm on my way," Garcia answered.

"Where are you?" Doc barked.

"Damn, I'm just entering the lobby. I had to log out."

"Don't go outside till I reach you. Someone just took a fucking shot at me," Doc exclaimed. He was pissed!

Garcia drew his weapon as well. The glass lobby door was ten feet in front of him. He froze and pressed his back against the wall, concealing himself just within the hallway that led to the lobby restrooms. He told Doc where he was.

Doc tucked his handgun under his jacket as he rushed across the manufacturing floor. He exited it without speaking to anyone and then redrew his weapon. He hurried through the corridor, coming up on Garcia's position.

"Call Cooper and tell him what happened. I'll call the Sheriff's department as soon as he says if he wants DEA or FBI to report this."

Garcia hit dial. He filled Cooper in. "No law, just DoD auditor," Garcia told him.

"Son of a bitch! I'm not waiting on the Sheriff. I'm going out there to find the asshole who took a shot at me."

"It's colder than fuck outside. He's probably long gone," Garcia said. "Call the Sheriff. Report it like a normal citizen would."

"Like a normal fucking citizen." Doc shook his head. "Coop doesn't want our cover blown yet."

Garcia shrugged.

Doc and Garcia stayed within the building, feeling like pussies hiding from danger until the Sheriff arrived. He was what Doc expected, a burly man with a grizzled beard and tons of attitude. His men were checking the area. They stayed within the building until he was given the all clear.

Once he got it, Doc and Garcia followed him from the building. He led them to the door Doc identified as the exit he was using when the shot was fired. "Was this where you were at?" The Sheriff asked, pointing at the door with a five-foot pattern of birdshot pitting the metal.

"Yes. I stepped out, looked at our car across the parking lot," Doc said pointing to the car, "saw he wasn't there yet," he said pointing to Garcia, "and thought it was way too cold to wait for him, so I ducked back into the building. Next thing I know, I hear the shot and the impact on the door."

"Yep, as you can see, the birdshot messed the door up pretty good. It's lucky you didn't want to get too cold. You'd be at the hospital right now had you been hit."

Doc flashed a 'you've got to be fucking kidding me' look at Garcia.

Garcia looked around. There was no camera covering the outside of this exit, not from the outside, anyway, just interior cameras that recorded who came into the building.

"Did you see or hear from which direction the shot came?" The Sheriff asked.

"No," Doc replied. "I wish I did."

"There's an awful lot of ground to cover in the dark to try to find the spent shell or the wad. That's if the shooter didn't pick them up. My men and I will be back in the morning to take a look."

"That's not acceptable," Doc argued. He pointed at the door. "I'd assume the shooter was between thirty and forty yards away based on the spread pattern. That narrows the search grid down considerably."

"And what do you know about spread patterns and search grids?" The Sheriff asked.

"We audit a lot of things, weapons manufacturers included. Check a perimeter thirty to forty yards out and I'll be satisfied. Then you can search the rest in the morning if you don't find anything," Doc said, his voice forceful.

The Sheriff's deputies were gathered around. The Sheriff exchanged glances with a few of them. "You heard him. Go walk that perimeter."

Doc and Garcia moved out towards the correct distance, as well. The wind was colder than a bitch. They understood why the Sheriff wanted to postpone this till morning.

"I've got a casing," one of the Deputies yelled. He picked it up with his gloved hand and dropped it into the Sheriff's also gloved hand.

"Well, I'll be damned," the Sheriff remarked. His eyes locked with Doc's. "I didn't think we'd find anything."

"You going to take that to the lab and run it for prints?" Doc asked.

The Sheriff laughed. "We don't have our own forensic lab. We send all our evidence into the police lab at Great Falls. I'll send it in the morning, and we should know if there are any fingerprints on it in about a week."

"A week?" Doc demanded. "Oh, son of a bitch. We don't have a week." He knew Cooper would be pissed, but a week was not acceptable. He knew he could expedite those results, or rather, his FBI cover could. His eyes met Garcia's. Garcia shook his head no.

"You have to understand, no one was hurt, so this is low priority," the Sheriff said.

"Step back inside with us for a moment, Sheriff." Doc pulled the door open. He dialed Cooper and filled him in.

"You want my permission to identify yourself and take custody of that shell, don't you?" Cooper asked.

"You know it," Doc replied.

"Oh, fuck, Doc," Cooper swore. "Do you think we can trust that Sheriff?"

"As much as the next guy."

"Fine, we can't wait a week. Bring the shell back to the hotel and I'll have Jackson bring it into the federal facility in Great Falls. I'll make sure it's rushed through."

"Thanks, Coop," Doc said. He disconnected the call and turned back to the Sheriff. He withdrew his FBI credentials from his back pocket. "I'll be taking custody of that shell, Sheriff."

The Sheriff looked dumbfounded. "You're FBI?"

"That's correct. I can't disclose my mission, but I will be taking that shell. I can have it run through the federal facility in twenty-four hours."

The Sheriff read the name on the credentials. "Agent Williams, do you think the shooter knew who you were?"

A smirk formed on Doc's face. "I don't think so. I think it was motivated by something else."

"You know, from the distance the shot was fired, none of the pellet strikes would have been life threatening. It looks like the shooter just wanted to mess you up a little and send you to the hospital."

"I still consider this attempted murder and I insist you do as well."

The Sheriff nodded.

"And don't disclose my identity to any of your deputies. This stays between us. For all they know, you'll be sending the shell off to Great Falls in the morning," Doc ordered.

"You should have checked in with me, to notify me you were operating within my jurisdiction," the Sheriff said. "I don't like this, not one damned bit."

Doc didn't even blink. "It wasn't possible, Sheriff. But I need your help now. You know your locals. Which of your people could have been behind this? Who owns a twelve-gauge? Who's unhinged enough to take a shot at a person? I got into a verbal altercation with the company doctor today, Dr. Rod Stanley. What do you know about him?" He fired the questions off in rapid succession.

"I know him. We've pulled him over a few times on a Friday night leaving his favorite watering hole, but the highest he ever blew was a point-zero-seven, just under the legal limit of point-zero-eight. He's not your shooter. He doesn't even own a gun. He's about the only one in town that doesn't. As far as who owns a twelve-gauge, who doesn't?"

That wasn't terribly helpful. "Okay, we'll touch bases with you tomorrow," Doc told him.

Doc took the keys from Garcia. "Get on your computer while I drive. Get me a location on that Dr. Rod asshole and dump his phone records. I want to know if he called or text messaged anyone after he left tonight."

"What kind of altercation did you get into with him?" Garcia asked as he opened his tablet.

"The fucker falsified piss test results. Four failed but he passed them with a doctor's override, coached several on their excuses. I called him on it, and he told me to meet him in Janey's office in the morning, that I'd understand. Then the asshole walked out on me."

Garcia laughed. "And you didn't stop him?"

"DoD auditor didn't have the authority to, but believe me, I wanted to put the fucker through the wall."

Garcia pulled Dr. Rod's cell phone number from the list he had. He ran it through his programs. "Dr. Rod left the facility and went straight to Mel's Tavern. He's still there. He's not your shooter." With a few more clicks of his keys Garcia pulled his phone call records up just as Doc pulled into the hotel parking lot. "I've got one call made right after he left the facility. I'll run it when we get inside."

They joined the others in Cooper and Madison's room and filled them in. Doc gave the shell to Jackson. Cooper still didn't like that Doc's cover was blown with the Sheriff. It only took Garcia a few minutes to track the number Dr. Rod had called. It was the landline to Mel's Tavern.

Cooper's trademark smirk set across his lips. "What do you say, Doc, you want to go get a beer and have some greasy bar food?"

"Yeah, let's pay Dr. Rod a visit and see who he's drinking with this evening."

Cooper threw his set of car keys to Jackson. "Get that shell to the FBI lab in Great Falls. Shepherd already called Whiting. You should be expected."

Jackson nodded. "I'll check in with you after I've dropped it. Good luck with Dr. Rod." He slipped from the room. He'd be on the road for a few hours. He'd give Angel a call.

Cooper came to his feet and grabbed his coat. "Garcia, you and Madison will be our backup in the parking lot. Sorry, it's colder than hell out there. You better layer up."

Romeo

Doc pushed open the heavy door to Mel's Tavern, a dive bar on the outskirts of town. The parking lot was full. They did a good business on a Thursday night. As they walked towards the bar, they recognized half of Walters Tactical Equipment's first shift. Within, they found Dr. Rod seated alone at the bar talking with the bartender, a young-looking Willie Nelson wanna-be. Doc took the barstool on his right, Cooper the one on his left.

"So, what's good here, Rod?" Doc asked.

Dr. Rod glanced nervously between the two of them. "Depends what you want." He held his beer mug up. "Thursday night is three-dollar draught night."

There was a plate with a half-eaten cheeseburger and fries in front of Dr. Rod as well. Doc took two French fries from the plate and took a bite. They were still warm. "A little salty for my taste."

Dr. Rod moved to get up. Cooper grabbed him, forced his ass back onto the barstool, and held him in place. "You're not going anywhere yet. Now stay the fuck in your seat and look like you're having a beer with your buddies," he growled in Rod's ear.

"How dare you," Rod protested, his face getting red.

"Look asshole, someone took a shot at me when I was leaving the factory tonight. You're the only one I've had words with. And by the way, my entire audit team knows why."

The bartender was watching the scene cautiously.

Cooper made eye contact with him. "Barkeep, two draughts for my friend and I." His eyes flickered to Dr. Rod's mug. "And our friend, Rod, seems to be getting low. Get him another and put it on my tab."

The bartender looked to Rod for guidance. Rod nodded, and the bartender moved away to get the beers.

"I've been here since I left work. I didn't take that shot at you. Anyone here can confirm that. Besides, I don't even own a gun. But, with your winning personality, I can't say I'm surprised. I can't be the only one you've rubbed the wrong way."

Doc leaned into his face. "But you and the four who failed their drug tests are the only ones who have a motive to shut me up."

"You're barking up the wrong tree. It wasn't me," Rod insisted.

The bartender sat the beers in front of them.

"Give us a couple burgers and some fries too," Cooper ordered.

"But no salt added to the fries. His exceeds the recommended daily allowance, I'm sure." He faced Rod. "I'll assume too much alcohol tonight will explain why your face is red. You better make sure you're not over the legal limit before you get behind the wheel, friend."

"How did you know I was here?" Dr. Rod demanded.

"We didn't, just stopped in for a beer and some burgers," Cooper said.

Dr. Rod shook his head.

"Are these guys harassing you? Do you want me to call the Sheriff, Rod?" The bartender asked.

"No harassing, we're just having a beer with our buddy here," Doc said, his heavy hand patting Rod's shoulder. "I didn't get your name, friend," Doc said to the bartender.

"You didn't ask, and I didn't volunteer it," he replied. His eyes were darting between the three of them. He had his hand on the landline phone on the bar.

"You been working all night?" Cooper asked him.

"Yeah, what's it to you?"

"Just making conversation. You keep that phone pretty close to you."

"We get takeout orders."

The man sitting a few seats down from Cooper yelled to the bartender. "Billy, I need to pay and get going." The bartender moved over to him. He took his cash and made change. Then he came back over in front of Dr. Rod. "Billy, make sure Cec is in tomorrow night. Debbie is coming in with me."

The bartender waved dismissively at him, but his eyes looked guilty as sin when they swept between Doc and Cooper again.

"Cec, as in Cecily?" Doc asked. "Are you Cecily Mays' husband, by chance?"

The bartender's eyes snapped to Dr. Rod.

"It's easy enough for us to verify, asshole," Cooper said. "So, don't lie to us."

"You need to leave. Right now, you need to leave," Billy the bartender stammered.

Doc laughed. "I'll take that as confirmation. How's your back, Billy?"

"What? My back?"

"His medical status is none of your business. He's not an employee," Dr. Rod interrupted. "He's right. You need to leave."

"No, I think we do need to call the Sheriff," Doc said. Billy's hand moved towards the phone. "Oh, don't bother. I will," Doc said, pulling his cell phone from his pocket. "And we'll have one of his deputies pick your wife up too. I hope she's taken a recent dose of her drug of choice so she's not in too much pain, of course, it doesn't matter, she can be held for up to twenty-four hours without any charges. I don't think she'll be okay. I know she's using an opioid."

"Wait, none of this is necessary," Billy said. "Yeah, Cec is my wife, and neither of us have done anything."

"Did your wife tell you she failed her drug screening today and good old Dr. Rod here covered it up?" Doc asked. The bartender's eyes locked with Dr. Rod's again. "You have two seconds, Billy, then I dial the Sheriff, and you're all going to jail tonight," Doc said.

"Go ahead and call the Sheriff," Dr. Rod challenged. "You can't prove any crime. I legally can make a physician's override to any test results, and you have no proof of who took a shot at you tonight. You've got nothing."

Cooper nodded, so Doc hit dial.

At the station, the Sheriff shook his head. "I appreciate your gut instincts, boys," he paused and nodded to Madison, "and ma'am, but there's no proof of anything."

"You've got Billy Mays shotgun from his car, loaded with the same kind of birdshot that was fired at me," Doc said. "We'll get it to the forensic lab with the shell. We've got Dr. Rod Stanley's call to Mel's Tavern as soon as he left work, where Billy Mays would have answered the phone."

"Which you still haven't told me how you got the warrant for his phone records that fast. Or didn't you? Will that call even be admissible in court?" The Sheriff asked.

Garcia's lips tipped into a grin. "If we do our jobs right here, we'll get a confession and it won't matter."

"If I wasn't pissed enough to learn an FBI Agent was in my town, finding out there's a whole damned task force of you guys from different agencies investigating whatever it is you still won't tell me about, is enough to burn my britches! So, watch it, boy," he warned Garcia.

Garcia laughed out loud. "Sheriff, Cecily Mays is a junkie. You let her sit long enough and the need to use is going to outweigh her need to stay silent. She'll make a full confession of whatever she knows to get a hit."

"And if she doesn't, watching his wife suffer will be enough for Billy Mays to make a deal," Cooper added.

"They're your weak links. Dr. Rod won't give anything up, unless it's to save his own hide. That's why we told you to put him in interrogation and the other two in separate holding cells," Doc said.

The Sheriff's cell phone rang. He raised it to his ear. He listened to his deputy's report. "Okay, photograph it, bag it all up, and get someone over to Mel's to search behind the bar too." He disconnected the call. "My boys searching the Mays' house found drug scales and product packed up for distribution. Is that what this is about?

I'd understand DEA investigating it," he said pointing to Garcia, "but that doesn't explain FBI or CIA."

"You can have that bust, Sheriff. It's only part of what we're investigating," Cooper said. "But now we have some leverage over the Mays'. We'll wait till your boys get back and print up some pictures. Then the interrogations are ours. We'll consult you before we offer them any deals." Cooper checked his watch. It was after midnight. "Leave Rod Stanley alone in interrogation. No one goes in."

Cooper walked over to the sofa in the Sheriff's office. He dropped himself onto the far-right cushion. He rested his head against the back of it and closed his eyes. Madison sat beside him, Doc on the far end. Garcia sat on the floor and leaned his head back against the seat cushion between Doc and Madison.

"What are you doing?" The Sheriff demanded.

Doc opened his eyes. "We assume it will be several hours before your boys are back with the evidence and the photos. We're going to grab as much sleep as we can, so we can go at the suspects. Wake us when your boys are back."

At four a.m. The Sheriff woke the Feds. He'd laid down on one of the cots in the deputy room and he wasn't happy about it. "Rod Stanley has been a royal pain in the ass all night. After the third time he demanded he be brought to a toilet, I told him that was it. I gave him a bucket in the interrogation room and the bastard used it."

"When did your men get back?" Cooper asked.

"They just walked in. Tommy is printing off the pictures for you now and I have a fresh pot of coffee on." He shook his head. "I can't believe Billy Mays was selling that shit in my town and I didn't know. Jesus! He's got over a hundred packets ready for distribution."

"Welcome to the epidemic all the other towns in the U.S. are facing," Garcia said, coming to his feet. "Now, where's that coffee?"

Doc and Madison entered the interrogation room.

"You?" Rod spat.

Doc and Madison took seats across the table from him. They both flashed their FBI badges and credentials.

"FBI?"

"Tampering with drug tests for federal contractors is a federal offence, just as blackmailing a DoD supplier is," Doc said.

"Whoa, whoa, who said anything about blackmail?"

"We did," Madison said. "Billy and Cecily may be smart enough to pull off selling drugs, but neither one of them is smart enough to pull off an attempted blackmail scam."

"And neither of them has the access to cause Walters Tactical Equipment to fail their audit. But you do," Doc added. "And, you're the only one there capable of covering up failed piss tests. Our counterparts are with the Sheriff talking with the Mays' right now. Whoever talks first gets the deal. The question is, will it be you or one of them?"

"Billy and Cecily will never do anything to hurt the other. Neither of them will take any deal that doesn't include them both," Dr. Rod said.

"Oh, I'm sure as soon as Cecily needs a hit, one of them will talk," Madison said. "My bet is on Billy. Most men don't like to see their wife suffer."

Rod Stanley shook his head no. "I want an attorney."

Doc smiled and came to his feet. "Good. I didn't want to offer you any deals, asshole."

They joined Cooper, who watched the interrogation of the Mays' couple on the monitor in the Sheriff's office.

"Yeah, you're getting sick. How long's it been since you've had a hit, Cecily?" Garcia asked, watching the woman through the bars to the holding cell she was in. Two over, her husband stood, holding onto the bars, staring their way. Garcia put his DEA badge away and then turned the folding chair he had, straddled it, and sat facing the bars of Cecily Mays' cell. "Here's how this is going to work. The first one of you who tells me what I want to know gets the deal, and Cecily, that deal for you is to be taken to the hospital or rehab to get treated."

"The Sheriff just got done showing them the pictures from their house of the drugs. They were also told that the Sheriff's Department found a box with similarly wrapped drugs at Mel's Tavern, behind the bar," Cooper filled them in.

"Here's what I want to know. Who all was in on the scam at Walters Tactical Equipment to hide failed piss tests, how was it done, and who was blackmailing the owners? Who took the shot at my partner with the twelve-gauge when he was coming out of the building last night? And who is your supplier. You had a hell of a lot of drugs in your basement."

The couple stared at each other.

"Tick, tick," Garcia said. "Cecily, I have it logged that you were brought in at two minutes till midnight. You'll be held for twenty-four hours."

"The Deputy came to my house before nine last night," Cecily argued.

"Oh, well, maybe I falsified the time. You know all about falsifying records, don't you Cec?" Garcia mocked.

It took until two in the afternoon for Cecily and Billy to crack. Cecily had been barfing her guts out for over an hour. "I need help!" She screamed.

"You have ten more hours," Garcia said.

"Fine, whatever you want to know," she moaned.

"End this and get her help, man," Billy said. "It was Rod Stanley. All if it was Rod Stanley."

"He didn't take the shot at my partner," Garcia argued.

"No, that was me. But I used birdshot and as far away as I was, it would only hurt him. It wouldn't have killed him. We just needed him to back off. Rod called me panicked. He knew the auditor was close to putting it together. He told me if I didn't go do it, he'd throw Cec under the bus and turn me in for the drugs. Now get her help, man. You promised."

After taking their statements, the Sheriff booked Billy Mays on a multitude of charges. Cecily Mays was transferred to the hospital, as a prisoner, and an FBI Agent from the Great Falls office came and took Dr. Rod Stanley into Federal custody. The team went to give their report to their clients, Rick and Janey Walters.

"That son of a bitch!" Rick exploded. "If he wasn't in custody, I'd kill the fucker!"

"I trusted Dr. Rod," Janey said in disbelief. "I can't believe he did any of those things."

"According to Cecily Mays, when the employees were selected each week for screening, he would text message the ones he knew used. It would cost them a hundred dollars for an alternate who was clean to fill their cups. Dr. Rod didn't put names on the cups until after the sample was collected, so none of the alternates knew their name hadn't come up," Doc said. "The same held true if a person got popped during the screening. Dr. Rod would shake them down for the money to slip in a clean sample."

"Did any of my Shift Managers know what was going on?" Rick demanded.

"Not according to Cecily Mays and we tend to believe her. Because the entire list of employees that was selected was not shared with the Shift Managers when it spit out, none of them knew. So, if eight from their shift were called down, they couldn't verify if they had all been selected or not. That is the first thing I would change in your process," Doc said, staring at Janey. "When the list spits out each week, it needs to go to all three Shift Managers as well as you both and whoever you hire to conduct the tests."

Janey nodded. "There is a lot we need to change. Does this make us fail the audit?"

"We are passing you for all aspects except the drug screening. For that, given the circumstances, you have two months to get your process cleaned up. A real DoD auditor will be back then for that portion only," Cooper said.

"So, was it Rod Stanley who was blackmailing us?" Rick asked.

"Stanley hasn't given a statement or admitted to anything, but we believe so. Billy and Cecily Mays didn't have the access needed to cause a fail. Only Rod Stanley did," Cooper said.

"Oh, and I'd stop the shell game of money transfers going forward," Madison said. "It's highly unlikely your original audit team will be back next year, and any other auditor will flag it."

Both Rick and Janey nodded.

"You have some housecleaning to do," Jackson said.

"You have at least three more people we know of who work for you using. And this is a small town. Half your first shift was at Mel's Tavern when the Sheriff took Dr. Rod and Billy Mays away in cuffs. If they were there or not, your entire staff more than likely knows about the arrests. Some may even know why. You need to get in front of this," Doc said.

"I'd recommend a mandatory piss test for all employees immediately," Garcia said.

"And given that you consider your employees family, that great policy you have of offering FMLA for drug treatment, with no job repercussions, needs to be offered to anyone in lieu of the screening," Doc said.

"But it does need to be noted in their employee file," Jackson said. "You haven't done anything against DoD procedures, but you sure as hell have skirted them."

"Well, we surely will make the changes," Janey drawled. "I thank you for uncovering what was going on." Her eyes then went to her husband.

"We have just enough time to call first shift together before they leave for the day and have our meeting with them. And then we can meet with the second shift as soon as they are in. Most of third shift is pulling some overtime tonight, so we can meet with them too," Rick said.

"We'll get an approved DoD screener in here Monday and screen the entire staff, well any who don't request FMLA," Janey guaranteed.

The team came to their feet. Their job was done, and they would head home immediately. Doc checked his watch. It was already past nineteen hundred in Chicago. It would be a late arrival home.

It was past midnight when Doc pulled into his garage. He was tired, but knowing Elizabeth waited in their bed reenergized him. Garcia's words to 'claim his territory' brought a smile to his face. No, he couldn't be his normal sexual self with Elizabeth yet. He was sure it would scare her. But she was his wife and he would make love to her tonight.

After dropping his bags in the kitchen, he came into the bedroom quietly. "You awake, honey?" He said in a normal speaking voice. He sat his gun and phone to the nightstand and then began to disrobe.

"I'm glad your home," her sleepy voice answered from the bed.

He stripped naked and slid beneath the covers, taking her into his arms. He heard Garcia's voice again tell him to claim his territory. *No, keep it slow and gentle,* he told himself. Her hand caressed over his face, down his neck, tickled him as it traveled down his chest and abs until it grasped his dick.

All thoughts of keeping it slow and gentle left his brain. He knew in that moment that he would uncage his beast, as Garcia said. Then he pushed all thoughts of Garcia from his mind, laughing to himself. He wouldn't tell Garcia he thought of him while in bed with his wife, her hand on his cock!

Then he made love to his wife, for hours. He told her what he wanted her to do to him, and she did. He placed her in his favorite positions, none of them missionary, and spoke provocative words to her. He banished from his brain any thoughts of her prior experience level, believing she would be okay with what transpired. And she was. He brought her to orgasm six times. And after, as he held her tightly to himself, he felt at peace. He felt satisfied in a way he had not during prior sexual encounters with her.

Elizabeth opened the car door and winced as she slid into the front seat beside Sienna. She smiled pleasantly and greeted both her, and Angel, who sat in the back beside Sammy's car seat. Elizabeth was glad they had this outing planned, but she wasn't sure how to broach the topic that weighed on her mind.

"I'm glad the guys only have to be at work a half day," Sienna said. "I understand debriefing and all they have to do after a mission, but jeez they were gone nearly two weeks!"

"That was the longest you and Anthony have been separated, isn't it? Even the mission to Africa didn't last that long," Angel said.

"Yes, it is the longest and I will admit I really missed him," Sienna said. She smiled at Elizabeth. "Since we've only been together since July, I'm still getting used to all this, myself. I'm glad you stayed with me. It was fun."

Elizabeth nodded and smiled. "Me too. I hope Alexander and I can find a place in your neighborhood soon."

"Until then, you are welcome at my house anytime," Sienna assured her.

They pulled into the parking lot of the restaurant. They were sat in a quiet back corner, per Angel's request.

"Coffee, yes, and keep it coming," Sienna said to the server. Her grinning gaze shifted between Angel and Elizabeth. "After last night, a full pot won't be enough."

"Why can't they ever get back before midnight? That's all I want to know," Angel added.

"And after two weeks gone, jeez, we were up all night," Sienna said.

"Well, *he* was anyway," Angel added with a hearty laugh. Her eyes met Elizabeth's. "I'm sure you know exactly what we're talking about. I'm sure Doc was the same last night. They're always like that when they get home from a mission," Angel said.

Elizabeth was surprised by the openness of the conversation, but she shouldn't have been. During the two weeks she spent with these two ladies, she discovered that few topics were off limits. She'd gotten to know them both very well, learned their stories on how they came to be with their men. She was inspired by their strength, learning what they had each gone through, what they had each overcome. And she shared with them what happened in Africa.

She was glad they had brought this up. She found Alexander's appetite when he joined her in bed, startling. When they had gotten the call that the team was on its way back from Montana, Alexander told her they'd be back late, but asked that Sienna bring her home. He wanted her waiting in their bed for him. Looking back, Elizabeth knew she had been naïve. She hadn't thought it was for sexual reasons.

"I wonder if both Cooper and Madison are like that with each other too? Wow! Can you even imagine what went on in their bedroom last night if they are?" Sienna said laughing.

"So, that's normal?" Elizabeth finally forced herself to ask.

"Oh, yes, trust me. Very normal!" Angel answered. She giggled. "I think Sammy was conceived on one of those post-mission nights!" Her eyes shifted to Sienna. "So be careful, or don't be." She laughed obnoxiously. "By the way, when are you two going to get married, anyway?"

"Funny you should ask," Sienna replied. "We talked about that this morning." Sienna took a drink of the coffee the server just brought.

"Seriously, you can't keep me waiting on that," Angel complained.

Sienna giggled. "As soon as there can be a break and everyone can have the day off, we'll get married. We're going to get the marriage license Monday after work so it will be ready to go when the day presents itself."

"Oh, yay!" Angel oozed. "And then how soon till we can talk babies?" Her smile shifted to Elizabeth. "It would be nice to have a third baby amongst us, wouldn't it?"

Elizabeth couldn't help but laugh. She really liked Angel. She was very unlike her mother, Sister Bernice John. But the fact that she was the Sister's daughter created a bond between them. She liked Sienna too, and she knew Sienna really wanted a baby, soon. They'd talked about that too.

Sienna laughed. "Not long. I'll go off the pill after this pack is done. Anthony finally wore me down." Her eyes shifted to Elizabeth. "Plus, I'd like my child to have others from the agency to grow up with whom are close in age."

Elizabeth nodded. The three women had talked about that too, about how isolated as a new mother Angel felt. It wasn't like she could talk with any other new mom outside of the agency about her feelings and fears when the team was in the field. There was one woman she met at a 'Mommy and Me Yoga Class' whose husband was a cop, who Angel had bonded with, but the woman obviously didn't know what Angel's husband did.

"You look like you have more to say, Elizabeth," Angel prompted.

Elizabeth felt herself blush, her cheeks burning hot. No, she couldn't talk about the intimate details of her and Alexander's lovemaking, not even with these two women who she counted as close friends. He had not forced her to do anything, but what she did do, was quite a bit outside of her comfort zone.

When Alexander slid between the sheets beside her, he was already naked. She grasped his manhood with her hand and was rewarded with an erotic moan from him. "Your mouth, Elizabeth. Please let me feel your mouth around me."

She knew she couldn't say no to him. He had brought her immense pleasure with his mouth on her, several times. It felt awkward though, and the thought of it was gross as she did it. She felt clumsy and was not sure what to do. He told her what felt good though, even begging her to gently use her teeth on him. He stopped her before he came, thankfully, but the multiple positions he placed her in to make love to her were surprising and a few were even uncomfortable, both physically and emotionally.

His preferred position for her to orally pleasure him was with him standing and her on her knees in front of him, which felt wrong, dirty. And two of the positions he said were so he could watch his dick slide in and out of her, which he did with great focus. That felt even dirtier. But when he bent her over the bed and took her from behind, she felt the worst about it. It didn't feel like making love. It felt like what others described as fucking, sex for the sake of sex.

He reciprocated the oral expression of affection so many times, in between the different positions that she still felt raw and swollen, though at the time, the physical ecstasy she felt had been incredible. She never knew someone could orgasm that many times in one night. And hours later when they were both worn out, he held her so tenderly and so tightly to himself that she had to believe he loved her.

She brought her thoughts back to the table. "No, not at all."

Angel smirked. "Let's see if I can figure it out. You were a Sister, probably not very experienced when you met Doc in Africa. He was only home a few days with you before they left on this mission, and last night you had post-mission sex for the first time." She paused and laughed. "I'm surprised you can even walk normally this morning. You have to be sore."

By the surprised expression on Elizabeth's face, Angel knew she'd nailed it. She smiled smugly.

"After we drop you off at home, sit on a bag of frozen peas," Sienna said. "I wish I could have the first night Anthony and I were together. I was on the back of his bike the whole day and was in agony."

"Oh, wow, you really do know," Elizabeth said, her eyes nervously going back and forth between her two friends.

"We do," Angel confirmed. "Your body will get used to it, don't worry. Sex is normal and natural." She smiled wide. "And fun. Our guys work hard and play even harder," she said with sexual intent. "Very normal."

"They are not normal," Sienna argued. "You know, I was married for ten years before I met Anthony and I never once had sex like I did with him from that first night on. I can attest that it isn't normal."

Elizabeth found herself giggling. Yes, she liked these two women very much. "Good to know. And thanks for the tip about the frozen peas."

"Oh, and just so you know, you'll have a slightly less intense repeat when he gets home from the briefing at the office later," Sienna said.

"Unless they hear they're going back out right away, then it will be even more intense," Angel added.

"You better stock up on frozen peas," Sienna said with a hearty laugh as their breakfasts were served.

Doc sat facing Lassiter in his kitchenette. This was the first mission in a long time that he hadn't been required to meet with him immediately upon return to base. He considered this a milestone.

"So, the son of a bitch took a shot at you?"

"Yeah. I'm damn lucky he wasn't seriously trying to kill me." Doc laughed. "I still can't believe they thought they'd just scare me off. Who does that?"

"Did it bring back any negative feelings?"

"Just pissed me off," Doc replied.

Sierra

"Alexander, do you have a stamp?"

Doc pulled his shirt over his head. He had five minutes before he needed to leave for the office. It was Monday morning. They had a team meeting with Shepherd to discuss the next few missions in the hopper. He hoped none would be long ones like the Montana job they'd just returned from. "No, what do you need one for?"

"I wrote a letter to my brother, Bobby, and wanted to mail it. I can take the bus to the post office, no worries."

Doc tamped down what his natural reaction was and kept his facial expression neutral. "I can take it to the office and mail it for you. It's cold out this morning and I know you want to work on your assignments for class. I'm proud of you, honey, enrolling for both classes you need. Online classes have to be harder, but I know you'll crush them."

"Thank you." She handed the addressed envelope over to him and gave him a hug. "I do need to spend most of the day on my assignments. Not having to go out helps a lot."

The address to the condo was in the upper left corner. Oh, hell no! "You're welcome. I'll take care of it for you."

Once in the subbasement parking level at HQ, Doc tore the envelope open and read the letter.

Hi Bobby,

I am in Chicago and will be staying here. It worked out better than I hoped. Alexander, the baby's father, accepted responsibility and has made our marriage legal. He's a good man. Please do not harbor angry feelings towards him. As I told you when we last spoke, I am thrilled that God has blessed me with this life inside me. I love this child and regardless if its father would have been in our lives or not, would not change that.

Life will be easier for both me and this child now that its father will be in our lives. You, more than anyone, know how much that decides a child's life and future. I have to believe that if either of our fathers had been in our lives, life would have been very different for us both. I understand Mom more than ever now that I found myself in a similar situation. I hope you can forgive her at some point in time, for yourself. Bobby, she did the best she could. I believe that in my heart. I know you do not like it when I get religious or philosophical with you, so I won't say more, but you know how I feel about the path your life took. I pray for you every day, Bobby. I hate that you are in that awful place and I hate even more what you have had to do and what you continue to do to survive. I pray for those you hurt too. All I will say is that God loves you and there is hope for a better future if you open your heart.

Below is my new phone number for you to reach me when you have phone privileges. We won't have to coordinate times. I have a cell phone now, so that number will reach me anytime. Alexander is very kind and generous. He owns his own home. It is comfortable and safe. He has welcomed me into it with nothing asked of me in return. The address is below as well. I'm giving you this address to write to me only. Please do not reach out to him. He did not take advantage of me as you assumed. There is so much about him I'd like to tell you, perhaps in the next letter. What I will tell you is he has honor and pride. He serves his country, helps those who need help, putting himself in danger in the process. I don't know when I might get back there to visit, so I guess it is back to writing letters like when I was in Africa.

I am always here for you,

All my love,

Elizabeth

Doc returned the letter to its envelope. He tapped out a message to Shepherd on his phone requesting a meeting as early that morning as Shepherd was available, said he needed a favor. He gave him no other details. He was just very thankful Elizabeth had not written and mailed that letter while he'd been away on the mission.

An invitation to a meeting in Shepherd's office a half hour later came before Doc even made it to the stairwell. He took the stairs to his office and killed the time, rereading the letter a few more times. Yeah, he was very thankful she had not mailed it without him seeing it. He brought up the information on her brother that Garcia had dug up when Elizabeth first appeared and announced her pregnancy. He reread that too.

Doc approached Shepherd's office. The door was open. Cooper was within, seated at the conference table beside Shepherd. Shepherd motioned him in when they locked eyes. So, Shepherd invited Cooper. Doc wondered if Lassiter would arrive as well. He knew he was still on their radar as a concern.

Doc closed the door behind himself. He sat on the opposite side of the table. The informal seating area would have been his preference for this conversation.

"I need a day off and a favor," Doc said, his eyes fixed on Shepherd.

He could see the irritation in Shepherd's features. He'd taken a lot of time off since the mission to Africa and he'd asked Shepherd for a lot of favors. He wasn't sure how much more goodwill he had left with his boss.

"Tell me," Shepherd prompted.

"Elizabeth's brother is in the state pen in Washington. She wrote him a letter, wanted a stamp this morning."

Shepherd and Cooper exchanged glances.

"Elizabeth understands what we do is classified, knows she can't say too much about me, knows it could put her in danger. But with her brother, there is a whole other layer of issues to address. She handled it as well as she knew to in her letter. I need to meet him. But I don't want her to know I'm going out there. I want to fly out early tomorrow morning and then be home after work. And I want to enter the facility with my federal credentials as a law visit."

"Anything else?" Shepherd asked.

"Elizabeth gave her phone number to her brother in the letter. He can't have it. I could get her a burner phone strictly for calls with him."

"Or we could set up a second decoy number on her phone like on the Operators phones," Shepherd completed where he thought Doc was going with his previous sentence.

"I don't know what to do about him Shep, and I don't think I will unless I meet him."

"Do you have that letter on you?" Cooper asked.

Doc nodded and pulled it from his pocket. He scooted it across the table, so it was between Cooper and Shepherd.

Shepherd opened it. His eyes focused on the paper and he took the time to read both sides. Then he handed it to Cooper. He too read the entire letter.

Doc sat quietly and patiently as both men read it.

When Cooper finished reading it, he sat the letter onto the table between himself and Shepherd.

"She obviously loves her brother. From what Garcia dug up on him, I have to wonder if she really understands how bad of a dude he is," Cooper said.

Doc shrugged. Yes, he'd had the same thought. "She has this big, forgiving heart. That's why I need to meet him for myself."

"Were you planning on letting that letter go to him in its current state? Or will you have the two sections redacted?" Shepherd asked.

Doc sighed. "It has to be redacted or rewritten."

It was as though Shepherd could read his mind. "But you're not sure if you should be the one to have that conversation with her or not. Or maybe not even how to go about it."

"I need to meet him first. Then I'll have that conversation with her. If he's as bad as I think, she cannot have too much contact with him, and he surely cannot know where we live or know anything at all about our lives. But I don't want her to know I'm going to see him. Can you help me arrange the trip for tomorrow and give me the day off?"

Shepherd nodded. "Angel will make your travel arrangements and I will make the call to DC to arrange your visit."

"Thanks, Shep," Doc said.

Cooper handed the letter back across the table. "Handle this."

Doc nodded.

Doc drove onto the penitentiary grounds. The foothills rose behind the guard towers and barbed wire. He'd flown out of O'Hare early, changed planes in Seattle, and arrived at the Walla Walla Regional Airport at thirteen-hundred, local time. He picked up the rental car and drove it to the prison. Thank you, Angel for the travel arrangements.

He badged his way in with his FBI credentials. Doc entered the room where Elizabeth's brother sat in the beige pants and white t-shirt, the standard prisoner uniform. Robert 'Bobby' Shaw sat facing the door, staring at him with a cop-hating air. His rap sheet was extensive. He had many years to build up his opinion of law enforcement.

Bobby Shaw had long, straggly hair, the same color as Elizabeth's, and he had the same vibrant blue eyes. That was where the physical similarities ended. His complexion was darker, his face pock marked from what had to have been a horrible case of acne in his youth. His nose was large and misshapen, probably from more than a few broken noses over the years that hadn't been fixed properly. His lips too showed signs of previous injuries that hadn't healed well. And he had taken advantage of the weights in the exercise yard. His muscles were well developed.

He had gang tats on his neck. On the left, was the shield with the letters A and B with a dagger running through it. On the right, were large script letters, ACAB. Doc had to wonder if Elizabeth knew the meaning of his tattoos. The prison file on him indicated an affiliation with the Aryan Brotherhood. On his chest were the swastika and SS tats all the gang members wore.

All Bobby Shaw had been told was that a member of federal law enforcement was visiting him. Why? He didn't know. Nor did he care. He hated cops, all cops, and had nothing to share with them, no matter what they were looking for.

Doc had a file folder in his hand with nothing inside but a pad of paper with no writing on it. It was for show. He sat it onto the table and then took a seat. "Robert Shaw?"

"You know I am. They have me in this fucking room, don't they asshole?"

Doc's lips twisted into a smirk. Pleasant guy. He wondered if he talked to Elizabeth that way. "I've come to talk with you about your sister, Elizabeth."

Robert Shaw tensed. Doc saw worry momentarily wash over his face. Then he hid it. "What's up with Elizabeth?" He threw out casually.

"The last she visited you was nearly a month ago," Doc said. "What were her plans following that visit? And what did she discuss with you at that time?"

"Didn't Elizabeth tell the penguins that she was going out of town? Is that what this is about? She's not one of them no more, what she does ain't their business. Did someone from the convent report her missing? She's not. She went to Chicago."

Doc's jaw set in frustration. "Did you know from your last visit she planned to travel to Chicago?"

"Yeah, she told me she was going to go hunt down the fucking scumbag who knocked her up."

Doc's gut twisted at that categorization of himself. He knew that would not have been the way Elizabeth presented it. "And he lives in Chicago?"

"She was pretty sure he did. Look, I'm not telling you no more, until you tell me who the hell you are and why the fuck you're asking about Elizabeth. Is she okay?"

"Yes, Elizabeth is okay. What can you tell me about the man she went to find?"

"Ask her yourself if she's okay," Shaw spat.

"I'm asking you."

"He's some kind of jarhead, a GI Joe, or something like that."

"What else did she tell you about him?"

Robert Shaw sat back and crossed his arms over his chest. His eyes stared daggers through Doc. Doc noticed how cold his eyes were. They may have been the same color as Elizabeth's, but this man's dark soul reflected from the icy depths.

"What did she tell you about this man?"

Robert Shaw rested his elbows on the table and leaned over it. "Who the fuck are you, and why are you asking?"

Doc pulled his FBI badge from his pocket. "I'm an FBI Agent." He didn't give his name on purpose. He was pretty sure Elizabeth would have told her brother his name during her visit.

"And why are you asking about Elizabeth?"

"I need to know what she told you about the man, where did she meet him, and if the sex was consensual."

Robert Shaw looked confused. "Are you telling me Elizabeth lied to me and she was raped or something? I'll kill the bastard!"

"No, that's not what I'm telling you. But you're going out of your way not to tell me anything. I'm trying to help your sister. Why aren't you?"

"Maybe if you tell me why she needs help. You've given me nothing, man, and I sure as hell don't trust you or any other cop."

"That's right. All cops are bastards," Doc said, pointing to the tat on the right side of Bobby Shaw's neck. "Well I'm not." Doc was thoughtful for a moment. "Elizabeth is special, trusting, and kind. I have a great deal of respect for your sister. She's been through a lot and I want to be sure she doesn't get hurt by anyone, even her brother."

"I'd never do anything to hurt my sister. I've spent my life protecting her. How do you think she made it, growing up in the neighborhood we lived in? No one got up on her. I made sure of it."

"Is she aware of your lengthy criminal history?"

"Yeah, Elizabeth knows all my crimes. She forgives me and prays for my soul." He paused and laughed. "She's one of the good ones. Now who the hell are you and why are you asking about her?"

"Did Elizabeth tell you about her last few days in Africa?"

"Yeah," he ran his hand through his disgusting hair and shook it back from his face. "She almost died there, fucking penguins put her in a hell hole. She deserves better than that."

Doc nodded. He agreed. "Elizabeth's in a good place now. You need to leave her alone."

"Wait, you're the guy, aren't you?"

Doc made his decision in that moment. He nodded yes once. "Yes, I'm her husband."

In one fluid movement, Bobby Shaw stood and dove over the table. "You fucking sonofabitch!"

Doc deflected him and helped his face meet the floor faster than his body had been en route to. Then he planted his knee firmly in the small of the man's back. His hand gripped Bobby Shaw's neck, all his weight, holding him to the floor. Even though Doc had him completely immobilized, he struggled.

"Fucking stop," Doc commanded, pressing down more firmly to make his point.

Just then, the room door flew open and two guards rushed in.

"It's okay," Doc told them. "This was just a misunderstanding."

The guards helped Doc pull Shaw to his feet and re-sit him in his chair. Then Doc retook his seat as well and stared at him across the table. They stared at each other for a few minutes. Doc's eyes scanned the gang tats on his neck. He couldn't figure out how different the siblings were. Elizabeth embodied love and forgiveness. Bobby Shaw was a picture of hate and lawlessness.

"At least you married her," Shaw finally said. "You better treat her right." It was said as a threat.

The corner of Doc's lip ticked up. "I'll treat her like a queen. Her happiness and health are all I care about."

"If you ever knock her around and I know about it, I'll find a way to end you."

"I'll never lay a hand on her. You have my word."

"Why are you here?" Bobby Shaw demanded.

"I needed to meet you. Elizabeth wrote you a letter." He pulled it from his pocket and passed it across the table.

Shaw opened it. Several sections were blacked out. He examined it. He couldn't make out what was beneath. He read the letter, a small smile curving his lips. "She sounds happy and believes she's safe with you."

Doc nodded. "She is. Probably safer than she ever has been in her life."

"After our mom died, the nuns took Elizabeth and promised they'd keep her safe. The streets took me."

Doc knew Bobby Shaw had an extensive juvenile record before his mother died. He doubted the streets took him; he had surrendered to them years before.

"But the nuns sent her to that place. She wrote me and told me about the bad situation the people there lived in, diseases, not enough food, war. And I get to see the news and watch some movies. I know how bad it is over there. Somalia, fucking Black Hawk Down, man."

"Yes, it was a dangerous place. But she made it better for those people, helped them. I promise you, Shaw, I will always keep her safe."

"She said you took her in and asked nothing from her in return." He shook the letter at him. "No one does that. Everyone fucking wants something, man."

Doc smirked. Maybe in Bobby Shaw's world. "She's one of the good ones and deserves a break in life. We thought we were going to die. During that time, we shared something that bonded us together and created the life inside her. What do I want from her? Just for her to be happy and raise our child with me."

"Are you going to let her write and call me?"

"That's why I'm here. To decide that."

"You're a fucking fed, and you're afraid of me," Shaw said with a knowing smile.

"Yeah, I don't need any of your gang-brothers showing up at my house, and mostly Elizabeth doesn't need that."

"I'd never do anything to hurt Elizabeth, man. Haven't you been listening to a fucking thing I've said?"

Doc handed a piece of paper across the table. It was a secure mailing PO Box address in DC that would automatically redirect letters to HQ, without anyone knowing it. "You may write Elizabeth at that address."

Tango

Doc's flight from Washington didn't arrive at O'Hare until nearly twenty-three hundred. Doc was beat. He had a hard time falling asleep though. He would have the conversation he was dreading with Elizabeth in the morning. He held her close, listening to her even breaths. He was sure she wouldn't understand his visit with her brother.

Shepherd knew he'd be in late the next morning. He still set the alarm at the normal time. When it went off, he dragged himself from the bed and stood under the hot downpour in the shower, trying to wake up. He brought Elizabeth a cup of herbal tea but made himself a cup of caffeinated coffee to try to wake himself up.

After they ate breakfast, he took hold of her hands. "I need to talk with you about something."

"What?" She sensed something was wrong.

"I went to the Washington State Penitentiary and met your brother yesterday."

"What?" She repeated. "You met Bobby?"

"Yes, before I could let him read your letter, I had to meet him."

"My letter?" She asked, even more confused.

"I read your letter, Elizabeth. It was redacted so that our address and your phone number were removed, as well as a few other areas that were not appropriate details to share with him."

"Why?"

"He's a member of the Aryan Brotherhood, Elizabeth. Do you even understand how bad of a gang that is? I need you to understand that if he wanted to, he could send them after us."

"Send them after us? My brother would never do that."

"He's a career criminal and a card-carrying member of a very real, very bad gang. I had no idea of what he would or wouldn't do and I wasn't going to risk it."

"He's my brother! And you had no right to read my mail!"

"Stop and listen for a moment."

"He's my brother, Alexander. Do you understand? My brother!" She screamed.

"Victoria, just stop!" Doc blurted. Elizabeth's stunned expression slapped him across the face.

"Victoria?" She repeated.

"Elizabeth, honey, I'm sorry."

"Who is Victoria," her small voice asked.

Doc felt a churning in the pit of his stomach. This wasn't the way he wanted to do this. He pointed to the couch. "Let's sit."

She didn't move. She crossed her arms over her chest and stared at him with that hurt expression on her face.

He stepped into her and took both her hands in his. "Please come sit down with me. It's time I told you why I pushed you away when we left Africa."

Elizabeth let him lead her to the couch. Doc made sure they sat close together, facing each other.

"I was married a long time ago. Victoria was my wife," he began. Elizabeth looked stunned. She'd never asked, so technically he hadn't lied about it.

"I see. I guess I shouldn't be surprised you're divorced."

"Not divorced, widowed."

"I'm sorry," she said, looking more shocked than when he'd called her Victoria.

"I haven't had one serious relationship since," Doc confessed. "Until recently, I blamed myself."

"How did she die?" Elizabeth asked after a long silence.

"She stuck a gun in her mouth and pulled the trigger."

"Oh, dear Lord," Elizabeth gasped. "Did you find her?"

"No, some poor cop doing a well-being check did. I was in the Middle East on active duty with the Rangers. I was a medic and I was seeing way more death than any person should."

"Why did she do it?" Elizabeth asked. She saw tears in Alexander's eyes.

"Six months earlier the car she was driving was hit by a drunk driver. She was six months pregnant with our son. The baby didn't make it. She nearly didn't either. I thought she was seeing a counselor. She was supposed to, but she didn't. She slipped into a deep depression. I only saw it in hindsight. She was alone, dealing with it. I wasn't there for her. I stayed in the Middle East when I didn't have to because I couldn't bear the thought of going home. I thought I'd dealt with it, my feelings, the grief, and self-blame, but I hadn't. I buried it and pushed it out of my thoughts. But after I was with you, it came back, and sucker punched me in the gut. We said vows to each other, much like the ones I said to Victoria. That's what started it. By the time I said goodbye to you at Andrews Air Force base, I had so many twisted dark thoughts running through my head."

"Do I remind you of her?"

Doc cackled out a burst of sarcastic laughter. "Not in the least. You couldn't be any more different. Which is good."

"Did you love her?"

"Before I went to the Sandbox, I did with all my heart. I was young, just a few years older than you are now. Where I was, had very active fighting. The wounded never stopped coming and there was so much death. Little kids carried bombs up to our troops. Their parents detonated them, killing their own children to take as many of us out as they could. I'd been a paramedic in Houston and saw more than my fair share of violence and hate, but I'd never seen hate like I did over in the Sandbox. The whole place made no sense. Even before the car accident, I know I'd changed. And after it, I poured everything into my work, trying to save those I could, because I couldn't save Daniel. That's what we were going to name him, after my father. After Victoria took her own life, I felt numb to all of it, to all the death. I signed up for several more tours over there. When I came back, I did several rotations at various bases until Shepherd recruited me."

"I'm sorry saying those vows to me did that to you," Elizabeth said after a few quiet moments.

"I'm not. I needed to deal with it. We have a team shrink, Joe Lassiter. He's been helping me finally deal with Victoria and our unborn child's deaths. Well, he's been trying to, but I've been a pain in the ass. It all hit me really hard after Africa and I was just starting to get my head on straight when you came back into my life."

"I would never have guessed any of this. You've been a Godsend, Alexander, in Africa and since I told you I was pregnant."

"I'm really sorry I left you the way I did. I haven't been with anyone since you and I made love in Africa. I tried to convince myself those vows meant nothing and that we had no relationship. That too ate at me the last few months. I wasn't anyone you would have wanted to be with since Africa."

"What changed? You've been so good to me since I've been here."

"I didn't want to screw it up a second time with you. You deserved better from me and after you told me you were pregnant; I knew I had to try to make it right. Plus, to be honest, I couldn't bear the thought of not being there for my baby. I already lost one. I couldn't lose another."

Elizabeth leaned into him and wrapped her arms around his neck and held him tightly. Her heart broke for him, for what he'd endured. No parent should ever lose a child, born or unborn. He was a strong man who had suffered in silence and alone for many years. She knew in that moment that she loved him.

"That's why I had to meet Bobby, to be sure he wasn't a threat to you. I don't care if the Aryan Brotherhood takes me out, but damn-it Elizabeth, I'd never be right again if anything ever happened to you and our child."

"It's okay. I won't communicate with Bobby if you don't want me to."

"I gave him a special address that will reroute his letters to HQ. It's not traceable. For now, no phone calls though."

Elizabeth nodded. "It'll be a month or more before he gets his phone privileges back, anyway. He got into a fight and hurt someone."

Doc nodded. Yeah, Bobby had beat the shit out of a rival gang-member, putting the man into a coma. "We do this together, Elizabeth. You don't give anyone information on us without telling me. It's to keep us safe."

"I won't give him our address or tell him anything about our life. I understand." She embraced him again and held him tightly.

The next morning, Thursday, Doc felt a level of excitement he hadn't felt in a long time. He had the morning off work for their first prenatal checkup with the obstetrician. He was sure they would be able to hear the baby's heartbeat and he couldn't wait to see the sonogram.

Elizabeth felt a strong connection to Alexander, now that she knew about his past, about the loss of his wife and unborn child. A lot more made sense to her now, even his visit with Bobby. She was glad she knew about it prior to this appointment. They held hands in the doctor's waiting room. It was a fancy office, quite different than the free clinic where she'd taken the pregnancy test and talked with Sister Abigale.

"Mrs. and Mr. Williams," the nurse called from the doorway.

Elizabeth smiled at the sound of it. She still needed to get her ID changed to the name Williams. Alexander pulled her to her feet. They followed the nurse through the door. After getting her weight and her vitals, the nurse left, promising the doctor would be right in.

Dr. Norman came in five minutes later. He was a bald man, with a gray mustache and goatee on his round face. He was in his mid-fifties. He had an easy smile and a calm demeanor. He shook both their hands and congratulated them on their pregnancy. Then, he spoke with them about the pregnancy, their expectations, and asked them what was important to them.

Doc could see why Jackson and Angel liked the man.

"Do you want to take a look at the little bugger?" Dr. Norman said with a smile, motioning Elizabeth to the exam table. "Let's do the sonogram before I examine you. I find that putting the main event first makes everything else we have to do today easier for the mom-to-be."

The image was clear and incredible. Their baby was on the screen and captured in pictures. The fast washing machine sound that was indicative of a healthy fetal heartbeat broadcast over the speakers. Even though Elizabeth had seen it and heard it before when working at the free clinic, seeing her baby and hearing her baby's heartbeat was overwhelming. Tears of joy flooded her eyes. She glanced at Alexander. He was similarly affected. Her heart swelled in her chest, knowing he'd never had this experience when his first wife had been pregnant with his son.

"Do you want to know the gender?" Dr. Norman asked. "It's a simple blood test on the mother's blood and we're taking some today. You'll know next week, if you want to."

Elizabeth's eyes focused on Alexander's. They still hadn't discussed if they wanted to know or not.

"Run the test. We can decide when you have the results," Doc said, seeing the uncertainty in Elizabeth's eyes. This was something they needed to discuss. The decision should not be made spur of the moment like this.

Alexander kissed Elizabeth's knuckles; her hand clutched in his. They stopped for lunch after her OB appointment on the way to the office. She was training with Angel today for the afternoon. After today, she should be ready to fill in the next day Angel needed off. She liked working at the office and would be able to do her homework there too. She felt good about the classes. Her life was meaningful and full of purpose. She was excited for the future.

Her cell phone buzzed a text message. Angel. "What time are you and Doc getting in?"

She tapped out her reply. "Within the hour. We just stopped for a quick lunch." Her eyes met Alexander's. She smiled. She marveled how she felt comfortable with everything about her life with him in just the few short weeks they'd been together. "Have I told you how much I like my life with you?"

Doc smiled. His heart was full. "No, but you can't like it any more than I do. I'm glad you're here, Elizabeth. It feels right in every way."

Her smile widened. He noticed that she actually glowed. He was glad they had had the discussion about Victoria and Daniel. It wasn't the way he would have liked for it to come out, but it was out now, and that was all that mattered. Things felt very comfortable with her and he realized he hadn't thought about the age difference in weeks.

"So, do you want to know the gender?" Doc asked her.

She took a bite of her sandwich. "I don't know. Do you?" A part of her wanted to do it opposite of how he had the first time. And a part of her prayed it would be a girl so it would be different than when his first wife was pregnant with a boy.

"I don't know," Doc admitted.

"But you had wanted to know when Victoria was pregnant?"

"No, the sonogram clearly showed a stem on the apple. We weren't going to find out, but it was obvious."

She thought about it for a second. "Well, Angel said it made it easy planning and shopping for things, knowing Sammy was a boy. There aren't a lot of gender-neutral things. I guess it would make sense to know to buy the appropriate clothes and bedding."

"And to think about names," Doc added. "Have you thought about names at all?"

Elizabeth shook her head no. "Before I came here to tell you, I didn't even allow myself to wonder if it was a boy or a girl, but ever since, that's all I've thought about."

"Then I think we should find out," Doc said, but the truth was, he would be fine with whatever her choice was.

Saturday morning, Elizabeth gave Alexander a kiss goodbye as he went out the door, heading to the office. Madison would be there in an hour to pick her up for the spa day. She was a bit nervous about it, even though she had confided in Angel that she had never had any of the services they would enjoy. Angel explained how they did everything and assured her it would be fun.

After they checked in, they were sent to the locker room to hang their clothes for the evening out and to change into wraps and robes. Then they were each whisked into separate treatment rooms. Facials and full body massages were the first services. Ninety minutes later when Elizabeth rejoined the others, feet in the pedicure bowl, she felt incredibly relaxed. Every inch of her skin felt soft and the warm oil they used to massage her was infused with a light, fresh scent.

She chose a pale gold for her nail color to match the dress Angel had lent her to wear to dinner. Madison's nails, both toes and fingers, were painted bright red. Sienna went with a sparkly purple on her toes and a French Manicure on her fingers, citing the need to keep her hands toned down for school. Angel had both sets of hers, painted a royal sparkling blue.

In between the pedicures and manicures, they were treated to lunch on couches in the waterfall room, a serene space with waterfalls on three of the four walls. Madison hadn't been kidding when she raved about the finger sandwiches. Elizabeth devoured so many she was stuffed. Elizabeth took one sip of the champagne during a toast to her and the baby, but the other ladies drank it freely.

After their manicures, the four of them moved into the hairdresser's chairs. Elizabeth hadn't thought about having anything done. She'd only planned to trim the ends. Her hair though, became the topic of discussion between her friends and her hair stylist.

"Highlights, definitely highlights," the stylist said. "And you should think about cutting off about twelve inches. The bottom half is thin, and your hair is not thick to begin with. Cutting it will make it look fuller and healthier."

"You think I need to cut twelve inches off?" Elizabeth demanded.

"I think it will look great," the stylist said. "Combined with the highlights, it will give you a new look, a more mature look. It will bring it to about here." She held her comb up to just above Elizabeth's breast.

"I don't want that much of my hair cut off," Elizabeth complained.

"Twelve inches can be donated to Locks of Love," Sienna chimed in. "It could really help a child who has lost their hair from a medical condition."

"I think it will look great shorter," Angel said. "And it will be easier to take care of which will really matter once the baby comes."

Madison shrugged. "I wish I could go shorter, but these curls are even wilder without the weight."

Elizabeth thought about it for a few seconds. The stylist showed her a picture of what she had in mind. The model did look great. Her hair was styled just so, and the blond highlights created a beautiful effect, one that Elizabeth would never have dreamed she could pull off.

"Sure, let's do it," she said bravely.

Elizabeth couldn't keep her eyes off her reflection during the cut, blow dry, and style. She changed into the dress, speechless from her appearance. After the makeup artist finished with applying the pallet of colors to her face, she gazed into the bright blue eyes of the stranger returning her gaze. The girl in the mirror was beautiful.

"Wow, Doc is going to be bowled over when he sees you!" Angel said, giving her a hug. "Elizabeth, you are stunning."

Elizabeth felt her cheeks heat. "I can't believe the difference."

"Holy hell," Doc said aloud.

"Fuck," Garcia seconded. "That's your Elizabeth?"

"I'm going to say yes, given that she's with the other women, otherwise, I'd never have recognized her," Doc replied.

"Close your mouth and stop drooling," Garcia said.

"I'm not fucking drooling," Doc argued.

"She doesn't look young or innocent any longer, does she? You're welcome, by the way," he remarked.

Doc gave Garcia a sideways glance. Then his eyes slid to the other women. Yeah, they definitely had something to do with this transformation. He rose and met the women half-way, taking Elizabeth into his arms. He placed his lips beside her ear and whispered. "Don't take this the wrong way, but damn do you look beautiful."

A wide smile spread over Elizabeth's peach tinted lips. "Thank you."

Doc let his eyes take her in. Her hair was cut, falling to just above her breasts. It looked thicker and there were highlights of lighter blond in it. It was parted on the side creating a sexy effect on her face, which literally glowed. She wore tinted, shiny lip gloss, her eyebrows were defined in a perfect arch, and she wore eye makeup. When his gaze lowered down her neck, he found her creamy white skin was exposed from the off the shoulders, deep cream and gold sweater dress Angel had lent her. It hugged her pregnancy-blossomed curves. Thank you, Angel!

"Please tell me you bought some of the makeup they used on you."

She giggled shyly. "I bought the moisturizer only because it is a very good product and I loved how it felt on my face. I also bought the lip gloss. I've never worn color on my lips, but I really like how it looks."

"You could have bought everything," Doc said, disappointed she hadn't.

"Well, Angel bought me the eye shadow pallet. Madison said I needed the face powder to set the moisturizer, so she bought me that, and Sienna insisted on buying me the eyebrow kit. They said it was because they didn't get to give me a personal shower before we were married."

Doc smiled wide. Thank you, ladies! "That was nice of them. Did you enjoy the day?"

Elizabeth wrapped her arms around his neck. A fresh, delicate scent wafted from her and invaded his senses. "I did. It felt absolutely decadent to have all the beauty services, but what I enjoyed most was spending the day with the three of them. They are all such wonderful people."

"Hum, hard to believe sinners who spend that much money on self-pleasure can be so wonderful," he said jokingly as he embraced her more tightly.

"Okay, you were right about that. I'll admit it."

Doc laughed. "Let's go eat as fast as we can. I can't wait to get you home and feel for myself how soft these lotions and oils have supposedly made every inch of your body."

Elizabeth laughed. "I do feel incredibly soft."

Doc groaned. She had no idea how turned on he was. This would be the longest dinner of his life. As they ate, he had a hard time keeping his hands off her. He noticed his teammates had similar difficulties. The atmosphere in the private dining room was definitely sexually charged. You'd think they'd just gotten back from a long mission. The other thing he noticed was how comfortable Elizabeth seemed. She smiled and laughed, looked confident and sexy. She had come a long way in the three weeks since she'd reentered his life.

The drive home though short, was painful for Doc. His mind imagined in detail what he planned to do to her once they were through the door. Even though it was ten degrees out, he was hot. His pants were uncomfortable with his swollen member straining against the zipper.

After they'd passed through the door from the garage into the kitchen, he helped take her coat from her, and then he took the remainder of her clothes from her as well, right there in the kitchen. His hands glided over her silky soft flesh, over every inch of it. His lips took hers in what he knew was an aggressive kiss. No, there was no way he could hold anything back tonight.

"Oh, fuck, Elizabeth, if you aren't the sexiest thing I've ever seen," he groaned. "I've been hard all night."

A smile curved Elizabeth's lips, appreciating that she did that to him. "Let's take this to the bedroom."

"No, right here," he insisted. "I want to put your ass print on the fridge by making love to you against it and get hard every time I see it." His hands roamed over her naked body more. "You are so damned soft. I can't get enough of feeling you." Then his lips followed his hands and she exploded in two intense orgasms, one after the other.

He begged her to get on her knees and orally pleasure him, which she did, feeling more okay with the act than she had the first time she had done it. "We didn't have dessert at the restaurant," he said. He took a bottle of chocolate syrup from the cabinet and squeezed some over his hard penis. "Lick all of it off, slowly, tease me, and make me plead with you to let me come."

She wasn't sure how to do that, but she tried her best. Judging by his moans and his imploring, painful groans to go faster, she knew she had done what he asked. He let fly a string of curses unlike she'd ever heard, pulled her up and pressed her against the refrigerator. Then, he did what he said he would. He drove into her hard and was relentless until he came and collapsed against her.

After he recovered from one of the most intense orgasms of his life, he sat her on the kitchen counter and poured chocolate syrup on her pussy. He licked her, making sounds of enjoyment, his eyes locked on hers. She watched him with intrigue, and he knew she'd never seen anything like it, had never watched porn, and he had a momentary resurfacing of those gut-wrenching feelings of taking advantage of her. Where had that come from? He hadn't felt that way in weeks. When her eyes rolled back in her head and her body quaked, those ridiculous feelings of his disappeared. This was his wife, pregnant with his child and there was nothing wrong with having sex with her the way he liked it as long as she liked it too, and she obviously did.

The intensity of doing the act in the kitchen, was startling to Elizabeth. Why did it feel so different out of the bedroom? All that was missing were the words of love that she longed to hear from him. They had gotten so close through the phone calls and text messages while he was away on the mission. Their conversations were honest and meaningful. And even the love they'd made since he got back from the mission was connecting. If this wasn't fueled by love, she wasn't sure what drove it to be so different than the love they'd made daily, before he left.

Doc swung by the OB's office on his way home from work after receiving the call that the blood test results that would indicate the gender of their baby were in. The receptionist handed him a sealed envelope. He knew a lot of people did what was called a Gender Reveal Party, in which the envelope was given to a baker to have the color blue or pink baked into the center of the cake, so no one would know the gender until the cake was cut. Or, a trusted friend was given the envelope to get a mini cannon that would fire pink or blue confetti to make the announcement.

He and Elizabeth would do none of those things. They would tell their friends personally, with little fanfare. He brought the envelope home and sat it in the middle of the kitchen table. Elizabeth made a special dinner for them, a roast with potatoes and carrots. The table was set beautifully. He was amazed daily by the household skills she was acquiring.

Elizabeth wrapped her arms around Alexander's neck. "Are you as anxious to know as I am?"

Doc chuckled. "You want to open it right away, don't you?"

Elizabeth smiled wide. "Yes. I'm not going to be able to eat, not knowing."

Doc sat, pulling Elizabeth onto his lap. He handed the envelope to her. "Open it, but we view the results together."

Elizabeth ripped it open and pulled the slip of paper out, holding it up in front of their faces. Relief flooded her. A girl! They were having a baby girl. Not that she wouldn't have loved a baby boy, it was just that she didn't want any reminders to Alexander of the family he had lost.

Doc embraced her. A part of him wanted a son, not that one would have replaced Daniel, but what man didn't want a son to carry on the family name? But he was thrilled with a girl. He suspected Elizabeth wanted a girl. Didn't all women want a little girl to deck out in pretty pink dresses and bows in their hair?

Valentine's Day was a few days away, creating a dilemma for Doc. Standing in the card aisle reading all the cards, none were right. He did not love Elizabeth and all the cards to 'my wife' spoke of love. No matter how badly he wanted to love her, he did not. He liked her. He was content living with her. He was proud of the woman she was becoming, confident and comfortable in his world. He was thrilled she was pregnant with his child. But that was where his feelings ended.

He finally found a card that was appropriate. It talked about looking forward to the future with heartfelt joy, but the word love was never mentioned. Now a gift. He wracked his brain on that one. He ended up at the jewelry store on the first floor in the Shepherd Security Building. He picked out a plain gold cross on a delicate chain. He'd bring her flowers too. Certainly, that would be enough.

Doc reached the conference room for the briefing. Both Alpha and Delta Teams were there, as was Yvette. Doc knew Delta was heading back out for an assignment the next day. He hoped that didn't mean they were heading out with them, not that he should complain. Since the first of the year, besides the two weeks in Montana, his team had one, three-day mission close to home, so close, he was able to sleep in his own bed. They had a second personal security four-day mission in South Beach at a resort, that had been more like a vacation. Three weeks away during a five-week period of time was nothing to bitch about.

"Let's get started," Shepherd announced, quieting the group. "As you know, Delta was scheduled to leave tomorrow to test out a new Rapid Response Team that was recently put together. These Operators have never worked together, so we are going to put them through multiple simulations. The majority are newly graduated from several different training establishments. Due to several other nonoperational constraints, I have decided we will put it off one more week and deploy both Alpha and Delta next Monday. The simulations will run more smoothly with eight of you putting them through their trials. Jackson, you will remain in Ops with Yvette for this one."

Jackson nodded. He appreciated the accommodation to allow him more time at home, though this one would be fun, and it was a no-brainer. Simulations were great, paintballs instead of real bullets being fired was always desirable.

Cooper smiled at Garcia. "This weekend all teams will be inhouse. If you still want to get married, Saturday would be the day."

Garcia grinned and nodded. "It's about fucking time!"

Everyone at the table laughed. They all knew how much he wanted to marry Sienna and have a baby, but Sienna wouldn't try to get pregnant until they were married. As a teacher, it was frowned upon.

"And Doc has a birthday this weekend too that we'll celebrate. The big four-oh!" Cooper added.

Doc groaned. "If it's all the same," he began.

"Not happening," Garcia interrupted. "I've already got the 'Doc is older than shit' balloons. We *are* celebrating it." His voice was firm.

"That number is something. Not many men can do this job at the level you do it at, at your age, Doc," Jackson threw out, an obvious barb.

Doc flipped both him and Garcia the bird. Laughter erupted in response.

Shepherd continued, pulling them back on topic. "The simulation exercises and our timeline for this job has been pushed to all your tablets. Memorize them and your role in each of the six drills. Cooper, Lambchop and I have put a lot of work into them. You will leave the following Monday at zero-six hundred, full tactical gear, both black and desert fatigues, and paintball loads. Plan on being gone a full week. Jackson, you and Yvette will pull shifts in Ops that align with the simulations."

Saturday morning, February fourteenth, Valentine's Day, would be a busy day. It was Garcia and Sienna's wedding day as well as the evening of Doc's fortieth birthday party. So, Doc brought the flowers home Friday night and gave Elizabeth her card and gift then.

"This is such a beautiful cross, Alexander. Thank you," she said, gazing at it with admiration. It was plain but the edges were beveled. The chain it hung on was delicate and very feminine. She reread the card.

She went into the closet that held the washer and dryer and brought the card and gift out that she bought for him. She had been out with Angel when they stopped to buy the cards and gifts. Elizabeth found the perfect card for Alexander right away. It talked about being grateful for having him in her life and praised him as a husband. Coming up with the gift idea was harder.

When Alexander finished reading the card, he glanced up at her and smiled. "That's very nice, thank you."

"I mean every word. You have already proven yourself to be the best husband I could have asked for." She held herself back from saying I love you, words she felt, but had not vocalized.

Doc pressed a kiss to her lips. "Thank you." Then he opened her gift. "Oh, wow, Elizabeth, this is nice." In a five by seven frame was the Fisherman's Prayer over a beautiful picture of a calm lake at sunrise.

"It's for your office at work. Or you could take it out of the frame and roll it up to take on missions with you to always be able to feel at peace like you do when you're fishing."

A pang of appreciation hit Doc's heart. "Thank you. You've always gotten it, even when we were in the cave talking about it."

Elizabeth smiled and nodded. "Everyone needs to do what feeds their soul. I will try very hard to be understanding and support your fishing trips, but I do hope once in a while you will take me with. I'd love it if you teach me to fish."

Doc embraced her tightly. "It's the perfect gift. Thank you. Yes, we'll go in the early fall and take the baby to my favorite spot."

Angel and Madison helped Sienna with the arrangements for the wedding and looped Elizabeth in to help plan Doc's fortieth birthday party that would occur the same night, following the wedding. Elizabeth was embarrassed. She didn't remember that his birthday was approaching. They were able to book the clubhouse in the townhome complex for the event. BT and Caleb Smith were tasked by Garcia with providing security and a tie-in to Ops.

They got access to the clubhouse that morning and positioned battery operated cameras at strategic locations. It was always risky, having an event that was attended by most of the personnel off-site. The women arrived shortly after it had been secured to decorate. One side of the room was decorated for the wedding, the other with black balloons for Doc's fortieth birthday party.

There was a side room the ladies would use to change into more formal attire. Although Sienna wanted it kept simple and informal, Anthony insisted she wear a white gown and wanted to see her walking down an aisle with a bouquet of flowers. Sienna would of course give Anthony the wedding day he wanted.

Both her parents had died years before, her father suffering a fatal heart attack, what is known as a widow maker and her mother following a year later from an undiagnosed brain aneurism that ruptured. Sienna had a brother. They had a falling out after their mother's death and hadn't spoken in years. She didn't even know where he lived now. She had a few close friends outside of the agency but knew how much complication it would add if nonagency personnel were there. She'd tell them that she and Anthony eloped.

Garcia wasn't close to his family. They knew nothing about his life since he had joined the DEA prior to being recruited by Shepherd Security. He wouldn't even tell them about his wedding. As far as he was concerned, his coworkers at Shepherd Security were his family. They were the only ones he cared about being there to celebrate his wedding to Sienna.

Michaela and Yvette joined the other ladies to help decorate when they were about half-way done. Elizabeth didn't know either one well, so she welcomed this chance to get to know them. Although they had very different personalities, Elizabeth liked them both.

Landon Lambchop Johnson stood in his Dress Blues with his Wedding Officiant Clergy Stole draped around his neck. He held his Bible in his hand. He stood beneath the arch the women had decorated with red and white balloons to celebrate the Valentine's Day wedding.

The groom and other male guests wore dress pants, dress shirts and ties. The women all wore dresses. The bride had a lovely long-length white gown she'd bought as soon as the couple had gotten their marriage license. It was a designer gown that she would be able to wear for any other formal occasion.

Gazing at Sienna after she put her gown on, Elizabeth recalled the vows she said to Alexander in that room they were locked in, vows that meant everything to her. She wished she had kept the beautiful dirac she wore. She'd left it in the bathroom at the hangar in Djibouti when she'd changed into the fatigues Madison lent her. At least they had a confirmation of their vow's ceremony that Lambchop had insisted on to sign their marriage license. A few of Alexander's friends had snapped pictures on their phones of them with Reverend Johnson. Angel had printed out a few, framed them, and gave them to her, so she had something to commemorate their union.

In a nontraditional procession, all the ladies, in no particular order, filed down the aisle to the waltz music that played over the speakers. When they reached the chairs that were positioned in an arc around the arch, where Lambchop and Garcia stood, they sat wherever they wanted. Elizabeth took a seat beside Alexander on the left side. Moments later, the Wedding March boomed through the room, bringing everyone to their feet.

Sienna walked down the aisle alone, carrying a bouquet of red roses. Elizabeth watched the expression of joy spread over Sienna's face as her eyes remained locked with Garcia's. Then she gazed at Garcia. Wow! His eyes were focused on Sienna. She was all he saw. The look on his face screamed how much he loved her. Their pictures would be beautiful, Elizabeth thought as Sienna joined him. He wore a white shirt with a red tie, matching her in every way. She looked beautiful and happy.

"Please be seated," Lambchop said. "Friends, we gather here today to celebrate the love of this couple. It is not enough for either one of them to love the other, they wish their union to be blessed by God and celebrated by those close to them. The joining of a man and a woman in the bonds of holy matrimony is one of God's most sacred ordinances. God calls upon everyone present to support and nurture this union. When I was speaking with Sienna and Anthony about this ceremony, we went over several Bible verses. One stood out to each of them, representing how they felt. Sienna identified 'I thank my God every time I think of you' from **Philippians 1:3** as a verse that represented the love she has for Anthony. And he told me that the following verse from **Song of Solomon 3:4,** summed up his feelings for Sienna, 'I have found the one whom my soul loves'. Indeed, to have found the one person who you know you love deeply, who you thank God for their presence in your life, is a rare gift!" He closed his Bible and kissed it.

Elizabeth felt a pang of emptiness. She knew she felt love for Alexander, but they never spoke the words to each other. Though wrong, she knew, she felt a jealousy that Sienna and Garcia had that love and openly professed it the way they did. And how she wished one day she could see Alexander look at her that way. She prayed that someday, she and Alexander would share what this couple had.

Lambchop nodded to Madison, who sat beside Cooper in the front row. Madison took Sienna's flowers.

"Please join hands," he said. "Sienna, do you take Anthony to live with as husband and wife, to love him and to cherish him in sickness and in health, for richer and poorer, forsaking all others until death do you part?"

Sienna smiled with tears moistening her eyes. "I do."

"Anthony, do you take Sienna to live with as husband and wife, to love her and to cherish her in sickness and in health, for richer and poorer, forsaking all others until death do you part?" Lambchop repeated.

"You better believe I do," Garcia replied, garnering laughter from their guests.

"The rings," the pastor prompted. Sienna took Anthony's off her thumb and handed it to Lambchop. Anthony grabbed Sienna's from Madison, who had held it for him and gave it to Lambchop as well. He sat them on the Bible. "God, bless these rings as the outward symbol of the pledge these two children of Yours have made. If the ring is on or off your finger from this moment forward is irrelevant. God sees you joined as one." He handed Garcia's ring to Sienna.

"With this ring, I take you, Anthony, as my wedded husband. I promise to love you with all my heart as I know tomorrow is never guaranteed. I promise I will always be honest with you. And I will always, with my actions, make sure you know how much I do love and appreciate you." Her voice became more unsteady as she spoke. She slid the ring onto his finger.

Lambchop handed Garcia Sienna's ring.

"With this ring, I take you, Sienna, as my wedded wife. I promise that I will always love you as I do today. I too promise my honesty. I will show you every day that I am grateful that you are in my life." His voice was strong and full of emotion as he spoke. He then slid the ring onto her finger.

"Let love and faithfulness never leave you; bind them around your neck, write them on the tablet of your heart, from **Proverbs 3:3**. And one last reading, 'So, they are no longer two, but one. Therefore, what God has joined together, let man not separate', from **Matthew 19:6**." Lambchop paused for dramatic effect, smiling at those assembled. "By the power vested in me by God, I pronounce you husband and wife. Garcia, you may kiss your bride."

Cheers and claps serenaded the couple as they shared their first kiss as husband and wife. Then they went into the seating area and greeted their friends. The marriage license was already signed and sitting on Angel's desk. Madison and Cooper had signed as the witnesses. Angel would file it at the county building for Lambchop on Monday as the team would be gone early.

Dinner was catered in and a self-serve bar was set up. Lambchop said a blessing before Garcia and Sienna followed by Doc and Elizabeth began serving themselves at the buffet. The remainder of the guests followed. Shepherd covered the cost of everything, one of his gifts to the couple. He also had an envelope in his pocket of an expense paid honeymoon vacation, the date to be determined. He knew Sienna could not take off when school was in session. It would be up to the couple if they wanted to go over the upcoming Spring Break or wait until the summer. He also had a second envelope with the same gift for Doc and Elizabeth, realizing their wedding had happened so fast, he'd done nothing to acknowledge it.

After dinner, the birthday party went into full swing. His friends all got Doc gag gifts jabbing fun at his age. He handled it well even though he realized the number did bother him. His birthday was the next day. Forty years old and he was about to become a father for the first time. He should have felt blessed, but all he could think about was that he would be nearly sixty years old at his daughter's high school graduation, probably one of the oldest parents there.

"Hey old man," Cooper said in jest, slapping Doc on the shoulder. He handed a gift wrapped in black paper to him. "From Madison and me."

Doc shot him a glare. "You guys get away with this today and today only," he warned.

Cooper and Madison laughed.

"Open it," Elizabeth prompted him. She knew what was inside as Madison had told her. They didn't go the route of the gag gift.

Doc opened the package. Inside, wrapped in tissue paper was a newborn baby outfit. The pink short-sleeved onesie had the phrase 'Daddy's little fishing buddy' on it. The light-weight pants had pink fish against the water-blue background.

"Oh hell," Doc swore as a smile curved his lips. It was the cutest damned outfit he'd ever seen.

"Little girls love to go fishing with their daddies," Madison said with a smile.

"Thanks, this is awesome," Doc replied.

Joe Lassiter made his way over next. "Happy Birthday," he said. Then he turned to Elizabeth. "It's nice to finally meet you, Elizabeth. I'm Joe Lassiter."

"You're the team," she paused, not sure how to refer to him. Everyone who had mentioned him to her referred to him as the team shrink. She didn't think that was an appropriate thing to say to his face.

"Shrink, yes." Lassiter laughed.

Elizabeth shook his hand. "I've heard about you. Alexander told me you helped him." She didn't elaborate any further. She didn't need to.

Lassiter nodded. "I tried. That's my job. You've got a good man, here," he said, clasping Doc on the shoulder.

"I know I do," Elizabeth replied.

She was sure this man knew intimate details about them, and probably knew Alexander's thoughts and fears more than anyone else did, herself included. She didn't feel jealous or insecure realizing this. If anything, it made her feel a warmth towards him. Alexander had said he was messed up after Africa, no one she would have wanted to be around. It was this man who enabled Alexander to be the person he was with her when she arrived in Chicago.

Angel and Sienna came and dragged Elizabeth with them to the corner where they had a karaoke machine. Doc watched her from across the room. She talked and laughed with the other women. She looked confident and sexy, a part of the group in every way. She had come a very long way in a short period of time. She truly was one of them now.

Madison unboxed two small cakes, one a wedding cake decorated with white frosting, red flowers and a wedding couple standing in the middle of it. The other was his birthday cake, black frosting with aqua writing wishing him a Happy 40th. Then she lit the candles.

Over the loudspeakers, Doc heard her, and the other women sing Happy Birthday to him. He heard Elizabeth's voice over everyone else's. She had a beautiful voice. He couldn't wait to hear her sing lullabies to their daughter.

After he blew out the candles, the ladies broke into Angel and Sienna's signature song, *If You're Going Through Hell*, by Rodney Atkins, damn Jackson and his country music, but appropriate to the ladies' pasts. He'd give them that. He was surprised to see and hear Elizabeth sing along with them. She knew all the words. The next song they sang, Elizabeth dedicated to him for his birthday, Tom Petty's, *I'm Learning to Fly*. She again knew all the words. He couldn't help but smile. He knew she had learned the song for him.

He felt pride as he watched her, even though it wasn't his doing that she was becoming this wonderful woman. He credited the other women for that and Elizabeth herself for wanting to be a part of his world. He knew she was brave from the moment she had told him she was leaving the Sisterhood and had to figure out the rest of her life. After twelve years, it would have been easier to remain rather than face the unknown, but she knew she didn't belong there, and she faced her future with courage.

The next morning Elizabeth got up early and made Alexander breakfast. She served it to him in bed. She had his birthday card on the tray, her gift inside. If coming up with a Valentine's Day gift hadn't been hard enough, coming up with a fortieth birthday gift was even harder. She took Angel's suggestion and got creative. Angel had done something similar as a gift for Jackson.

Doc opened the card. It was a heartfelt 'Happy Birthday Husband' card. It spoke of love. She only had her name signed at the appropriate space, nothing else. Inside was a book of coupons. He flipped through the first few of them. They were handwritten by Elizabeth. His grin spread wide.

"There are forty of them. You may only use each once, and you may only use one a day. They expire one year from today." She sat cross legged across from him with a proud grin on her face. "The first ten are get out of doing something for the baby, that is your turn to do, like changing a messy diaper. The next ten are fishing related, go off alone for a day or splurge on yourself and buy something fishing related you don't really need, but want. The next set of ten are for me to do something specific for you, like a massage, make you breakfast in bed, or something." She blushed red knowing she had sexual favors written in there as well. "And the last set of ten are for you to ask me to do anything for you."

"Anything?" He asked with a leer curving his lips.

"Yes, pretty much anything," she agreed.

Doc laughed out loud. "Oh, honey, you have no idea what you just agreed to." He tore off one of those coupons from the last section and handed it to her. They stayed in bed for hours.

Doc kissed Elizabeth goodbye Monday morning. "I'll text and call when I can."

She nodded and smiled. Then she embraced him again. "I'm glad this is a simulation mission."

"Yeah, this one should be fun. I think Jackson is pissed he won't be going."

"I think Angel would prefer he does the missions like this too, rather than the dangerous ones."

"But that's our job." Doc shook his head. "It's who I am, Elizabeth."

"I know," she agreed. "I told you I could be fine with all this, and I am."

Doc embraced her again. Yes, she had handled it very well, what she knew about, anyway. "I have to go. I'll see you in about a week."

After Alexander closed the door and left, Elizabeth stared at it for a few seconds. She was disappointed. She wasn't sure what she expected him to say as he left, but he hadn't said it. Okay, to be perfectly honest, she was hoping he would say he'd miss her or that he loved her. She felt they had gotten closer the last few weeks. The love they made was different. It was intense. Certainly, it was driven by emotions.

Uniform

The mood on the Lear on the flight to Virginia was light, even though the accommodations were jam-packed with both teams and all their gear aboard. Even though they were going to test the training of the new teams, this would be an excellent training exercise for them too. Doc suspected Cooper or maybe Ops would file a report with Shepherd on the team as a whole and on each team member's performance.

When they landed, they were escorted to an unoccupied barracks on the base, the Joint Expeditionary Base Little Creek-Fort Story. Its former residents, SEAL Team Four, had just deployed to the Middle East. Both Gary 'the Undertaker' Sloan and Brian 'the Birdman' Sherman had spent time at this base when they were with the SEALs as they were part of the Atlantic Fleet. Landon 'Lambchop' Johnson's time was spent in Coronado assigned to the Pacific Fleet. This barracks would be their base of operations.

"Home sweet home, huh Sherman?" Sloan said, glancing around the rec room.

Brian Sherman smiled. "Yeah, I don't think our team was ever billeted in this particular barracks, and this is a whole lot nicer than I remember it being when we were here. This room is actually heated. I remember it never being over fifty degrees in the winter inside the barracks. I froze my nuts off at night."

"Yeah, and then over in the Sandbox we sweated our asses off," Sloan said.

Cooper went over to the table that had been set up in the center of the rec room. Maps of the base territory where the exercises would take place were stacked on the table. "We're going to go over the first exercise now, then grab some sleep, then we'll hit it again. As you know, the first simulation will be against what has been designated as Fire Team Red, at twenty-three hundred hours."

General Seyller, the officer who had contacted Shepherd for their assistance in conducting these tests, came into the room, halfway through the briefing.

"Atten Hut!" Cooper called as he came to attention. The others followed suit.

"As you were," the General said, his eyes sweeping over the team. "As of nine hundred this morning, the four teams were brought together for the first time and have been switched to paintball loads. They know this next week will hold multiple simulations. They do not know how many each team will face or from whom. And they will not know the scenarios they are facing until they are scrambled to respond.

I'm sure they are expecting the tests to come from teams they are familiar with and associated with this base."

"Yes, sir," Cooper acknowledged. "I know Shepherd worked with you to identify for us what they have been trained on. We are going to throw our own little spin on it."

The General nodded. "That's what I'm counting on."

"Yes, sir," Cooper repeated.

Then, Cooper filled him in on the particulars of each simulation and the timing planned. The second exercise would occur immediately after the first, when the next team coming on deck would least expect it. They would no doubt know of the first simulation as the first team would be allowed to return to the barracks all sixteen men were housed in, but they would not be allowed to talk with the first team. The Shepherd Security personnel would only have time to change out of any paint-splattered clothing and arm themselves with fresh loads.

Each of the four teams would be tested alone twice, and there would be two simulations that all four teams responded to at once, a first for them. That meant ten simulations to be run by the Shepherd Security personnel in just under five days. It was a tight schedule.

"Eight against sixteen, hardly seems fair," Lambchop remarked with a laugh. "I hope the four teams can figure out how to operate together quickly. We've been doing this together for so long, we'll destroy them if they can't."

"That's the idea," the General said. "That's one of the reasons I reached out to Shepherd rather than using regular military to test this team. You boys have operated outside the teams for enough years that you've picked up some tactics that will be new to these boys," he paused as his eyes landed on Madison. "They need to be tested with the worst you can throw at them. We'll grade them for their tactical cohesiveness, response time, and if they choose a frontal or multi-side response."

"Our first simulation isn't till twenty-three-hundred hours. They've given us four rooms down that hallway," Cooper said to the team. "Pick a room and get some sleep. We'll reconvene at nineteen-hundred in this room."

The sleeping accommodations were two-man dormitory-style rooms. Knowing Garcia didn't snore, Doc followed him to a room to drop their gear. Besides, Sloan and Sherman always roomed together, and he knew for a fact that both Trio and Johnson snored. He wanted to get some decent sleep while they were here.

"Cooper," General Seyller called as the team headed towards the hall.

Cooper returned to the General.

"You have a female. I wasn't aware of that. Do you require a fifth room for her?"

Cooper laughed. "Miller's my wife. She doesn't need a separate room."

"No shit?" The General remarked. "Shepherd must be softening in his old age."

Cooper's lips tipped into a smirk. "He wasn't thrilled about it, but we can work together and keep it separate. Plus, she's a hell of an Operator."

The General nodded, still surprised. "Carry on."

As Doc laid on his rack, his thoughts wouldn't quiet. His memories of his birthday, the day before, and the time spent in bed with Elizabeth kept him up. Elizabeth was becoming more comfortable with sexual exploration every day. The coupon he redeemed the previous morning showed that she fully trusted him. Well, the fact that she even wrote the coupons for him, proved that. His request of her for that coupon? Simply that he laid still on his back and that she would make love to him, anyway she wanted, until he came.

In all previous erotic play, she had never straddled him. She had never taken the lead. He knew she felt awkward, at first, but she proved she had been paying attention to what he liked, to what got him off. Lying there, he knew his lips were fixed in a grin as he recalled what it looked like, what it felt like, what it sounded like.

"You want a hammer to pound that wood down?" Garcia's sarcastic voice broke into his thoughts.

Doc opened his eyes and sure enough, the blanket over his cock was tented. He flipped Garcia the bird. "Fuck you. Have your own erotic dream."

Garcia laughed. "I was trying, but you were moaning over there. Jesus Christ, Doc, either you're not getting any or you finally turned your beast loose!"

Doc laughed. "Let's just say my birthday yesterday was a day to remember."

"Well, then, fuck this. I'm putting my earbuds in so I can get some sleep. Have at it." He did just that, rolled so his back was to Doc and then let his mind recall his own incredible encounter Saturday night with his wife. 'We just got married sex' was the hottest sex he'd ever had.

At nineteen hundred, the eight of them gathered around the table in the rec room. Doc and Madison were dressed in street clothes. Madison's hair was left loose. The others were in black fatigues. This first scenario would test one four-man team's response to a hostage rescue. The team would be scrambled and told that A VIP and his secretary were being held. A training building on the base would be used. Since the exercises were simulations, small firecrackers would be used rather than flash-bangs. It was understood by all that the disruption would be nowhere near the disorienting effect as in live fire.

The team went to the single-story structure to set up a half-hour before Red Team was scrambled. It was a mockup of a house, with a front and back door, an open kitchen and living room area, a bathroom and two bedrooms, all full of furniture. Garcia rigged a few motion detectors at various entry points. The Undertaker hooked up a fake detonation device to the main entry point. They picked their room to defend, one of the bedrooms. They sat Doc and Madison in chairs in the center of the room. They had Sherman stand in the back corner. And then they waited.

The first indication Red Team was onsite was the registering of movement from the detector at a back window. Then they heard movement on the roof. There was a skylight over the living room area. Standard procedure would have them insert flex neck cameras into at least two locations in the structure. Doc assumed that would be one point, to get a birds-eye view of the main room and the doorways into the three other rooms. It would be where he would put one.

Doc looked at Madison through his safety goggles, which they all wore. They all wore helmets too, including the two hostages. "Good luck. If you have to hit me, I'd prefer it in the helmet than the heart," Doc whispered.

Madison grinned. "A headshot is all I'd take. At close range, I'd go for the greater chance for a fatality."

"That's comforting," Doc joked quietly.

He felt Cooper's hand on his shoulder. "Here we go. I do believe they have breached the house."

Garcia stood behind Madison. The Undertaker and Lambchop were on the floor to the left, their weapons aimed over the bed, one aiming at the window, the other door. Mother was in the corner to the right of the door. His position would be concealed when the door was opened. They waited.

Red Team avoided the main door, finding the explosive device with the camera they'd inserted through the skylight. Two members entered the house through the rear and cleared the other rooms first. The doors to the bathroom and the other bedroom were left open. A second flex neck camera was inserted through the cold air return vent that spanned both the bedrooms side by side. They saw about half of the target room, enough to plan their assault.

Red Team performed their initial breach of the room well. The door to the bedroom crashed open from the force of a battering ram at the same moment the bedroom window exploded in with the first of two team members crashing through it followed by the second immediately. The firecracker went off simultaneously mocking the flash-bang they would normally use. They took out Sherman, Cooper, and Garcia, the paintball rounds striking them each in the head and chest.

The two men who entered through the door fired at Sloan and Lambchop, who returned fire on them all, hitting one of them. Mother came from behind the door and shot a second, before he was also hit. A third member of Red Team was hit at the same time he hit Sloan in the helmet. The fourth member shot Lambchop.

"All Tangos neutralized," the man broadcast. "Three team members are down. Send in backup." He approached Doc and Madison; his weapon trained on them. "Are you both okay?"

Madison waited as he approached. She produced her gun and plugged him with three bright pink rounds in the center of his chest. "You're dead. Assume nothing," she told the stunned trainee.

At the onsite debrief, it was pointed out to Red Team that Sherman, who stood in the corner, had no weapon. They assumed Miller was the secretary, when in fact, Sherman was. They failed the exercise as they killed one of the hostages in addition to getting themselves injured or killed. Many of the rounds the Shepherd Security Team had hit them with, struck their body armor. The hits wouldn't have been fatal, but some would have been.

They reran the same scenario with Green Team. In this run, however, the Shepherd Security Team had the mattress flipped over the window, with the dresser up against it. They were all in the corner, except Mother, who was once again behind where the door would cover him, and Sloan was in the opposite corner. Both Cooper and Lambchop had guns to Doc and Madison's heads and were concealed behind them when Green Team breached the room, all four rapidly coming in through the door.

The first man in took a hit from Sloan, but also hit him. The second man through had clear shots that took out Sherman and Garcia. Mother hit him, but he was then hit by man number three coming through the door.

"Weapons down or I kill this hostage!" Cooper yelled; his body concealed behind Madison.

"Not happening, release the hostage!" Man number three yelled.

"Drop it!" Cooper ordered.

Man number four saw an opening, a tiny part of Lambchop's head beside Doc. He fired. It whizzed past Doc and struck the side of Lambchop's helmet. It wouldn't have been a lethal hit, but enough to incapacitate the bad guy.

"Drop your guns or I kill her!" Cooper yelled again.

Man number three kept his weapon trained on Madison with Cooper shadowing her well enough that there was no clear shot. Man number four stepped to the side, trying to get a better shot. "Put the gun down and we all live to see tomorrow."

Mother, only injured, and left unchecked, took that moment to fire on both members of Green Team.

"Oh, fuck!" One of them exclaimed.

Mother stepped closer to show them the paintball splatter. His left shoulder was hit. He'd gone down and they assumed a more incapacitating wound. They debriefed onsite pointing out that Sherman had no gun and that Madison did. They too had killed a hostage assuming Sherman was one of them. They too failed the exercise.

"Always look for a weapon. Your bad guys will make their hostages dress the same as them. Or your bad guys may be in street clothes too, just as your hostages," Cooper said.

"And don't assume a woman is not your Tango," Madison added.

They ran the same scenario that night into Wednesday morning with the two remaining teams with twists on both. While the Shepherd Security Team slept, the trainees were finally brought together and were allowed to speak about their simulations. They were debriefed as a group, going over all four simulations.

The trainee groups were ran through training that day as well by the base personnel while Shepherd Security planned for the next simulation. The next set would have the trainees transporting a prisoner or high value figure and the Shepherd Security Team would attack to free that prisoner or take that VIP. There was a road that wound through the training area of the base, through the sandy area and the tall grass landscape. It had hills, dips, curves, and intersections.

On Thursday, each four-man team was attacked at various locations during their transport. Their vehicles were disabled in a variety of methods, pinned in with two or three trucks, run into the hillside, even cut off with a school bus. The Shepherd Security Team hit them hard. At the end of the simulations, only one team failed, Red Team. It was proving to be the weakest of all four teams.

Friday brought the two simulations with all sixteen trainees functioning as a unit together, beginning at zero-four hundred. They were dropped in the wilderness area of the training base as though they were in enemy territory. Their target was a building four clicks away. The Shepherd Security force was dug in, hidden between the trainees and their target, lying in wait to ambush.

As the sun rose, Doc saw the trainees moving in. They moved in formation right from the training book. *Come on boys, show some originality*, he thought. His eyes were pressed to his scope watching them. "Two o'clock from my location, I've got four moving in."

"Roger that," Cooper replied through their comms. "I see them, and I have two more a few hundred yards to their west."

The Undertaker was in sniper position in a tree. "And two more a few hundred yards to their east."

"Does anyone have eyes on the others?" Cooper asked.

The reply was negative from all. Madison and Lambchop were dug in nearest the target building. The minutes dragged into a half-hour. No one had eyes on the last eight of the trainees. The first eight inched closer but kept themselves concealed well when moving.

Through her scope, Madison saw something odd looking near where Danny Trio was positioned. The sun was rising behind his location and tall grasses that swayed in the breeze surrounded him. "Mother," Madison broadcast. "Check your perimeter. There's something not quite right in how the grass is moving to your east."

"Roger that, Xena," he replied.

This made all the Shepherd Security personnel do the same. Just as Doc was scrutinizing the tall grassland to his west, while crouching with his back against the bark of a tree, shots rang out. He felt the impact of four paintball rounds in his chest. The threat was only feet within the dense underbrush, and he hadn't seen him until he fired.

Besides Doc, Mother, the Birdman, and Razor were all ambushed in similar fashion by four of the missing trainees. The Undertaker took two of them out after the fact. At the moment they fired, four more rushed the target building, firing on Xena and Lambchop. The pair hit two of them but were hit themselves by the others. The attack plan the trainees had used was good. They won the exercise.

The second exercise occurred later that afternoon. The trainees had returned to their barracks. They could shower and change and were told to report to the range at sixteen-hundred hours. Alpha and Delta attacked them in their barracks.

It was the definition of chaos for the trainees. Several were caught in the showers, their weapons on their bunks. One trainee slept soundly in his bunk with music blasting through his headphones, so he didn't wake at the sound of the attack. One trainee on Red Team outshined all the others, rushing the attackers and striking Sherman, Trio, and Garcia, before pulling one of his teammates to a position of cover.

Cooper and Madison went room by room, together, clearing each room or shooting those within until they too were hit by four of the trainees who happened to be in one room. They ducked for cover upon hearing the attack. They did not respond and seek out their attackers. They waited for them to come. Only then did they venture into the hallway, covering each other as they moved towards where more gunfire came from.

At the end of the exercise, just twenty minutes after it had started, all but four of the trainees were hit, the four who had waited in the room. On the Shepherd Security side, everyone but Doc and Lambchop had been hit, who retreated from the building, without being seen. This was considered a draw. Neither team won. After the exercise was officially called as over, there was a debrief with all in the room. Then the Shepherd Security personnel mingled with the trainees.

"Good job," Doc said shaking the hand of the trainee from Red Team who had shined. "You moved in and got your teammate to safety."

"I'm a medic, sir, it's my job," he replied.

Doc smiled. He should have known. These trainees all looked so young. *Of course, they do, because they are*, Doc thought. "Mine too," Doc replied. "You need to evaluate though your odds of survival before you move in. You can't save your teammate if you're hit, yourself."

"Yes sir," the trainee replied. "Can I ask you something, sir?"

Doc nodded, bracing himself.

"You've been doing this a long time," the kid said. "Or at least I assume you have based on your age."

Ouch, Doc thought. "Yes, I have."

"Does the adrenalin spike ever stop? What I mean is, for the hundredth time hitting a building, does it ever get routine?"

"Never," Doc told him. "And beforehand, mentally preparing yourself for the injuries you might face that you have to treat, that never ends either. I won't tell you how many bullet wounds I've treated, some made it, some didn't. Seeing it and going into treatment mode after you've engaged the enemy and wounded or killed them, to shift to lifesaving mode always quickens my heartbeat and spikes my adrenalin. I guess the day it stops doing that is the day I'll retire."

The kid nodded with a smile on his face. Doc guessed he gave him the answer he wanted to hear.

"Thank you, sir."

The team ate dinner at the mess hall. They were treated to a couple of beers at the Officer's Club by General Seyller. And they were then brought back to the airfield. Their plane took off, streaking across the dark sky towards home.

Doc woke as the plane descended. The sun rose in the cloudless sky behind them. It was a crisp four degrees outside, February in Chicago. As Doc stepped from the plane, he noticed the moon to the west hanging low in the darkened sky. To the east, the fiery oranges and yellows glowed bright.

His mind recalled the sunrise over the lake during his last fishing trip, the brilliant colors reflecting off the water, the peace and serenity he found there. So much in his life was different now. He was heading home to his wife, his pregnant wife, who waited there for him. And he couldn't wait to get home to her and redeem another birthday coupon.

Friday morning rush-hour traffic was light. They made it to HQ, stowed their gear, and met Shepherd in the conference room just over an hour after landing. Doc sipped his coffee as Shepherd went over the overall team evaluation of their performance from the exercises executed during the simulations. Individual evaluations would be given to each team member over the next few days.

Doc sent a text message to Elizabeth when he reached his car in the parking garage to let her know he was heading home. Then he followed the long line of cars exiting the garage. Alpha Team was due back at the office the next morning at zero-six hundred to prep for their next mission.

Upon entering his condo, he found Elizabeth in the shower. A grin formed on his lips as he viewed her through the glass doors. "Do you mind if I join you?"

Her head shifted so her eyes landed on him. "You're home faster than I thought you'd be."

He took that as a yes and disrobed.

Elizabeth watched Alexander strip through the shower door. He stepped in and her eyes were drawn to the four purple bruises on his chest and abdomen.

"Paintball rounds," he said as he moved in close, wrapping his arms around her. He kissed her,

"Does it hurt?" She asked as she gently ran her hand over them.

He relocated her hand farther south. "No, but this feels better."

A smile spread over her face. "I'm sure it does. But, the bruises?"

"Later," he murmured and then engulfed her in a kiss that would keep them in the shower for quite a while.

Victor

Life proceeded with no hiccups over the next few months. Doc and Elizabeth fell into a comfortable routine. The team was away nearly eighty percent of the time, the normal rotation for a field team. The two online classes Elizabeth took, consumed a good forty hours a week. The amount of reading required was overwhelming. Between her classes and helping at the office a minimum of one day a week, she was kept busy.

He called and they text messaged as much as he was able to while away, which over the two months, forged an even stronger bond between them. When he was home, it was as though he'd never been gone. They were like any other couple. They prepared for the arrival of their daughter. They were both excited as the pregnancy progressed. Life was good.

Even though both Angel and Sienna kept feelers out, so far, a unit in the same townhome complex had not come on the market. Several of the single-family homes in that portion of the development did, but with his schedule, the maintenance-free townhomes just seemed smarter to Doc. Plus, he really wanted their place to be within a few blocks of his teammates.

When he was away, she usually stayed with Sienna or Angel. And since Jackson was on a reduced mission schedule, he was home fifty percent of the time the team was away, so Doc knew Jackson was looking out for her too, not that the rest of the agency wasn't. With Elizabeth helping at the office, it gave her an understanding of what he did and gave her a connection she would not have otherwise had.

Although she easily passed the rules of the road test and got her temporary driving permit, she wasn't anxious to drive anywhere but in parking lots and on little used, side streets, which was fine with Doc. He had nightmares of Elizabeth driving and getting into a car accident as Victoria had. He kept those nightmares to himself. The last thing he wanted was to get back on Lassiter's radar, who had pretty much declared him emotionally stable.

Everything at work was good and Doc felt normal again, no longer the odd man out. His relationship with his teammates was back to how it had been before Africa. He liked having Elizabeth live with him and he liked the growth and changes he'd seen in her. She had become a confident equal, a wife in every way, but he still couldn't say that he was in love with her. He wasn't sure that word would ever be part of his vocabulary again.

Doc packed his bags, feeling uneasy about leaving Elizabeth at home alone for the next, maybe five days. Something felt different this time, something he couldn't put his finger on. Maybe it was his own anxiety about this mission. This would be his first mission back to Africa since he'd met her. Maybe it was because Jackson would also be on this mission. He wouldn't be there to look out for Elizabeth.

He knew that she had plenty of food in the house and that Angel and Sienna would both invite her out to do things. They would give her a ride anywhere she needed. She understood his issues with public transportation and hadn't mentioned it in months. He suspected Angel had something to do with that too.

He embraced her as she came into the bedroom, his hand finding its way to her expanded abdomen. At five months pregnant, she sported a large belly as she carried the baby completely out in front. It had been a healthy pregnancy, which he was grateful for. Elizabeth pressed his hand to the other side of her tummy. He felt the kick. He'd been home for nearly a week and was fascinated with feeling the baby's many movements. The 4D sonogram at the doctor's visit the previous day was amazing. They saw in detail the features of their little girl.

"Be safe," she said, embracing him.

"I promise I will," he replied. "You too. I'll call and text when I can. Remember, I'll be dark the first sixteen hours."

She nodded. Sienna had theorized that meant a mission to the Middle East or Africa. The possibility that was his destination was unnerving and worried her. She knew it was his job, but the thought of him in danger bothered her tremendously. She wasn't scheduled to work at the office over the next five days, so she wouldn't be able to find out firsthand where they were going or what the mission was. It was very likely though that Angel would fill her and Sienna in.

"I love you," she said to the door after Alexander closed it behind himself as he left, like she had done for the last two months.

That was the only thing missing in their relationship, his declaration of love. So many times, she nearly told him to his face how she felt, but she always stopped herself. It would be horrible if she said it and he did not in return, or worse, if he'd admit he didn't love her. She knew it would crush her, so she took the coward's way out and didn't tell him how she felt.

Elizabeth finished the online exam, scoring one hundred percent. She closed the textbook beside her and breathed out with relief. The test had been a tough one. She logged out of the student portal and checked her phone. There was a text-message from Alexander. They were finally 'engaging' and would be out of contact for a day or two. But then he should be home after. He'd been gone four days. He'd call her as soon as he could but would be 'dark' till then.

When she stood, she felt a warm gush between her legs like she'd peed her pants. But she knew she didn't. She rushed to the bathroom, peeling the black leggings off as she reached the tile. Her white panties beneath were saturated bright red.

"No, no, no," she said aloud in a panic to no one. Her cell phone was still in her hands. She dialed 9-1-1.

"9-1-1 what's your emergency?" The woman's voice asked.

"I'm five months pregnant and am bleeding, vaginally," Elizabeth said. Just saying it out loud made the reality even worse. Panic overtook her. She began to feel lightheaded and she couldn't breathe.

"Is anyone there with you?" The 9-1-1 Operator asked.

"No. I'm alone."

"I want you to unlock the front door and then lay down on your left side. I've dispatched an ambulance." She confirmed the address. "And stay on the line with me."

Elizabeth unlocked the door, grabbed her purse from the kitchen table, and then spread a towel on the couch and laid on her left side as instructed. "I'm going to put you on hold. I need to make another call to a friend." She dialed Ops.

"Hello, Elizabeth, this is Yvette. What can I do for you?"

Relief flooded Elizabeth just hearing Yvette's voice. She told her the situation.

Yvette relayed it to Mother, who stood beside her. He brought up the tracker app to view who was nearest to Elizabeth.

"I'll send Sloan. He lives near Doc and is home."

"Elizabeth, we're sending Gary Sloan over. He's a few blocks away."

"Thank you, Yvette," Elizabeth said. "Don't tell Alexander anything yet, until I know if I'm losing this baby or not. I'm only five months, she won't make it."

"Hey, think positive. You're not losing the baby," Yvette said. "There are a lot of reasons for bleeding."

"I know," Elizabeth agreed quickly, without thinking about it. "I need to switch back to the other line. The 9-1-1 Operator is holding and wants me on the line until the ambulance arrives."

"Okay," Yvette said. "Sloan will be there in a few minutes."

The wait until the ambulance arrived seemed like it was hours. Every minute or two, the 9-1-1 Operator would ask if she was still there, if she was in any pain, or if the friend she'd called had arrived yet. Yes, she was still there, no she wasn't in any pain, and no, he hadn't arrived yet.

When she finally heard sirens, she relaxed just a little. "I hear the sirens."

"The ambulance is just arriving. I'm going to disconnect now," the 9-1-1 Operator said. "Good luck."

"Thank you for staying on the line with me."

The red and blue glow of the ambulance lights radiated around the edges of the closed blinds over the front window. Then, the front door opened and two men with a stretcher, in EMT clothing stepped through. The flashing lights from the ambulance shined brightly behind them.

"My name is Luke, and this is Steve, what's your name darling?" One of them asked.

"Elizabeth."

He smiled as he knelt down beside her. "We're going to take good care of you and get you to the hospital," he said. "Tell me what's going on tonight."

"I stood up and felt warm fluid run down my legs. It's blood. I'm five months pregnant. I'm a nurse, so I know how bad this is."

"Easy there, Elizabeth, one step at a time. Let's get you on the stretcher. We're going to get you out into the truck and then I'm going to start an IV."

Gary Sloan pulled up in front of Doc's condo. He parked beside the ambulance. He didn't need to grab his medical kit with the EMTs on site. He rushed to the door and entered. They were getting Elizabeth onto the stretcher. He saw the towel on the couch. It was stained bright red with blood.

He pulled his ID and badge out and identified himself. "Agent Gary Sloan, ATF. I'm a friend and colleague of her husband, who is away for work right now. I'm also a former Navy Corpsman." His gaze shifted to Elizabeth. Her face was as white as the sheet over the stretcher. "How are you holding up Elizabeth?"

"I'm afraid. I'm losing the baby, Gary."

He came in close and took her hand. "You don't know that. Let's wait till we get to the hospital and a doctor takes a look at you." His eyes went back to the EMTs. "I'd like to ride along. I promised her husband I'd take care of her like he would."

The two EMTs exchanged glances. He did have a badge. "Sure," the EMT who stood closest said.

Sloan road in the back of the truck and held Elizabeth's hand. She squeezed it hard when the paramedic inserted the IV needle in her other arm. He did everything he could to help calm her down. Some color returned to her cheeks by the time they arrived at the hospital.

He had to badge his way into the treatment room too. The doctor came in immediately. After a short question-and-answer session he squeezed the gel on her abdomen and pressed the ultrasound head against her baby bump. His smile spread wide when he saw the baby with her strong heartbeat. He turned the monitor so she and Sloan could see.

"We've got a strong heartbeat and an active baby," the doctor said.

The relief brought tears to Elizabeth's eyes. "She's still okay?"

"She's great. Now, let's figure out why you bled." The doctor moved the instrument around. "Ah-ha," he said. He pointed to the screen again. "Right there is the culprit. The placenta is too low. The baby is laying on it. Placenta previa, usually discovered around the five to six-month mark, right on time."

Elizabeth knew what it was. She also knew it meant bed rest either until it resolved or until she delivered. And it very well may mean delivery by a caesarian section. "Is it partial or completely covering my cervix and why didn't the sonogram scans at my obstetrician show it?"

"It looks to be a partial, but your OB will monitor that. These things usually resolve. As the uterus grows with the enlarging baby, the placenta is pulled up and off the cervix. If it doesn't, you'll just be on bed rest longer and the baby will be delivered via a caesarian. As long as you rest, laying down as much as you can, you and the baby will both be fine," he assured Elizabeth. "That means you only sit up to eat and you only get out of bed to use the bathroom and to take a very quick shower."

"Will you be admitting her?" Sloan asked.

"No, we'll let this bag of fluids finish and then you can take her home. But she needs to call her OB tomorrow and follow up with them per their direction. We'll be sending the report over." The doctor stood. "I'll have the nurse come check in on her in about twenty minutes. The fluids should be done by then."

Elizabeth was relieved, but she was also worried. How would she manage bedrest with Alexander away on missions? And school? She was only half-way through the semester. She needed to finish these two classes. She needed them to start nursing school in the fall.

"Hey, this is good news," Sloan said. She was in deep thought and frowning.

She had forgotten he was there. "I know," she agreed. "I'm just wondering how I can possibly be on bedrest for maybe the rest of my pregnancy. I don't even know when Alexander is going to be home. And then what about during the next mission?"

"We've got you," Sloan said, taking her hand again. "Don't worry. We'll figure it out."

His voice was confident. Elizabeth looked into his eyes. There was something about them that never failed to capture her attention. They were eyes like Alexander's, eyes that had seen way too many bad things. They didn't reflect his soul, though. They were cold, hardened, haunted. But she knew from the first she'd met him on that helicopter after she and Alexander had been rescued, that he had a sense of humor, was a great friend, a trusted and loyal team member, and tonight, he had provided her comfort when she needed it.

"Thank you for being here, Gary. I appreciate it."

"I always have the team's six, yours included." He pulled his phone from his pocket. He dialed Ops.

"What's your status?" Mother's voice answered.

"Elizabeth isn't being admitted. She'll be released in about a half hour. I left my POV at Doc's. Can you have someone from the team pick us up? And clear with Shepherd her staying in the apartment on nine until Doc is back. She can't be alone."

"Roger that," Mother replied. "Shoot me a text when she is cleared to leave. I'm off in just under a half hour. I'll head over and pick the two of you up."

"Thanks, Mother," Sloan said.

"Why is he called Mother?" Elizabeth asked after Sloan ended the call.

"He's our Mother hen, has always been that way. Just wait till you see how he fusses to help take care of you." Sloan winked. "You won't be asking after you see him in action."

The hospital lent Elizabeth the bottoms of scrubs to wear when she left. Sloan draped his coat over her shoulders. Mother's pickup truck was warm, but he didn't want Elizabeth to get chilled for the brief time she was outside, transferring from the wheelchair to the backseat. Once at the Shepherd Security Building, Sloan retrieved a wheelchair to give her a ride to the apartment on nine. She would not be walking any further than the bed to the bathroom.

Doc unrolled the Fisherman's Prayer verse and photo. He read it and then stared at the calming scene behind the words. This had become part of his pre-mission ritual. The team was flying in, on a V-22 Osprey in the airspace above South Sudan, heading in to rescue an American reporter who had been kidnapped and held for three weeks. This woman they were going in to get was lucky. Intelligence identified her location quickly, and they had been dispatched to go in and get her.

Doc tucked the photo away in his bag and then mentally went over what types of injuries she might have. Jackson would carry her out if she wasn't mobile. He had pain killers, splints, butterfly bandages, and skin glue to use on site if she was in such bad shape that he'd have to stabilize her to move her. In the second equipment pack he'd leave on board, he had bags of both IV solution and O Negative blood. Hopefully none of these things would be needed.

He felt the vibration of the aircraft change. The Osprey was slowing, preparing for its transition from the turboprop plane to the rotors assuming a vertical position needed to land.

"New thermal imaging scans shows six heat signatures in the house. Since we assume one is our target, that leaves five Tangos," Cooper's voice came through everyone's comms, startling Doc's thoughts from the mental checklist that he was running through. "Two minutes till go time."

Doc watched as Cooper and Madison gave each other a fist bump, the most intimate of gestures the couple ever shared while on duty. He wasn't sure how they did it, Operating together. He knew he wouldn't be able to focus if Elizabeth was anywhere near danger.

He got up, secured his weapons and his pack, and waited behind Garcia. The five of them jumped out the second the aircraft's forward momentum ceased. Three steps off the firmly packed road, their boots sunk ankle deep in the muck of the swampy ground.

The Osprey rolled forward. The whir of the rotors was deafening as it moved a lot of air, gaining purchase to vertically raise back up into the dark night sky. Cloudy skies obscured all heavenly light. Doc watched the craft gain altitude through his night vision goggles. The rotors tilted forward, in an engineering feat that still baffled him, and fully locked into place. It again functioned as an airplane. Its speed increased, and it quickly put distance between them and itself.

Assault rifles held at the ready, the team made their way towards their target, a little farmhouse that was three clicks away. It was hot, over ninety degrees. And it was muggy. It wasn't quite the rainy season yet, but it felt like the sky could open up at any moment. Within minutes, Doc was drenched with sweat. They didn't encounter anyone on their trek through the tropical rainforest, which reeked of dead and decaying flora and fauna. This was an unpleasant place.

They steered clear of one farmhouse that lay in their path, the only structure within a mile of their target building. It was dark and quiet. The satellite showed eight heat signatures within, no one they would want to mess with if it could be avoided. They continued, at a fast pace and soon came upon their target. Calling it a farmhouse was generous. It was a twenty by fourteen three-room shack. Doc wasn't sure how it remained upright.

Because of its tiny size, they would all go in from the front, in classic assault formation. Once inside, they would neutralize all threats while searching for their target, pretty much a textbook rescue operation. Except nothing was ever textbook. Going into a building blind, not knowing if someone had a gun trained on the door, not knowing if there were boobytraps, not knowing your target's location, was never textbook. The second an Operator forgot that, was when that Operator would be dead.

"HQ, we're in position," Cooper spoke softly.

"We've got you, Alpha," BT's voice replied. "All is quiet in the neighborhood. Headcount remains at six within the target building. You are a go to engage."

"Roger that," Cooper replied. He led the others, swiftly approaching the building, rifle up, surveying the building and the surrounding area through his sights. It was dark within and quiet.

Doc fell in line and followed the others up to the structure. He pressed his back against the building. He'd be fourth in, behind Cooper, Jackson, and then Garcia.

Madison had her sights trained behind them. Even though HQ's Ops Center watched them from the satellite feed, they took nothing for granted.

"Breach, breach, breach," Cooper said softly, pulling his back from the structure. He squared up in front of the door and kicked it open with a powerful thrust of his leg. He threw the flash-bang in, which shattered the soundless night.

Cooper propelled himself through the doorway, going low, rifle up sweeping to the right. Jackson was through right behind him, his rifle trained to the left. Two men laid on rugs on either side of the room. They both grabbed their AK-47s. Before Garcia had flung himself through the door, Cooper and Jackson had taken both the threats out.

"That's one and two," Cooper broadcast.

The door to the left opened. A muzzle flash lit the void, shots struck near the team. The team returned fire as Doc came into the house, hitting at least one target within. Doc concentrated on the door to the right, rifle up. It remained closed. Garcia shifted over and approached the door with Doc while Jackson and Cooper invaded the other room.

Garcia raised his leg and kicked the door in. It broke in half, rotted wood.

"Don't shoot," a female voice shouted in English. "There's a child in here."

Doc heard more gunfire from the direction Cooper and Jackson were, small caliber fire. Then he heard the unmistakable, AR full-automatic reply. "That's three and four," Jackson added.

There was movement in the room in front of Doc and Garcia. "Get down, hands, let me see your hands," Garcia barked.

Within, Doc saw their American target, huddled with a local woman and a small child, maybe four years old. "Get on the ground, get down," Doc ordered. "Got the target, a woman and a small child," Doc broadcast.

"That's all six," BT's voice came through their comms. "Get your target and move to extract, Alpha."

Doc watched their target soothe and direct the South Sudanese woman to assume the position. She did so, clinging to the child. Then their target, on her knees with her hands raised into the air, prostrated herself on the ground too. Doc glanced around the small room. There was no furniture, no windows, no doors, no place for anyone to hide.

Garcia covered him as he moved to her. "You got any weapons?" Doc asked.

"No, of course I don't," she replied.

"What about her?" Doc asked.

"No, and neither does the child, asshole."

Doc ignored her. "Are you hurt anywhere?" He asked, feeling over her, searching her for himself.

"No, just dehydrated and hungry," she answered.

"We're getting you out of here. Can you walk?" He moved over to the other woman and searched her as well. She had a knife which he relieved her of.

Their target was up on all fours, watching him. "Yes."

He pressed his hand down firmly on the other woman's back. "Stay," he said.

"Albaqa', Fiza," their target said. Her eyes were focused on the goggles of this mystery man wielding the automatic weapon. "I told her to stay."

"You've got incoming, Alpha. The eight from the neighboring farmhouse are closing in."

"Let's move," Doc said, taking hold of her arm. "Stay close to me and do what I tell you to do." He led her back to the main room. Cooper and Jackson had just finished up in the other room. All Tangos were neutralized.

"Let's get the hell out of here," Cooper said. "Xena, we're coming out."

"Roger Coop," she replied. "No sign of movement yet."

"Your ride is coming in hot. New exfil location, your twenty. They will make a pass firing on the unfriendlies and then sit down. Don't waste time getting on board," BT advised.

"Roger," Cooper acknowledged.

They went back out the door in the same order they entered. Doc held onto their target, keeping her crouched down. She was a sturdy woman, who topped out at five eleven.

The minigun rounds announced the arrival of the black Osprey that approached low and fast from the west. It sat down just to the north of the structure. The team ran towards it. Gunfire erupted, hitting the ground around the team and pinging the aircraft. The door gunners returned fire. Madison and Cooper both turned and fired at the incoming threat to help provide cover while Doc got their target on board.

Doc was nearly to the aircraft with their target in tow when he heard, through his comms, Madison's deep grunt. He turned his head and viewed her lying on her back on the ground. At the same moment, he saw Cooper's body jerk backwards. Then Cooper's voice came through his comms. "Fuck!"

"Man down," Doc broadcast.

Jackson returned cover fire as Garcia, ran back towards his downed teammate. When he reached them, Cooper already had Madison by the vest, and was pulling her to her feet. Garcia looped an arm around her and helped Cooper drag her towards the chopper. After a few steps, her legs helped to propel them forward. Meanwhile, Jackson and the door gunners eliminated the threat.

"Xena's hit," Cooper declared.

Doc knew Cooper was too. He pushed the target on board. He climbed up beside her, moved them both within the belly of the bird, and got both his packs open and the supplies ready to treat his teammates. His mind was already running through the steps needed to treat their injuries and potentially save their lives.

Garcia lowered Madison to the floor beside Doc. Cooper dropped himself next to her. Doc's initial evaluation of Madison confirmed she was breathing and had a pulse. He removed her NVGs and her helmet. Her eyes were open, but unfocused. He felt over her neck, no blood, no wounds. His hands slid down her vest. Square in the center, a slug.

"Help me get her vest off," Doc said to Garcia. "Where are you hit?" He then asked Cooper.

"Left upper arm," Cooper admitted.

"I'll be to you shortly." Doc and Garcia wrestled to get the bullet proof tactical vest from Madison. "Vest stopped the round," Doc said after he had checked beneath it, cutting her fatigue shirt open to reveal the black sports bra she wore as always. He quickly checked over the rest of her. No injuries. She'd have a hell of a bruise from the impact on the vest though. "Get an ice pack and put it on her," he ordered Garcia, pointing to the purple contusion that was already forming.

Madison's eyes were more focused, gazing at him.

"Hurt like hell, didn't it?"

She breathed out hard, swallowed even harder and nodded her head.

"You'll be fine. Just lay still."

"What can I do?" Jackson asked.

"Get Miss Moore some water and a protein bar." He pointed to their target, who sat nearby, watching them intently.

Doc moved onto Cooper. He cut the sleeve away, exposing the wound. He examined it from both sides of his arm. It was a deep flesh wound. It didn't even look like too much of the muscle was hit. "It's just a graze." He poured disinfectant on it.

Cooper screamed out curses.

Doc applied a QuikClot dressing to stop the bleeding and then bandaged it. Then he made Cooper lay beside Madison.

"Are you okay?" Madison asked, her eyes locked with her husband's.

"You heard Doc, it's just a graze." He raised his fisted hand, holding it out to her. She grinned and tapped it with hers.

"Jesus, you two," Doc said taking both their hands, making them clasp. "If I take one in the vest or through the arm one of you better hold my hand."

Cooper flashed a smirk at him. "I'm not ever holding your hand. You're not my type," He raised Madison's hand to his lips and placed a kiss on her knuckles. "Don't ever scare me like that again, Blondie." Then he clutched her hand to his chest.

"Back at you," she said, breathing a bit easier.

Doc moved over to their target, Christine Moore. "How dehydrated do you think you are? I can start an IV to get fluids in you."

She downed the rest of the bottle of water Jackson had given her. "I think a few more bottles of this and I'll be fine." She ate all the protein bar too. "Are they going to be okay?" She pointed to Cooper and Madison.

Doc nodded. "They both got lucky." He handed her another bottle of water and another protein bar. "Let me just check your vitals quick."

She nodded.

Doc gave her a quick exam. Her heart rate was a little high. Nothing odd about that given the situation. Doc was sure his still was too. Her pulse was a little weak, dehydration and exhaustion would do that. And her respiration was quick and shallow, what he'd expect.

"You have no unit markings," Christine Moore said.

"That's right," Doc replied.

"Who are you, SEALs? Marine Raiders? Rangers?"

"We are no one you need to be able to identify and absolutely no one who should end up in one of your articles," Doc said.

"Oh, come on. This is a story that people should know."

Garcia leaned into her face. His voice was low and gravelly when he spoke, a definite warning. "You heard the man. This isn't your story to tell and if it weren't for us, you wouldn't be here to tell it. So, lady, you owe us."

"And you shouldn't have been here, anyway. There is good reason there is a travel advisory for this region. Can you say Level Four Designation due to crime, terrorism, civil unrest, kidnapping, and armed conflict? Do you understand what that means? That means do not travel there," Doc said.

"I wasn't traveling, asshole. I was working," she spat. "The truth of what's going on in these areas has to get out, and it's people like me who get these stories to the rest of the world."

"You shouldn't have been here without a security force protecting you. No one in this hell hole respects the press. You're nothing but a big dollar sign to these assholes," Doc lectured.

"Maybe you'd want the job then," she replied.

"You couldn't afford us," Garcia said, shaking his head. "And lady, there're easier ways to earn a paycheck."

Doc watched him as he moved to the bench and sat. He plugged his earphones back in and rested his head against the fuselage. His eyes flickered to Jackson, who sat beside Cooper and Madison. Yeah, they'd been very lucky.

The V-22 Osprey had already converted back to a turboprop aircraft and flew at its maximum speed out of the South Sudanese airspace heading back to the U.S. base in Djibouti. It would land and do a quick refueling on the way.

"Give me a Sitrep for Big Bear," BT's voice came through everyone's comms.

"Coop has a graze to his arm, Xena took one to the vest. Both are stable and mobile," Doc reported.

"Good to hear," BT replied.

When they landed in Djibouti, they turned Christine Moore over to the base personnel. As they carried their gear to their ride home, an Air Force C-130, Cooper received a text from Mother. "Doc needs to call the Undertaker, ASAP," the text read. Cooper knew right away something was wrong.

Sloan's phone vibrating in his pocket alerted him to the incoming phone call. Even though he had his ringer on high, there was so much noise in the room he didn't hear it. He checked the display, Doc. He stepped towards the door as he answered it.

"Doc, hold on a sec." Once he was in the quiet hallway with the door closed, he continued. "Okay, sorry about that. First of all, Elizabeth and the baby are fine. But there was a situation tonight."

Doc's gut clenched. This couldn't be good. Even though it was over a hundred degrees out, his blood ran cold. "What happened?"

"Elizabeth called into Ops. She was bleeding vaginally. She'd already called 9-1-1. Ops called me and I went to your place. I rode in the ambulance with her and stayed with her the whole time. She has been diagnosed with placenta previa. But as long as she remains in bed, there's no danger to her or the baby. Lying down stopped the bleeding. The ER doc said it looks like it could move up on its own, but her own OB will keep tabs on it and be better at predicting the likelihood it will resolve itself before delivery."

"Where is she now? What hospital?" His four team members, who stood nearby, all stared at him with concern.

"They didn't admit her. I brought her back to HQ. She's going to stay in the apartment on nine. This way we can all help take care of her till you get back. She's supposed to stay in bed and only get up to use the bathroom."

"Oh shit. She must have been so afraid," Doc remarked.

"Yeah, but once the ER doc told her she and the baby would be fine if she stayed in bed, she noticeably relaxed. Before that, I was going to ask for a sedative or an anti-anxiety pill for her. All she wanted was you to be there, man. I think she's worried you will think she did something to cause this."

"Does she have her phone with her? I need to call her, so she knows I'd never blame her."

"I'll carry my phone back in, and you can talk with her on mine. It'll help me clear the room."

"You were in with her when I called? All that noise was in the apartment?"

Sloan laughed. "Yeah, everyone wanted to be sure she was okay and let her know they are here for her. Shepherd even visited her, to assure her she is welcome to use the apartment for as long as she needs to. It's better she's there as Angel can help, bring her meals, you know, be a mom." He reopened the door. It had quieted some. "Okay, everyone out. I've got Doc on the line for her."

Elizabeth couldn't wait to hear Alexander's voice.

"You'll be fine, little momma," Lambchop said, grasping her shoulder. He pressed a chaste kiss to her forehead. "Let me know if you need anything." He nodded to her phone.

"Thank you, Landon," she said, watching the big man move towards the door to follow everyone else out.

"I'm sleeping in my office," Mother said. "You've got my phone number now. Call me if you need anything at any time."

"Thanks, Danny," she said as Gary handed her his phone. She pressed it to her ear. "Hi."

"Honey, are you okay?" Alexander's voice came through the receiver.

Relief flooded her, just hearing his voice. "I am now. I just needed to talk to you."

"Sloan said the doctor said you'll be fine as long as you stay in bed."

"Yes. The bleeding stopped soon after I laid down. When will you be home?"

"In about twenty-four hours."

"Okay," she replied. On one hand she wanted him home sooner. On the other, she was glad it wouldn't be days. "Gary has stayed with me. He was at the hospital with me, but I wish it had been you."

"I'm sorry I wasn't there. I'll be home soon though."

"Danny was going to take Angel to our place to get me some things, clothes, my laptop and my textbooks. But if you'll be home tomorrow, maybe he should hold off."

"No, have them go ahead. We'll probably stay in the apartment at the office for a few days. It'll be easier not knowing my schedule yet." He anticipated that with Cooper and Madison's minor injuries the team would be out of the rotation for field work for at least a week.

"Shepherd said I could stay in the apartment for however long I needed or whenever you were gone. Everyone has been so nice, offering me their help."

Doc smiled. "That's what a family does for each other. I'd expect nothing less from them."

"I'm glad you're on your way home," she said.

"Me too." He paused. "I'll be home soon, honey. Let me speak to Sloan again."

"Okay, bye," she said. She handed the phone towards Gary, who stood near the door.

"Yeah," Sloan said into his phone,

"You'll make sure someone is with her till I get home?" Doc said as both an order and a question.

"Yeah, we got her. Don't worry about it."

"Thanks, man. I owe you," Doc said.

Doc opened the door to the apartment. The low lighting from the hallway spilled into the pitch-black room. He glanced at his watch, zero-one-forty, about four hours later than he'd anticipated. There had been bad weather in Germany, delaying their departure after refueling. He slipped into the room and reclosed the door as quietly as he had opened it.

"Hello?" Elizabeth's soft voice came from the direction of the bed.

"Hi, honey. It's just me." He crossed the room, stopping when his thighs made contact with the mattress. "I'm sorry I woke you."

"It's okay. I don't think I've slept very soundly since I've been here," she said.

Doc followed her voice to the head of the bed. His hand searched the mattress until it found its way to her body. His touch ran up her arm, over her shoulder, and up the soft skin of her neck until his hand cupped her face. Then he bent over and kissed her, and he perched his behind on the edge of the bed.

"I'm sorry I wasn't here with you," he said when their lips parted.

"Me too. I missed you."

Doc embraced her. "I missed you too. I'm going to talk with Shepherd and see if I can reduce my mission time, at least until this condition resolves or the baby is born."

"Do you think he'll let you?"

"It's all in my presentation of the request, and what value I can bring the agency if I'm here. I gave it a lot of thought on our trip back. I think my justification is strong." Doc stood and started to peel his clothes off. "Scoot over and make some room for me."

Elizabeth wiggled to the center of the bed. Warmth surrounded her as he pressed his body against hers, taking her in his embrace.

"I was really afraid when I started to bleed," she said softly. "Gary was great, held my hand and stayed with me the whole time, but he wasn't you."

Doc embraced her more tightly. "I'm sorry I wasn't there, Elizabeth," Doc repeated. "When Sloan told me what happened, my heart stopped beating for a few seconds. All I could think about was how scared you must have been and that I wasn't here for you." There was a long, silent pause. "I love you, Elizabeth. I knew in that moment that I truly do."

Tears filled Elizabeth's eyes. "I love you too, Alexander. I've known for a while I do, but I didn't want to put pressure on you by telling you."

He tightened his hold of her.

She felt his erection press into her. "I can't have sex with this condition," she whispered.

"I know." He arched his back, so his pelvis didn't press to her. "It'll go away. I just need to hold you. I missed you and I really am sorry I wasn't here for you. I'll convince Shepherd," he repeated. "Go back to sleep. We'll talk more in the morning."

She relaxed into him, feeling safe and loved. She sighed her contentment as she nestled in close, her head against his chest. She breathed in the scent of him, comforted by it. Then she drifted into a deep, restful sleep.

Doc held her, heard her even breaths, and knew she was asleep. He felt at peace, for the first time, in what he realized was over a decade. This woman, pregnant with his child, meant everything to him. The realization that he was in love with her came to him like a missile impacting its target with an Earth-shattering concussion and a fireball that seared everything near it with intense heat. There was nothing subtle about the realization. It was explosive and obvious. How could he not have seen it before? And once he saw it, realized what it was, and accepted it, the peaceful feeling that settled in his soul was overwhelming.

Whiskey

"How is Elizabeth?" Shepherd asked looking up from the screen of his laptop.

"She's good, thank you for asking. If it's okay with you, I'd like us to stay in the apartment so that Angel can continue to help with Elizabeth when I'm working."

"That's probably a good idea," Shepherd remarked. He noted Doc had not taken a seat yet. He eyed him carefully. Something was up. "Is that all you wanted to talk with me about?"

"Partly. The medical condition could resolve itself in the next few months and then she'd be off bedrest, or it could stay right till she delivers. Then it would be by a C-section. Shep, I'd like to reduce the amount of time I'm away on missions until after this baby comes and she's fully healed, if I can."

Shepherd didn't interrupt. He raised an eyebrow, his intense gaze focused on Doc, urging him to continue.

"If I took over the oversight of every team member's medical, that would bring continuity and reduce the burden on each team's medic. Charlie Team has been in the field so much, I know Powder hasn't had the opportunity to even think about the team's medical status and immunizations. I checked the logs, and it doesn't look like any of them have had a physical in over six months. PT logs are not complete with the level of activity on any of the Shepherd Security personnel. And that's on me. As senior medic, I'm responsible for that, but haven't had the time to follow up on it. We talked before about getting some automation in place with Apps that we would push out to everyone's phones and we could then monitor it to be sure all members were meeting the requirement. I could get that done too."

Shepherd pointed to the chair in front of his desk. "Sit."

Doc took the seat, watching Shepherd carefully. As usual, Shepherd's facial expression gave nothing away. That's why he would never play poker with the man.

"Do you anticipate this mission reduction to be just until the baby comes, or do you think you will not want to be away as much after she's born?"

Doc could tell by the way Shepherd said it, he already believed it was to be a permanent situation. Doc sighed and dragged his hand through his hair. "I guess I won't know till I hold my daughter in my arms, but I have to believe I'll feel as Jackson does, and I won't want to be away as much as the team usually is. I know it's my job, but." He paused and blew out another sigh.

"I anticipated this," Shepherd said. "We made accommodations for Jackson. We need to do the same for you." He lifted his cellphone and tapped out a message. Then he sat his phone down. "I just asked Cooper to join us. He's already in this morning, figured you would want to check his wound."

A few minutes later, Cooper came through the door. He closed it behind himself. "Hey Doc, how is Elizabeth?"

"She's good. I'm glad we're back though. How's the arm?"

"Hurts like a bitch," Cooper replied. "Madison's bruise is nasty."

Doc's lips tipped into a grin. "You both had horseshoes up your asses."

Cooper shrugged then he turned his attention back to Shepherd. "I thought our mission debrief was at thirteen-hundred."

"Doc requested less field time, the same as Jackson," Shepherd reported.

Cooper's lips set in a smirk. "Will fifty percent be enough?"

"I'd prefer less while Elizabeth is confined to bed, but I will be happy with whatever you can work out." His eyes swept between Shepherd and Cooper.

"We need to work this out for him, like we did Jackson," Shepherd said, his eyes on Cooper. "I think we need to recruit another medic for the teams." His eyes focused back on Doc. "Fifty percent is what we can do for now, but you'll get scrambled for an emergency, just like Jackson."

Doc nodded. "I appreciate that, Shep, and of course I'd always report during an emergency. I like my job, always have, and I don't want to stop doing the field work. I just need it reduced so I can tend Elizabeth. It's not fair to dump it on Angel."

"She doesn't mind," Shepherd said. "And I can put Jackson on the same rotation as you, so you're both away at the same time. Angel is welcome to use my guest room. I always love to have Sammy around."

Shepherd filled Cooper in on the in-office projects Doc would be working on. "Can you think of any other administrative work we can throw his way?"

Cooper smiled. "I'd love to push a few of the end of the month reports off on him. I spend way too much time on them."

Shepherd's lips tipped into a grin. Of course, Cooper would. "We'll see about those. If anything else comes to mind, let me know." Then his gaze shifted back to Doc. "I expect you to put in full days, while tending to Elizabeth and don't hesitate to ask Angel for help. Get to work on your projects. I want weekly updates."

Doc knew he'd just been dismissed. He came to his feet. "Thanks," he said as his eyes slid between the two of them.

After Doc left, Shepherd let out a rant of curses. "Lassiter warned me not too long ago that I may have to reconsider the makeup of the teams. I've always believed having the same four men work together provides the greatest continuity and bond between them. Alpha and Delta work great together, as does Bravo and Charlie. With

Jackson and now Doc requesting reduced field time that makes it harder to cover, especially since Doc is the medic."

"Sloan handled the call to notify Doc well. Doc didn't freak out after he was told about Elizabeth bleeding and her condition because of how Sloan delivered the news. If it were me, getting that news about Madison I sure as hell would have."

"Since you brought it up, do you and Madison have any plans to change the status quo any time soon?"

Cooper laughed. "Is that your way of asking me if we too are going to dive into the parenting pool?"

"Well, while we're talking about team coverage, now seemed like a good time to. If there are any more shifts in staffing coming, I'd prefer to know now."

"No, we have no plans anytime soon. Madison is happy with the amount of time she spends in the field and in Ops. If we need to increase her time in the field, she's okay with that."

"And you are both still alright working in the field together?"

Cooper's expression was unreadable. He shook his head. "Honest to God, Shepherd, operating together is the only way we want it. After what just went down, I think I'd go nuts if she were on a different team. Plus, we'd see each other a lot less and neither of us wants that."

"Okay, good. I just had to check." Shepherd sighed and blew out a breath. "I need to run some numbers and see how many more Operators we can hire. I was planning to add a more technical guy for the field, some sort of engineer to help with the Power Grid Project, but Doc's status bumps up the need for another medic."

"My brother, Michael, is getting out of the Navy in three months. He's been bugging me for an interview with you. He's a nuclear engineer on a sub, knows advanced electronics. I think he could handle the government contract to protect the energy plants that Charlie Team is working on. He'd need a lot of training for any other conventional mission, but he could learn. He's a good shot but has never been in an active combat zone. If we add him there, we could bring Taco or Handsome up to either Alpha or Delta. If you find another medic, we could put him on Charlie and bring Powder up to Delta too."

"So, you think we should bring Sloan up to Alpha then?"

"He'd backfill both Doc and Jackson's positions. Sloan is just as good of a sniper as Jackson is," Cooper said.

"We all know Garcia and Sienna want to start a family. Garcia would prefer to be in Ops as it is. He's just too damn good to not have in the field," Shepherd said.

"Well fuck, maybe Madison and I should have a kid or two, then all of Alpha could be part time in the field and we wouldn't have to disturb any of the other team rosters."

"Yeah, we'd just have to find enough for everyone to do in the office and be able to afford to hire three more Operators."

"Don't forget, you'd need to cover for us all when we are in the field." Cooper rubbed his forehead. "This is giving me a headache."

"Welcome to my world. If you were in the office more, you could take over more of the administrative shit from me. After I was shot, you did a damn good job with it."

"Yeah, and I hated every minute of it too."

Shepherd laughed. Then he turned more serious. "In all actuality, if we hire two more men, your time could be spent training them as well as helping out with more of the administrative shit on my plate. We could have Miller pull more shifts in Ops, and that is one way to maintain Alpha as the five of you."

"So, we'd make Alpha more of a part-time in-the-field team."

"More like split fifty-fifty between office and field work."

Cooper's jaw set in a tight clench. He didn't like it. And he certainly didn't want to become an office paper-pusher. "Do you really think two more operators would fill our staffing needs if Alpha is only in the field half the time?"

"Alpha would be reserved for the most important cases only. If we can swing hiring three more Operators, one a medic, the other two with strong electronics knowledge, we can have Charlie Team train them on the power grid protection project. We then give Charlie Team more traditional cases fifty percent of the time, leave them on the power grid the other half, and we might actually catch up on the schedule. We are way behind."

"So, this new team would be a three-man team?" Cooper shook his head. He didn't like this either.

"No, Echo Team would be a four-man team. BT has good technical skills. He could handle the power grid project just fine. He'd be the team lead."

"BT?"

The corners of Shepherd's lips tipped into a grin. "I already spoke with him. He's open to it. You'd need to give him full Operator training though."

"And he could still provide back up in Ops when Madison, Jackson, and Garcia are in the field. I guess it makes sense to develop in-house talent."

"With Alpha providing three team members to cover Ops, we're overstaffed there. BT has proved his leadership in Ops, and he is very strong technically."

"So, Miraldi can work more with Michaela, and provide backup coverage in Ops too, when Alpha is in the field?"

"That's what I've been thinking," Shepherd confirmed. "Just don't tell your brother he has the job. I want to put him through the full interview process. Unless he really fucks it up, he has the job."

"Shepherd approved my field time reduction. I'll only be away fifty percent of the time," Doc told Elizabeth. He watched a smile brighten her entire face. "I love you, Elizabeth. I'll be here as much as I can be."

Elizabeth's heart filled. "I love you too." She beamed a smile at him. "Thank Shepherd for me. He was so kind when he came in here to see me. He assured me I could stay here as long as I needed to and that everyone would pitch in and help me any way I needed."

"Didn't I tell you we were a family?"

"You did."

Doc took hold of her hand. "Honey, I need to tell you, on this last mission, Madison took one in her vest and Cooper's arm got grazed, but they are just fine."

"They got shot? Are you telling me they both got shot?" She demanded.

"They're fine, honey, but yeah, they both got shot. I wanted you to hear it from me."

Elizabeth didn't know what to say. Her thoughts raced. She knew what they did was dangerous, but this put it into a whole new perspective. She embraced him tightly. "I'm glad you'll be on a reduced field schedule."

"I need you to understand, Elizabeth, we are highly trained, take a lot of precautions, we wear body armor, but getting shot is always a possibility, even on what is classified as low risk operations." He paused, and for some reason he thought of Daniel and Victoria. "I was in a warzone when my unborn child was killed by a drunk driver. No one is safe anywhere, Elizabeth."

"I know. Just hold me, Alexander."

As he held her, he realized that here in this bed, she was safe. A sense of relief washed over him. As long as she stayed in bed, Elizabeth and their daughter were safe. This was a blessing in disguise. He wouldn't have to worry about her.

X-Ray

The rest of March and all of April flew by. Cooper's brother, Michael, came to town and was put through a grueling interview process that all the members of Alpha Team, Shepherd, and BT took part in. They were told to be hard on him, and they were. In the end, he was offered a position by Shepherd.

Doc brought Elizabeth to the OB every two weeks. It was the only time she left the apartment on the ninth floor of the Shepherd Security Building. Doc insisted they remain there, so it was easier for Angel to help care for her while he worked. The truth was, he didn't want her to be alone even at his condo.

At the OB appointment in the beginning of May, the news that the placenta had pulled up enough, resolving the placenta previa condition brought a huge smile to Elizabeth's face. When the OB said she could resume somewhat normal activity, dread settled in Doc's stomach.

"Just take it easy," Dr. Norman warned. "You're no longer confined to bed, but no running any marathons, don't go dancing, and no exercise classes. You are just allowed to walk. That's the best exercise."

"Thank you," Elizabeth said. "Are you sure it's safe?"

"Absolutely. You can even resume sexual relations," he said with a smile at Doc. "But that too, go easy."

Now a smile spread over Doc's face. It had been nearly two months since he'd made love to his wife. He couldn't wait to get her home to their condo, to their bed.

It was a beautiful late May morning. All the flowering trees that lined the streets in the townhouse community were in full bloom. It was sunny and warm, a seasonal seventy degrees. Doc parked on the street in front of the unit. They stepped out of the SUV and onto the sidewalk that was covered with the light pink petals from the flowering crabapple tree that arched over the sidewalk.

Elizabeth smiled as she took in the view. It was magical, like a fairytale or a dream. A light floral scent filled the air. The ground and the trees were still wet from the light rain that fell overnight. The sun hit each droplet, which made them glisten like diamonds. A bird landed in the tree overhead, making the leaves rustle, dropping a brief cascade of sparkling showers.

They walked up the driveway. Elizabeth studied the home in front of her. It was a middle unit. Its face was brick. A large, three-pane, floor to ceiling window was to the right of the black front door. She could see couches within, the living room. On the second floor above, were two large windows. This unit's two-car garage was on the right, with windows above. It was flush with the front door. On Angel and Sienna's homes the garages protruded from the face of the house. She liked this better, gave the unit a longer driveway.

The front door swung open and an older woman with short gray hair stood with a smile behind the full-length screen door.

"Hi, I'm Doc Williams and this is my wife, Elizabeth."

"Hi, Dorie Mulvey. Thank you for coming so early." She opened the screen. "Please come in."

They stepped within, their feet landing on the dark gray hardwood floor. The living room before them held a large black sectional couch that didn't make the room feel small. It faced a flat screen television that was mounted on the wall beside the stone front fireplace that was in the middle of the wall. Beyond it, a breakfast bar with four stools separated the living room from the kitchen at the far end of the room. A window over the sink on the far wall looked out over the back yard.

"That's a wood-burning fireplace," Dorie Mulvey said.

"Very nice," Elizabeth said. "I like the stones rather than bricks like most have."

"Yes, brick was standard. My husband nearly put us in the poorhouse with the upgrades he wanted for this place, including the stone finish on the fireplace. We are original owners. There are not too many of us left in this complex."

"Why are you selling?" Elizabeth asked.

"We're moving near our daughter. She lives in Missouri, has four children. We don't get to see our grandchildren often enough. My husband just retired. I'm retiring at the end of the school year. Of course, you already know that because you know Sienna."

"That's very nice you can," Elizabeth said. "Your home is beautiful," she said glancing around.

"Thank you," Dorie said. "Let me show you the rest of it." Dorie pointed to the four barstools. "Our new home in Missouri has no breakfast bar. We will have no need for the stools. We are leaving them with the house."

Elizabeth smiled and nodded. It would be nice to not have to buy replacements if they bought this house. This home was quite a bit bigger than the condo. They would have to buy more furniture than she would like for Alexander to have to spend.

They moved into the kitchen. It too had many upgrades, stainless steel appliances, new cabinets, and granite countertops with specks of silver that sparkled. Off the back was a small four seasons room that Dorie and her husband had added. It acted as an eat-in kitchen as this model did not have room in the kitchen for a table and chairs. Windows with screens ran from the ceiling to the thigh-high bottom wall. A sliding glass door was on the left, leading to a brick patio.

"The sunroom ate up a portion of the yard which isn't too big to begin with. And there's the patio which leaves very little grassy area for kids to play, but the park is just a half block over," she pointed to her right.

"This backyard is very cozy," Elizabeth said as they stepped onto the brick patio. It was cute and more than Elizabeth had ever had.

They went back in and Dorie showed them the first-floor powder room, garage and finished basement. Then they went upstairs. At the top of the stairs the master bedroom suite was to the right and filled the entire space over the garage. To the left was the door to one of the two bedrooms.

"This whole master suite was an upgrade too. We did take a little space away from the third bedroom and I downsized the laundry room too, but I didn't need a big laundry room. It was oddly oversized and included the furnace which we moved to the basement preconstruction."

The master bedroom was huge with a vaulted ceiling. At the far end of the room was a large master bathroom. It had a separate large soak tub with jacuzzi jets, which sat up on a tiled pedestal. A large shower stall was beside it, its tilework beautiful. There were double sinks. And the toilet was hidden behind another door. An enormous walk-in closet completed the master space.

They returned to the hallway. They went into the first bedroom. It spanned the living room and overlooked the front of the house. It had two windows with a built-in padded bench below them. It was cute and had a large closet with built-in shelves and drawers.

"My two girls shared this room," Dorie said.

The hallway curved to the left. A good size hall bathroom was there. Across the hall was the laundry room. Tucked in the back was the third bedroom, which sat atop the kitchen. Its two windows overlooked the back yard. It was much smaller than the other spare bedroom.

"When were you and your husband going to list the house with a realtor?" Doc asked Dorie.

"Saturday morning, but we do have two more people coming to look at it for sale by owner before then. We're hoping to avoid having to pay a realtor commission."

Doc didn't like to be strong armed, and he wasn't sure if that was what she was trying to do. But he didn't want to lose the opportunity of getting the house either. "Would you mind if Elizabeth and I sat on your patio for a few minutes and discussed it?"

"Certainly," Dorie said, motioning them back towards the stairs. "I must share with you we do have one offer already. We have not accepted or declined it. It is contingent on the sale of their home and it's not even on the market yet. We'd prefer to have a noncontingent offer."

"Thank you for telling us that," Doc said. More strong-arming?

Doc and Elizabeth sat together on the swing. "This is very nice back here," Elizabeth said.

"The yard is small, not much room for kid's stuff, but I think it would be okay," Doc said. "Do you like the house?"

Elizabeth smiled wide. "It's perfect. I absolutely love the sunroom dining area. And I especially love the master bedroom suite. Alexander, I love this house, but it's so much money."

"Don't worry about that. I can swing it."

"But you would have to sell your condo yet too and it doesn't sound like she'd accept our offer either."

"She'll accept our offer," Doc guaranteed. "I don't need to sell the condo first. Cooper's brother, Michael, will be moving here and joining the agency next month. Cooper said he'd rent my condo for at least six months, which would cover my expenses there. I have a few accounts I can cash in for the down payment on this place so it's a noncontingent offer. If you want this house, we're buying this house."

"That sounds financially reckless."

"Elizabeth, you are seven months pregnant. This unit is for sale. We don't know when the next one in this complex will come on the market. I like the idea of being this close to Garcia and Jackson, for me as well as you when I am on a mission."

Elizabeth nodded.

"So, we're agreed. You want this house, right?" Doc asked.

Elizabeth flashed him that excited smile again and nodded her head. "If you're sure you can afford it; yes, I want this house."

They went back inside and made the offer to Dorie. It was not contingent on anything besides the house passing a home inspection. Doc even already had his financing approved. Closing date was thirty days out. He wanted them settled before the baby came.

Later that afternoon, they got the call from Dorie. She and her husband accepted their offer. They went back over and signed the contract. They dropped by Jackson and Angel's after they were through to share the news. Garcia and Sienna were there as well.

Angel wrapped Elizabeth in a hug. "I'm so excited you're going to be just down the block! We'll all help you pack and move."

"Thanks. It's a great home. I could see Alexander and me living there as soon as I stepped through the front door."

Garcia opened a beer and handed it to Doc. "Congrats. This will be good having most the team on the block. Now we just need to get Cooper and Madison to move."

Jackson laughed. "Good luck with that. Cooper loves his condo."

"Speaking of Cooper, does anyone know the real reason his brother is joining the agency next month?" Garcia asked.

"Like Shepherd said during the interview with him, he is adding him to the Power Grid Protection Project. They're way behind on the schedule," Doc said.

"Yeah, I think it's more than that," Garcia said. "There're changes coming. Don't ask me how I know, I just do." He didn't look happy about it. Sienna wrapped her arm around him and snuggled in close to him.

Jackson shrugged. As long as he had his reduced field schedule, Shepherd could make all the changes he wanted to. Put his ass on another team, or assign him to Ops full time, he didn't care, as long as he got to be home with Angel and Sammy more than he was away.

Angel knew that Shepherd was looking to add a few more men to the agency. She had handled some correspondence for him that indicated he was looking to recruit a medic and another field engineer from the active duty special forces teams. She didn't know the full scope of what Shepherd was doing, and she knew to keep the confidence, even from Jackson. When Shepherd wanted the team to know, he would tell them.

Yankee

Elizabeth's due date was one week away. Her belly was huge, and she was uncomfortable.

"Okay, you can get redressed," Doctor Norman said, patting her leg. He'd just finished an internal exam. His eyes flickered to Doc. "Meet me in my office when she's dressed." He stepped from the room.

Doc pulled her into a sitting position, something she hadn't been able to do herself for several months. She wore a light-weight summer top. He slid her panties over her feet, followed by her maternity shorts. Then he helped her up.

In Dr. Norman's office, they settled in the two chairs facing his desk. "Everything looks good. You're dilated to three and about fifty percent effaced, but what you're feeling aren't real contractions. You were correct in classifying them as Braxton Hicks. You're not in labor. I would say though that you could go at any time." He paused and his eyes focused on Doc. "So, you won't want to go too far away from home, Mr. Williams."

Doc nodded. He didn't plan on it. He'd been on a mission-hold status since the beginning of the month. "Walking is still good for her, isn't it?"

"Yes. It's a beautiful day, go out and enjoy it. Walk around, see if you can get anything moving. It's a full moon tonight. For some reason, I tend to see more women going into labor when there is a full moon." He shrugged. "Maybe you can be one of them."

After their doctor's appointment, they drove into Chicago. Doctor Norman was right. It was a beautiful July day, not too hot, not too humid. After walking around Millennium Park, Grant Park, and the Lakefront for a few hours, they returned to the car. Elizabeth was tired. The baby had dropped, and she was beyond uncomfortable. The traffic was heavy. It took longer than expected to get out into the suburbs.

"Alexander, I have to pee again."

"We'll be home in twenty minutes," he said.

A grimace formed on her face. "I can't wait. Please pull off at the next exit and we'll hit that convenience store I like on the corner." She pointed out her window. "They have those cinnamon mini bun things I like, and I could go for a package or two." She shot him an instigating smile.

Doc took the exit. He pulled up in front of the store. He wondered if she really had to pee or if she just really wanted a package of those mini buns. He got out of the car with her. "You don't have to say you have to pee to get me to stop for a package of sweets for you, you know." He smiled as he teased her.

"I do have to pee. Your daughter is jumping on my bladder. I can't even describe to you what I've been feeling from her on it all day. It's been terrible."

"Okay, okay." Doc laughed as he swung the door open. "Let's get your cinnamon buns."

"Really, the cramping in my abdomen from her sitting on my bladder is really uncomfortable."

The clerk wasn't at the counter. Doc found that odd but didn't give it too much thought. He was concentrating on what Elizabeth had just said. He followed her through the aisle. The restrooms were near the back. "Elizabeth, describe these cramps. Could they be contractions?"

"I'm just uncomfortable, not in pain," she said as she turned the corner around the end cap.

Then Doc heard her scream. Coming around the corner himself, his heart nearly stopped. Elizabeth was being held in front of a man, a gun to her head. Three other people laid face-down on the floor. Doc recognized the clerk as one of them. The other two were women.

Doc raised his arms into the air. "Don't shoot, please."

"Shut up!" The gunman yelled, grabbing Elizabeth more tightly. "On the ground!"

"Okay," Doc said. "I'll get down. Just stay calm." He dropped to his knees as he assessed the situation.

"Don't tell me what to do!" The man yelled.

This assailant was clearly getting agitated. He appeared to be the only gunman. His eyes were dilated, bloodshot, and a sheen of sweat coated his face. He was most likely high on something. If there was a distraction, Doc could unholster his weapon and fire on him. He had a clear shot at the man's head as long as Elizabeth remained still.

Doc's eyes locked with Elizabeth's. He shifted them to his left, hoping she understood to drop left if she could.

The front of Elizabeth's shorts got saturated with liquid. It ran down her legs and splashed to the floor. "My water just broke!" Then she screamed out and clutched her abdomen, drooping to the left in his grasp. The assailant's eyes focused on her.

Doc took the opportunity the distraction provided and unholstered his weapon from the small of his back. In less than a second, he brought it up and centered the gunman in his sights. He squeezed the trigger once. The round tore through the man's forehead; his lifeless body crumpled to the ground.

The three who were face down on the floor jumped up after the assailant hit the floor. Elizabeth screamed.

"You shot him!" The clerk exclaimed.

"Go call the police," Doc ordered as he moved to where the assailant laid on the floor. He kicked his gun away from him. Then felt for a pulse. As expected, there wasn't one.

The clerk took off towards the front of the store. One of the women who had been on the floor came up to help Elizabeth.

"Are you okay?" Doc asked Elizabeth as he took her into an embrace.

Her eyes were focused on the dead man. She couldn't look away. He would have killed her. In those few minutes he held her with the gun pressed into her, all she could think about was how heartbroken Alexander would be if anything happened to her or their baby. She prayed he wouldn't have to go through losing his family again.

"Elizabeth, right here," he commanded, turning her so she no longer gazed at the dead man. She had tears in her eyes. "Are you okay?" He repeated.

She nodded; her eyes locked with his. She was so thankful he was armed, that he was who he was. He saved her, again. He was her hero, and she loved him with all her heart.

"Elizabeth, that was genius peeing your pants and saying your water broke!" He hugged her tightly.

"I didn't pee my pants," she argued. Then another contraction hit, and she grabbed her abdomen again grunting out.

"Breathe, honey, breathe," Doc said, coaching her, his face leaning into hers. He checked his watch. The two contractions were less than three minutes apart. He pulled his phone from his belt and dialed Ops.

The woman who was beside them saw a chair in the back corner near the doors to the restrooms. She got it for Elizabeth and prompted her to sit. "I've had three kids. I can help."

"Ops, go," BT answered.

"I've been involved in a shooting. Elizabeth and I walked into a robbery at a convenience store. I killed the perp. Local LEOs have been called. I need DC to be aware of the situation. And I need an ambulance stat. Elizabeth is in labor and her contractions are about three minutes apart."

"Oh shit," BT swore as he typed commands into his console. Two minutes later, he spoke again. "Okay, DC has been notified and I've tapped in to the local 9-1-1 center requesting an ambulance for a woman in labor. I made an update to advise this was an officer involved shooting so the local LEOs will be aware when they get on site. I've also just dispatched Miller with her creds to be on site to interface with the LEOs while you go with Elizabeth to the hospital."

"Thanks BT." Doc heard the sirens approach.

"Let me know if you need anything else."

Doc pulled his badge and FBI credentials out to have them ready. He had re-holstered his gun. The sirens got closer until he could identify that they were right outside. Elizabeth had another contraction. It appeared to be stronger than the last. He knelt in front of her and coached her through it. He heard the police talking with the clerk in the front of the store, their voices getting louder as they approached.

"He's the one who shot the robber," the clerk said pointing at Doc.

Doc held his badge and credentials up. "Agent Williams, FBI."

One of the two uniformed officers bent down and checked the perp. The other came in close and examined Doc's credentials. Then his gaze focused on Elizabeth. "Your wife is in labor? We got notified and a second ambulance is en route for her."

"You won't need the ambulance for the perp," Doc said. "Just the coroner."

The officer who knelt by the robber's body nodded. He spoke into his radio, cancelling one of the ambulances and summoning the coroner. "The detective is on his way."

"Her contractions are less than three minutes apart," Doc said. "When the ambulance arrives, we're leaving. The detective can get our statements at the hospital after our baby is born. One of my counterparts will arrive to interface with your office."

"And if he doesn't arrive before the ambulance?"

"She, Agent Madison Miller. And if she doesn't get here by the time we're loaded on the ambulance, we're leaving."

The uniformed officers recorded the ID from everyone, beginning with Doc and Elizabeth. By the time sirens wailed out again, Doc was coaching Elizabeth through another contraction. She was still panting and following Doc's breathing directions when the detective came around the end cap of the aisle. Doc barely glanced at him.

"Agent Williams," the plainclothes detective announced as he stepped up to him. "The ambulance for your wife is two minutes out."

Doc looked up at him. He looked familiar. They'd crossed paths before. "Thanks. The contractions are holding at just under three minutes apart, but she doesn't have the urge to push yet." Doc told him the hospital they would be at. "Give me your card and I'll call you when we can give our statements. That bastard had a gun to her head and was getting agitated. It was a clean shoot. Ask any of these people."

The three others who stood around, all nodded their heads. "He was going to kill us all, I'm sure," the clerk said. "And he was jacked up on something. His eyes were wild."

The detective nodded. The coroner would confirm that.

Madison came around the corner, badge and creds in hand. Her eyes took in the situation. "The ambulance is a block out. How are you doing, Elizabeth?"

Elizabeth blew out a few breaths. "Okay."

The detective smiled. "I know you. The condo shooting downtown last year."

Madison smiled too. "Detective Russell, it's nice to see you again." She extended her hand towards him. "Madison Miller, FBI."

Russell nodded. He looked back at Doc. "You were there that night too."

Doc nodded. Another contraction gripped Elizabeth. The ambulance arrived, and the EMTs were coming through the aisle with a stretcher by the time the contraction ended.

"Contractions are two minutes apart and lasting ninety seconds," Doc advised them. "Water broke approximately twenty minutes ago. I'm a former EMT, and Army Medic."

The two men wasted no time getting Elizabeth onto the stretcher. Doc followed them to the front of the store.

"Madison, a minute!" Doc yelled from the front door. Madison met him there. Doc handed her his car keys. "Have someone from the office bring it to me at the hospital later, will you?"

"Of course. Good luck. Let us know when your baby girl arrives." She took the keys and gave him a quick hug.

Doc climbed into the ambulance and it sped away, lights and sirens on, all the way to the hospital.

Zulu

"Are you ready to do this, honey?"

Elizabeth forced a smile. She blew out three quick puffs. The contractions were nearly continuous. The pressure of the baby crowning was horrendous. She gripped Alexander's hand more tightly. "Ready."

"Okay, on this next contraction, Elizabeth, push, with everything that you've got," Doctor Norman said, his brown eyes locked with Elizabeth's. Then he nodded at Doc.

It only took five minutes for Elizabeth to push the baby out. Doctor Norman suctioned out her nose and mouth, loosely wrapped her in a pink blanket, and then laid her on Elizabeth's chest.

"Meet your daughter," one of the nurses said, patting Elizabeth on the shoulder. "You did it, momma, and she looks perfect."

Elizabeth cried tears of pure joy. Their baby girl was beautiful, breathing, and the most precious baby she'd ever seen. She had a barely there coating of blond hair on her tiny head. She had bright blue eyes, that were open and staring into Elizabeth's and the cutest little heart-shaped mouth. She had perfect little fingers that were long and slender with fingernails.

"You did it, Elizabeth," Doc whispered. "You brought our baby into the world." Tears streamed down his cheeks. "She's beautiful. She looks just like you."

Elizabeth's gaze shifted to Alexander. She saw the tears on his face. She'd never seen him cry. "We did it. We did it together," she said with a soft crackling voice. "I love you so much. Thank you for being here, and for saving me from that man in the store. I've never been so afraid in my life."

"I would have died before I let anything happen to the two of you." Doc shook his head, shaking the image of that gun to Elizabeth's head from his mind. "I love you more than you will ever know, Elizabeth and I love her like I never thought was possible, just meeting her. Thank you for this gift. I love you, honey."

He kissed her and then his eyes returned to the eight-pound, three-ounce miracle cuddled on her mother's chest.

"Do you have a name for your daughter yet?" The nurse asked.

Elizabeth's eyes met Alexander's. "So, you're really okay with Olivia Bernice?"

"Yeah, she'll be a tough cookie like her mom."

Elizabeth laughed. "You'll teach her to fight. She'll be her daddy's little girl in all ways, I'm sure."

"Does Angel know you planned to name her after both your mothers?" Doc asked.

"No, but it's only right. Thank you for letting me name her. Bernice John is such a wonderful woman, so loving and full of faith. And Olivia, my mom, she did the best she could. She was strong in her own way and she left this world way too young." She teared up.

Doc pressed a kiss to Elizabeth's forehead. "It's okay." It was only natural she would be thinking about her mom after just giving birth to her own daughter. Doc flashed a smile at her. "Besides, you did all the work. But I get to name the next one, okay?"

Elizabeth laughed again. "Great, our next kid will probably be named trout, pike or walleye."

Now Doc laughed. "Pike Williams, sounds good."

They spent another half hour just staring at their little girl as the medical staff did all they needed to do post-delivery.

"I want to call the team and let them know she is here and that you are okay," Doc said.

Within the hour the maternity floor waiting room was filled with Shepherd Security personnel, including Shepherd, himself.

"I'm sorry," the nurse said. "The rules for visitation allow immediate family only in the new mother's room."

"This group *is* our immediate family," Doc told her. "We both have very large families." He stared her down.

She glanced over the many who gathered in the waiting room, counting ten, and then back at Doc. There was no way this group of people were related. His jaw was set, and his eyes were fixed on her with determination. She had a moment that she looked undecided. "Fine," she finally said. "But no more than two visitors at a time."

Doc grinned, his eyes shifting to his team. "Shep, why don't you and Lassiter come back first."

Shepherd rolled past the nurse. "Thank you."

His tone was pleasant. She had the distinct feeling he could be anything but, if he wanted to be. The nurse who attended this couple during the delivery told her this new father was armed. He was some sort of law enforcement. She figured most of these people in the waiting room were cops too, she could always tell. Her ex-husband was a cop. After living with him for ten years and hanging out with his coworkers, it was like she had an innate cop-radar.

Elizabeth still stared into her sleeping daughter's face, cradled in her arms. It would be a long time before she laid the baby in the bassinet beside her bed. The tidal wave of emotions had just about receded. The fear from the convenience store, the exhilaration of her water breaking and knowing she was in labor, and the pain and exhaustion of going through labor, culminating with the elation of her daughter being born and sat in her arms brought her highs and lows unlike she'd ever known. And the intense love she felt for Alexander, her hero yet again, saving her from that gunman in the store, as well as the instant all-consuming love for this baby, surprised her that they were such strong emotions.

The curtain by the door swept open and Alexander followed by Shepherd and Dr. Lassiter came into the room. Elizabeth smiled wide. She was hoping Angel or Sienna would be the first in, but she was fine with it being these two men.

"Hello, Elizabeth," Shepherd greeted. His eyes went back to Doc. "She's definitely tough enough to be married to a Shepherd Security Operator. Look at her, just hours after being held by an armed crack-head, labor, and delivery, and she looks great!" He smiled at Elizabeth. "You are a true champ. Now let me get a look at this little one."

He rolled closer. Elizabeth tipped the baby so he could get a good look.

"May I hold her?"

An irrational fear swept over Elizabeth. She knew it was irrational. "Of course." She handed her over. She watched this powerful man hold her little baby so gently. It was an insane contradiction.

"She's beautiful. What did you name her?" His eyes glanced up into Elizabeth's.

"Olivia Bernice."

Shepherd nodded. "That's nice. I know Olivia was your mother's name. Does Angel know you were also naming her after her mother?"

Elizabeth shook her head no.

"Then she and Jackson should be the next to come in and meet her. You have a full waiting room out there. They'll only let us in two at a time." He placed a gentle kiss on the top of the baby's head. "You've got a hell of a set of parents, little one. You'll do great in this world."

Doctor Lassiter came in close. He smiled at the baby and then at Elizabeth. "Well done. If you need to work out any issues from being held at gunpoint, just let me know. But I'd say just focus on this little sweetie and you will be fine."

Elizabeth smiled. "Thank you."

Lassiter took the baby from Shepherds arms, cradled her for a few seconds and then returned her to her mother. Both men congratulated Doc. "Touch bases with me towards the end of your two-week leave," Shepherd told Doc. "Or sooner if you need anything."

"Thanks, Shep," Doc said, gripping his hand and drawing himself down to Shepherd for a shoulder bump.

Jackson and Angel came in next. "Oh, she's beautiful," Angel gushed.

"Meet Olivia Bernice," Elizabeth told her with a proud grin.

"Oh, you named her after my mom too!" Angel's eyes leaked tears. She had known Olivia, Elizabeth's mother's name, was in the top two names being considered. She hugged Elizabeth. "My mom will be so thrilled and honored to know you think this much of her."

"Of course, I do. If it weren't for your mom, I wouldn't be the person I am. She was like a second mother to me."

"That makes us sisters," Angel said with a smile.

"Congrats, man," Jackson said, embracing Doc. "It's incredible, isn't it? Knowing you created that little being."

Doc shook his head. "I had no idea how I'd feel, seeing my child for the first time. Indescribable!"

Jackson smiled knowingly. "Angel and I are talking about when we should try for baby number two. I'm sure her holding your little newborn is going to make her want to do it right away," he whispered. "I'm so screwed."

Doc laughed. He could think of a lot of ways to be screwed that would be worse. He also realized he was in the perfect place in his life, surrounded by the best people, to be beginning this parenting, family man thing. He was one lucky man.

Sienna and Garcia came in next. Hugs all around and coos over the baby, a congratulatory shoulder bump, followed by a hug passed between Garcia and Doc.

"Man, she's so tiny," Garcia said as he held the tiny blanket-wrapped bundle in his large hands. "I didn't see Sammy till he was three months old and damn I thought he was small, but she is like half of what his size was."

Doc chuckled. "Not quite half."

Garcia laid his hand to Sienna's abdomen. A knowing smile passed between them. Then he nodded.

Sienna took hold of Elizabeth's hand. "We haven't told anyone yet, but I'm pregnant." She smiled wide, her adoring eyes then flickering to Anthony.

"You are?" Elizabeth exclaimed.

"Nine weeks," Sienna said. Then she took the baby from Anthony. "I can't wait to tell everyone. I planned to wait until I passed the twelfth week." She shook her head. "But I guess I don't need to."

"Congrats!" Doc embraced Garcia. Then he hugged Sienna. He wasn't surprised. He knew Sienna wanted children, lots of children. He imagined his friend would have them pretty quickly, like one a year until Sienna decided they'd had enough. He chuckled at the thought of it.

"I'm so happy for you," Elizabeth told Sienna. "We won't say anything to anyone. Tell the rest of the team on your own time."

Cooper and Madison came in next. Elizabeth was beginning to get tired, even though each group only stayed five or ten minutes. Madison held Olivia for a long time. "I'm not ready to give my job up quite yet, but maybe in a few years," she said, much to Doc's surprise.

Cooper pressed a kiss to Madison's cheek. "It'll be whenever you want it, Blondie. We have plenty of time."

Madison glanced back at Elizabeth. "I love kids, think we'll probably have one or two at some point, just not yet. I love what I do in the field too much to give it up just yet."

Elizabeth nodded. She didn't understand. "So, you can't do your job if you have a baby? Not even after it's born?"

Madison shook her head no. "It can't work that way. Cooper and I go out in the field together. We want it no other way. We know we cannot ever have a child, and both put ourselves in danger at the same time. That wouldn't be fair to any child, to lose both its parents like that."

Her statement shocked Elizabeth. The fact that she had given it that much thought and consideration was surprising. "But you also work in Ops, don't you?"

"Yes, and I could still do that job. It's just that," she paused and blew out a breath. "It's so unfair the men don't have to make this choice." She handed Olivia back to Elizabeth. "But I have several years before I have to worry about being too old to have a healthy baby. And I do love my life just the way it is, for now."

Cooper embraced her. "Congrats again, guys," he said, his eyes sweeping between Doc and Elizabeth. "We're going to get out of here so you can rest. Let us know if you need anything."

Doc embraced Cooper and then Madison. He followed them out. There were only two more left to come see the baby. He'd make sure they only stayed a few minutes. Elizabeth was looking very tired, and truth be told, so was he. He escorted Lambchop and the Undertaker in.

Gary Sloan rushed to Elizabeth and embraced her. He took the offered baby from her arms, holding the tiny bundle close to his own chest. "I'm so glad you made it safely, little one," he whispered. "She's beautiful," he told Elizabeth.

Lambchop congratulated the new parents as well. He took the baby from Sloan and said a prayer over the child thanking God for this precious life, her safe arrival, and the health of her parents. "You will still let me baptize her, won't you?"

Doc clapped him on the shoulder. "We wouldn't let anyone else. We'll talk about when to do it after we get home with her."

"Who are you thinking for the Godparents?"

Doc smiled at Elizabeth. "Jackson and Angel."

Lambchop nodded, a smile curving his lips. "Seems appropriate."

Elizabeth watched the three men, these three brave and fierce warriors. Gary had a strength and gentleness that coexisted behind his haunted eyes. He was quiet and intense, but caring and thoughtful. He had stayed with her when she thought she was losing Olivia, afraid and in a panic. He promised her he'd remain with her until Alexander returned to her, and he did.

The pastor, Landon Johnson, a hulk of a man who was as tender as he was tough. He was a man of God, who was also a soldier. She wasn't sure how he reconciled that, killing men while worshiping the Lord. He never seemed conflicted. He always appeared at peace and steadfast in his faith. He was an amazing person who she was glad she was lucky enough to know.

And Alexander, her Alexander, she saw the joy in his features as he took their daughter back from the other men. He was her hero and the love of her life. She thanked God for bringing him into her life and blessing them with Olivia. Her life was better than any life she could have envisioned for herself.

Even their friends who surrounded them today, Alexander's teammates, his family, she knew this group that she was lucky enough to be a part of, were a special group of people. She smiled, her head resting against the soft pillow, and then she fell asleep.

Doc said goodbye to the Undertaker and Lambchop, thanking them for coming today. Mother and the Birdman would be by in the morning. They were working an overnight detail with Bravo Team. He'd call his blood family in the morning. It was late. He laid Olivia in the small baby bed that was beside Elizabeth's bed. He dropped his exhausted body into the recliner and stared at both Elizabeth and Olivia.

He felt a contentment in his soul that was foreign to him. He realized that for the first time in over a decade and a half, his world was in harmony. He had a woman who loved him, flaws and all, a woman whom he loved deeply. And he had this little miracle, this little baby that he and Elizabeth had created during moments when they both thought they would die horrendous deaths.

This little life was a symbol of their lives spared, of faith, and of strength. He'd protect both her and her mother with everything he had in him, to his last breath. And he'd live every day to its fullest, enjoying this God-given life that he had been blessed with, for as long as he lived. He knew he was in the right place in his head to be the best husband and father he could be.

A month later, after they settled into their new life as a family, they traveled to Doc's hometown, Houston. Doc proudly introduced his wife and baby to his family, who he hadn't seen in over five years. He had pushed them out of his life, claiming to be too busy at work. He had four sisters. They still lived in the Houston area with their families, as did his parents. Dan and Peggy Williams were in their late seventies and healthy.

The Williams clan all gathered at the house they'd grown up in, where his parents still lived. He was sure his sisters and their families had regular gatherings at this house. He hoped there'd be enough years left that he and Elizabeth, and their children would be able to spend holidays with his family in this house that raised him.

"We never gave up hope Alex would find his way back to us," his mother told Elizabeth quietly. "We knew he was in a dark place after Victoria died. It broke my heart to know that he was so alone, but we couldn't force him to communicate with us. The more we pushed, the further away he got."

"He wasn't alone. He had his team. They're a special group of people who love him," Elizabeth replied.

"We missed him and wanted to be there."

Elizabeth nodded. "He's a good man. You raised a really good man, Mrs. Williams. He may have been blaming himself for Victoria's death, but he is kind, a man who risks his own life to save others, including me."

"It's Peggy, my dear." Her gaze fell back on her granddaughter. "The mother of my grandchild should call me by my first name. I'd given up hope Alex would find love again and have a child."

"He's a good father, a good husband," Elizabeth said. "I love him with all my heart, Peggy."

She nodded and forced a smile. "I hope I can get to know that man."

Doc sat the flowers on top of the headstone and then stepped back. "I forgive you Victoria, and I'm sorry I wasn't there for you. I am finally at peace and hope you have been all these years. You've had Daniel with you, and I've missed you both. I'm ready to move on now and I was lucky enough to find a woman who loves me. She gave me a little girl. I'm going to be okay." He gazed into the bright blue sky and allowed the happiness of his life to fill his heart as the tears filled his eyes. "I'm going to be okay," he repeated.

The End

The Shepherd Security Series:
Book 1, Operation: Protected Angel
Book 2, Operation: Recruited Angel
Book 3, Operation: Dark Angel
Book 4, Operation: Fallen Angel

Books 5-8 (Delta Team's stories)

Book 5, Operation: Departed Angel

 Gary 'the Undertaker' Sloan, Navy SEAL, sniper and corpsman on Shepherd Security's Delta Team, left the Sloan Family Mortuary and Funeral Home in Cleveland, Ohio in the hands of his brother and joined the Navy after the death of his father.

 When he left Cleveland, he also left his high school sweetheart and fiancé, Kennedy Bristow, who was more interested in pursuing a career in music than she was in being a military wife. The parting was somewhat mutual, at least that was what Sloan told himself over the years.

 When Gary gets a call from his brother that Kennedy is laying on their prep table, the victim of an execution-style shooting, he immediately returns home. He soon discovers that things are not what they seem. It will take all his skills and the help of the entire Shepherd Security Team to get to the bottom of the murder and bring those responsible to justice.

Book 6, Operation: Bayou Angel

Book 7, Operation: Unknown Angel

Book 8, Operation: Beach Angel

Acknowledgements

I truly say thank you, to you, the reader, for choosing this book. If you enjoyed it, would you please leave a review, so others might find this book to enjoy, as well? As an Independent Author, without a publishing house to help advertise my work, I rely on reviews from readers such as you and followers on social media to promote me. Thank you! I would greatly appreciate it.

Thank you to my ARC Team, readers who volunteered to read this book before it was released and give me a private, honest review, before leaving a public review after I made revisions based on their feedback.

The model for this cover is a husband and a father of two school-aged daughters, Olivia and Brielle. Olivia is such a beautiful name, I had to use it in this book. I loved the name Brielle so much, that I decided to name a main character in an upcoming book Brielle as an added thank you to him for modeling for this cover. You will meet her in Operation Bayou Angel. The photo shoot was fun! Thank you, Kirby!

I mentioned the Infants Remembered in Silence website in this book. IRIS is a 501(c) 3 non-profit organization that is dedicated to offering parents, families, friends and professionals support, education and resources on the death of a child in early pregnancy (miscarriage, ectopic pregnancy etc.), or from premature birth, stillbirth, neo-natal death, birth defects, sudden infant death syndrome (SIDS), illness and all other types of infant and early childhood death. Please go to their website for additional information if you are interested at: https://www.irisremembers.com/

The Shepherd Security Team has mental health protocols as my way of acknowledging the fact that PTSD is very real and many of our Service men and women struggle with it. In this book, Doc faces ghosts from his past that he works through with Dr. Lassiter. I recently learned about a wonderful organization that is helping our veterans. Mission 22 is a non-profit who combats the ever-rising veteran suicide rate. Every day, more than twenty veterans are lost to suicide. Mission 22 wants to bring that number to zero. It does this with three main programs; veteran treatment programs, memorials and national awareness. Mission 22 provides treatment programs to veterans for Post-Traumatic Stress, Traumatic Brain Injury and other issues they might be facing. For more information: https://www.mission22.com

Thank you to my editors, who gave of their time selflessly to help me with the grammar, which is not my strongpoint.

Thank you, my friend, photographer, and graphic artist Harry R. who shot all the covers for this series. Thank you, Harry!

Thank you to Norm E. my friend and resource for the fishing references. The lake Doc went to is one of his favorite spots. Yes, Dr. Norman was named after him as a thank you.

Also thank you to two other authors who read and critiqued various sections of this book as I wrote it. Daniel Giallombardo and Thomas Dorsch, both of you are true gentlemen and amazing writers. Both of them have books on Amazon, different genres than mine, but check them out.

Thank you to my sisters, RK Cary and Charlie Roberts, who are writing their own romance books. RK has finished up her Destined & Redeemed series and has several other Science Fiction/Fantasy stories in the works. Charlie is working on a contemporary romance series, the Stevens Street Gym Series. Both have been wonderful friends with the honesty and encouragement that only a sister can give. Check out their work on Amazon! Links directly to all our books on Amazon can be found on our website. That link is below.

Thank you to my wonderful and supportive husband for his patience and love while I spend hours upon hours to research and write this story. Also, for advising me on any parts of this story requiring knowledge of the military or weapons that I did not have.

Thank you to my mother who shared with me her love of books. As a child, the wonderful example my mother set for me as an avid reader led my sisters and me to write our stories. She has encouraged me to publish and I thank her for her support.

Lastly, a big thank you to my girlfriends who have encouraged me and made me feel that I could do this at the times I felt insecure in my ability to accomplish this. You know who you are ladies! You hold a special place in my heart.

About the Author

Hello! I am Margaret Kay. They say being a Military wife is the toughest job in the Armed Forces even though there is no MOS for the position. As the veteran of more than a few deployments, I have to agree. My husband proudly served 8 years in the United States Navy in the 80s. That was before cell phones and the internet.

For anyone who's never had a loved one who's served, being associated with the military is being part of a special community of people who support each other, who understand what the day to day is like when your loved one is deployed half-way around the world.

Saying goodbye to your loved one as they leave on a lengthy deployment is unlike saying goodbye to someone for any other reason. It's not like dropping a son or daughter at college or hugging an aging parent after a visit. Your military member is being deployed, part of a mission. You cannot go visit when you miss them too much. You know it's different. You plan for it differently. They may be getting deployed into harm's way. And even if they are not, you know what their purpose is and that they could be in harm's way at any time.

The emotions you feel when you stand with other families, when the unit, boat, or flight returns after many months of separation cannot be described in words that bring adequate justice to it, but I will try. There is a level of excitement equaled only by a child's wonder on Christmas morning. A pride in your country, in the unit, and in your loved one that courses through your vein's as you, your children, and all around you hold American flags and signs welcoming them home, waiting all together sometimes for hours before they appear and make their way towards you. As a spouse, you're hungering for your partner's touch, for their lips to meet yours, and for the reunion that will occur later, when you're alone. With that excitement also comes nervousness because it has been so long since you've been together as a couple, sharing your bed.

My husband honorably separated from the Navy and easily transitioned to civilian life, but I never forgot what it was like while he served. Many of our returning servicemen and women have not had it so easy. Please keep them in your thoughts and prayers as they recover from physical and emotional injuries. Many struggle to find employment. If you have the ability in your work to encourage the hiring of a Vet, please do.

Our military members are special! I honor all past, present, and future members of our military with my stories. Salute the flag, stand for the national anthem, and thank a Vet for their service. Freedom is not free, a lot of people sacrificed for the freedoms we enjoy.

Don't ever forget!
Margaret

Please stay in touch. I have more books in the Shepherd Security Series in process plus two more, separate stories I think you will enjoy. And remember to check out my sister's books. You can be kept abreast of my sister's work and mine, see upcoming book covers, sign up for our newsletters to be kept informed of when our next books are due out at our website:

Visit our website at: www.sistersromance.com

Email me at: MargaretKay@sistersromance.com

Follow me on Facebook at: @MargaretKayAuthor

Manufactured by Amazon.ca
Bolton, ON

18839875R00155